NMU FF

enjoy
due
D0589080

Joss was born on the b[illegible] Essex. Leaving [illegible] careers in British [illegible] and along the way [illegible] from Oxford Universit[illegible] written [illegible] children and young adults, winning awards in both categories. She has published over fifty novels that have been translated into many languages. She lives in Oxford.

goldinggateway.com

twitter.com/jossstirling

facebook.com/JossStirling

Also by Joss Stirling

The Jess Bridges Mysteries

Black River

White Horse

Red House

Standalones

Don't Trust Me

The Silence

GREY STONES

JOSS STIRLING

One More Chapter
a division of HarperCollins*Publishers*
1 London Bridge Street
London SE1 9GF
www.harpercollins.co.uk

HarperCollins*Publishers*
1st Floor, Watermarque Building, Ringsend Road
Dublin 4, Ireland

This paperback edition 2021
First published in Great Britain in ebook format
by HarperCollins*Publishers* 2021

1

Copyright © Joss Stirling 2021
Joss Stirling asserts the moral right to
be identified as the author of this work

A catalogue record of this book is available from the British Library

ISBN: 978-0-00-842267-7

This novel is entirely a work of fiction. The names, characters and incidents portrayed in it are the work of the author's imagination. Any resemblance to actual persons, living or dead, events or localities is entirely coincidental.

Printed and bound in Great Britain by
CPI Group (UK) Ltd, Croydon CR0 4YY

All rights reserved. No part of this publication may be reproduced, stored in a retrieval system, or transmitted, in any form or by any means, electronic, mechanical, photocopying, recording or otherwise, without the prior permission of the publishers.

To Jamie and Clare

'Silent, remote, for ages,
Weather beaten and grey,
Army and knights and King Stone
Have stood there to this day.'

The Rollright Stones: History & Legends in Prose and Poetry, F.C. Rickett

Chapter One

The Rollright Stones stood in their three-thousand-year-old circle waiting for the February sun to rise. Mist wound between them, slinking close to the ground. Muffled in a heavy coat, scarf and hood, a lone figure stood in their midst, as still as the limestone rocks. Some stones were as tall as a man, some huddled close to the earth like creeping beasts. No one ever managed to count their number the same twice because where one rock began and another ended was hard to fathom. Legend said they were the army of an ambitious king turned to stone, a punishment for his overweening ambition. His stone stood alone across the road on the next rise, frozen in place by a witch's curse.

Or that was what the folk tale said.

The visitor now moved, turning slowly to revel in the silence after days of so much noise. This circle always drew you back, lodged inside you once visited. It was a place between things at this bleakest time of the year. A place of resolution. If you faced away from the road behind the trees, quiet at this hour, you could see was the sweep of the Swere Valley. That way lay Oxfordshire. Behind you, sprawled Warwickshire, birthplace of that critic of kings, William Shakespeare. The stones marked the border between the two counties, as well as the watershed between the Severn and the Thames. They divided kingdom from kingdom. Past and present. Living and dead.

The sun crept over the horizon, flushing the sky pink. If you stood here at the spring equinox, that light would fall straight through the hole bored on one of the circle rocks. Lying down, humbling yourself, to look through it, you would discover that it lined up like a rifle sight with another monument. This was a cluster of megaliths called the Whispering Knights, a field away, leaning in to plot treason, a second crime scene. The two stone clusters might seem unconnected but the traitors had also been hit by the witch's curse – though that seemed unfair if their plans had been laid against a king who deserved petrification.

The grey stones could be read as monuments to ambition, betrayal, and collateral damage. The watcher walked back to the car. It had been an excellent place to come to terms with murder.

Chapter Two

Leo

What was the worst that could happen, wondered Leo, when he introduced Jess to his university friends? She could hate them. They could hate her. Being locked away for three days in a lakeside retreat would be an intense introduction to his old circle – some of whom, to be honest, he no longer knew that well. One of whom he had never even liked.

He flicked the indicator and pulled out to overtake a green-clad cyclist, giving her plenty of space. So why was he doing this? He found relationships like playing blind man's buff in a field of open mine shafts: he never knew when he was going to make an irreversible misstep. He supposed he had agreed to bring Jess because he was trying hard to be more open with his girlfriend of two months, having had other relationships founder on the rock of his introverted nature. He wanted Jess to get on with them, particularly Freddie, Lauren, and Rainbow; but now he came to think of it, this was a huge gamble.

He glanced in the driver's mirror, wondering if there was still time to do a U-turn and head back to Oxford. He could always say work had called him away. Life as a detective inspector in Thames Valley was never predictable so the excuse would be entirely believable. However, there was a Range Rover right on his tail, making a sudden brake impossible, and maybe Jess would think he was ashamed of her?

Relax, Leo. It was only for a weekend, he reminded himself. There was lots to do at the clubhouse if the lakeside cottage got too much. The two of them could always escape for walks in the Cotswolds countryside if it was really going badly. This was a beautiful spot even at the tail end of winter – rolling green hills, little woods, and clusters of thatched cottages and limestone churches. No wonder so many of the rich and powerful, from former prime ministers to media stars, chose to live and socialise around here.

A sigh came from his companion. It seemed he was not the only one anxious about the reunion. Jess was staring out as the frosted lanes zipped by. Bare oaks stood sentinel in scraped fields. Sheep huddled around feeding troughs. Brown hedges. Little birds seeking refuge. She pulled down the mirror in the sunshade and he saw her frowning at her reflection. Not that Leo could see anything wrong: Jess had a sweetly rounded face, shoulder-length blonde hair, currently kept back by Art Deco butterfly slides from the V&A exhibition they'd gone to last month. She had curves under her powder-blue lambswool jumper that he knew to be soft and inviting. All this packed into a small frame. She was only a few inches over five foot and refused to own up to exactly how many. His professional guess was three.

'What if they take against me?' she asked.

'They won't.' Leo slowed for a junction as a supermarket lorry made a slow turn.

'They will. I didn't go to that fancy schmancy college of yours.'

'You've got a master's in Psychology from UCL. You're probably the most academic among us.'

'But I didn't live in a castle while I did it, eating dinners in a hall that looks like Hogwarts.'

'Castle is just like an Oxford college. You're used to that, aren't you?'

'As a humble member of the admin staff.' Jess worked in the Development Office of St Nicholas' College, a temporary job while she established her missing persons agency as a going concern. Work had picked up lately, but she'd not yet felt brave enough to swap a reliable income for that of the self-employed.

'Jess, you're doing it again.'

'Doing what?' She nibbled on her bottom lip.

'Playing down your own success. You got me to read *Lean In*. I know the signs of female disempowerment,' he teased. Jess had been going through a Me Too self-education phase. Leo thought that a lot of quiet men like him could learn from it as well.

She perked up at the mention of the book on women in

positions of power. 'You think I just need to "lean in" to your friendship group?'

'I think you just need to be yourself. They'll love you.'

'Aw.' She smiled now at her reflection and snapped the sunshade back up in place. 'Inspector George, I can't wait to get you in our four-poster bed tonight. I think it's my turn to be in charge?'

He grinned at that. 'Only for round one.'

'You're on.'

Perhaps the weekend wasn't going to be so bad after all?

They drove through the estate gates, following the gravel road past the stately home that was now the clubhouse, and drew up outside one of the lakeside cottages at eleven, an hour later than the agreed arrival time. Jess had inevitably been running behind when he collected her, caught up arranging for a willing neighbour to dog-walk her spaniel, Flossie. This meant Leo and Jess had missed the start of the weekend's activities.

Jess's mouth dropped open at the prospect before them. 'This is a cottage? Sure you've got the right address?' She wriggled out of her seat, grabbed her phone and opened the maps app.

Leo got out his side. 'Definitely the right place. And I guess it is a cottage – just a super-sized one.' Leo began laughing, as surprised as she was. The online photos hadn't done justice to the scale of the place. It looked like a Nordic log cabin, but huge – more of a feasting hall – complete with a decking area that jutted out over the lake. Smoke rose from the two chimneys either end of the building. 'I hope this gives me boyfriend points?'

'You bet! You didn't tell me it was one of those Birbeck clubs! Oh, my God: listen to this! "Stay in one of our luxury lakeside lodges, or in our woodland cabins. Then enjoy the five-star amenities in our clubhouse, where you can choose from our three restaurants, bar, casino, library, games room, swimming pool and spa."' She gave him a hug, then did a little boogie with her phone. 'You've set me up with my dream, Leo. I know the Birbeck brothers have the reputation in the media as pretty ruthless business moguls but you have to admit that they know how to do luxury.'

Her delight made everything feel so much better. 'I live to please my lady.' Three cars and a club van were already parked outside their one. 'Come on – I think we might be the last to arrive.'

'I'll murder your friends if they've stolen the four-poster.' She grinned up at him. 'I know that's not fair, what with you being a murder cop and all, but I'm just saying. Prepare to arrest me.'

Leo got their case out of the back of the car. 'Don't worry. I won't need to crack out the handcuffs. It was all agreed in advance.'

She pretended to be disappointed. 'When we get home then?'

He laughed. Only Jess.

'How can we afford this, Leo? Are your friends loaded?' Her worried look had returned.

He shook his head. 'Not really, but the manager of the

club is a good friend of Freddie and Lauren. Rebecca – we'll probably meet her too. It's low season so she's been able to upgrade us.'

'So who's sleeping where?'

'Freddie and Lauren are at the far end. Janice and Phil are with us down this side, each taking one of the twin bedrooms. That leaves us the last double.'

'We'll have a view out over the water? Fabulous.' They paused to take in the lake with its mercury-tinted surface, fringed by willows and brown sedge. Two swans flew overhead with their strangely squeaky wings. They skimmed the lake to land on the far side.

Leo held out a hand. 'Ready to face them?'

She took it in hers and squeezed. 'I'm sticking to you like glue.'

They went up the short flight of steps to the decking area by the front door. A jumble of walking boots already lay there. Leo opened the door and they walked straight into a noisy gathering around the dining table in a high-ceilinged living area. It occupied the centre of the lodge, going the whole height to the rafters, dividing the two bedroom areas from each other. The smell of bacon and coffee hit, making his mouth water. The counter that divided the dining area from the space-age kitchen was covered with breakfast dishes. A chef in a white hat was tossing pancakes over a steaming stove. A waiter in a green uniform ferried the food to the guests. An auburn-haired woman restocked plates of pastries and fruit – that was Freddie and Lauren's friend, Rebecca.

'Leo! You made it!' Freddie bounded up from his place

at the head of the table, almost spilling his orange juice in his hurry. Fortunately, Lauren was on hand to catch it. 'And you must be Jess!' He arrowed towards them, looking as fit as ever, his friendly blue eyes twinkling. The main difference from the rowing-mad twenty-year-old Leo best remembered from college was the receding nut-brown hair and slight softening about the jaw. Freddie wasn't bald yet, but was certainly baring more of his forehead to the battering of time.

'Sorry we're a little late,' Leo said, wincing slightly as Freddie gave him an enthusiastic hug. His friend had the energy of a Golden Retriever. 'Jess, this is Freddie Forrester.'

'I'd quite despaired of ever getting you to one of our bashes, Leo,' Freddie declared, giving him an extra squeeze. 'I'm so pleased the new lady changed your mind about that.' He turned to Jess. 'May I?' He held out his arms.

Unlike Leo, Jess was the hugging kind so didn't turn him down. 'Nice to meet you, Freddie.'

Freddie broke away and beamed. 'I like this one. We'll try not to do anything to scare her off.' He linked his arm in Jess's and moved her to the table. 'Jess, this is my wife, Lauren.'

Lauren greeted Jess. She still had her pale, elfin face, though she had chopped off the long hair of her twenties to a sleek bob, longer at front so it emphasised her cheeks by coming to a point either side. A straight fringe set off her dark-blue eyes. Slim to the point of painfulness, Leo found it hard to imagine she was the mother of three young children.

'Hello, Lauren. What have you done with the children?' he asked, accepting a kiss on the cheek.

'At the grandparents', no doubt being spoiled rotten,' said Lauren.

'Our tribe,' said Freddie proudly. 'Three children in eighteen months. What were we thinking, Lauren?'

'Well, I certainly wasn't thinking "twins" the second time around.' She smiled up at Leo. 'You've hardly changed, Leo – it's not fair. Portrait in the attic? It's so lovely to see you again. I was just saying to Janice that it's been too long.'

Leo felt a little tightening in the pit of his stomach. First mineshaft. He'd meant to mention to Jess that an old girlfriend from college days was going to be at the weekend but had never found the right moment. To say something might've made it sound like it meant too much and now it was too late. He turned to his old flame who was sitting at the other end of the table. Her beauty hit him afresh. Had he really ever dated someone who looked like that?

'Janice, how are you?' he asked, aware he sounded a little too formal.

She gave him a wave. 'Good, but jet-lagged.' Her voice had a transatlantic drawl these days. 'I flew in from LA yesterday and I've still not adjusted.'

Janice, an actress, was now building a career in American TV. She wore her black hair in a long, sleek mane curled over one shoulder. Big gold hoop earrings brushed shoulders bared by the boat neckline of her white top, a stunning contrast with her dark skin. She didn't look the least tired. She looked catwalk ready.

'This is Jess,' Leo said gamely. He didn't hold out much hope that the two women would like each other. They were too different.

'Hello, Jess. I googled you.' Janice popped a strawberry in her mouth. 'When I heard you were coming.'

Jess's hand twitched in his grasp as if she was thinking of running. He gave her a reassuring squeeze. There was some embarrassing stuff about her if you dug deep online, as well as the more recent involvement in a number of murder cases in Thames Valley. How much had Janice found out? Leo wondered.

'I hope the pictures were flattering?' Jess tried a brave smile.

'They made you look younger.' Janice dabbed her mouth with the napkin. 'Missing Persons Agency? Is that, like, a job?'

'Trying to make it into one,' Jess said, leaning forward in a parody of their remarks in the car. Leo smiled. She was up to this battle.

'Good for you.' Janice flicked her wrist towards her breakfast buddy. 'Phil, aren't you going to say "Hello" to Leo and Jess?'

Leo steeled himself. He and Phil Harwood had never got on, even at college when they sometimes played squash together. They were the two remote planets either end of this solar system with Freddie, Lauren, Janice, and Rainbow in the middle, holding them together. 'Good to see you again.'

Phil just nodded, barely looking at him.

Freddie clapped his hands. 'Enough with the

introductions. We've a whole weekend to get to know Jess. Pull up a chair and dig in before Phil and I eat all the pancakes.'

Jess wisely chose a chair next to Freddie. Leo sat next to her, which put him opposite Phil and closest to Janice. Not ideal but it was the only seat open next to Jess and he'd promised not to abandon her.

'Where's Rainbow? Isn't she coming?' Leo asked Janice. Rainbow was the one he was hoping Jess would really take to. She had developed to be very much like her fanciful name, always shining in cloudy moments, relentlessly optimistic and finding a kind word for everyone.

'We're going on a walk to meet her after breakfast,' Janice said. She had the oddest ability to sound bored by herself and the person she was talking to. A sigh never seemed far off. 'She's driven here in a motorhome but they don't have permission to park it on the club grounds.'

Leo selected a croissant from under the heavy white napkin that kept it warm. 'Are you saying she's finally living her dream of being on the road?'

Janice sipped her fizzy water. 'Seems so. She's got together with Lloyd. You remember him, Lloyd Rumbold? Freddie and Lauren's Lloyd?'

Leo had a clear and not very positive recollection of the city broker who was a friend of Freddie and Lauren's. After Durham, their close-knit college friendship group had been diluted with new additions from London, Lloyd foremost amongst them. Leo had met Lloyd at various dinner parties and clubs, always in the company of his old friends, never by choice. He couldn't see the man's attraction, never sought him out as a friend, finding him too brash and self-confident.

'Rainbow and Lloyd? How did that happen?' he asked.

'The usual – Lauren and Freddie matchmaking again.'

Leo couldn't think of a worse fit than Rainbow. Lloyd had joined their social circle in the early days of the Durham graduates all starting their first jobs, leaving the north of England for life in the capital. Leo was an exception, opting to join the police and train in Thames Valley, something they all teased him about for years. Of the new London friends, louder-than-life Lloyd had been known to splash his money around and brag about his earnings on the stock market. At that age (mid-twenties), there had still been that feeling that they were all really playing at being grown-up, half expecting a responsible adult to come in and tell them to behave. That moment had never come so they'd grown used to these new versions of themselves. Low-paid civil servant Freddie had been in awe of bullyboy Lloyd and that, Leo had often thought, was the real source of their friendship – Freddie as acolyte to Lloyd's sun king. From everything Leo remembered, Lloyd didn't seem the sort to live in a motorhome.

'Isn't he something in the city?' asked Leo. 'Where does the motorhome fit in?'

Janice laughed, throwing back her head with sensual abandon. He suddenly pictured her doing the same at eighteen and twenty-one – a disconcerting time-slip moment.

'Of course it doesn't fit with old Lloyd. But new Lloyd?'

said Janice archly. 'He's given it all up to find himself, if you can believe that?'

Phil, who had been eavesdropping, snorted and refilled his cup of coffee from the pot without offering it to anyone else.

'Struggling,' admitted Leo.

'He'd fit right in in California,' Janice smirked. 'The new, bohemian, vegan-preaching Lloyd won't come here, so we have to go to them. They're parked up by the Rollright Stones, having bunged fifty quid at the farmer, living the good life, so I hope you've got your walking shoes with you?'

'We have. But isn't that taking principles a bit far?'

She shrugged. 'I thought you were a detective. You should know it's more complicated than that.'

Leo had little time for Lloyd's complications. 'Tell me, Janice, how's the acting career going?' he asked, changing the subject to safer territory.

Chapter Three

Jess

If Janice threw her head back and laughed in that orgasmic way one more time at the slightest joke from Leo, I was liable to do something drastic.

Stabbing a piece of blueberry pancake on the end of my fork, I shovelled it in and chewed vigorously to stop myself saying anything. Leo had neglected to mention that among the guests this weekend would be one of the most beautiful women in the world. I'd seen her on TV – not that I was going to tell her that – in an American series called *Ann Droid,* which you could find if you dug deep in the Netflix menus. As the title suggested, this was a programme about human-looking robots. She wasn't the lead droid – Ann – but she played one of her best friends, another AI construct called Ava (short for avatar). It had run to three seasons and I'd found it thanks to the algorithm deciding my life for me.

Because you watched Westworld, *why not try…*

Who was the machine-controlled person in that transaction? Faced with such competition, my heart was down in my boots, jumbled up like the ones on the porch.

'How did you meet Leo, Jess?' asked Freddie.

Our first meeting had been over the dead body of a college bursar and I'd not been wearing any clothes at the time, just a few sheets of newspaper. With great difficulty, I restrained my usual urge to blurt out too much detail.

'We met on a crime scene.' I leant back to make room for my cup and thanked the waiter for the cappuccino he'd made for me.

'It's hard to imagine him as a serious policeman.' Freddie's smile turned thoughtful. 'I always thought him too gentle for that line of work.'

'But if you know Leo well, you'll be aware that there's a toughness to him. He's a perennial, not an annual.'

Freddie chuckled. 'Yes, he's survived the frost. So nice to see him talking to Janice again.'

It really wasn't. 'Hmm.'

'They didn't get on very well for years after she ended things.' – *What?* – 'More pancakes, Jess?'

Lauren must've caught my deer-in-headlights expression. 'Freddie, I think you might've put your foot in it.'

'What've I done now?' He looked around in all innocence.

'I don't think Jess knew – about Leo and Janice.'

Why didn't I know?

'Oh, that?' Freddie waved it away. 'Ancient history. It must be… what, fifteen years ago? I mean, I had wondered if they might… but you're on the scene now and clearly he's very happy with you.' He beamed at me. 'Another pancake?'

'Er, no, thanks, I think I might unpack.' I picked up my cappuccino to stage a strategic retreat while I came to terms with this new information. 'Which room are we staying in?'

Freddie beckoned the manager. 'Rebecca, this, as you've probably guessed, is Jess. Jess, Rebecca.' He gave what was clearly another old friend a one-armed hug. 'It's all thanks to Rebecca that we've got these classy digs for the weekend. I keep asking her to sit down with us but she's always on duty.' He lowered his voice. 'Don't worry, we'll get her drunk later and make her relax.'

This had to be the woman Leo had mentioned, the friend of Lauren who had got us the discount. I gave her a friendly smile.

'I'm off tomorrow,' Rebecca said, patting Freddie's shoulder. 'Just let me do my job for now.'

'We'll keep you to that. Would you be an angel and show Jess to her room?'

'Of course, Freddie.' She helped me up by moving my chair back so I didn't spill the coffee.

I followed Rebecca to the opposite end of the cabin. I grabbed the suitcase we'd abandoned just inside the door.

'Let me take that,' said Rebecca. She had a great voice, like a BBC programme announcer. Everything about her was classy, which I suppose fitted the job. Pale-skinned with blue eyes and tousled collar-length auburn hair, she was pretty but not very smiley. A few inches taller than me, she shared my tendency towards a fuller figure.

I kept hold of the handle of the case. 'No need. You're the manager. You shouldn't be carrying stuff.'

She gave me a pinched smile. 'Manager or gofer? Sometimes the roles seem very similar.'

'No gofering for me, thanks. You're a friend of Freddie and Lauren's?'

'That's right. I met Lauren at a yoga class way back when she and Freddie first moved to London.' She led me across an area given over to black leather sofas and low coffee tables.

'Nice of you to get them this deal.'

'My pleasure. I've been an honorary member of the Durham group for a few years, even though I didn't go to college with them.'

'You're like me then?'

She gave me a patient half-smile. 'I think you'll need a few more years before you reach "honorary".'

Ouch. Was that a little mean-girl coming through? 'Meaning I'm at "plus-one" status?'

'No bad thing to be.' She opened the door at the far end of the corridor. 'This is yours. Oh—'

I poked my head into the room. There was the promised four-poster, looking splendid, but on it lay an open suitcase with two others at the foot of the bed – a matching designer set in cream and tan, the kind that cost a couple of thousand even before you put anything in them. A silky nightgown lay on the covers and the bed had been slept in.

'Just give me a moment.' Rebecca went back to the table and whispered in Janice's ear.

'Oh, that was meant to be Leo's room, was it?' Janice

said loudly and unrepentantly. 'But when I arrived the rooms were all empty.'

'Janice—' Leo threw an apologetic look at me.

'I'm in the middle of moving back to the UK, and I have so much luggage with me.' She fluttered her false eyelashes at Leo. 'You're always so accommodating. I was sure you wouldn't mind.'

The cow. But I was the plus one so I was hardly in a position to kick up a fuss. It wasn't my reunion.

Showing she was used to dealing with awkward customers, Rebecca regrouped. 'Well, that does leave one twin room free.'

She had to be kidding me. The big appeal of coming this weekend was a sexy time with my guy, not dormitory beds.

'I'll see if we have a mattress topper and can push them together.' Rebecca walked away to pass on a message to housekeeping.

Janice placed a hand on Leo's wrist. 'Of course, I had imagined that maybe someone might like to join me. That was before Freddie broke the news that you were bringing a guest.'

Oh, no, she didn't! *Get your beautiful manicured claws off of my man!* Before I could storm over and say something unwise, Leo pulled his hand away and stood up. Coming quickly over to me, he took the case from my grip.

'Jess, are you OK with this? We can always just stay for the day and go back to Oxford.' He sounded as if he very much wanted me to say 'yes'.

'Oh, Leo!' protested Lauren.

'That one backfired rather spectacularly, didn't it, Janice?' said Phil. He appeared to be relishing the upset.

Rebecca returned to calm troubled waters. 'I'm sure you'll find that there is no such thing as a bad room in this cabin. Phil, are you in the one facing the boathouse?'

'Yes. Next to Janice. Not budging.' He grabbed a piece of toast off a silver rack.

'Then that leaves the one upstairs. It's smaller but it does have the nice feature of a balcony. I think you'll find it cosy.' She led Leo, who was carrying our suitcase, up the open wooden stairs. I didn't protest. It was just a room. And I still might get a chance to murder the bed-stealer.

Freddie rubbed his hands together, trying to dispel the bad atmosphere with his positivity. 'Everyone eaten enough? Right, meet here in ten minutes, coats and boots on.' Being a parent had obviously become ingrained.

'Yes, Daddy,' Janice replied, smirking. She glided to her room and shut the door in my face.

When I reached the upstairs room, Leo put the case down by one of the narrow twin beds and gave me a hug. 'I'm sorry.'

'Not your fault.' I rested my head on his chest. Janice might have the four-poster but she didn't have this. 'It's just for two nights.'

'Cosy' was one way of describing what was clearly meant as the room for junior guests who didn't require full headroom. There was a tiny en suite where the shower door would bang against the toilet if you pushed it all the way open and a handbasin rather than a full-sized sink.

I flopped back on the bed and looked up at the roof beams. Accentuate the positive. 'Heidi's attic.'

Leo opened the door to the balcony, letting in a draft of cold air. 'Heidi, who?'

'*The* Heidi, from the book. She lives in a hayloft of her grandpa's chalet in the Swiss Alps. That's what this reminds me of.'

Leo lay down next to me, staring up at the same view. 'I'd forgotten about Janice.'

I turned to look at him – a much better view – my gorgeous officer of the law. Leo had an aquiline nose, dark brows, and a strong jawline. My very favourite feature though were his eyes. Slightly hooded, hinting at an Asiatic forebear on the family tree, his eyes always looked out at you as if he suspected you of doing something – that was until he smiled and then the suspicion vanished and he became almost boyish. That was a side of him that only a very select few saw, certainly none of his colleagues or the people he dealt with at work.

'Forgotten as in, forgotten she existed?' I asked hopefully.

'No, as in how she can be so selfish. I think the lifestyle of an actor doesn't help, but she was always like that even before she started to make a name for herself.'

I ran my finger over his chin, touching the little dent at the end. Not quite a Henry Cavill cleft but the suggestion of one. 'How long did you date?'

He winced. 'You heard about that?'

'Within about five seconds from Freddie. That guy is a terrible gossip.'

'He's always had the tendency to just spill what he's thinking without considering the audience.'

'And you told me he works at the Ministry of Defence in procurement? That means he's signed the Official Secrets Act?' I dropped my hand and chuckled at that prospect.

'I've not heard him spill any official beans. Probably because he doesn't think about work once he goes home.'

'Thank God, for the sake of national security.'

He caught my hand and kissed my knuckles. 'He's a nice person.'

'I got that too.' I left a pause. 'You didn't tell me?'

He clasped his palm to his forehead. 'I know. That was stupid. I was going to but then I thought that would look like I was making too much of it.'

'Basically, you wimped out?'

'I wimped out.'

Was I going to make him pay or let him off the hook? I know Leo fretted about relationships. Sure-footed in investigations, he overthought his moves when it came to me because he'd had a few catty girlfriends tell him he wasn't enough for them. I imagined Janice lay near the front of that short line of women who didn't know a good thing when they saw it.

I kissed the place on his forehead that he'd squeezed, which had the nice side benefit that he could nuzzle my breasts.

'It's OK, Leo. She's incredibly hot. I'm impressed you pulled that at college. Go, you.'

He tugged me on top of him so we lay sandwiched in a full body stretch. 'She's nothing compared to what I have now.'

Two months into our relationship and he still thought I was a good thing. I kissed him on the lips for that completely biased remark, then levered up to mock-scowl at him. 'But if I catch you walking down memory lane with her, I'll cut up your favourite suits, poison your plants, and push her into the lake.'

Chapter Four

Jess

Trying to incentivise me, Leo assured me that I'd like Rainbow. When I asked about Lloyd, Leo grimaced and said it might end up as an even hit and miss.

'You need to aspire to a better hit rate for friends, Leo,' I advised him, tucking my trousers into my boot socks.

'Lloyd's not my friend – only Rainbow. Making friends isn't easy for me.' He zipped up a dark-blue fleece with the Thames Valley police shield on the breast. 'I appreciate that they're loyal. Freddie never lets me feel left out, never gives up.'

I kissed him, understanding completely how you could just fall into unwise relationships in the hothouse of university first week. It was a lottery that could decide the rest of your life. 'I'll sort you out. I make friends easily.'

He smiled and brushed my hair behind my ear. 'I've noticed – too easily, some would say.'

'What?'

He tapped my nose. 'Your boss, Paul, who still makes your life difficult at work? Kristie, your housemate, whom you won't tell to shut up when she's speaking loudly on her phone at night? The homeless man outside the supermarket who tells everyone you're his girlfriend?'

OK, maybe I was a bit soft-hearted. 'I don't want to be rude.'

'Occasional rudeness is necessary.' He knotted my scarf, making sure I was going to be warm. 'Somewhere between your extroverted "love the world" and my introverted "distrust everyone" attitude is the perfect human.'

'I don't love everyone. I have quite the talent for hating certain people,' I said in my defence.

'Oh, yes? And how long does that last?'

In my father's case, a lifetime, but I didn't want to dampen the mood by bringing him up. Early in our relationship, before we started going out, Leo had had to arrest him for stalking, or as I put it, being a terrible human being.

As urged by Freddie, we returned to the ground floor, wrapped up for a winter walk. We joined the others putting boots on outside.

'I'm walking with Jess,' said Lauren, curling her arm through mine. 'Leo, please go and talk Freddie out of his latest madcap idea. I think it must be the looming big four-oh that's getting to him. Forty? How did that happen to us?'

'Please, it hasn't happened yet,' I replied with a mock-shudder. I was still comfortably at the other end of the decade.

'Freddie's a few years ahead of us,' explained Lauren. 'He had some years out before college, crewing, and that's seeded some romantic delusions.'

Over by the clubhouse, I could see a string of ponies as guests went out for a ride. The building itself was a converted manor house, Georgian style with the obligatory accessory of an oversized portico with a frieze of mythical figures. Apparently there was a spa and swimming pool and a restaurant and several bars. A casino was open after dark in the basement if we wanted to pretend we were extras in a James Bond film.

Were me and a casino a good idea? It sounded like petrol and a match.

Leo stood up from tying his bootlaces. 'What's Freddie thinking of now?'

Lauren blew on her fingers. 'His latest plan is that we should take a career break and sail around the world with the children.'

'Seriously?' I asked. I'd been expecting her to say he was thinking of getting a motorbike or growing a goatee.

She pulled on what looked like a home-knitted hat in gold and black stripes, turning herself into a queen bee. 'It would be serious if he had the logistical skills to organise the home schooling and all the practical stuff. He's a good sailor. Been doing long voyages since he was a teenager and could probably manage to get us through it alive. He says he wants the children to experience the freedom of the high seas while it's still easy to take them out of school.'

'And you?'

'I get seasick on a boating lake.' She gestured to a blue

dinghy moored outside the house in case any of us wanted to freeze our butts off on the water. 'Apparently I'd get over that.' She laughed dryly. 'Then I say, "Somali pirates, tropical diseases, storms, and missed schooling," and he goes quiet. And he fails to take into account I've only just got back into my career after taking a five-year break for child-rearing. Hardly the time to hare off on a new adventure.'

I could tell there and then that there was no way the Freddie-Lauren clan were getting on board a yacht to cross the Atlantic.

Our walking party set off, OS map in capable hands (not mine). Freddie and Leo took on guiding us to the right footpath, tailed by Janice and Phil who seemed quite close in the dynamics of this friendship group. Had they ever been an item, I wondered? There didn't seem to be any chemistry between them, but there was something intimate, almost conspiratorial. Lauren and I brought up the rear.

'Ah, this is the life: no kids to worry about, outside in the fresh air, good company!' Lauren smiled at me. 'I love our reunions. They kept me sane when the kids were babies.'

I wondered how she could think like that when there were clearly tensions among so many members. Maybe she and Freddie skated by not noticing? That was my mother's attitude to life. 'It's nice that you make time for it each year.'

'I can't see how you maintain real friendships if you don't invest the time. Tell me about looking for missing people,' Lauren urged.

Picturing my motivational Post-its on my computer, I

reminded myself not to downplay my skills. 'My research background is in psychology and I always loved behavioural studies. I guess this is a logical extension. I tend to be brought in when the police or social services have lost interest or reached a dead end. They very often don't have the resources to devote to it.'

'What do you do that's different from the authorities?'

'I usually start by drawing up a detailed profile of the person. I mine their social media for clues, follow up with interviews of friends and family, find out everything I can from open sources. The main thing is I have the time to really dig, to give the problem the attention it deserves.'

Lauren bounded over the stile. I followed more gingerly because the lower step rocked in the mud. The others were already ahead, entering a copse of skinny birch trees.

'Do you track their phones?' she asked. 'Triangulate them from the nearest phone mast?'

I laughed. 'I wish. You've been watching too much TV. I can't do that – and I can't hack into financial records either.' Though I did have a few shady contacts who could for a price, but that wasn't something to be admitted out loud. Leo would find it problematic as it wasn't exactly legal. 'Mostly, the breadcrumbs are there, if you're persistent at asking the right questions. And you get a feel for it after a time, especially with the kids.'

'I suppose they are the most likely to go missing, aren't they?'

Passing under the birches, I unwound my scarf, warming up from the brisk pace. 'You wouldn't know it from the news, but children go missing with surprising regularity – older teenagers mostly. A lot of them these days are in care because they were trafficked into the country and ended up in foster care – then they just… *poof!*'

She frowned, brows almost meeting beneath the yellow and black stripes. 'Where do they go?'

'Regrettably, that's the deal with the traffickers. *Come find us once you're in country or else.* They end up in sweatshops, nail bars, prostitution, and so on. It's happening all over the country.'

'Sounds fascinating. I wonder if anyone's ever done a programme about it?' she mused. 'Who asks you to find them?'

A light rain began to fall, cold on my hot cheeks.

'Sometimes the social workers or foster parents, more often friends or concerned teachers from their school and very occasionally family from abroad if they get suspicious something is up. Then there're the ordinary runaways.'

'What counts as ordinary?' She held back a bramble so it didn't whip my jeans.

'Good question. No one's really ordinary once you look hard at them.' I was embarrassed by how out of condition I seemed compared to everyone else on this walk. I really should be less relaxed about my fitness regime. 'You sound very interested, Lauren.'

'Hazard of my profession. Always on the hunt for ideas. I'm a series editor for Bellwether TV. We specialise in drama documentaries.'

The path widened so I moved up beside her. 'What are you working on at the moment?'

I let her talk for a while, eager to turn the attention away from my very unimpressive little business. I wouldn't want a TV person to get the wrong idea about me. 'Leaning in' was OK until you toppled over with the weight of your self-misrepresentation.

The path eventually emerged from the wood into a field bordering a country road. Freddie shook raindrops off the plastic cover of his map.

'That was Whichford Wood. Covered in bluebells in the spring, apparently. A few more fields and then we'll be at the stone circle.'

Our walking party shuffled after this pause and I found myself beside Phil. I had to make the effort, didn't I?

'What do you get up to, Phil?' I asked. Leo had been very unforthcoming about this member of their group. Phil's features were fine taken individually but didn't quite add up to handsome. He had hard eyes, quite deep-set and a little too close together, like Ryan Gosling's, and a clipped beard that had more red in it than his tawny hair. He styled his hair swept back, leaving his forehead very square, as if someone had ruled a line across the top. Comparing him to Leo, who was over six feet, I guessed Phil was a little shy of that.

'I have my own construction company,' he said, answering my icebreaker, a little Brummie in his accent.

'You're a builder?'

He looked peeved to be described in that way. 'I develop new housing. We built forty executive homes last year.'

The pause he left suggested the correct response was 'congratulations, housing magnate', but he sounded like a builder to me. 'That must be satisfying.'

'Would be if I didn't have to spend all day hacking through red tape. This country is so full of regulations, it's impossible to get anything done.'

'Apart from building forty executive homes.'

He frowned, not sure if I was teasing (I was). 'Apart from that, obviously.'

'I always have a problem with rules too. They usually appear to me as a great suggestion of things to try.'

'Exactly.' His expression became more open. 'What gives society the right to make up our minds for us? We're adults: we can assess the risks.'

'Unless we're drunk. I have to admit some of my worst decisions happen when I'm half-cut.' A sheep bleated an agreement from a field away. My adult form of ADHD made me pro-risk so even without the alcohol my choices were often not the safest.

'But you still can decide for yourself and take the consequences, can't you?'

'I suppose so.'

'Me? I like to think of myself as a sovereign citizen.'

'Like super loyal to the Queen?'

He snorted. 'The exact opposite. I was born here without any say in the matter so I don't recognise the power of anyone over me – not the state, not my family, not the police.' He cast a look at Leo's back, now walking with Janice. They weren't touching, I was relieved to see.

Quaint. Phil was an English survivalist. If he were American, I could just see him up in the hills somewhere with his assault rifle and 'get off my land' attitude. Hard to picture him in Birmingham though.

'I guess you and Leo get on like a house on fire then?' I made no effort to hide the irony.

'Leo always liked his rules, even when we were at Durham and were at our freest. At nineteen, twenty, he hated to see anyone cutting corners.'

By which he meant 'cheating'. 'Hmm.'

'I wasn't surprised when he decided to join the police. That job was tailor-made for him. Finally he could do something when he saw someone breaking the rules.'

All of which had probably been a natural reaction to Leo's chaotic upbringing. 'You do need the police when there's a violent crime involved, surely?'

'Do you? What's wrong with those that are wronged exacting their own punishment?'

'Well, if you're dead, you can't.'

'In that case then it's left to the family or friends to hand out the punishment.'

'Not so good if you're a kid who can't protect themselves from an abusive parent.' *I've been there,* I added silently.

'Then others should step forward and do it for you.'

It really wasn't so easy. How would you even reach out for help at that age? Not everyone had someone in their corner. 'That's mob rule, Phil. Next stop, lynching.'

'Instead, we get legitimised lynching by the police. Just look at America.'

He was enjoying this, I realised. His 'no rules necessary' stance had probably provided him with lots of lovely debates down the pub for years, but no one actually lived that way.

'You are against the social contract then? "Down with Rousseau!" your rallying cry?'

He curled his lip. 'Who?'

OK, he wasn't coming at this from a philosophical stance after a careful consideration of the western tradition of human rights. I guessed this was something cooked up on conspiracy-fuelled social media. 'What about speed limits?'

'Infantile. I should be able to decide what's safe.'

'One-way streets?'

'If it's clear, go for it.'

'Theft?'

'If you try and take anything of mine, I'll thump you.'

'But if I'm bigger and stronger and have the bigger thump?'

He shrugged. 'Then I suppose it's my tough luck. It's unrealistic to expect life to be fair for everyone.'

'OK. I'll send my biggest mates round to your depot and drive off with all your white vans.'

'I'd like to see you try.' He actually thought I was challenging him.

I burst into laughter. 'That's ridiculous, Phil, but I guess you know that in your heart of hearts. Even you don't live in such a caveman society. I bet there are a million rules you obey each day without being aware of it.'

'Not if I can help it.'

'Then you're obeying your new rule of breaking rules. QED.' I grinned at him and marked a point to me in the air.

He shook his head, not wanting to concede that I'd argued him to a standstill. 'You're crazy.'

'But in your system, that's good, right? No more rebellious person than the mad one.'

He edged away from me, annoyed and maybe a little scared that I'd called him on his bullshit. 'Hey, Leo, did you know that your girlfriend is insane?'

Leo glanced round and smiled at me. 'Oh, yes, completely aware of that.'

'It's the attraction between us.' I offered Phil a mint from my pocket as a peace offering, which he declined. 'Tell me about your executive homes. What is it that makes them so *executive*?'

Phil recovered a little talking about himself. We arrived at the spot where the motorhome was parked off the road, right by the ancient monument. The Rollright Stones stood in a huddled circle, about the circumference of a medium-sized roundabout, but obviously far older and nothing to do with ancient traffic regulation. In the daylight, their mystery was diminished. From what I read about them on the web, they could have served many purposes in the Iron Age, from ceremonial space to market place. Maybe all of the above. But we weren't stopping to visit them just yet. Freddie went up to the door of the van and knocked.

'Rainbow, Lloyd! Make yourselves decent. You've got company!' he called.

Chapter Five

Jess

A woman – it had to be Rainbow – opened the door and flung out her arms in a happy greeting. Tall, slender, with long blonde hair, centre parted, all she needed was a beaded white gown and silver circlet to complete the Cate-Blanchett-does-Galadriel impression. In reality, Rainbow was dressed in patchwork trousers and a thick-knit purple jumper that went to her thighs. Leo had not mentioned that here was another old friend who scored a solid ten on the attractiveness scale.

'Guys, it's been too long. So glad you made it out here. Aren't they something?' She gestured to the stones as if she were somehow responsible for them.

'They're certainly something,' said Janice, sourly.

'Oh, Jan, only you could look at such ancient history and find it lacking!' She stood back. 'Come in. There's plenty of room but if you don't mind leaving your boots outside…?'

Following the elf queen's orders, we one by one kicked off our walking boots and climbed the metal steps into the motorhome. Plenty of room actually meant a bit of a squeeze on the white leather sofas that converted into beds. Everything seemed very high spec, not at all the bohemian interior I'd expected – no incense sticks or dream catchers. It reminded me of the Winnebago I'd got used to when working undercover on a film set during the wild swimming case.

I ended up wedged between Phil and Leo. Our host, Lloyd, was enthroned on the driver's seat that he'd spun round to face us. He looked to have a big build, though I couldn't tell how tall he was. His face was just losing its youthful good looks, going soft around the jowls – probably the result of years of wining and dining in the city life that he had recently left behind. A retired lion. His collar-skimming hair was brushed back, held by gel or maybe he'd just showered? I hoped that was the reason rather than styling product because otherwise someone should mention that it was only a good look for an otter.

'Hi, everyone,' said Lloyd, his voice a gravelly bass. 'I would get up and greet you but then we'd probably all be committing six acts of public indecency, and Leo would have to arrest us.'

Leo shook his head but just smiled slightly, not really amused.

'Bow –' Lloyd clicked his fingers at Rainbow – 'rustle up some coffee for our guests, would you, sweetheart?'

What was she, his maid? 'Already on it,' she said, far more patient than I would've been. She moved to the sink where she had a little tray already set. 'Anyone got any allergies? I made almond biscuits. Eat at your own peril.' She put the tray on the table between us.

Janice took her coffee black and refused a biscuit. She grabbed her friend's hand in passing and gave it a tug. It looked like there was a genuine warmth between them. 'How's living on the road treating you, Rainbow? I've been worried.'

'It's great, especially in good weather.' Janice gave her a strained smile that said otherwise. 'Harder at this time of year of course. Much more intense.' Once she'd served us all, she sat cross-legged on a floor cushion. 'It helps having some new heaters – I got so cold at Christmas we decided to treat ourselves. Everyone warm enough?' She was looking at me.

I was finding it quite sultry inside the van with all the bodies packed together. 'I'm fine. It's a lovely home you've got here.'

She looked pleased. 'As you can see, we're not exactly slumming it. Lloyd said we shouldn't stint on size and quality and he was right.'

'Got this one shipped in from America,' Lloyd said proudly. 'Widest legally allowed in the UK. Difficult on some of the roads round here but we manage.'

'*You* manage, you mean. I'm too scared to drive Goliath. All's well until we meet a tractor and trailer. The fur has flown a couple of times,' Rainbow said with a roll of her eyes.

'If they can't bloody well back up, they shouldn't be on the road,' grumbled Lloyd.

'Great biscuits,' I declared, thinking that there was nowhere but down for that subject to go.

Rainbow beamed at me. 'They're vegan, but you can't tell, can you?'

'What did you use?' asked Lauren, joining in the Women for Peace initiative.

The room broke into two factions: those intent on discussing the versatility of coconut oil and those listening to Lloyd holding forth on the wonders of cutting ties and living on the road. As my cooking-related conversation was limited, I joined in the latter.

'Hey, Phil, this sounds right up your street – a new market,' I said in a teasing tone, elbowing him. 'Forget the executive homes, build executive caravans for the exhausted middle management – those who want to jack it all in and reconnect with their rebellious youth.'

Phil curled his finger around his cup to make it a rude sign in my direction.

'Oh, Phil would never do that. He likes his bottom line too much,' said Lloyd, enjoying our little interaction.

Phil added a shot of something from a hip flask to his coffee. 'Anyone want some?' Freddie held out his cup with a boyish grin. Phil did not stint, then screwed the lid back on, ignoring my proffered mug. 'And you never paid enough attention to the bottom line, did you, Lloyd?'

'Phil.' Leo's tone was quelling, indicating he didn't want old arguments revived.

'You did well to keep out of that, Leo,' persevered Phil.

Leo appeared to understand what they were discussing

even if I didn't. 'I've never been one for investments beyond my pension.'

'And it's a nice one, I have no doubt. The government looks after its law enforcement. You can retire after how many years' service?'

'Thirty is normal.'

'Then in a decade and a half, you can join Lloyd here on the road, living off the rest of us for the remainder of your natural life.' Phil sounded as if he found that a personal insult.

'That's not my plan,' Leo said quietly. His dignity compared to the other two blusterers was very plain. Freddie just sat looking a little distressed by the turn of the conversation. Watching the four of them, I thought it proof that excessive testosterone was a poison. Only two seemed to have their hormone levels in balance.

'Leo would never go on the road,' I deflected. 'He's got an amazing garden – though I guess you all know that?'

Freddie seized on the change in subject with relief. 'We absolutely do. It's a marvel. How is the pond coming along, Leo?'

Forced out of his reticence, Leo had to come up with an update about his bog garden and pebble path. He became quite eloquent, especially as Freddie also had a passion for gardening – relatively newfound in his case.

'Of course, we've only got a little patch front and back in Richmond but we do have an allotment now,' Freddie said happily. 'The kids grew runner beans last year – and sunflowers. Huge success. I'd love to have more time at home to really have a go at it.'

Lloyd didn't have anything to add to this discussion, seeing how he'd made the exact opposite lifestyle choice. There wasn't even a pot of herbs by the sink. He looked for a new audience for the gift of his wisdom and foolishly picked me. 'And you, Jess, what's your take on life? Have you considered being vegan?'

Phil put his hand on my knee. 'Don't answer that. Plead the Fifth.'

I laughed and dislodged Phil's hand. 'Why? Is it a secret?'

'Should bloody well be. What we eat is our own business. And if you say you're a meat eater, he'll spend the rest of the weekend trying to convert you, and if you are vegan, he'll not let the rest of us forget it.'

'I think I'll risk it. I'm not scared of any of you. That's the benefit of being the outsider. No, I'm not vegan. Not intending to become vegan, though I'm happy to give being vegetarian a whirl.' Leo put his arm around me which I took as moral support for any dietary stands I chose. 'But good for you, Lloyd, if you go the whole hog – well, not a hog, obviously. The whole soya burger. I respect your decision.'

Lloyd opened his mouth to argue.

'Uh-uh. On holiday here.' I tapped my chest. 'Tell me about yourself. What made you give up the city?'

Lloyd settled back, one ankle resting on the opposite knee. 'In the end, I just couldn't stand it – the constant chasing after money which, when you look at it, is all just some glorified gambling. None of it is real. We weren't doing anything that did a fucking bit of good to the world, just lined our own pockets with obscene bonuses. My colleagues were pricks, the people we worked for were pricks, I think I became a prick.'

'You always were, mate,' said Phil, taking the obvious opening.

'Takes one to know one.' Lloyd and Phil grinned humourlessly at each other. That gave me a shrewd idea of how their friendship worked: a mutual ragging society.

'Old insults are always the best,' said Phil. 'Why bother to come up with any new material when nothing's changed?'

'Actually, I'd say I have changed. I've gained a new lease of life cutting free. I feel twenty-five again. Isn't that what you've been preaching for the last few years? No rules? No laws? And I got the girl too. Took me long enough.' He smiled over to Rainbow. She tilted her head then gave him a wary smile back.

'Don't know what it is she sees in you, mate,' said Phil. 'She's too good for you.'

'It's not my money, that's for sure. Maybe I had to get rid of that before she'd give me a second look? And I flatter myself that maybe I've always given the ladies other compensations.' He winked at Rainbow.

Ugh. 'You keep on telling yourself that, hun,' I said mock-consolingly. 'It's possible she might have fallen for your great big... motorhome.' I looked up at Leo. 'We should hire one. Escape Oxford for the open road. What do you say?'

'Unlikely,' he said dryly.

'You're right, I'd drive us into a ditch and you'd miss Goldemort.'

'Goldemort? Is that big fish still alive?' asked Freddie. 'The kids love him.'

'He is,' confirmed Leo.

'He's lurking in the mud at the bottom of the pool,' I said, 'like an assassin, just biding his time until spring. And where are his fishy friends now? Leo blames the heron but I'm not so sure. Inside job – or in-pond job – is my theory.'

'Is your girl always this sassy?' said Lloyd. 'I must say she's a bit of a surprise. Not who I expected you to be with.'

I eyed the plate, still feeling hungry after our walk. Could I reach over? 'Sassy is my middle name. Why do you find me a surprise?'

'You're not very quiet.' Lloyd took the last biscuit, foiling my plans for it.

'She suits me perfectly,' said Leo gallantly.

'And that's what he keeps telling himself,' I confided to Lloyd. 'Don't disillusion him, please.'

Chapter Six

Leo

Sitting cramped on the motorhome sofa between the sink and Jess, Leo died a little inside from acute embarrassment. He'd forgotten how macho his friends could be – well, not really *his* friends, he corrected, Freddie and Lauren's friends. He would long ago have shed Phil and never picked up Lloyd. It was pleasing though that Jess wasn't upset by them, even with Phil's blatant rudeness. He knew her well enough now to understand her expression as horrified enjoyment of these specimens of masculinity.

Just then his phone buzzed in his pocket. He pulled it out and grimaced. 'Work.'

'I thought you weren't on duty?' asked Jess.

'Not supposed to be. I'd better take this.' Muttering apologies, he squeezed past Jess, stepped carefully over Rainbow, and went outside. As he only had boot socks on, he sat on the steps rather than get them wet on the grass. In front of him, the stone circle they were yet to visit seemed to be waiting for him to do something, like an audience at a comedy club determined to be a tough crowd.

'George, here.'

'Leo, apologies for interrupting your weekend.' It was his superintendent, Claire Thaxted.

Leo sat up a little straighter. 'No problem. What can I do for you, ma'am?'

'I have a situation. Karl Fosdyke has called in sick. He's just back from an Italian skiing holiday, feeling under the weather, and what with this new virus in circulation, thinks he'd better stay at home.'

'I understand.' Karl was his counterpart and the senior officer on duty that weekend. 'How can I help?'

'There's an unattended at Chipping Norton. I immediately thought of you as I know you mentioned you were at the Piccadilly People Club. Could you call in and see that it's being handled correctly? There's not a lot of experience in that station for dealing with this kind of thing. Flag me if there're any suspicious circumstances, but initial indications from the senior officer on scene are that it's a straightforward self-termination.'

Just what he didn't need on his weekend off. 'Will do.'

'I'm sending you the address now. Hopefully, that will be it for this weekend. See you on Monday.'

'Tuesday, ma'am. I'm on leave on Monday.'

'Right. Tuesday.'

The details came through. Leo called the local station to send him a squad car. Jess was going to hate this. He went back inside.

'I'm so sorry but something has come up at work and I have to go in for a few hours.'

'Oh, Leo!' protested Lauren. 'Can't they let you have any time off?'

'Unfortunately, death doesn't take a holiday.'

'That sounds like an Agatha Christie novel,' said Jess. She squirmed past Rainbow to tug at the strings of his fleece. 'Is everything OK?'

'A suicide. My boss thinks it shouldn't take long.' He had his own doubts on that. 'Will you be OK?'

'We'll look after her,' said Freddie. 'See you back at the club, later? I'm going to persuade Lloyd to darken the doors of the clubhouse and join us for dinner, then a spin down in the casino. Jess, you'll help me, won't you?'

Jess dropped the strings and turned so her back rested against Leo's front. 'You bet. Just think of all the fun you can have, Lloyd, demanding the most difficult vegan dishes on the menu and grilling them as to how everything is… well, grilled?'

Lloyd's face did light up at that mention of opportunities to annoy.

'And Rebecca wouldn't find it the least bit awkward. She told me already this morning that it wasn't a problem for her,' added Lauren.

Lloyd's expression soured. 'I'm busy tonight. My team's playing.'

While the others attempted to argue him out of a date with the footie, Rainbow handed Leo his coat from the stack on the countertop. 'I like your Jess. She has a bright spirit.'

Not always, was the truthful answer. Jess had had some

very dark times, but right now she was the sunshine to go with Rainbow. 'She's good for me. Keep an eye please? Don't let Phil and Lloyd bully her.'

Rainbow smirked. 'Haven't you noticed? I don't think it's going to be that way round.'

The whoop of a police siren announced the arrival of the squad car.

'See you later, everyone,' said Leo. He kissed Jess then headed out. The feeling of relief slipping clear of old friends told him he'd made a mistake coming for this weekend. He was different now, more confident, and could admit to his own needs. He only wanted to keep up with Freddie, Lauren, and Rainbow. This annual reunion of misfits wasn't the only way to do that.

The unattended death had taken place in a cottage on Church Lane. This was opposite the historic almshouses in the Cotswolds market town of Chipping Norton. Hidden behind the main square, Church Lane was the kind of road that could be dressed to look like a location for a Dickens adaptation with very few changes, particularly with the church tower at the bottom of the hill. An elderly lady sat muffled up in a coat and hat on the little area in front of her door in the row of almshouses. The arrival of three police cars might well be the most exciting thing to happen to her road in years. The almshouses were seven identical terrace cottages, each with a pitched roof and light-blue door, sharing an open lawn for a front garden. As they had a good view of the property where the fatality had taken place, Leo made a mental note to ensure every occupant was followed up by the uniforms.

The officer who had driven him from the Rollright Stones drew up outside the house. 'Sir, you can go straight in. Sergeant Wilmot is inside. He's waiting to hand over command to you.'

Leo nodded. 'Thank you.' He felt at a disadvantage not knowing the faces of the local officers. CID rarely got called out to Chippie, as it was affectionately known in the area.

A red Corsa was parked right outside across the gateway, so possibly that belonged to the deceased. The cottage was narrow and neat, a tiny front garden of lavender and stalks of what would regrow as fuchsia. A pruned rose arched over the doorway, bared for winter but it would be a riot of blooms come June. The brick path was weeded and had been scattered with salt to make it safe in the frosty mornings. A tender plant – a cabbage palm, he thought – was wrapped in a fleece. All these signs showed that the owner had expected to be there to see the fruits of their autumn tidy-up. This wasn't a slow decline and a letting go of day-to-day life; this was someone who anticipated spring.

An officer came down the steep staircase. A short man with a shock of red hair and a belligerent expression, it was easy to expect him to have an irascible temper to match, but he seemed friendly enough when he spoke. 'DI George? Sergeant Wilmot.'

Leo held up a hand in greeting. 'Good to meet you. Give me a moment. I'll leave my boots outside.'

'Got called in on your weekend off, I hear? Bad luck.' Wilmot waited while Leo toed off his walking boots and left them by the milk bottles. Who still had deliveries these days? wondered Leo. This person did, it seemed. A pint of semi-skimmed sat in the rack.

'What have we got?' he asked, pulling on a white coverall so he didn't contaminate the scene.

Wilmot recited from memory. 'The victim is the householder, Kelly Ann Porter. Single. Forty-four. Lives alone. Works at that posh club near here – Piccadilly People. You know it?'

'That's where I'm staying,' said Leo. He would have to go back not as a guest but interview the staff, including Rebecca – not how he thought this weekend would go.

'They must be paying CID more than us uniform muppets, then.'

Leo didn't rise to the jibe. 'How did she die?'

'Best if I show you. If you'll follow me?'

Wilmot led him upstairs, passing the open door to the master bedroom – neat, bed made, scatter cushions in shades of lavender – to the bathroom, done in white and blue tiles and frosted glass in a fern pattern. 'She's in there. I'll stay back as it's a bit tight for two.'

Leo could already smell the tang of blood. Experience told him what he would find. Female suicides usually chose the least violent forms of death – pills or slit wrists in the bath being common. Stepping inside he saw the body slumped in crimson water, skin deathly white by contrast, chin tucked against her chest. Her arms were draped by her side, caught on her hips where there wasn't enough space between them and the tub. The water reached her chest but her face wasn't submerged as the bath was too short. Her hair – a light brown – was dry except for the tips that touched the water. These were stained almost black with blood. Her eyes were closed. She could almost have been asleep. The lividity indicated that death was some hours ago.

'Who found her?' Leo took care not to touch anything, noting that her clothes weren't in the bathroom and the towel was out of reach on the radiator. A burned-down candle sat at one end of the tub, an empty wine glass on a stool near her head, a sharp box-cutter knife beside it. Why hadn't she just dropped that in the water when the job was done? And how had she put it there without dripping blood over the side? Everything was very orderly, apart from the insult of the bloody water.

'She was found like this by a neighbour who has a key. The woman said she didn't touch her as it was clear from the condition of the body that she had been dead a while. She called us and the ambulance. Once they confirmed it was too late to do anything, I sent them away. We're waiting for the pathologist.'

'What made the neighbour drop in?'

'Kelly Ann's sister was worried when she didn't join in on their usual Friday-night call. Deciding she might've been caught up at work or forgotten to mention that she would be out, the sister left it until this morning and, when she still didn't get an answer, she rang Mrs Randall, the neighbour, and asked her to pop in and check on her. I've got one of my team sitting with the neighbour.'

If Kelly Ann missed a call on Friday night, it was likely death was well over twelve hours ago. Leo stepped out of the bathroom. 'Any note?'

'I found it on the bed.' Wilmot held up a plastic evidence bag. On what looked like a sheet taken from a Piccadilly People branded notepad, someone had written 'I'm very sorry' then a line underneath, arching slightly in a flourish. The sheet was half A4. Looking more closely, Leo could see that it had been neatly torn in half, leaving just the top part for the note.

'What do you reckon, sir? Kelly Ann here had had enough for whatever reason, comes home, decides to take the easy way out? But because she doesn't want to bother anyone, she leaves a note and does it in the bath where it will be dead simple to tidy up?'

That was neat – like the house – but Leo wasn't ready to accept that version. 'Any sign of drink or drugs?'

'Wine in the fridge – and the empty glass by the bath. A few boxes of pills downstairs in the medicine cabinet. Not had a proper look through them yet but at first glance they're the usual – aspirin, paracetamol, antihistamines.'

'Bag up the glass and flag the body for a full toxicology report. I want to know what she ingested.'

'If I were going to top myself, I'd take a few tranqs to make it nice and gentle.'

'Maybe. Let's see what the postmortem tells us.'

Leo headed down the stairs, Wilmot following.

'You don't think it's suicide, sir?'

'It might be suicide, but there are just enough off-notes to make me wonder. Let's find out what her family and friends knew about her state of mind. Do we know who her GP was?'

Wilmot pepped up at the possibility that this might be a bigger case than he had anticipated. 'Living here, she probably was a patient at the West Street surgery. I'll see if I can get hold of anyone on a Saturday. My wife knows one of the practice nurses socially – I'll try her, if I've no joy ringing them up.'

Leo walked into the kitchen that was at the back of the cottage. Facing west, it opened out onto what looked like a well-cared-for garden. There was a chicken coop at the end. 'Any residents?' he asked, pointing.

'I had a quick look and I could hear clucking, but they're inside the hen house.'

Another detail that didn't sit well. 'They should probably be let out and fed.' He opened the fridge and saw that it was neatly ordered, the wine opened but hardly a dent made in the level.

'I'll get animal welfare onto it. Perhaps the neighbour knows what to do.'

'After the body is removed.' He checked the recycling bin. No empty wine bottle.

'Of course. There's a side gate. She doesn't need to come into the house again.'

Leo folded his arms and took in the kitchen. A magnetic notepad on the fridge marked 'Lists' with some items already added for the next grocery shop. A calendar with appointments for the following week. A wire chicken with eight eggs inside, one with a fluffy grey feather attached to the shell – from the hens at the end of the garden probably.

Fresh flowers on the table. A neat pile of post. Organised. Normal. Nothing showed a person in despair, pushed to the edge.

'Did you find the pad the note came from?'

Wilmot shook his head. 'I haven't looked yet, sir.'

'Add it to the search. She could have written it at work but that seems a very long time to wait before taking action. It would be far more likely that she would write the note at home. It was a quiet, private death.' Leo checked the handwriting on the fridge pad. It matched that on the note. There was even a similar line struck across the shopping list, separating food from household cleaning items. 'And that's all it says? "I'm very sorry"? That's not much of a note.'

'Maybe she was too distraught to say any more than that?'

'Perhaps.' Leo pinched the bridge of his nose. It would be so much easier just to agree that this was a self-termination and go on with his weekend but he couldn't do that. 'I'm calling this in as a suspicious death, sergeant. Let's contact SOCO and start the canvas of the local area.'

'You think someone else was involved in her killing herself?'

'Keep an open mind and follow where the evidence takes us, sergeant. I'll call in my team. We need to start the investigation again, looking this time for any indication of foul play.'

Wilmot grimaced. 'I'm sorry, sir. What did I miss?'

'You haven't missed anything, because you called me in.'

'No, really, tell me. You've seen something I haven't. What is it?'

Unzipping his crime-scene suit, Leo got out his phone to make the necessary calls. 'A neat woman and a neat death. So why write your note on a torn piece of paper, neglect to cancel the milk, and leave your chickens uncared for? I'd say that was out of character, wouldn't you?'

Chapter Seven

Jess

This was not how I anticipated the weekend to go. Instead of snuggling up to Leo and being largely a spectator as he reconnected with old friends, I found myself thrown in their midst without him to act as a buffer. He messaged at lunchtime saying that the case he'd been called away to was more complicated than first thought and that he couldn't say when he'd be back. I asked if I should head home, but he said he still hoped to make it back for the evening. That left me to make the best of it until then.

On our return from the Rollright Stones, most opted to sit with laptops and books, nap, or chat by the log fire. Rainbow had walked back with us, but Lloyd was still refusing to enter the grounds of the club, preferring to stay in his motorhome and watch football. He made a bit of a scene about her abandoning him but wouldn't budge from his resolve. I think she was relieved to escape.

His stance seemed at odds with having a fun weekend but I came to understand more as I listened to the three Durham women gossip. The piece I'd been missing was rapidly revealed: Lauren's friend, Rebecca the manager, had been married to Lloyd in the late noughties.

'This is entirely your fault,' Janice told Lauren. 'You have to admit you and Freddie are terrible matchmakers.'

Lauren shook her head. 'We merely invited them to the same dinner party. They were married for four years and apparently parted on good terms – I don't count it as a failure.'

But still... awkward – especially if Lloyd had enough resentment left over not to want to come where Rebecca was in charge, I thought.

I studied Rainbow, who seemed to be listening to this squabble with no sign it disturbed her. She clearly knew the history of the prior relationship and hadn't been deterred from following the same path ten years on.

'Do you mind me asking something?' I ventured to the trio as we sat on the sofas with our feet up.

'Of course not,' said Lauren. 'Ask away.'

'Why are you holding the reunion here on Rebecca's turf if it makes things uncomfortable with Lloyd?' I can be a little too blunt but I wanted to know.

Janice shrugged. 'Pass up the chance to experience the Piccadilly People Club at a bargain price? We'd be mad not to take Rebecca up on the offer. They've branches all over the world – *très exclusif*. I'm thinking of joining the one in London.'

She was missing my point. At least Rainbow got what I meant.

'It's really not a problem,' she said, sweetly. 'Lloyd and Rebecca divorced long ago. It's all very amicable now. We'd put off taking up Rebecca's offer for a few years. This time, Lloyd said he didn't want to stop the others enjoying the club.'

But he was happy to make everyone feel bad about him not wanting to join in. What a hero.

'Let me get this straight: Freddie and Lauren married each other?'

Lauren smiled and nodded.

'Janice used to date Leo?'

'We were practically children,' Janice said, moving in her slinky cat way to pose sideways on the couch.

'And Lloyd was married to Lauren's friend Rebecca but is now dating you?' I asked Rainbow.

Rainbow laughed, a little nervously. 'Well, we are all friends: where else do you meet people than in your friendship circle? It's not unusual – is it?'

'Not an expert. Have I missed anyone?' I glanced around the room and saw the executive home builder leafing through the brochure on the other properties in the club portfolio, a covetous gleam in his eye. 'What about poor Phil?'

Janice rolled her eyes. 'Please.'

'Me. A few months – at college,' admitted Rainbow.

I shook my head in wonder. 'Wow – your relationships make love lives in *The Crown* look straightforward.'

'And your relationships are straightforward, I take it?

Funny: that's not what I read about you,' asked Janice, sticking the stiletto in nicely between my ribs. Well, that shut me up, didn't it?

They moved on to discuss the tangled love lives of other friends from college days. I felt excluded as their talk was all about things they used to do, other Durham friends – apparently, there were some couples who couldn't make it this weekend –and funny tales from the past. There was a fair bit of complaining and laughing about men. Lloyd's and Freddie's ears should be burning. That's what these reunions were for really, not for awkward conversations around the new girl. I went in search of Freddie, thinking he would be persuadable to take me out in the dinghy. And I was right: he leaped up like a Labrador seeing the lead brought out.

Our progress as adventurous sailors was aided by a light breeze so, apart from chilled hands and feet, I had a lot of fun with him. We didn't stop giggling. He had a good line in silly jokes. I was afraid that I had to report to Lauren on my return that I had undone any good work Leo might've done persuading Freddie not to follow his dream of sailing around the world with his family. After thirty minutes on the boating lake, I was sold.

High tea was the next event and it was as good as, if not better than, breakfast. Rebecca was back, without a chef but with a tea trolley and waiter, to make sure we were all served our choice of speciality tea. Sikkim Second Flush Muscatel black tea, anyone? I'm not sure Rebecca appreciated my joke about it being a drink for the menopause but Freddie, Phil, and Rainbow laughed and all put in a loud order for it. We also could select teatime favourites themed around local beauty spots from tiered cake-stands. There were Blenheim Palace cucumber sandwiches, White Horse eclairs, Oxford Victoria sponges, and the centrepiece was a clever circle of iced gingerbread made to resemble the Rollright Stones.

'How much does this place cost per night?' I whispered to Lauren, looking guiltily at my eclair.

'Don't ask,' she replied. 'On our salaries, we'd have to get a second mortgage to afford the membership. Or sell one of the kids.'

I held up my hand. 'I'd buy them. They look super cute in your photos. Shame I don't have any money.'

She smiled and patted my hand. 'I think I'll keep the kids. Enjoy this as a one-off.'

'God, yes, wouldn't you get bored having to put up with this luxury everyday?' I said it as a joke but I was actually speaking the truth. I'd lived in an oligarch's mansion for a few months and it was odd how used you could get to such things as swimming pools in the basement.

Lauren smacked her lips. 'This is so sinful – so many calories. I wouldn't mind taking home the chef who made these cakes.'

'Well, he was quite dishy.'

She choked on her gingerbread finger.

'Didn't you notice him this morning? Wasn't he all kind of Joe Wicks as he tossed his pancakes, muscles shown off nicely by his black T-shirt?'

'I'm a happily married woman.' But she was grinning.

'That doesn't stop you having eyes. I mean, I'm perfectly satisfied with Leo.'

'Who wouldn't be? He's as lovely as he looks.'

I gave her a nod for that nice compliment. 'But I still can appreciate a man with skills… in the kitchen, Lauren, the kitchen!' She was fun to tease. 'Anyway, Janice seems very interested in joining the club,' I noted, seeing Janice was talking animatedly to Rebecca between nibbles of cucumber (avoiding the bread).

'She's probably the only one of us who can afford it. Funny how things work out.' Stretching back on the sofa, Lauren scrunched her hair at the top of her head and let it fall back down. 'We all thought she'd be scraping by on next to nothing – you know, the usual story for wannabe actors? Happily, they get paid well in the US, once they land a job. She must've put quite a lot away by now having been in a successful series.' The waiter refilled her cup – only bone china for Piccadilly People. 'Thanks, Daniel.' I liked that she'd learned the young man's name. 'Janice has done far better than any of us would've predicted. Phil always said she'd be a drama teacher by thirty in a comprehensive in the inner city, having to give up her dreams for a real job.'

'Phil does like to put you all down, doesn't he?' I watched him poke at the log fire, telling Freddie the best way to keep it lit.

'Telling it like it is, he says.'

'He's a bit of an idiot.'

'But he does have a heart of gold underneath it all, as he's proved on a number of occasions. You have to dig deep.'

To Australia, I'd've thought. 'But going back to Janice, is it true that she's coming home to stay?'

'That's what she said. She told me on the walk this morning that it looked like her show had been cancelled – but that's hush-hush.' Lauren was as good as Freddie at keeping a secret.

'Wouldn't she do better staying in LA' –and far away from Leo –'to get another part?'

'I think she wants to burnish her image back home. In America, she's a known quantity, nothing to excite the casting directors. She comes back to England as a big star, so she can probably land a part on the West End stage or a lead in a TV series, then fish around for the next big thing having proved her chops as a serious actor.'

'I see. Good luck to her then.'

Lauren caught my less than hearty tone. 'She's kinder than she looks, too.'

'Really?'

'She might pull stupid stuff like stealing your room – I gave her grief about that, I can tell you' – Janice hadn't offered to exchange, I noted – 'but when I had a miscarriage – before having Josie – she was my rock. So sensible, so sensitive. She didn't brush it off like others did. God, I could've strangled the next person who said not to worry, that I just had to get pregnant again, like one child replaced another.'

I had the sinking suspicion I would've been that kind of insensitive friend. 'I'm sorry.'

'Thank you. Having my three certainly helped. But I do still mourn that first. It was a late miscarriage, you see. I was in an accident, so it could've been prevented. Twenty weeks. You've not...?'

She was fishing to see if I had any children. 'No, not yet. I'm pleased Janice was there for you. And maybe that will help me forgive her for stealing my four-poster.'

Lauren nudged me in a friendly fashion. 'There are compensations to having to squeeze up with Leo in your Heidi room.' Back at the motorhome, I'd told Rainbow and Lauren about my childhood dream bedroom as we raided Rainbow's scarves for dress-up. I'd instigated this bit of madness as I felt we weren't paying the monument sufficient interest. That's how I roll if you hadn't yet realised. We then had danced around the Rollright Stones in our approximation of a Druidic rite. The others hadn't joined in. 'Leave it to the pagan maidens!' Freddie had called, cheering our impromptu ceremony.

If ever I form a heavy metal band, that's the name I'd choose.

'Compensations if Leo ever gets back,' I said sombrely.

'True. Have another cake.' Lauren passed me a gingerbread.

You would have thought with so much cake inside me, that I wouldn't have managed dinner. You would be wrong. Leo had already warned me that dinner would be 'posh' and, without him there, I was worrying how I was going to pay for it – that was until Freddie took me aside and mentioned that Leo had already covered my share. Where was Leo? No more messages. Either he was on his way or too busy to answer my texts. We gathered in the lounge to walk over to the clubhouse. Phil and Freddie looked fine in their dinner jackets. Janice was stunning (of course) in a red pantsuit with plunging neckline. Lauren had a lacy dress that was a little mother-of-the-bride but still pretty in pink. I wore an above-the-knee layered dress from the Oxfam online store. Its main claim to fame was that it resembled The Dress that the world could not decide which colour it was. (White and gold in my case, not blue and black). I'd been looking forward to seeing Leo in his dinner jacket so I was genuinely upset that as time ticked by it was looking less and less likely.

My saviour from single-doom came in the shape of Rainbow, who emerged from Janice's room decked in a maxi-dress that I was pleased to see did fade through all the colours of the spectrum in a nod to her name. She held it out and gave a twirl when I applauded.

'Are you my date?' I asked as Janice had already bagged Phil's arm.

'Looks that way.' Rainbow slipped on a patchwork coat, tugging her hair out from the collar. 'Who needs men these days?'

We followed last in line for the short walk across to the stately home that was the clubhouse. Our breath was foggy in the cold air. It was very quiet, just the occasional night sound, a distant dog barking or owl call from the woods, the crunch of tyres as taxis purred down the gravel drive, delivering other dinner guests.

I glanced across at the perfect profile of my companion, a pale outline against the black glass lake. 'What do you do besides travelling, Rainbow?'

'I paint ceramics, when Lloyd lets me have the space –

he's rather proud of his white sofas.' She hugged herself. 'That's the downside of living on top of each other!'

'I can imagine.' And white was never a good choice if you wanted actually to live in a space and not just photograph it.

'I had to give up my studio but the gains outweigh that.' She sounded as if she was convincing herself of that.

As a self-employed person, I wondered how that all worked. Without my computer and hook-up to WiFi, I'd have no business. 'How do you get the commissions?'

'I've a friend in Wales who makes the pots and deals with the orders. I collect them and personalise them.'

'Like doing a portrait of their favourite pet?'

She laughed and shook her head. 'No, nothing like that. My art isn't figurative, more gesture based, like calligraphy. I go for something to express their soul. That's the interesting part of the process. I interview the client and come to an agreement as to what should be on the piece.'

'So Freddie here would be…?' I gestured to her friend, bounding up the road with his characteristic energy.

'He would be something funny on the surface but serious and loving underneath – a selkie, maybe.'

'From Hebridean mythology? Right, I see. What about Janice?'

'A dragon. A beautiful one, obviously, but with glowing red scales.'

'You came up with that very quickly!'

She nudged me. 'I've had plenty of time to think about it.'

'What about Leo?'

'Ah, that would be a challenge.'

'It would have to be something to do with gardens.'

'You're right. Maybe there's a tree that would suit?'

'He loves his bonsai.'

'Then one of them? Something controlled yet bursting with life.'

I knew the perfect thing. 'Japanese winterberry. I got him one for Christmas. It bears berries like beads of blood, and has light-pink blossom.'

'I should paint him one for his next birthday.' She linked arms with me. 'It sounds to me like you suit him.'

'He definitely suits me.' It was a relief to find there was another one of his friendship circle who I could relate to. 'How would you paint yourself?'

'Oh?' She gave another laugh, a little brittle this time. 'I really don't like thinking about myself much. I'm such a mess.'

'But you're living the dream!'

'Am I? It's kind of you to say that.' She wrinkled her nose. 'It isn't exactly what I expected. Not the life, but the person I am when living it.'

The restaurant was in the converted stable block, attached to the manor house by a glass walkway. The main room had a vaulted wooden ceiling rather like the pictures I'd seen of their old college in Durham. Two long oak tables stretched the length, their polished surfaces laid with tall black candelabras, dark roses, glasses, and cutlery. That, added to the black iron chandeliers dimly lighting the space, made for a very medieval atmosphere. Sadly, the waiters weren't dressed as jesters or troubadours, but in the usual green livery of the club.

I took a seat next to Lauren at the end of our table. Hoping against hope that I wouldn't be stood up, the chair opposite was left for Leo.

'Do you know why they're wearing black armbands?' I whispered to Lauren as I saw that everyone on the staff had one on their arm or a black ribbon pinned to their shirt.

'Rebecca told me that they've heard of a sudden death of a colleague this morning.' Lauren buttered her roll.

I made the connection. 'Do you think…?'

Lauren nodded. 'She said not to say, but, as it's Leo, and he's yours, you'll find out anyway. A suicide. Totally unexpected. The woman was fine on Friday and then, just like that, she's gone.' She took a bite. 'I didn't think I could possibly be hungry again today, but homemade bread...!'

I tore off a piece from my roll. 'I know. It's a killer of self-control.' If the death was a suicide, then why wasn't Leo back yet? I decided that it was best not to say that to Lauren. Anything I said to her I had to be happy to have shared with everyone and it sounded like Rebecca knew the person, or at least worked with her. But I could get a head start for Leo's enquiries, couldn't I?

'Time to order a bottle of wine to go with the bread, I think, and drown life's sorrows. Did Rebecca say anything else?'

'Just that Kelly Ann was the last person you would think

would take her own life: efficient, cheerful, not noticeably moody or prone to depression.'

The waitress filled my glass with a red that Freddie had chosen from the long wine list that had scared the bejabbers out of me. I took a sip.

'Hmm, each sip rolls on the tongue like velvet. I'm getting hints of blackberry, oak, and stacks of cash,' I said, using my best Jancis Robinson manner.

Lauren smiled and put her hand over her glass. 'White for me,' she told the waitress. 'I sometimes have a funny reaction to red,' she explained.

I clicked my fingers in the air. 'Quickly, a Chardonnay for the lady! It's an emergency.'

The waitress actually brought her a Sauvignon Blanc.

'I was just joking,' I told the girl, thinking maybe she might've thought I was acting like a self-entitled trust-fund chick. 'Sorry.'

'No problem, madam.' She leant closer. 'The tag is sticking out of the back of your dress. I thought you might like to know.'

'Oh, my God.' I nudged Lauren. 'Make sure we tip her. Would you mind ripping it out?'

Lauren got a tiny compact out of her bag and found a pair of nail scissors. Discreetly, she snipped off the tag and handed it to me without a word.

Chapter Eight

Jess

I was still sitting solo as we finished dinner and were ready to move on to the casino. Leo had texted an update, saying he still hoped to get back that night and sorry he had to miss dinner. I already knew that police enquiries, particularly at the start, were complex operations that involved lots of moving parts. The scene-of-crime officers. The pathologist. The forensic teams. The gathering of statements and logging of these into HOLMES, the police computer system. The preservation of evidence. Notification and family liaison. Dealing with any interested press or matters of wider public interest. And someone had to oversee it to ensure all these parts worked together, and that was my guy, the senior investigating officer.

'Ready to splash some cash?' I asked Rainbow, shaking water off my fingers as we freshened up in the ladies' before heading down. This was one of those chichi lounges with a basket of flannels to use as hand towels rather than pull-it-from-the-wall paper dispensers. Some kind of feng-shui arrangement with pebbles and twigs arched between the sinks. I resisted the temptation to disturb it.

Rainbow smoothed her already perfect hair. 'I don't think I've ever been to a casino before. I'm sure I'll make a complete hash of it.' She was curiously low on self-esteem for such a gorgeous woman. 'I didn't expect a country hotel to have one.'

'Ah, but it's not a country hotel; it's a playground for the rich, a version of the American country club.' I tweaked a wayward strand of hair in the mirror. 'Though to be honest, I think it's more like a posh person's version of Center Parcs.'

'But what do you have to do in a casino? It's so far away from my ordinary life.'

'I think it's the game equivalent of falling off a log. I mean, if all those bachelorette parties in Las Vegas can grasp the principles, I'm sure a sober gaggle of Durham graduates can.' I put away my lip-gloss. 'From what I can see, you decide how much you can afford to lose, then go and lose it, trying to have fun along the way. Don't expect to come out on top as the house always wins in the end.' I turned and grinned at her. 'Hey, that almost sounded grown-up! I surprise myself sometimes.'

'How much are you going to spend?' Rainbow glanced into her beaded bag.

'Fifty quid. That's my limit.' I was temporarily solvent, having earned a decent amount from my two jobs, but I was saving up for set-up costs for an office space. Working on missing persons from my bedroom in my shared house was not very professional and people just didn't do Skype calls with their duvet as a backdrop if they wanted to be taken seriously.

'Do you think they'll mind if I only put down twenty?' asked Rainbow.

Was this frugality or was she even more strapped for cash than I was? 'Rainbow, it's money. They'll take anything off you.'

I took her arm and together we went to the cash desk where we exchanged our money for chips. I was given a false sense of my own riches as I asked for small denominations.

We entered the underground chamber, tables spotlit by low-hanging shades that reminded me of snooker clubs. There'd been a time and a boyfriend when that had been the kind of place I'd hung out. This was definitely more upmarket than the offerings off the Mile End Road and the smoky clubs always on the point of violence. Rather than chewing-gum-speckled lino and grey walls, there was a crimson carpet, velvet hangings, and gold swirls on the red Moroccan wallpaper. It was a little too dictator-kitsch to me. None of the players, apart from Janice and Rainbow, were James Bond-extra standard, so it didn't quite reach the level of sophistication I'd hoped for. This place needed something. What was it? Oh, yes. Leo in a dinner jacket.

I let that little vision mature in my mind for a moment. Where was he?

'What do you want to try first?' asked Rainbow. 'I don't even know how to play.'

My knowledge was taken from films so I was only a little more clued in. 'Let's try roulette. That seems the basic throw-your-money-away game, requiring no skill.'

We wove our way through the guests to the nearest roulette wheel. There was something enticing about the rattle and clicks that came from the table, pushing a button I already suspected I had for wild gambles. Janice was there, putting her chips on the outside edge where you were given groups of numbers at lower odds, a safer strategy than stacking everything on a single number.

'Place your bets please,' the croupier announced.

After much deliberation, Rainbow went for a range: one to eighteen. Never one to do something half-arsed, I piled a little stack on my lucky number (thirty-one– my age) and got ready to lose it. The wheel spun and the ball rattled around, tantalising us with its dance, then dropped into 7.

'My number!' cawed Janice. I then noticed one token of hers on that square. My bet got ignominiously scooped up and winnings were shovelled towards the others, a large portion going to the actress who had already come out on top so much in life.

As Rainbow seemed happy to carry on with the game and keep Janice company, I wandered off to find more entertainment before I ran out of chips. I settled on blackjack, which I knew was possibly the simplest card game in existence after snap. I slid into the free chair next to Freddie.

'Where's Lauren?' I asked.

'She's a fan of baccarat.' He jerked his head over to the far end of the room where a discreet curtain obstructed the view of that table. 'It's too intense for me.' He patted his heart. 'The engines canna take it, captain.'

I grinned. 'Yeah, you got to be careful now you're almost forty.'

He groaned.

'Any luck so far?' I asked, noticing that his pile of tokens was not much bigger than mine.

'None. Bust each time.'

'Ladies and gentlemen, are you ready?' The dealer asked. We each placed the table minimum down as our bet and readied ourselves for the cards. I had a five and a ten. Freddie two eights.

'You wave your hand like this if you want another one,' Freddie told me.

'OK, hit me.' Wasn't that what they said?

The dealer handed me a 7 of hearts.

'Unlucky,' commiserated Freddie. He then split his two eights apart.

'What are you doing?' I hissed.

'If you get a pair, you can take them separately, double your chances.'

'That doesn't sound very fair.'

'This is gambling. It doesn't run on fairness, but luck.'

The dealer handed him a ten to add to one, where he stuck, a five and a six on the other.

'I'm happy with that,' said Freddie. 'Let's see what she's got.'

The dealer turned over a ten, which added to her seven, meant Freddie was the winner on both hands. He raked it in.

'Beginner's luck,' he said to me.

'In my case, bad luck.' I took up my remaining chips and headed for the dice game. Phil was blowing on his fist and flinging the dice down the table with every indication that he knew what he was doing. From his 'yay!', he too was on a winning streak.

'How's it going, Jess?' he asked me.

I grimaced. 'Crap.'

He made room at his side. 'Then this is the game for you.'

'I have not the faintest idea how to play this,' I admitted, looking at the list of craps rules that seemed fiendishly complicated.

'How about I tell you what to do and you just throw the dice?'

Following that advice, I did make back some of my losses. The game seemed to involve trying to throw one number, say seven, and then when you failed, trying to throw that new number instead. Between the croupier with the little rake thing and Phil, I managed a few rounds. I think they were humouring me.

Finally, the joy of chucking dice exhausted, I picked up my modest stack of chips and backed away. 'Thanks, but I'm out. See you in the bar.'

Having had enough of this subterranean existence where everyone was a winner but me, I went over to the baccarat table to see if I could find Lauren, hoping to lure her away to the bar upstairs. She wasn't there. Deciding to call it a night, I went back via the roulette wheel, placed my remaining chips on number seven, and promptly lost them all when the ball landed on thirty-one. *Now, Lady Luck, you're just messing with me.*

Fifty quid washed down the drain in record time – or into the silk-lined pockets of the owners of Piccadilly People, I should say. I headed upstairs, saw the waitress just on her way out for the night and persuaded her to stay for one drink – on me – as a thank you. We were joined by the Joe Wicks chef going off-duty (her boyfriend) and we actually had quite a nice time chatting. As I was a complete stranger and not being judged by them as a partner of someone they had all known far longer than me, I was able to relax for the first time that day.

All I needed now was for my policeman to come home.

Chapter Nine

Leo

Leo slid in beside Jess, negotiated the hump between the beds not disguised by the mattress topper, and pulled her into his arms. At last.

She mumbled and tucked her head under his chin.

It was two-thirty and he was exhausted. Everything had taken far longer than he'd liked, partly because it was a weekend, but also because he'd had to stay to argue his case that this was no commonplace suicide. With his boss really preferring he wouldn't 'complicate matters', a friend at the lab had done him a favour and put a rush on the blood results. The superintendent had backed down when they came through. The victim had ninety-five milligrams per hundred millilitres of blood – enough to make driving illegal but by no means blind drunk. There were, however, very high levels of a prescription sedative. That was not unusual for a suicide but Kelly Ann's GP had confirmed that he had never prescribed her these drugs. In fact, he said he hardly saw her apart from routine checkups as she was a healthy single person with no mental illness or suicidal urges that she had ever brought to him.

How had the drugs got into her then? In alcohol, according to forensics. The glass by the bath showed traces of drugged wine. The wine in the fridge was uncontaminated. And Leo still couldn't reconcile the levels in the bottle and her blood results. She could have started drinking before coming home – they'd check the local bars, pubs, and her place of work – but the fact remained that the glass by the bath was a large bulb-shaped one. Would you bother to take just a centimetre or two up to your candlelit soak? It wouldn't have even been enough to down the number of pills she had to have swallowed to reach the level of sedatives they'd detected. In any case, wouldn't you, on a Friday night, think it was time for self-indulgence and give yourself a generous serving? Especially if you were easing your way out of life. So where was the other bottle?

Jess turned over and muttered something. Leo held still, waiting for her breath to even out. The only one awake in the dark, he ran the two scenarios: suicide and foul play. Scenario One: Kelly Ann decided to kill herself. He still couldn't see a motive for that, or any sign her thoughts had turned that way apart from the enigmatic note. But, he had to acknowledge, people did the strangest things. She finished off one bottle of white for some Dutch courage and disposed of it, how? Household waste had been checked and no bottle found. The bins had not been emptied that morning as it was a Saturday. That left… what? Someone clearing the bottle away after she was dead? The neighbour who found her swore she didn't touch anything in the house. No one else was known to have been inside, no one else local had a key. It wasn't working as a description of the facts.

Scenario Two: there had been another person with the victim on Friday. They drank wine together, probably at the victim's home. Kelly Ann's had been spiked. In her woozy state she's persuaded to take a bath. But by whom? A lover? It had to be someone she trusted, surely?

Fast-forward: she falls asleep in the tub and the murderer slits her wrists, having staged what they believed was a perfect suicide. The gush of blood into the water would've been shocking but otherwise it was a quiet death. They leave the blade so the message of self-termination would be crystal clear; but they make one big mistake by taking the bottle and the glass they had drunk from, to avoid leaving identifiable DNA traces or fingerprints. Leo had counted the victim's glasses in the kitchen cupboard and she had five including the one by the bath. Unless Kelly Ann had broken one (and she seemed too organised not to have replaced it), that meant one of the set was missing. The idea of another person being involved solved some of the inconsistencies in the manner of death, but opened up a whole new set of questions. The biggest being, why?

'Hmm, stop it. I can hear you thinking.' Jess pawed at his chest, sleep-dazed.

He smiled up at the ceiling. 'Bad habit. I'll tell my brain to switch off. Did you have a good evening?'

She snuggled closer. 'Not without you. Gambling sucks. I lost fifty quid.'

His smile broadened. 'Sorry.'

'Stop apologising and sleep. You can make it up to me in the morning.'

This probably wasn't the time to mention that he had a full day of interviews scheduled. He kissed the top of her head and let his busy brain shut off and sink into oblivion.

Up at seven, Leo got dressed, intending to make an early start.

'Leo?' Jess's voice was raspy, coming from deep under the duvet.

'You're going to hate me.' He donned one of his work suits, grateful he'd had the foresight to bring it with him in the garment bag with his unused dinner jacket.

'Doubtful – unless you're abandoning me again.' She lifted her head from under the covers and her eyes registered her disappointment. 'You are, aren't you?'

'Yes.'

She threw his pillow at him.

He caught it and carried to back to the bed. He sat down beside her. 'This is not the weekend I wanted to give you. I'll arrange a lift home for you this morning.' He stroked the hair from her forehead. 'I'm really sorry.'

Jess mock-pouted. They'd had this discussion before when death had spoiled their weekend plans, but he knew she understood even if she didn't like it. 'I hate your job sometimes.'

'I'll make it up to you. We'll go away again, but on our own.'

She smiled sleepily. 'Four-poster? No Janice?'

'Absolutely. Just you, me and room service.'

'OK. Go catch the bad guy – or gal.' She gave a histrionic sigh.

'Thank you.' He bent down and kissed her. 'You are the best.'

Tucking his tie in his pocket, he went quietly downstairs only to find Rainbow, Freddie, and Lauren already at breakfast.

'*Leo!*' exclaimed Freddie. 'The wanderer returns.'

'Not for long, I'm afraid. I've got to go back into work.' He took a seat next to Freddie at the breakfast counter. A selection of breakfast cereals, fresh fruit, and pastries had been laid out by the staff. He hadn't even heard the kitchen team come in. He must've been tired.

'You look good in a suit, Leo,' said Rainbow, 'but aren't you too well-dressed for crime?'

'You can never be too well-dressed for crime.' He was glad he'd left off the tie. 'You're all up early.'

'Trained by our children,' said Lauren.

'I still find it odd to eat breakfast without cartoons playing. I could even listen to the news if I wanted. Imagine that!' said Freddie.

'And you, Rainbow? Are you always an early-riser?' asked Leo.

Rainbow peeled an orange. 'Definitely, since being on

the road. The dawn chorus strikes up and I always feel I have to get moving.'

'You walked over that early?'

She shook her head. 'Crashed with Janice last night. Lovely four-poster bed like something from a Disney film.' Luckily, Jess wasn't up to hear this. 'It was seriously late when we called it a night.'

'And we'd all had too much to drink to drive Rainbow back,' admitted Freddie. 'Bit of a miscalculation there.'

Leo checked the newspapers set out on the sideboard. Nothing about his case on the front pages of the nationals. The local paper was a weekly so that would take a while to pick it up.

'There's cooked food in the warmer if you prefer,' said Lauren, pointing to some silver domed dishes on the counter with little burners underneath to keep the food hot.

'Just coffee, fruit, and cereal will be fine.' Leo piled muesli into a bowl and added a generous portion of fruit salad.

Lauren rose to get him a coffee. 'I thought policemen were all about doughnuts and full English breakfasts?'

'Which leads to an arrest at forty – a cardiac arrest.' He took the coffee from her. 'Thank you.'

Rainbow giggled. 'It's nice to hear you joking. I think you've lightened up since you got together with Jess.'

Lauren patted his arm. 'We like her. She can stay.'

'I was rather hoping she'd stick around – with me that is.' For how long, he wasn't sure. This conversation was making him feel uncomfortable. His other girlfriends had only lasted a year or two at most before tiring of him. 'As

I've got to work, I'll arrange a lift home for her today. Bit much to expect her to put up with you lot without me.'

'No need to do that. We'll look after her!' Freddie protested.

Leo just smiled.

'Leo's right. She did well without you here but it must be hard being the stranger in our group. She's clearly head-over-heels for you to do that,' said Rainbow. 'She watched the door the whole night, hoping you'd come in.'

'And left early when you didn't,' added Lauren. 'She missed you.'

'It couldn't be helped,' he said awkwardly.

'We all know that. She knows that. But it was nice that she missed you.' Lauren looked to Freddie and they shared that matchmaking smile that was just a little smug.

'But the timing couldn't be worse. I hope the rest of you had a good night without me?'

'It was fun. I came away only five pounds down,' said Rainbow. 'Janice made a killing.'

'I lost my shirt,' admitted Freddie. 'I should've quit while I was ahead.'

'How much of a shirt?' asked Leo, commiserating.

'A hundred quid.'

Not too serious then. 'Bad luck. Rainbow, I've got to drive into Chipping Norton to pick up a colleague. Would you like a lift back home?' he asked.

'Oh, would you?' Rainbow offered him a segment of orange, which he took. 'The others are going to drive over later and join us for a walk and pub lunch but that saves Lauren an extra journey.'

By car, it was only a short run to the Rollright Stones, just ten minutes compared to the hour it had taken them to walk it the day before. Leo noticed that Rainbow was frowning as they drove through the white sparkling lanes.

'Everything OK?' Leo asked.

'Lloyd's going to be annoyed. When I left, I said I'd be back last night.' She scratched at her trouser leg, removing a burr that had caught on the patchwork seam.

'You told him you weren't coming? He's not going to have been up all night worrying?'

'Of course I told him. I messaged him three times. But he didn't reply. I think he's punishing me for having fun without him. He can be childish like that sometimes. Not keen on me having my own life.'

'Jealous?' Leo worried for her.

'Crumbs, yes. He always is when he's in a relationship, according to Lauren. I knew that before we started living together and mostly I handle it just fine.' She rubbed at a mark on the window, exhaled on it, then drew a star in the mist. 'And he knows that there're no rivals among us lot. We all know far too much about each other – we know where all the bodies are buried, so to speak.'

'Hmm.'

She slapped her hand to her mouth but a snort escaped. 'Sorry, unfortunate metaphor. Mind you, of us all, you are the one who always kept your secrets.'

'That's because my mother didn't know the meaning of the word discretion.'

'Oh, God, yes, I remember.' Her tone changed as she recalled the mess Haven Keene had made of her son's life.

'Seeing the damage she did, I'm not one for oversharing.'

'That's really understandable and I'm sorry for… well, we all love you as you are. You know that, don't you, Leo?'

'I appreciate that.' He pulled up beside the motorhome. It was now eight but there was no sign that Lloyd was up, curtains and door still closed.

Rainbow put a hand on his where it rested on the gear stick. 'Come and say "Hi", will you? It might divert him from being in a huff with me.'

'I'm not exactly his favourite person, Rainbow.'

'Oh, but he likes you!' Her blue eyes, the colour of forget-me-nots, were round with earnestness. 'He said as much yesterday. He says you're "the genuine article".'

This didn't sound likely to Leo. 'Meaning?'

She furrowed her brow, thinking. 'I believe he meant it in contrast to Phil – he can't stand Phil. Oil and water, those two.'

Or maybe people with too many traits in common, thought Leo. 'OK, I'll just drop by for a second. I really do have to get to work.'

'I know, I know.' Rainbow got out of the car and hurried over to the steps. She tried the door but it was locked. She tapped lightly.

'Lloyd? Are you awake yet? It's me.'

Leo joined her. 'Don't you have a key?'

'I didn't bring one with me. Lloyd? *Lloyd!* I've got Leo with me.'

Leo didn't feel he could leave her on the step. Perhaps they'd got their wires crossed and Lloyd had walked over to meet her?

'Try ringing again?' he suggested.

She did, and now they could both hear the mobile ringing inside. Rainbow pressed her ear to the door. 'The TV is on.'

Leo crouched beside her. Over the hum of the generator, he could hear the murmur of some discussion programme. He caught the word 'menopause' and thought it was unlikely viewing for Lloyd.

'He's probably gone out, hoping to meet up with you on the footpath.'

'Not without his phone.' Rainbow sounded worried now and Leo picked up some of her unease.

'I'll check the windows.' Leo went round the van but all the curtains were tightly closed and the air vents shut. He could hear Rainbow hammering on the door. When he got back to her, she had a rock, which she was bashing at the handle, doing a lot of damage to the paintwork.

'Hang on, if you're determined to break in, there's a better tool for that.' He got a crow bar out of his toolkit in the boot. 'Stand back.' He wedged it between the frame and the door and heaved. The door popped open, in no shape to close again. Lloyd would be furious when he saw that. They could both hear the television now, but no Lloyd emerged from the shower to ask what they were doing. The only light was from the flickering screen.

Rainbow bounded up the steps and plunged inside.

'God, Lloyd, why didn't you hear us? You had us both worried for a moment.'

Leo went to the top step but didn't enter. He could see an empty bottle of Scotch on the coffee table, which suggested one reason why his host might not want visitors.

Rainbow shook Lloyd's arm. He was asleep on the sofa. 'Lloyd? Wake up, Lloyd!' She slapped his cheeks.

Suddenly, Leo understood what he was looking at. He crossed the short distance and moved her back. 'Go outside quickly and call an ambulance.' Lloyd was uncommonly flushed – a cherry-pink colour Leo knew all too well from attending a recent death on a canal boat. Putting his scarf over his mouth, he felt for a pulse. Nothing. The body was already cool.

Rainbow hadn't moved. Grabbing her arm, he towed her outside to get clear.

'What—' she asked, bewildered.

He braced her, hands holding her upper arms. 'Look at me, Rainbow.' Her eyes were skittering all over the place, from the stone circle, to the busted door, to what lay within. 'I think it's carbon monoxide poisoning. You can't go back in there.'

'But Lloyd—' Her voice cracked as she realised what he was saying. 'CPR – can we try that?' She pulled away to go back in.

'I'm really sorry but he's dead. He has been for a while. There was nothing you could've done.' Except die with him if she'd been there the night before. 'And nothing we can do now. I'm so sorry.'

'No.' Rainbow shook her head, her face blank, not wanting to accept it. 'You must be wrong. It's a mistake...'

He dug out his phone, making sure he kept hold of her. He hadn't shut off the source of the fumes so the interior was a death-trap. 'I need an ambulance and tell Sergeant Wilmot we've another'—he couldn't say 'body' with Rainbow right by him—'incident. I need a team sent to the Rollright Stones. Yes, I'm standing by.'

Chapter Ten

Jess

The sun was up long before me. I hadn't fully roused when Leo headed off to work, only enough to grasp that he was sending the escape vehicle to rescue me this morning. I rolled out of bed and splashed water on my face in the little bathroom. Digging through the contents of our suitcase, I selected warm clothes for the February day. I borrowed Leo's fleece. If I couldn't have him, I'd at least have his scent with me.

Time to face his friends and say my goodbyes.

Skipping down the stairs, I entered the lounge and saw immediately that something was very wrong. Lauren and Freddie were huddled together on a sofa, her head on his shoulder as she sobbed. Janice and Phil were sitting in separate armchairs, both with shocked expressions. Rebecca the manager was talking on the phone in a lowered voice, but she too looked ill.

'What's happened?' I asked.

'It's L-Lloyd.' Freddie's voice hitched and he cleared his throat. 'Lloyd… He's dead. Died last night. Something about the heater in the van. Carbon monoxide.'

'Oh, my God.' I searched the room. 'Where's Rainbow? Is she OK?' I seemed to remember some idea that she'd sleep over with Janice.

'She's all right – as much as she can be, considering. Leo's bringing her back. He was with her when she found him.'

'Oh, guys, I'm so sorry.' I wrung my hands together, then tucked them under my armpits. 'What can I do?'

Rebecca hung up the phone and stood at the counter, head bent. He'd been her ex-husband, hadn't he? This had to be horrible for her. I went over to her and touched her arm. 'I'm really sorry for your loss. Is there any way I can help?'

'It's all such a shock. First Kelly Ann, now this.' Rebecca seemed completely at sea.

'Sit down with your friends. I'll make tea. I think everyone needs something to put some warmth back in them.' I steered her over to sit with Lauren and Freddie. Freddie put his free arm around her and pulled her into the hug. I switched on the kettle and tried to work out what this meant for our weekend. The selfish thought crept in that I just wanted to scurry back to Oxford. I made myself a milky coffee and tried to sneak a few bites of croissant where no one could see. I was shocked, but not that shocked. Does that make me a bad person? Probably.

'How can it have happened?' asked Janice to the room at

large. 'That motorhome looked top of the range. They'd been sleeping in it all winter.'

'I'm sure those are the questions the investigation will be looking at,' said Freddie, falling back on procedures. 'But I can tell you that portable generators are notorious. We've had problems at the MOD with mobile units. There's no way to smell or see carbon monoxide – you just go to sleep and don't wake up. That's why you need a detector. Didn't they have a detector?'

No one knew the answer to that, of course. I handed around a tray of tea. Everyone took a mug but I think they were just being polite. None of us knew what to do.

Tyres crunching on the gravel outside warned us that Rainbow and Leo were back. It was almost a relief. Freddie hurried to the door. The others stood up and waited in a huddle in the no-man's land between dining area and sofas. I hung back in the kitchen.

'Rainbow! Oh, my God, come here!' Freddie hugged her tightly while Leo hovered on the doorstep behind.

The others joined in the chorus of disbelief and sorrow. Rebecca and Rainbow exchanged a very long and tearful embrace, both rocking the other.

'He's gone,' sobbed Rainbow.

'I know,' said Rebecca.

'I can't believe it.'

'Neither can I. Such a strong man – it's all so wrong.'

'It's not fair, Becca, not fair.'

'Shh, love, shh.' Rebecca pulled Rainbow down beside her on the two-person sofa and let her sob.

The others came to perch like a disconsolate flock of

crows, balanced on chair arm and sofa back. No one seemed at ease with sitting. Leo came over to me.

'Are you OK?' he asked.

'I should be asking you that.' I poured him a black coffee. 'You look like you need something to warm you up.'

He ran his hand over his face, but then reached out and took it. 'Thanks. You're right. It's a mess.'

'I can imagine.'

'I can't be involved because I know the victim. Another detective is coming to take over.'

'But it's an accident, right?'

'Probably. No sign he intended to go that way.'

'God, no. Yesterday, it was quite clear he wanted to be around for many years to bug the hell out of meat-eaters.' Did that sound too flippant? 'Sorry, I don't know what's the right thing to say.'

'You don't have to worry what you say around me.' He rubbed the back of his neck.

'It's just...' I said, trailing off.

'I know. All wrong. But we can't just assume it was an accident. We have to investigate it as an unattended death.'

'Like the other one – the one you went off to handle yesterday?'

'That's what really makes this complicated. I've got to get back to that. I've already got interviews scheduled, Rebecca among them. I've explained to my boss what's going on, but she's so short-handed with people off sick, I can't pass it on.' He lowered his voice. 'That one from yesterday is looking like it might be murder, or at least assisted suicide.'

'Bloody hell. That's not good.'

'She needs someone to stand for her now and that has to be me.'

'I get it.' I straightened his tie for him. 'Should I go back to Oxford?'

He looked over my shoulder at his friends. 'Would you mind very much just sticking around for a little longer?'

'Me?'

'The detectives will want to speak to you and I can't now send you away – it would look as if I'm obstructing their work.'

Ah. I was a witness. Damn. I mustered a smile. 'Of course.'

'Give it a few hours. I'll call in after my first set of interviews and see how things are going. If everyone is told to go home by the investigating officer, I'll make arrangements for a car. Would you mind taking Rainbow back to mine?'

'Her home's a crime scene,' I realised. 'Poor Rainbow. The dream's become a nightmare.'

'Let me know if there's an emergency, otherwise just hold the fort, will you?'

I gave him a salute that shifted to tenderness as I reached out to caress his cheek. 'I'm sorry about your friend, Leo.'

He placed his hand over mine. 'Lloyd wasn't really my friend.'

'I was thinking of Rainbow.'

'Oh. I'm sorry, too.' He kissed me. He pulled away and met my gaze to check I was really all right before turning to the others. I could see the mental shift he made, walking the line between official and personal. 'Rainbow, Rebecca, everyone, I can't tell you how sorry I am at this tragedy. I know this has come as a terrible shock to all of us. For the moment, my colleagues dealing with the…with Lloyd would appreciate you staying here. They'll be over soon to interview you because we were all in the motorhome yesterday. They'll need to talk to Rainbow, too – sorry, Rainbow, but I'm not allowed to be there. Maybe Jess can sit with you? She knows about police work.'

She nodded but didn't look up from Rebecca's arms.

'And where the fuck will you be?' asked Phil, making no effort at politeness. He was angry and Leo was a convenient target.

'I'm still following up the case I was on yesterday.'

Phil shot to his feet. 'What's wrong with this fucking place? People topping themselves left right and centre!' He kicked a footstool, but as it was a solid stuffed piece it didn't shift.

'Lloyd didn't kill himself!' wailed Rainbow. 'He wouldn't.'

'You know he fucking would – only rational way out for a man who had fucked everything up.' Phil was working up quite a rage.

'*Phil!*' said Freddie, sounding much more assertive than usual. 'This isn't helping Rainbow.'

'Pretending otherwise won't help her either. Lloyd cocked up his life – we all know it. All that schtick yesterday? I didn't buy it, even if you did.'

'Shut up, Phil,' said Lauren, her eyes on Rainbow who was close to hyperventilating. 'It's not the time.'

Janice got up and took his arm. 'Phil, let's walk a little way around the lake. We're not running off,' she said to Leo. 'I just think we need to get some air.'

'Thanks, Janice,' said Leo. 'Good idea. I'm sorry to leave you all like this.' He went over and knelt beside Rebecca. 'Do you want to reschedule our interview about Kelly Ann? I know this news about your ex-husband must be especially hard for you.'

She looked up, startled. Her attention had been on calming Rainbow. 'I… I would appreciate that. Sorry, I'd completely forgotten we were supposed to meet.'

'Understandable.' He gave one last look around the room. 'I have to go.'

'Is there something… anything we can do?' asked Lauren.

Leo opened his mouth to say there was nothing but I knew we needed a task to get through the next few hours.

'How about we make a detailed timeline of what happened yesterday?' I suggested.

Leo nodded. 'That's a good idea but, please, write it out separately. The interviewers will want to know no one has influenced anyone else. I'm leaving an officer with you. She's just outside. She can help you with any questions you might have and keep you up to date. I'll be back as soon as I can.'

I watched him go, wishing with all my heart I could stride out with him. Instead, I turned back to the mourners and set about finding paper and pens.

Chapter Eleven

Leo

The Piccadilly People management had offered Leo and his team the library for their interviews with staff. Before taking his first one, Leo handed over the search warrant to Jamie Paxton, the head of legal affairs who turned up in a charcoal bespoke suit, suitably funereal. Leo began an initial check on the victim's office. It would be searched more thoroughly by the team arriving this morning but he wanted to see where the dead woman had worked. He found it was a chilly white box of an office at the back of the mansion on the ground floor; she shared this with another accountant and the person who managed membership communications. The door was marked BUTLER'S PANTRY and there were signs of its former use in the Victorian patterned tiled floor and the row of hooks along the wall by the door. A cardigan hung limply on the last peg. Hers? he wondered. He checked the pockets, finding only a neatly folded tissue. The windows were a little high, probably to prevent the below-stairs servants from looking out. There were portable heaters near each desk.

Heaters. These ones looked like they were electric, but it reminded him of what would be happening at the motorhome right now. His colleagues would be taking a very close look at the generator that ran the heaters. They'd tow the vehicle for closer inspection at the police pound.

That wasn't his case. Dragging his attention back to his victim, he checked her desk drawers. Pads of headed notepaper were stacked neatly inside, still in their plastic wrap. There didn't appear to be one in use in her work area but those belonging to her colleagues had to be taken into evidence just in case she'd written her note on one of theirs. The pads were ubiquitous though. He'd noticed one on the telephone table in the guest cabin as well as in the lobby area of the clubhouse. It wasn't unreasonable to imagine she took one home with her. What this visit did confirm for him was that Kelly Ann was as neat at work as she was at home.

The search team arrived and he briefed them before leaving them to it. Entering the library, he found DS Boston helping himself to the tray of pastries the kitchen had laid on for the police team. A burly man with the lumbering movements of a rugby player who'd done a few too many scrums in his career, Harry was always a big presence in any enquiry team.

'Inspector,' said Harry in an unusually happy tone, 'great grub. Prime location.'

Leo had to admit the library, with its rows of oak bookcases, gilded leather tomes, and leather armchairs, beat the characterless interview rooms at the various police stations around Thames Valley.

'Morning, Harry.'

'I heard you found another one dead on the way to work.' Harry added three spoonfuls of sugar to his tea.

'He was a friend – an acquaintance.'

'Sorry to hear that. Bad luck.' Harry's tone was gruff but not unsympathetic. He did have a heart then, despite his ongoing feud with Leo. Harry's resentment was based on the fact that he had to take orders from Leo, who was the younger man. 'Can I get you something?' He waved to the tray.

'Thanks, but let's just get started.' Leo helped himself to a water and checked the list. 'We'll begin with the two women she worked with. You take Nicola Hayes, the assistant accountant, and I'll take Elizabeth Benfield, the membership secretary.'

'Today's looking up. You've given me the glamour puss.' Harry rubbed his hands together and headed for the door to call them in.

Leo took his seat at the far end of the room in the windows that looked out over tennis courts. A pair of mixed doubles were playing, well insulated in designer sportswear against the cold. They looked very good, the match many levels above a casual knockabout.

'Inspector?'

Leo turned to find a small woman in a black shirt and grey skirt waiting for his attention, hands held clasped at chest height. He immediately thought of a gerbil waiting to be fed – a stray memory from primary school. 'Miss Benfield? Please take a seat.' Behind her, he could see Harry beginning his conversation with an elegant thirty-something in a yellow trouser suit. The colour seemed too frivolous for the occasion, even with the black armband.

'I don't know what you think I can tell you, Inspector,' began Miss Benfield, keeping her handbag on her lap in front of her. 'I just can't believe it. Kelly Ann was the very last person to commit suicide. I have no explanation.'

'You were friends?'

'Yes. Good friends, I would've said. How did I not know?' she appealed to him. 'I could've done something – I could've got her help.'

'Miss Benfield, can you describe what state of mind Kelly Ann was in when you last saw her? When was that, by the way?'

'Friday, at the end of shift. We were celebrating because the Christmas figures had come out and we had made a record profit this year: bookings in all areas were up, our waiting list increased ten per cent, and spending in all areas is building nicely. The management were very pleased with all of us and predicted 2020 was going to be even better.'

'How were you celebrating?'

'A staff meeting. Mrs Crawley and Mr Paxton'—by which she meant Rebecca and the head of legal—'called us all into the dining room in the break between afternoon tea and the evening meal and briefed us on the financial report. Kelly Ann was standing right alongside them as head accountant. Then those of us going off shift were sent home with a bonus and a pamper package.'

'What kind of bonus?'

'Ten per cent, in my case, because of the increase in the membership waiting list.'

'And the pamper package?'

'Again, that was personalised. I got a scented candle, handmade chocolates and a voucher for a midweek spa treatment in our beauty centre.'

Kelly Ann's last bath came vividly back to him. 'What kind of candle?'

'Vanilla cupcake. I know some of the men got a bottle of port, so I was a little jealous.' She met Leo's questioning gaze and shrugged. 'I never know what to do with scented candles. I'm not really into things like that. I worry about setting the house on fire.'

'What kind of basket was it?' Leo couldn't remember seeing one at the house but he hadn't been looking.

'Grey wicker. Very nice. I'm using mine in the bathroom at home for my soap collection. I collect novelty ones that look like something else – slices of water melon, lemons, chocolate cake and so on. But you don't need to know that. I'm sorry. I'm not myself today.' She got out a tissue from her sleeve which she mangled in nervous fingers.

'Please, don't distress yourself. You're doing fine. Tell me more about the pamper pack. Everyone got one? Including Kelly Ann?'

'Oh, yes. The management are good like that. Always make things personal, and remember big days like birthdays or a family celebration.'

'Did you see what Kelly Ann got in hers?' He made a mental note to track down Kelly Ann's gift basket. Rebecca or her PA would presumably have to know what was in it.

'It was like mine but she had a candle called something like Rainbow Cookie because she joked about how we could start a bakery together selling just smells. She loved to relax with them.'

Had that been the brand at the end of the bath? Leo thought he remembered a rainbow striped label. It suggested Kelly Ann had gone straight home to enjoy her gift. 'Would it be normal for her to use them then?'

Miss Benfield nodded. 'Kelly Ann liked her little rituals. Friday nights, she used to joke, she usually had a hot date with a big glass of wine, a bubble bath, and a soothing candle, then a chat with her sister. Saturdays she goes shopping in Reading. Sunday we walk.' Her lips quivered, tears welling again. 'Neither of us have... *had* a very exciting private life.'

'And did you see Kelly Ann after that meeting on Friday?' Leo kept his tone very gentle.

'No, we live in opposite directions. I'm in Banbury.'

'Did she leave with anyone?'

'I think she was planning a quiet night in. But we did arrange to join the Ramblers on Sunday if the weather was fine for a walk around Stratford-upon-Avon.'

'She had made plans for Sunday?'

'Yes. For today.' Miss Benfield looked down. 'We both egged each other on to join to meet new people. Not that we wanted partners, you understand? We were both happily single. Better than being with the wrong person.'

'I see.'

She felt she had to explain her statement, though Leo really did see. 'There are a lot of men looking at women like us for the wrong reasons – they see us homeowners, as being easily fleeced – but, you never know when your luck might change, do you?'

As she searched his face for a reaction, it appeared she needed him to say something. 'No, you don't.'

'It turned out the Ramblers wasn't a very good place to meet men of the right age and calibre but we had fun with the girls anyway.' She put her hand to her brow. 'Oh, my God, I'm going to have to tell them all what's happened. They'll be so upset. Everyone loved Kelly Ann. She had so much life in her. Such curiosity and get-up-and-go. So passionate about her good causes.' She looked up. 'I'm sorry, Inspector, but I just don't believe she killed herself. There has to be some other explanation.'

Leo met her eyes – a distressed dark brown, vivid in an otherwise ordinary face. 'And that is exactly why you answering my questions is so important. We want to get at the truth of what took place on Friday night and every detail helps. Now, what can you tell me about Kelly Ann's local friendships? Had she argued with anyone, or mentioned that anyone upset her?'

Miss Benfield's eyes widened as she understood what he was asking. 'Well, no. She had her views – strong views – about people but she never let that interfere with her professionalism. I'm not aware of her falling out with anyone.'

It was rather a relief to find some character attached to

the victim beyond the 'everyone liked her' chorus that he'd had to listen to up to this point. 'What kind of strong views?'

Miss Benfield's gaze went to the tennis players behind Leo. 'As you might imagine, not all the guests are pleasant to deal with. They expect a very high level of service as members of the club and can be difficult if disappointed.'

'And was there any particular guest with whom Kelly Ann had a conflict?'

'She wasn't in front-facing customer roles – not really suited to them – but she did have the task of following up membership fees. That's if people are slow to pay… or can't pay. She was normally tactful but it could be unpleasant.'

'And if someone had a complaint, where would they go?'

'Mrs Crawley oversees them – and above her, head office.'

Another thing to add to the list of questions he had for Rebecca.

'In what way then did Kelly Ann's strong views make themselves felt?'

Miss Benfield took a quick look over her shoulder. 'The majority of our members are lovely people but there are a few less savoury types.'

'Meaning…?'

'Ill-gotten gains behind their wealth.' She gave him a quick nod. 'I'm sure you know the type in your line of work.'

'Does anyone of them stick out to you? You can speak in complete confidence.'

It was like watching a diver preparing to take the plunge, toes lined up with the edge of the board. She wanted to jump, just needed the excuse. 'The Kanons and the Stanton-Milbecks.' She said it quickly, as if speed excused the indiscretion. 'She told me she didn't like them – money from pornography – adult shops, that kind of thing – and dodgy dealings respectively. About eighteen months ago, both couples fell behind with fees, and she argued with the management that they should be barred for nonpayment or late payment, but I don't think it went anywhere. They're still on my membership list. She was annoyed by that.'

'Who would've made the decision on that?'

'Either Mrs Crawley or Mr Paxton – or maybe even the owners: the Birbeck brothers. They're based in Guernsey. If the clients were important enough, it would've gone to them for a final decision.'

'But Kelly Ann would've started that process?'

'Yes, after the client failed to pay, of course.'

Had the modest Chipping Norton accountant made some powerful enemies? Ones with enough clout to stage a suicide because she'd dared to question their financial health? The fortunes of some businesses lived or died by reputation so it could be sufficient motive for someone if they felt really threatened. 'Thank you, Miss Benfield. That's it for now but if you think of anything else, no matter how small, don't hesitate to get in touch.'

She untucked her feet from under the chair and stood. 'You don't think she killed herself, do you?'

Leo couldn't say what he really believed. 'The investigation is open and ongoing.'

She gave him a no-nonsense nod. 'That's what I thought. Thank you.'

Chapter Twelve

Jess

Lauren and Janice took over care of Rainbow, carrying her off to Janice's room to have a bath and a weep, so I decided my duty was to concentrate on Rebecca. She seemed unsure if she should carry on in her service capacity as manager of the club or allow herself to feel she was one of the friendship group. My task was to help her with letting the emotions out.

'Come for a walk?' I suggested when I caught her cleaning the kitchen counter for the fifth time. 'I think you need a break.' Freddie was nursing a tumbler of whisky and staring into space, Phil had disappeared to the clubhouse, saying he'd be playing pool if anyone wanted him. At least you couldn't accuse him of hypocrisy. He wasn't pretending to be more upset than he actually felt.

'Do you think I can?' she asked, holding the cloth like it was a lifeline.

'I absolutely think you should.' I prised it out of her fist. 'Come on. Show me the path along the lakeside.'

Having something to do seemed to settle her. 'Yes. OK. Good idea.'

We put on coats and I pulled on my boots.

'Will you be OK in those?' I pointed to her work shoes which had a slight heel.

'We'll go along the wheelchair-accessible route.' Out on the porch, she took a deep breath, closed her eyes and shuddered. 'Oh, God.'

I took her arm and tugged her gently to start moving. 'Just take a step, then another.'

She glanced at me. 'You're so kind. I'm sorry if I was a little brusque with you yesterday.'

I'd forgotten that; indeed, I'd been so annoyed by Janice I'd barely paid any attention to Rebecca. 'It's fine. I understand. It's always hard when a new person pitches up to an old group. Takes a while to adjust.'

'But you mustn't think of us like that. We rarely get to see Leo so the dynamics aren't settled. My only excuse is that I was a little jealous.'

'Jealous? Of me?'

'I've always had a soft spot for Leo and he never noticed me.' She started walking, setting a brisk pace. 'Barely noticed I existed.'

She was probably right about that. Leo was blind to his admirers; it was one of his sweetest traits. 'I'm sorry about Lloyd. I know I said it already, but you were married to him once – there's a lot of history there. All the attention is on Rainbow as his current partner, but this must hit you hard. I can imagine that it brings back all sorts of conflicting feelings.'

'You're right.' She paused at the end of the deck and gazed at the dinghy for a moment. The water was so still it seemed to be suspended on the water. 'You're absolutely right. My head is spinning. I've been thinking of him as I first knew him – and how he was when we decided to separate. He could be wonderful and infuriating, all at the same time. I think I love-hated him for many years after we ended, until the feelings tailed away and I was able to move on.' She dug her hands in her pockets, shoulders hunched. 'Working here helped. It gave me back my self-respect.'

I knew what losing respect for yourself was like. 'Did you lose your confidence when you were with him then?'

'Completely. Lloyd was a very dominant person. Living with him was to realise you'd planted yourself in his shade.'

'And you decided to dig up and re-pot yourself here?'

'Not directly. I suppose this was where the real healing took place.' She started walking again.

'How did it end for you both? The others said you were able to be civil. And I've seen how sweet you are to Rainbow.'

'Who wouldn't be sweet to Rainbow? In fact, I spent a lot of time worrying that Lloyd would damage her spirit like he did mine. Sorry, I didn't mean that how it sounded.' She scrubbed a sleeve over her eyes. 'It wasn't his fault that he was so…so big in the way he occupied a room. I was annoyed when Lauren and Freddie set them up – not through jealousy but because I predicted it wouldn't go well for her. I suppose that's all academic now.' She sighed. 'He might've been the best thing that ever happened to her. What do I know? Just because he was one way with me, didn't mean that had to be repeated with another.'

Didn't it? I had the impression that a certain amount of damage had already been done to Rainbow from what I saw of her yesterday.

'It's bad enough losing Lloyd. Is it horrible of me to be relieved she didn't go home yesterday?' asked Rebecca.

'No, not horrible.'

She blew her nose. 'I'm such a terrible person. And do you know what else I've been thinking? I've been thinking thank God they didn't park up on our premises, because then I'd be dealing with a death on our property and all that this brings – bad publicity and the rest. How can I even think that?'

'I think our brains dredge up inappropriate but honest thoughts at even the most serious times. I'm sure that, come the end of the world, I'll think some stupid random thought like "see, diets *were* a waste of time".'

She gave a watery chuckle, no real humour in it. 'Thanks. Just don't quote me on anything I say now. I'm not myself.'

'It's OK. If you need a shoulder to cry on, I'm available.'

She gave me a warm look. 'Then I'm glad you're here.'

When we arrived back at the house, two police officers had taken over Freddie and Lauren's suite, the biggest private room for their interviews. I peered in as we passed the window. Plainclothes – that meant they were detectives – probably Leo's colleagues, but I didn't recognise them. They had started on the interview with Rainbow and from her expression it didn't look as if it was going well.

'Crap, I was supposed to be with her. Excuse me.' I left Rebecca in the entrance and hurried into the interview. Occupying the opposite end of the lodge to where I'd slept, the suite was easily the biggest bedroom, the size of the other three combined. The sleeping area was screened off by folding doors, leaving a seating and a coffee table arranged around a fireplace. There was no fire lit. The police officers were seated on hard chairs borrowed from the dining room while Rainbow sat on the chaise longue. 'Sorry, sorry, I was out by the lake.' I stuck out my hand to the officers. 'I'm Jess Bridges. DI George asked me to sit with his friend when she was interviewed.' I sat beside Rainbow and took her hand. 'What did I miss?'

'Miss Bridges, are you a lawyer?' asked the senior officer, a woman of around forty with curly black hair scraped back in a bun. She gave the impression of having no give in her.

'Er, no. I've been a police consultant though, on previous cases. Ask Leo – Inspector George – I'm sure he'll vouch for me.' I was quickly getting the message that my bursting into their interview was neither welcome or expected.

'Then you have no business here. Please join the other witnesses outside and wait your turn.'

Why were they being so hostile? 'Isn't that for Rainbow to say? Rainbow, do you want me with you?'

Rainbow just stared at me wide-eyed.

'We are interviewing Miss Williams under caution so no, it is not for her to say. She is entitled to legal representation, as she has been informed.'

This did not sound good.

'Why would she need a lawyer?'

Rainbow shuddered, her pale, skinny shoulders looking so exposed in the low neck of her off-the-shoulder top. I felt the urge to find her a scarf or tweak it up to cover her throat. 'They say Lloyd might have been killed on purpose. I think they think I did it.' She sounded almost as if she was talking about someone else.

'But that's nonsense. You were here with us. How can you have killed him? He died from carbon monoxide poisoning, didn't he?'

The female officer, who was still to introduce herself, stood up. 'Miss Bridges, if you don't step away, I'll caution you for interfering with a police interview.'

I got up and backed away. 'Fine, fine. I misunderstood. I was only trying to help. But Rainbow, word of advice? Call a solicitor and don't say anything until they get here.'

'*Miss Bridges—*' barked the police officer.

'What? You can't arrest me for telling her her rights. Just think how that would look on the charge sheet – and in the media.'

'You're obstructing our enquiries.'

'That's not true.' I turned back to Rainbow. 'A lawyer. Now.'

Rainbow nodded, looking close to passing out. 'I want a solicitor.'

The two officers exchanged glances. Clearly, I was

ruining the scenario where they pressured a shocked partner into confessing to things she didn't do in her haze of grief. 'That is your right, Miss Williams. We'll continue this at the police station. Tell your lawyer to join us at Banbury,' said the senior officer.

I took off Leo's police fleece and wrapped it around Rainbow as she was seriously shocked, literally shaking in her boots. 'We'll get you a lawyer. Just hang on in there and we'll sort this out.'

Nodding dazedly, Rainbow was led away by the officers.

As we came out of the bedroom suite, an awful silence fell among those waiting. Rainbow was quickly walked past them and out to a police car.

'What the fuck is happening?' exploded Phil. 'Rainbow? A killer? They have to be insane.'

For once I think I agreed with him.

Chapter Thirteen

Leo

The leader of the search team at Kelly Ann's house, DS Suyin Wong, came to the library to deliver her report in person. Most interesting to Leo was what they had found in the dead woman's home filing cabinet. As a neat person of meticulous habits, it was no surprise that Kelly Ann kept all her bills and bank statements in separate folders, making the job of the search team so much easier and quicker. DS Wong had already looked through these and flagged up some odd transactions.

Catching Leo between interviews, she spread the statements out on the library table. Leo scanned the last three years of transactions. Kelly Ann had marked off with ticks certain items that corresponded to purchases.

'There's a separate spreadsheet on her home computer. She was keeping a close eye on her outgoings,' said Suyin, her intelligent face waiting for Leo to spot what she had seen. Leo, perhaps unfairly, he had to admit, felt she had set him a test. The sergeant was an excellent officer, often making Leo feel inadequate. He would not be surprised if he turned round one day to find she had been made his boss. She had the promotable people-pleasing skills that he lacked. Him and Harry both, he thought glumly.

'I can see that.' None of the expenses were guilty secrets. Membership of various clubs and societies, purchases from online craft retailers, garden supplies, books, and music. Quite a few purchases made in Reading, which fitted with the pattern her friend had described. Why go all the way to Reading, not Oxford? Did she have other friends there? Was that what Suyin was waiting for him to see?

There were regular large payments going out to what looked like a pension scheme. Leo did a quick calculation. 'Where did the money come from to set aside that proportion of her wage?'

Suyin smiled. 'That's what I wondered. See, here's her pay coming in. Adds up to about fifty-five thousand a year after tax. She's got no mortgage – must've paid it off already – but with other household expenses, insurance, car, usual stuff, then she's spending about ten thousand before any big splurges, like holidays or a new car. And yet she manages to salt away a hundred thousand last year into what looks like her pension pot or some kind of trust.'

'Then she has another source of income. Other properties, inheritance, investments?'

Suyin shook her head. 'Not that I've found so far. She created the investment account last year. And look at the income stream back in 2018.'

Leo pulled the relevant pages nearer. Over the course of nine months, Kelly Ann's wage ballooned to triple its usual amount. 'She was acting up to a more senior role? Had another job?'

'Not according to her employment records.'

Leo ran his finger down the columns. On the thirtieth of each month, after she got paid, she moved the money out of her current account into her investment one; and a few months later she was moving it again into a pension or trust, using the current account as a staging post. It was like she wanted to see it all go in and out of one set of spreadsheets. 'She ran the accounts. Could she have cheated, inflated her own pay and hoped no one noticed?'

'But why declare it legitimately like this? I checked her payslips. She's reporting it to HMRC – that's hardly the mindset of someone putting their hand in the till.'

Leo rubbed his chin, thinking. 'It could be a bonus. Another employee told me that the club has a habit of rewarding their workers in personalised ways. Perhaps she did something spectacular in 2018, deserving the reward?'

'And then humbly went back to her not shabby but not lavish wage?'

'I agree, that doesn't seem to fit quite right.' Leo knew he'd have to talk to Rebecca. She would have the answers. The timing, however, could not be worse.

His phone buzzed. Pulling it out, he read the message from Jess. It was bad. Very bad. They were thinking of charging Rainbow?

'Inspector? Are you all right?' asked Suyin, gathering up the statements.

He couldn't believe it. The words felt strange. 'One of my friends is being questioned under caution in connection with the accidental death we found together this morning.'

'Oh, sir, I'm sorry. Do you need to go?'

Yes, but… Leo knew he couldn't officially get involved in a case in which he was a key witness, even though he wanted to be with his friends. Another message from Jess popped up on the screen. She was right to suggest legal advice. He couldn't help Rainbow, but he knew someone who could. 'I'll take an hour of personal time. I need to set my friend up with a lawyer.'

'Which one?'

'Brook Musgrave, if she's available.' He texted the details to Jess. He was sure that if Rainbow couldn't afford the lawyer, the rest of them would club together to pay the fee.

'Good choice. She's impossible in the interview room.' CID had an informal league table of their most effective adversaries from the legal community and Musgrave regularly finished in one of the top spots. Suyin returned the statements to the evidence box. 'I'll take your next interview if you want, sir. I've time before I have to take these back to HQ.'

'Thanks. I've made some notes already. It's the team from the beauty spa. See if anyone knows anything about 2018. Oh, and there are two sets of clients who potentially had it in for Kelly Ann. Their names are also on my notes.' Perhaps the two things were connected in some way? From what Miss Benfield said, 2018 would be about the time Kelly Ann was having her run-in with the

Kanons and Stanton-Milbecks. But how did that link together? Had she found out something that meant it was worth paying her not to publicise it? Looking around the library, which oozed an air of respectability and comfortable wealth that was meant to reassure and lull, Leo's instincts were pricked. He never trusted surface impressions; his mother's fakery had taught him that. He had begun to wonder quite what lay under the gloss of the Piccadilly People. If the secrets were dangerous, and they had got Kelly Ann killed, then how much did Rebecca know?

He left his car at the clubhouse and walked to the cottage. On the way, he shot a quick text to a colleague in Banbury to find out informally what was going on with the investigation into Lloyd's death.

A minute later, his contact chose to ring rather than put anything in a message.

'Leo, I was half expecting your call.' May Holland, specialist in working with victims of sexual assault and domestic violence, had transferred from Oxford to work out of Banbury.

'May, sorry to pull you in on this, but you might've heard—'

She cut him off. 'Yes, we all have. An old friend of yours. I'm sorry for your loss.'

'Thanks. He's more of a friend of a friend but still, I was with him just yesterday. It's a shock to us all. Look, I don't mean to put you in a tight spot, but can you tell me what's changed and why they're interviewing under caution?'

'The word is that SOCO think the generator was left

running with the ventilation deliberately blocked. Unless the victim did it himself as a suicide, it could be murder.'

Would Lloyd commit suicide? wondered Leo. There had been no signs of depression yesterday; the only behaviour that struck Leo as odd was Lloyd's resolute refusal to enter club territory.

'Thanks, May.'

'They'll want to interview you, you realise, so I can't say any more.'

'I understand. But I'm in the middle of my own investigation so they'll have to wait.' Which raised the question of what the chances were that there would be two deaths so close together that could be staged suicides. Ideally, he'd talk theories over with the investigating team on Lloyd's case, see if there were any links, but his own involvement made that difficult. 'Much appreciated. I'd better go.'

Tucking the phone away, he looked at the front door of the lodge, bracing himself to go in. His friends would want answers that he couldn't give, but he could offer practical help and explain police procedures. That would have to be enough.

Chapter Fourteen

Leo

His friends looked up from their seats in the high-ceilinged living room as he walked in, their faces hopeful. Janice and Rebecca were sitting either end of a long sofa, sharing a blanket; Freddie and Lauren were crammed together in an armchair; Jess and Phil occupied a window seat, a big gap between them. Jess ran over to throw her arms around him. He could feel her relief.

'Leo!' Jess squeezed him tightly. 'Thank God you're here.'

'Do you know what the hell is going on?' asked Freddie.

'I don't know much more than you,' he said, hugging Jess in response to her greeting. 'Did you get in touch with the solicitor, Jess?'

'Yes. She's gone to Banbury police station to help Rainbow. But why is that necessary? What do they think she's done?' said Jess.

'It's normal to start with the people closest to the victim, you know that.' He hoped it was just that.

'But it had to be an accident, surely?'

'There's enough doubt that they have to investigate.'

Phil swaggered towards them, a belligerent expression to go with the swishing cognac in his glass. 'Told you.' He stabbed a finger at Leo. 'It's a fucking stitch-up. The pigs always look for someone to blame. Lloyd took his own life and they want to pin it on an innocent. But choosing Rainbow as the fall guy? That's a fucking joke!'

'Why do you say that he took his own life?' Leo asked, ignoring the implicit invitation to argue that accompanied most of what Phil said. 'You said the same earlier but I don't get it.'

'Isn't it obvious? The guy was rolled up financially – lost all his money as well as ours. What was there left for him? Pretend all was sodding sweetness and light in his twenty-first century gipsy life? Look at me, the saintly vegan? He knew he was fucking done. Good for him for making his exit.' He raised his glass in a toast. 'Just wish he'd left us a note so Rainbow didn't get dragged over the coals for his decision. Honourable death. A fucking hara-kiri.'

'I had no idea.' Leo led Jess over to a spare sofa and sat down with his arm touching hers. Phil trailed them. 'It was that bad, was it?'

Freddie exchanged a look with Lauren. 'Things had got pretty rough,' he agreed. 'Lloyd didn't like people knowing but his house was repossessed and I think he was badly in debt. That's why we thought Rainbow was so good for him. A new start. She loved him anyway, without the money – in fact, that was even better for her as it freed him up. We thought they'd be perfect for each other.'

Phil collapsed into an armchair and snorted in disdain. 'She's a butterfly and Lloyd was a bloody great pin you drove right through her.'

'*Phil!*' Janice uncurled from her corner seat on a sofa. 'You're drunk and rude. You'd better sober up before the police get back here.'

'Why the fuck should I bother? I don't respect Leo's jack-booted friends and they certainly don't trust any of us.' Phil reached for the bottle of cognac but Janice was too quick for him. 'Fuck off, Janice.'

'This isn't about your issue with the authorities. This is about Lloyd and Rainbow. Just grow up.' Putting the cognac on top of the fridge, she went to the sink and filled a glass with water. 'Drink that and shut up until you've got something helpful to add.'

There was the Janice that he'd once fallen for, thought Leo, strong and standing up for what was right; it was timely that she had made her reappearance in their hour of need.

'Thanks, Janice,' murmured Lauren.

Leo searched his friends' faces. He'd assumed he knew them all to some degree but how well had he really kept track over the years? 'Look, I feel I've missed a few steps here. What exactly happened with Lloyd and the money? I thought that was all over six years ago?' Jess nudged him, indicating that she'd like to be included in the conversation. He turned to her. 'Six years back, Lloyd was drumming up support for an investment fund that he was heading up for his new firm. I declined but I think the others put a little into it – to encourage him.'

'A little? Leo, it was much more than that. I thought I was going to make a killing.' Janice studied her nails critically. 'And, yes, I know: horrible pun. I put into Lloyd's fund what I'd earmarked for a deposit on a house. It wasn't the right time for me to buy so I thought it a good place to park it. Phil put in a similar amount, didn't you?'

'How much are you talking about?' asked Jess. 'Fifty thousand? Seventy?'

'Sweetie, you can't put down a deposit of that amount – not in London. We're talking a couple of hundred grand to get a mortgage for a decent-sized apartment or house – in other words, most of my earnings from seasons one and two.'

Phil drained the glass of water. 'Should've known. Never give money to a friend. It always fucking backfires.'

'He lost the money?' Jess asked.

'I don't think he ever admitted to losing it. Just said the investments had lost their value. Told us to wait for an uptick in the market and we'd get it back. Eventually.' Janice sighed. 'That eventually is probably never. His firm must've thought so as they sacked him.'

'What did he invest it in, do you know?' Leo laced his fingers with Jess's.

'I think he blew it on the bloody gee-gees,' grumbled Phil.

'He didn't,' countered Janice. 'Didn't you read the paperwork? It was a share portfolio, various investments in the Middle East. Medium to high risk but supposedly high yield. But the political situation deteriorated, price of oil crashed, he had too many eggs in one basket and…' She tailed off. 'We weren't the only ones. Freddie, Lauren, didn't you invest with him too?'

Lauren looked a little uncomfortable. 'We did, but not in that fund. We have to be very careful, said we couldn't shoulder the risk. I think our investment was handled by a colleague of Lloyd's who was grateful for the referral. Our money hasn't made much but it didn't vanish like yours did.'

'I'm pleased for you,' said Janice, sounding pissed off, 'but I could've done with the heads-up that your friend was a maverick.'

'I think I knew more about investments than Lloyd did.' Phil closed his eyes. 'Still, I don't wish him dead for all that. The only payback I was going to get was to hold it over him for the rest of his life, make him choke on the humiliation of having failed us. Now he doesn't get to suffer.'

Leo checked the time on his phone, conscious of numerous messages having come in during even this short time away. He had to go. 'It might be helpful if you mention to the police why you think Lloyd might've killed himself, Phil. If they have reasons to think the death suspicious, they need the full picture. It will help Rainbow.'

'Oh, yeah? Tell them that and give them a motive to accuse me next of killing him? Like that's going to happen.' Phil pressed his temples with his fingers. 'Let the others do the psychological shit. I want nothing to do with any of this. As soon as your lot says we can go, I'm out of here. This was one fucktastic reunion – well done, Freddie.'

'This isn't Freddie's fault!' snapped Lauren.

'Yeah, well, maybe we should give these get-togethers a rest, hey? They don't seem very good for our wellbeing, do they, what with one of us topping himself?'

Leo loosened his hold on Jess's hand and stood up. There was nothing to do when Phil got into this mood. Only Janice had any hope of handling him. 'I have to go back. Rebecca, I know this is a bad time, but could I just ask a few questions? Some things have come up on my case and we think you'll know the answers.'

Rebecca, who had been sitting alone hugging a pillow until that point, looked up. 'Sorry? Now? Oh, er, yes, I suppose that would be fine. I'm not doing any good sitting here.'

'It shouldn't take long, then you can come back,' said Leo, fetching her coat from the pegs by the door and holding it up for her.

'I wouldn't come back if I were you,' growled Phil. 'Go home. Keep out of this.'

Lauren moved over to give her a hug. 'He's actually right. You didn't see Lloyd yesterday so the police request for us to stay here doesn't cover you.'

'I'll make sure they know where you are if they do want to follow up with you,' said Leo. 'You won't get in trouble for leaving.'

'That's unless you prefer to come back to be with us?' probed Lauren. 'I don't mean to chase you away.'

Rebecca held up empty hands, confused by too many options. 'God, I'm sorry. I don't know. I can't make up my mind.'

Lauren squeezed her shoulders. 'Then let's just say, come back if you want to, but don't feel guilty if you prefer to go home. I know you've got responsibilities.'

Rebecca nodded. 'Call me if Rainbow needs me.'

'We will. Now go with Leo.'

Leo opened the door for her. 'Let's go to your office, shall we? Jess, let me know your plans. I can still arrange for a lift back to Oxford if you need one later.'

'It's OK, Leo. I'll sort myself out,' Jess said. 'You get on with whatever you've got to do and don't worry about me.'

Leo and Rebecca started the walk back to the clubhouse. He couldn't think of anything he could say that would help, his personal and professional roles horribly blended.

'Do you think it's my fault he's dead?' Rebecca asked in a small voice.

'Sorry? What?' Leo almost stepped in a puddle, so distracted was he by her question. He avoided it just in time.

'I think I'm to blame. I invited everyone here. I wanted to show it off, this wonderful place where I've landed the dream job. God, I even wanted to rub Lloyd's nose in it a little, how the tables had turned. He used to go on about his great job in finance and now I'm running an elite club and he was pretty much bankrupt. That's why I insisted everyone came this year – why he had to pretend he was fine with it. I knew it would kill him to act like he didn't care.' She glanced up at Leo. 'Not literally kill him.'

'I know what you meant.'

'But, if he hadn't driven to the Rollright Stones so Rainbow could come to the reunion, then he wouldn't have been on his own last night while Rainbow was over here. Rainbow might've noticed something was up, might've opened a window, told him to switch off the generator when she started to feel woozy… something!'

'There are always "might haves" in any death. You can't blame yourself. We don't know what happened at this stage. If he did it to himself, then I doubt being here made any difference. It could've happened any night anywhere. At least last night Rainbow was kept out of harm's way.'

They walked into the echoing foyer of the clubhouse. Two women passed wearing towelling robes, on their way to the spa. They greeted Rebecca who managed a professional smile for them. It was bizarre to remember that normal life was going on around them while they were talking about such dark matters.

'Your office?' suggested Leo.

Rebecca nodded, seeming to find some solace in being back in her territory. 'I'll ring for some tea. I don't expect you've had time for lunch?'

'I'd appreciate that. I should ask if you want a lawyer present?'

'Why? Am I under caution, too?'

'No, but my questions are to do with the running of the business and I presume your owners will have interests to protect?'

She gave him a wry smile. 'Leo, I do believe you are trying to save my job. You're right. I'll call in head of legal.'

'Jamie Paxton?' Leo remembered the charcoal-suited man from earlier who had turned on the charm like it was a hundred-watt bulb and he was determined to dazzle Leo with it.

'You met him?' asked Rebecca.

'I was the one who served him the warrant to search Kelly Ann's office.'

'Of course you were.' Rebecca shook her head wearily. 'I'm getting muddled – Lloyd and Kelly Ann. Neither makes the blindest bit of sense of me. Forgive me for mixing them up.'

'That's completely understandable. Now, about that tea?'

Chapter Fifteen

Leo

In her office, Rebecca paused before she took her usual seat behind her desk.

'Would you like to sit here?' she asked.

'No need. I'm happy in the visitor's chair.' Leo took a seat across from her. It was a high-ceilinged office on the first floor overlooking a topiary maze. The yew hedges were netted with frosted webs and stood out darkly against the light gravel paths. An elderly couple was walking slowly along the low hedges, working their way to the centre. There was something incredibly touching about the way they held hands.

Rebecca adjusted the blotter in the centre of her desk. 'I've buzzed Jamie. He should be along any moment.'

'And I'm just waiting on a colleague to join us. As I know you outside of this case, it's better we do this by the book.'

On cue, DS Wong tapped on the door. 'Sir?'

Leo stood up to make the introductions. 'Rebecca, this is Detective Sergeant Wong. She's been leading the search team today.'

'Sergeant, can I order you some tea – or coffee?' Rebecca asked, one hand over her phone's mouthpiece.

'No, thank you, Mrs Crawley. Your staff have been very hospitable. I'm awash with coffee.' Suyin took the last free chair next to Leo.

'Let's get started then,' said Leo. 'Rebecca, first things first: when did you last see Kelly Ann and how did she seem to you?'

'That would be Friday night, at the end of the staff meeting.' Rebecca put the phone back on its cradle and contemplated her clasped hands resting in front of her. 'We walked out together. I have to say I didn't notice anything odd about her behaviour. She was happy about the results, talked of cracking open the champagne and celebrating.'

'Alone?'

'She didn't say. She's got lots of friends on the staff so I rather assumed she meant with others but I was distracted. I didn't ask.'

'Distracted?'

'By the weekend – you and the others coming to visit. I wanted it all to be perfect. Janice was arriving that night so I made a final check on the cottage.'

'Did you stay to greet Janice?'

'No, that was the night manager. Gill Granger was on duty. I popped back from home at about ten once I got word she'd arrived, just to say hello.'

'And where is home?'

'About five minutes' drive away in the village of Great Rollright.'

'Did you see anyone else that evening, between leaving work and returning?'

'My mother. She's living with me now. My father died last year. I always try to get back to have supper with her. I work long hours and she gets lonely.'

Leo didn't think Rebecca realised but he was asking her in effect for her alibi. 'My condolences. We're asking everyone where they were that night. Is it OK if we contact your mother to verify?'

'Of course.' She stiffened, her tone becoming more formal as the penny dropped. 'But I'd prefer if you didn't mention anything about someone dying. Mum is in a vulnerable state at the moment – a little confused. I'm looking for the right home for her but the good ones are so expensive, or have no vacancies. Tell her that we had salmon and she'll probably remember.'

Meaning that she might not be the most reliable alibi. 'Thank you. Right, moving on, next we need to ask you about Kelly Ann's professional history with the club.'

Rebecca's shoulders relaxed, showing she was at ease with this line of questioning. 'She was an excellent worker. I'm happy to share her performance evaluations with you if you wish to see what we thought of her. Consistently one of our top performers.'

'I've no doubt. From what I've seen, she was formidably organised.'

'Yes, she was. She leaves a big hole both personally and professionally.' Rebecca looked down, blinking away tears.

'In the course of our searches, we noticed one strange thing: she was paid much more in 2018 than in 2019. Do you know why?'

'She was?' Rebecca frowned and tapped on her computer keyboard to wake it up. 'I'm sorry, I don't keep the wages of all the staff in my head. I'm more big picture, but I'm sure we didn't decrease her salary. Do you know how much more?'

'Over a hundred and fifty thousand more,' said Suyin.

'No, that can't be right.' Rebecca tapped on a file on her desktop and received a bleep sound. 'Sorry, I can't seem to access the data at the moment. Where are you getting this from?'

'From Kelly Ann's bank deposits. The sums enter as her salary from Piccadilly People Holdings Ltd.'

'Rebecca, who administers the wages? Is it done here?' asked Leo.

'No, it's done centrally. All the HR for the clubs around the world is handled by the company HQ based in Guernsey. I mean, I know which wage band everyone is in, and what the annual budget is for this location, but I don't sign off on the money going into each person's account myself.'

'But is it feasible that Kelly Ann would've earned such a large bonus – many times her actual salary – in 2018?'

'I can't see how… We get bonuses for good results but the largest I've ever earned was twenty percent on top of my salary. That was this year in fact, not 2018. I don't remember that being a particularly good year in the membership department. 2016 was better, for example.'

'Who do we ask to find the answers?' Leo watched as she tried to access the file again.

'I don't understand why I can't get in.' This fact clearly annoyed her as she pecked at the keyboard. 'I think you'll have to apply to Jeremy and Chester Birbeck, our owners. They are famously reclusive though, so it might not be a straightforward process. I was hoping I could just give you the answer but for some reason… It's no good. It's saying I don't have permission to access the files. I'll have to get that sorted out before I can help you.'

Which she might not if someone was covering their tracks. 'Not to worry. We'll take this up with them. Another question we had was what did Kelly Ann get in her basket on Friday?'

'Oh, that I can answer. I do a lot of the choosing myself. One moment…' She clicked on a list and scrolled down. 'A nice bottle of champagne, not Prosecco, as she was senior management. A scented candle. Handmade chocolates from the kitchen here. And a pamper package at the salon. She wasn't the kind to be into beauty treatments so I suggested we gave her a hot stone massage and reiki session.'

There was no champagne at the victim's house. 'And this was all in a grey wicker basket?'

'Why, yes. Everyone got one – every member of staff. Sorry, I'm still struggling with what you told me about her wage. That really doesn't sound right. There must be a mistake.' She tried the file again and got another bleep.

'We'll look into it. Rebecca, we understand that part of

Kelly Ann's job was to chase up people who didn't pay their membership fees on time; she could also recommend they be cut from the list if they didn't follow through. Is that correct?'

She took her fingers away from the keyboard, giving up. 'Yes, more or less. Membership would normally lapse under those circumstances, unless there were extenuating circumstances.'

'Like what?'

'Temporary difficulties, for example. We like to think of our membership as a worldwide family.'

Who paid for the privilege of belonging. 'And who decides whether or not to give the person in question extra time or waives the necessity of paying their dues?'

'Each manager has three gift memberships annually. The idea is to use them for local influencers, however we might want to define that. The owners and board members obviously have much greater leeway. There are a number of Birbeck members in every club. I've always assumed their membership is sorted out directly with the brothers as it doesn't go through us.'

Leo could well imagine a patronage system of planning ministers and key business contacts being given the perk in return for favours. 'Did you ever come across problems with two families in particular – the Kanons and the Stanton-Milbecks?'

'Problems? No, not as such. They're not everyone's cup of tea, I know, but they're stalwarts of the club. The Kanons live in Chipping Norton, but make regular use of our sports facilities and restaurants. They're keen tennis players and have a daughter who's in the under-sixteens GB squad. The Stanton-Milbecks are from Bicester, I think. They're something to do with the designer village that pulls in all the tourists – suppliers of some sort. Sorry, I'm not sure of the details. Why are you asking about them?'

'Did Kelly Ann ever raise concerns about them with you?'

She wrinkled her brow. 'Let me check.' She searched her email. 'How far do I need to go back?'

'Try 2018.' Leo exchanged a look with Suyin. He wondered what his colleague was making of this exchange. Was she getting the same impression he was that in some ways Rebecca was cut out of the key decisions over club business? True, she managed this site, but it seemed the real tune was called by the elusive Birbecks.

'Hmm, you're right. I see I was copied into a note Kelly Ann sent to the central membership secretary about both of those couples, but I don't appear to have anything further from her after that initial enquiry.'

'And what does she say?'

'Only that they hadn't paid after several warnings and that she thought the club would be better off without them on the membership roll due to their questionable business activities.' Rebecca sighed. 'That wasn't very diplomatic – I'm afraid that was one of her few weaknesses, being susceptible to local gossip about our members. If she'd asked me before sending it, I would've cautioned a more emollient tone. The Birbecks don't like being told what to do.'

'Can you tell how they reacted to her recommendation?'

She clicked a few more files open. 'Looking at the current membership list, it seems both couples switched over at some point last year to being Birbeck members, so Kelly Ann no longer had anything to do with them. It would've all been handled centrally.'

At that interesting point, a waiter brought in a tray of tea, followed closely by Jamie Paxton, head of legal. Leo knew his window to ask sensitive business questions had closed. Paxton took in the gathering and grabbed a chair from just outside the office.

'Don't tell me, Rebecca, you've started without me?' His charming tone was a little more strained than earlier.

'Jamie, I believe you've already met Leo, Inspector George.' Even though he brought his chair to her side of the desk, Rebecca did not shift from the centre position. 'This is his colleague, Sergeant Wong.'

'Yes, I've met them both already.' Paxton took a cup from the waiter and motioned for him to leave. Once the door closed, he began speaking. 'I'm here as you must know to protect the legal interests of my employers. We have data protection laws we have to obey, as well as commercial secrets that need guarding, not to mention privacy issues. Our clientele is very exclusive.'

'We understand, Mr Paxton,' said Leo calmly. 'Our interest is purely in the circumstances around Kelly Ann's death.'

'But why so many questions, Leo?' asked Rebecca. 'Sorry, I should've asked this earlier but the events of today had rather muddled my thinking. What has her salary in

2018 and her queries about members got to do with her decision to commit suicide?'

'Her death isn't being treated as a suicide. We're looking into it as suspicious.'

Rebecca dropped her cup on her saucer, tea sloshing over the side. 'My God, you're serious! Not her too!'

'Not her too? What does that mean?' Paxton rescued her cup, while Suyin offered him tissues from a box on the sideboard to mop up the spillage.

'My…Lloyd…that's being investigated as a possible… I'm not sure, exactly.' Rebecca pinched the top of her nose. 'What on earth is going on?'

'Mr Paxton, what Mrs Crawley is referring to is that we think someone else was involved in Kelly Ann's death,' said Leo. 'We're trying to ascertain if Kelly Ann had made any enemies or had given anyone a reason to silence her.'

'But what could she know that would make anyone do that?' Paxton shook his head. 'No, no, you have to be barking up the wrong tree. We're a social club, not some secret government agency. What's the worst she could know about anyone?'

'You'd be surprised, Mr Paxton. The devil can be in the detail of people's lives. And for the record, if you could state where you were on Friday night?'

'Me? What possible relevance does that have to anything?'

'If you could just answer the question. We are asking everyone. It's standard procedure.'

'I was here all evening. We had a staff briefing and then I

had dinner with clients followed by a few hours in the casino, if you must know.'

'I'd appreciate their names.'

'And I'd appreciate not being treated like a criminal!'

'That's not my intention. This is for elimination purposes only.'

He gave a huff. 'Jozef and Marta Kanon. They'll vouch for my whereabouts.'

How…interesting. They asked a few more questions but with Paxton now blocking many lines of enquiry on grounds of client privacy, the most productive part of the interview was clearly over. Leo would have to go to the people who could possibly tell him what he wanted to know.

He stood up. 'Thank you. I'll let you both know if there are any more questions but it looks like the next answers we need are in Guernsey.'

Chapter Sixteen

Jess

It was not my first time in a police interview, but it was the first time that I knew I really had nothing to say.

It was also the first time I'd ever been interviewed in a lodge that was reminding me more and more of an Anglo-Saxon mead hall, complete with threat of some of us being carried off by the monster Grendel as had happened to Rainbow earlier. We needed our own Beowulf (Leo in my little mind drama) to return from the clubhouse to stop them making more inroads to our numbers and ideally return Rainbow to us.

'Miss Bridges, what was your relationship with the deceased?' asked the unfriendly Grendel-like police officer responsible for these attacks. She now introduced herself as DI Kesha Edmonds, her colleague DS John Connaught, both based at Banbury. They were conducting their interviews in the lodge 'for our convenience' but wouldn't tell us when we could expect Rainbow to return.

'I met him yesterday for the first time and spent about two hours in his company.' They had to know this already because they'd left me until last to interview, and the others had already explained the purpose of the weekend.

'You are here as the guest of DI Leo George, correct?'

'Yes.'

'What is the nature of your relationship with DI George?'

Could she sound any more stuck up, or was it just plain nosy? I sensed Banbury were somewhat resentful of their colleagues in the Oxford HQ. 'Clearly, we are friends. He isn't in the habit of dragging strangers off to college reunions.'

I wasn't amusing them, I could tell. Fortunately, being annoying wasn't an arrestable offence. 'Then you weren't here in your professional capacity?'

'No, we were here to have fun. Obviously not much of that has been had by anyone.'

'How would you characterise Lloyd Rumbold's relationship with Rainbow Williams?'

'You mean on the strength of two hours in their company?' Why were the detectives wasting their time on me? 'They both seemed happy enough. Rainbow isn't very confident and Lloyd had bags of the stuff, that was the main difference I noticed.'

'Was there any tension between them?'

'What kind?'

'Just answer the question please.'

That made me wonder what Rainbow had been saying. If she needed a defence (and why would she need one?), what had she gone for? 'You're asking me? Someone who has known them both for about five minutes?'

DI Edmonds flicked an imaginary piece of fluff off her black trousers. 'But you are a trained observer and have consulted on police cases before, as you pointed out.'

So she had been listening. 'Look, you'd be better off asking these questions of Leo. He's known them both much longer than I have.'

'Answer the question.'

I blew out a breath. 'OK, here's what I saw. Lloyd was the dominant one in the relationship. Evidence? Rainbow made the coffee while he ordered her around. My conclusion? Rainbow was a little under his thumb, looking to him for permission to do her own thing. If that's how she always behaves with men, or just with him, I have no idea. And that's not abuse as far as I know, just the way some couples behave. That's all I saw.' The door opened and Leo came in. 'There's the man you need to ask.'

Leo crossed the carpet in the bedroom suite to us. 'DI Edmonds, DS Connaught, I understand you want a word?'

DI Edmonds released me from her tractor beam of a stare. 'Inspector George, thank you for coming over. This is an awkward situation for us both but Superintendent Thaxted said you'd try to carve out some time from your own enquiry to assist.'

'I have that time now,' Leo replied coolly, 'but first, do my friends really need to be here any longer? You've interviewed them?'

'I was just finishing up with Miss Bridges.'

'Then they are free to go?'

'I suppose they are, though they said they wished to wait until we'd finished with everyone.' And she hadn't bothered to tell us that we could depart if we wished.

Leo nodded and went back into the main room to Freddie and Lauren, that move indicating, whether he knew it or not, that he considered himself the one in charge here. He left the door wide open. 'There's no need for you to wait for Rainbow. I'll make sure she's collected and has somewhere to stay while we sort this out.'

'Don't you think we should be here for her?' asked Freddie.

'It might take a while. Wouldn't you prefer to be with your children? We can keep in touch about developments.'

'If you're sure?' said Lauren.

Phil got up from his seat. 'You heard the man: time to go.'

Janice took his car keys from his hand. 'You're not driving anywhere, Phil, not with the amount you've put away today.'

'Well, I'm not bloody well staying here.'

'I'll drive you home. Can you put me up for the night? I'm not due in London until tomorrow evening.'

'I'll be fine.' He tried to take the keys but she didn't let go. I was impressed. Janice's Phil-handling skills were epic.

'Phil, show some sense,' she snapped. 'You're standing in a room with three police officers. We can all smell the drink on your breath. Do you really want to give them the excuse?'

'Oh all right then.' He cleared his throat. 'You might have a point.'

They went to pack their things. Janice had already got her suitcases lined up by the door. It struck me that association with a death was a reputation threat for her. No wonder she was in a hurry to leave.

Leo came back to me.

'Jess, I can drive you home as I've got work to do in the Oxford office.'

'Yes. I'll go and collect our things.' I exited the room where I'd been interviewed and hurried across the main living area. Leo hadn't really had the chance to unpack but I, as usual, had scattered the contents of my half of the suitcase around the room like a small bomb had exploded.

As I made my way up the stairs, I heard him question the Banbury officers.

'When can I fetch Rainbow? I take it you're not planning on charging her with anything? Not now you've met her.' His tone made it clear he thought them foolish to consider any other outcome.

'That remains to be seen. We were planning to speak to her once more today after we've finished these interviews,' said DI Edmonds.

'Right. I can come to Banbury at eight. Does that give you enough time?'

'We can't stop you coming but I can't promise she'll be released. Inspector George, if you'd like to take a seat? Let's start with this morning. What did you see when you arrived at the motorhome belonging to Rainbow Williams?'

'It belonged to Rainbow? I thought it was Lloyd's.' Leo

shook his head as if that thought was irrelevant. 'What did I see?' At that point, the door was closed.

I rushed into our room to finish packing. If I was quick, I might be able to listen into the rest.

Bags ready in record time, I stood by the closed door to Freddie and Lauren's suite and eavesdropped. I was helped by the fact that Leo was getting angry, his usually modulated voice raised. Leo's friends, gathered together waiting for their dismissal, looked at me half aghast half admiring at my boldness. I gave them a shrug.

'Let me get this right,' Leo was saying, his incredulity plain, 'you think it was murder and that you're not looking for any other suspects than Rainbow?'

'Look, Inspector, I know it's difficult for you to believe as you've known the suspect for a long time—' DI Edmonds was irritated too but trying to be polite.

'You say that as if it is a disqualification for having sound judgement on this. Might it not be exactly the opposite – the reason why I know she can't have done what you are saying?'

'All the evidence points to her. It's her fingerprints on the roll of duct tape which sealed the ventilation channels, her prints on the generator.'

'Along with the victim's?'

'His weren't on the tape.'

I now understood why they'd leant towards murder. Lloyd had been poisoned by toxic fumes while watching the football game. He probably hadn't suspected a thing.

'You do understand that they lived together,' said Leo, 'that it would be more surprising if her prints weren't on objects in the motorhome? This makes no sense. What's her motive?'

'Williams claims that she was subject to months of mental abuse by her partner. She says she was planning to leave him. Miss Johnson,' she meant Janice, 'confirmed that Williams had confided in her just yesterday that their relationship had broken down.'

They'd hidden that well for our visit but I wasn't really surprised the relationship had been trending that way.

'But does Rainbow say she killed him?'

The silence answered that.

'Planning to leave someone is the opposite of a motive for murder,' argued Leo. 'She had her way out, friends ready to help. She didn't need to kill him.'

'That's not how the evidence reads.'

'Then I think you're reading it wrongly.'

'This is not your investigation, Inspector George.'

'No, but have you considered the resemblance to the one I am running? I don't know how much you've heard about that, but I have a death that might have been staged to look like suicide. I'm certainly treating it as such. What you're looking at is similar. Maybe we have a single murderer who, for a reason we're yet to discover, is killing individuals when they are on their own and then tries to dress it up as suicide?'

'A serial killer? In Chipping Norton?' Edmonds's tone was mocking. 'I know you're desperate to help your friend, but this isn't the way. If you're really on her side then tell her that her best defence is to claim mental cruelty and plead manslaughter.' The subtext being that they could then close the case in record time with a confession.

'That's nonsense, as she's not a killer under any circumstance. You misunderstood. I didn't say serial killer – at least not in the sense you mean of a random psychopath. If these deaths are linked, they are carefully planned. There may be connections, not just geographic coincidence. Shouldn't we at least be exploring this possibility?'

'Inspector George, this is my investigation and I will conduct it in the manner I see fit. I will lodge a complaint if I think you are in anyway meddling in it because your judgement is clouded by your personal feelings for the suspect.' Her tone turned waspish.

'You've got the wrong person.' Leo dug in further.

'You've got the wrong police officer if you think you can bully me into buying this theory of yours.'

'Since when did stating that I think you are wrong become bullying?'

Leo was going to get himself into hot water if he carried on like this. In this era, another officer, especially a female one, claiming bullying could damage his career no matter how unearned. Time for some disruption to redirect her ire my way.

I bounced into the room. 'Leo, I'm ready to go. Have you finished with Inspector Lestrade and sidekick here?'

Leo turned to me, his eyes bright with anger. Is it wrong that I wanted to jump him there and then? He looked so hot. 'Jess, not now.'

'It's Inspector Edmonds,' the woman said curtly.

'Him Holmes,' I pointed to Leo, 'me Watson, you

Lestrade.' I shrugged at the detective sergeant. 'Sorry, you get sidekick as I ran out of Sherlock-related names. You both really should listen to Leo as you're just embarrassing yourself dismissing his deductions.'

'Miss Bridges, this is none of your business,' hissed Lestrade, sorry, DI Edmonds.

I poked my finger in my ear and wiggled. 'Hang on, I think I'm mishearing you. Not ten minutes ago, when I said it was nothing to do with me, you said you needed my psychological observations. Here's one for you now: mentally abused, truly *bullied* women do not make convoluted plans to murder their partner. They may take a while to summon up the courage, retreat to the kitchen to get a knife, for example, strike while the person is asleep or drunk so they aren't physically in danger, but they *don't* do what you're claiming Rainbow has done. It's too cool and there are too many steps in the plan. If she were that clever and clear-thinking about taking her revenge, she would've made sure no prints were found.'

Edmonds was looking at me with great dislike. The feeling was mutual. 'You shouldn't have heard that.'

'Then you shouldn't have discussed the case here, should you?'I folded my arms. 'Sound travels.' Particularly if you had your ear glued to the keyhole.

I think I weirded her out. Edmonds nodded to her colleague. 'We're done here. Inspector George, take my warnings seriously. Don't come anywhere near my investigation or I will make an official complaint.'

'When can we fetch Rainbow?' I asked, seeing Leo was still too angry to speak.

'If Miss Williams wishes to contact you when we've decided whether or not to charge her, then she will do so.' Edmonds gathered up her bag and coat and swept out, a sheepish DS Connaught on her heels.

Leo looked like he wanted to rip something to shreds. I passed him a cushion.

'Throw that. It will make you feel better.'

Instead, he chucked it aside and hugged me.

'That works, too,' I told his chest. 'She's an idiot.'

'But Rainbow—'

'We'll help her. Don't worry.'

'Edmonds is right. I can't go anywhere near that enquiry and, if they won't cooperate with me, there's little I can do.'

I leant back and tapped the dent in his chin as his friends came in to say goodbye. 'You might not, but no one said anything about me. I'm a private investigator of sorts. Hire me for the case – or get one of your friends to do so – and I'll look into it.'

Freddie glanced at the others, reaching swift agreement. 'You're hired. Jess, you can't let Rainbow be accused of something she absolutely didn't do. It would break her.'

'Do you really think the cases are connected, Leo?' asked Janice. 'How?'

Leo shook his head. 'I'm not sure yet, but there's something going on here and I think it's to do with money. Freddie, do you know if Lloyd had anything to do with the Birbeck brothers?'

'The Guernsey billionaires?' Freddie dug his hands deeper into the pockets of his unzipped Barbour jacket and flapped. 'Of course. They owned his investment firm – still do, in fact.'

I clapped my hands. 'There! We have our connection. These guys – the Durham gang – can be our Baker Street Irregulars to help me with my investigation. You work at it from your side and keep Lestrade off your back. Together we'll make sure Rainbow is vindicated.'

'And Lloyd's killer found?' said Freddie.

Of course, he had been a good friend, hadn't he? I gave Freddie a hug. 'That too. OK, Leo, cover your ears if you need to keep out of it – who's setting up the WhatsApp group?'

Chapter Seventeen

Jess

Back home in Oxford, I submitted to the rapturous welcome from Flossie the spaniel and a rather less exuberant one from my housemates.

'You're back early,' said Kristie, a little accusingly, looking up from the sofa where she was sharing a blanket with Sally. We couldn't afford our heating bills.

I contemplated announcing that murder had ended my mini break but decided they put up with enough weirdness from me without me adding to it.

'I'll take Flossie out for a walk,' I said instead. I'd obviously interrupted Kristie and Sally's plans for a binge-athon of Australian *Love Island*. Improbably good-looking people cavorted on the TV screen in mere suggestions of swimwear, reminding me of my dire need to do something about exercise. Flossie would have to rescue me.

My dog led the way at a cracking pace along the narrow

pavements of Southmoor Road. A suburban street of tightly packed Victorian houses, cars parked both sides, it always felt to me like a sclerotic artery in dire need of a dose of statins to clear the Volvo estates and skips. The individual houses were pretty though, with pleasurable little details like carvings over doorways or fancy tiled paths. The back gardens on the western side, like my house, tilted all the way down to the canal – a nice secret that you couldn't tell from the street. Many people had made the utmost of small front gardens and there was a community vibe that included even the shared houses like mine. Come the zombie invasion, it would be the kind of road where the citizens would band together, barricade either end, and fend off all attacks.

My dog knew exactly where she was going even though it was already dark. We left street lights behind and she took me over the canal bridge and then over the railway, out onto Port Meadow. Across the sky, stars turned out the dust from their empty pockets and the moon shrivelled to its last quarter – a cold, lean time of year. Below, the land was a dark expanse with only the reflected lights from the heavens to show where grass became water. Port Meadow was a spectacular area of common grazing, flooded to the brink of the paths at this time of year so that it resembled an inland sea stretching to the river. Sometimes, on the rare occasions of prolonged cold weather, it would freeze and form an amazing outdoor ice rink. Not today though. Despite the chill, it wasn't the bone-deep cold necessary for that transformation. In the distance was the Thames, a line of trees and boats marking the river winding in its youthful phase before it left Oxford. Up here, it has traditionally been called the Isis, but recent political developments had made that a nightmare for those businesses who had named themselves after it. The Isis Guest House? The Isis Retirement Home? That was a recipe for finding yourself blocked on most online searches. Or worse, misunderstood and mistakenly put at the nexus of international terrorism.

My phone buzzed. Leaning on the gate going onto the meadow, I let Flossie roam as I scrolled through the messages. I'd asked the Durham Irregulars to tell me everything they could remember about Lloyd and Rainbow, so I had a better grasp of the couple I was investigating.

Janice: *It's true what the police said: Rainbow did talk to me about leaving Lloyd last night. The road trip wasn't working for her. She couldn't paint – no space, and Lloyd didn't like it. They'd had some rows – and it takes a lot to make Rainbow argue.*

Lauren: *He never really understood women, did he, poor love?*

Janice: *But there was NO sign Rainbow had snapped. She was expecting to go back and tell him later today that she was coming to stay with me in London. She was going to leave him the van – that's typically generous of her.*

Me: *So, yesterday's visit was an act for our benefit?*

Janice: *That was the real reason why Lloyd didn't want to come to dinner. Too much tension between them.*

Phil: *He's not the only man who fails to understand women. You're all impossible to live with.*

Me: *I see that as our superpower.*

Freddie: *I have the deets for you, Jess. Lloyd was born 6 February 1984, in Enfield. Only child. Parents Laura and Mark, both still alive but divorced (I'll get their address so we can send condolences). Graduated from Sussex University in 2006 in Economics. Went into finance with BIF (that stands for Birbeck Investment Fund) straight from college. Flew high in their estimation until 2018 when he had a crash – his fund went belly-up.*

Phil: *Fucker. I know I shouldn't speak ill of the dead but still…*

Freddie: *He lived in Kingston upon Thames until that house was repossessed. House was worth a million by the time that happened – massive blow. Was in our spare room for quite a few months – that's when he met Rainbow properly. They've been together since early last year.*

Me: *That's the outline, but what about the shading? Known enemies? He clearly pissed off Phil and Janice losing their money. Anyone else?*

Phil: *We are legion.*

Me: *Unless that's a confession that you all did it, butt out, Phil. Any other partners between Rebecca and Rainbow?*

***Lauren:** A few. I remember a Shauna, a Raquel, and an Ellie.*

***Me:** Any of them serious enough to bear a grudge?*

***Freddie:** He did say that Ellie had a screw loose – that he was relieved to finally get rid of her.*

***Lauren:** Never liked her. Cruel to animals. Hated kids.*

***Me:** If you have a way of contacting her, that would help.*

***Freddie:** I'll take a look at my old emails.*

In the pause that followed, I watched as Flossie attacked a stick and won, leaving it in pieces. I'd have to head home in a moment. I wasn't sure how my next question would go down on this group chat, but I was interested in their impressions.

***Me:** And what about Rebecca? Was she really as over him as she claimed?*

***Freddie:** Married for about 4 years; divorced 6 years ago. Water under the bridge.*

***Janice:** A little angry but nothing more than that.*

***Phil:** Fuck if I know.*

***Lauren:** Definitely over. Married too young.*

Me: *He moved on, but did she?*

Lauren: *She's been dating a colleague on and off. A man called Jamie. He's a lawyer. She says he isn't the one but she enjoys his company. Life at home with her elderly mother is testing. She certainly can't bring men home.*

Janice: *God, yes, how embarrassing.*

Phil: *Definite buzz kill. You're about to get your leg over when old biddy walks in in her M&S nightie and offers cocoa.*

Phil was growing on me.

Lauren: *I think she's looking for a partner who wants to start a family.*

Me :*Please don't say biological clock.*

Lauren: *It's natural, isn't it, at our age?*

I wasn't going to touch that one.

Me: *And Rainbow?*

Lauren: *Born 14 March 1985, in Hollywood.*

Me: *Hollywood??*

***Lauren:** County Wicklow, Ireland. Large family. Three sisters. Came to England when she was 8. Went to school in Ely before Durham. Father died soon after she left college. Mother still alive and still in Ely. Bow is a genuinely nice person. Would give you the last Malteser in the packet.*

***Me:** Now that I don't believe.*

***Janice:** She would.*

***Phil:** Yep.*

***Freddie:** Not a shadow of a doubt.*

***Me:** Sigh.*

***Me:** Thanks, guys. Keep the info coming.*

I tucked the phone away and persuaded Flossie to accept the indignity of a leash.

'Just tell yourself it's your human you're taking for a walk,' I crooned to her, rubbing her chest.

Retracing our steps, I pondered what I'd found out. I was as interested in what each chose to share as in the actual information. Leo might be leaning towards money as a motive but I had to consider whether these old friendships might also conceal slow-burn grudges, things to which he would be blinded by bias. Janice had seemed resigned to her financial loss, but then, she was an actress. She could be a Lizzie Borden underneath all that. (OK, I admit it: I was struggling to like her so that was a tad ungenerous). Phil had been upfront about his dislike and equally clear that his own philosophy meant it was his duty to get his own revenge. Had the 'sovereign citizen' taken the law into his own hands and decided a death sentence was a fitting punishment? As a builder, he would have the technical knowhow too, able to sabotage the generator and block off the ventilation. He was at the top of my shortlist if I were looking close to home for my suspect.

Freddie and Lauren? Thus far, they'd not shown any motive and seemed too genuinely nice to be murderous. It wouldn't harm to dig a little though. Lloyd didn't seem a good fit as a friend for them; had there been something else keeping them together?

That left Rebecca, the one always slightly on the outside. Ex-partner, so that was an instant motive right there. If Lloyd was a bully she might have done it for revenge or in some weird way to save Rainbow from what she went through. If we were looking for links between the two deaths, she knew both victims. But could I see her as a killer? Two big things stood against it. Her affection for Rainbow appeared genuine and it was a cold move to frame an innocent by using the duct tape. The second was that I couldn't see a strong enough motive for killing her colleague, not unless Leo turned something up in his enquiries. If she was that crazy, she hid it well. But it wasn't unthinkable. She would have to stay on the list.

I decided to call her and get her take on Lloyd. What she said would lift the lid for a peek inside her mind too.

It took a few rings – probably because I was an

unknown number – but she did pick up.

'Rebecca, it's Jess.'

'Oh, Jess. Sorry, I thought it might be the press.'

'They've been bothering you?'

'It's inevitable. Give me a moment.' She put the phone on a surface and then her voice came from further off. 'No, Mum, not the blue ones. The red ones, remember? Yes, those.' Then she was back. 'I'm sorry. It's a full-time job looking after her these days. I always expect to come home to find she's burned the house down.'

'I can imagine. You must be under a lot of stress.'

'Tell me about it. Have you heard any more about Rainbow?'

'We're waiting to hear when we can fetch her. The police seem to be fixated on her as Lloyd's killer.'

'That's just rubbish. She'd no more kill him than I would. He could be infuriating but he always managed to make you love him despite his flaws.'

'Do you have any theories as to who might have done it?'

She took a moment, and when she did speak, it sounded like she was only just holding to together. 'I still think it was suicide myself. I didn't see him to judge if he was different, but Phil said he thought Lloyd was on the edge and maybe… maybe meeting up with everyone pitched him over?'

That was plausible. 'But if not suicide, then who might do it?'

She gulped. 'He had a talent for making enemies. Other people whose retirement plans he ruined by losing their money? A former lover? He had some colourful girlfriends before Rainbow – Lauren kept me informed. There was an Ellie, or something like that, who poisoned his dog.'

'What?'

She sounded more at ease on this subject, some pent-up resentment showing, I wondered? 'Yes, a real bunny-boiler that one. It would be worth finding out where she was yesterday. God, was it only yesterday? It feels like centuries ago.'

I had to agree with her. Today was turning into an epically long one and we weren't finished yet. 'Tell me more about the dog.'

'One of Lloyd's good points was that he had a soft spot for rescue animals. He took on this boxer with an attitude problem – and reputedly a farting problem.'

'Gross.' I patted Flossie. Her breath might set you back sometimes but she wasn't usually guilty of that canine sin.

'Ellie was living with Lloyd at the time in the Kingston house. I didn't meet her but I understood from Freddie that she was a gold-digger. A single man, big West London house, plush job with bonuses – you get the picture. Ellie was a lifestyle adviser, whatever that is. Doesn't sound like a proper job to me.'

OK, this was sounding just a little bitter.

'And the boxer?'

'Her ideal home reeked of dog, and it scared her friends with its growling. Then the boxer mysteriously sickened and when Lloyd took it to the vet they thought it had ingested rat poison. The poor thing died, but Ellie had a sweetly smelling home after that, didn't she?'

'Did Lloyd suspect her?'

'Maybe he did, but how could he prove it? Anyway, the relationship ended soon after. I know she got in contact with Rainbow and said some horrible things about Lloyd.'

'How do you know this?'

'Rainbow was rattled enough at the time to get in touch and ask me if they were true.'

'What kind of things?'

'That he was into pornography, the extreme sort. Like bondage and breath play, you know, erotic asphyxiation? He liked to act it out in his own sex life.'

Now this was getting more interesting. 'And was he into it?' She paused. I could feel her embarrassment. 'This is confidential, Rebecca. I won't tell anyone.' Maybe Leo, but only him. Possibly.

'He had his dominant side, but, no, not with me. What he got up to with a willing partner who was into that stuff, I don't know – don't want to know. I got the impression it was more about Ellie's taste than his. He'd've experimented but I doubt if he led the way.'

'OK, so Ellie is a bunny-boiler with a kinky side who likes to bad-mouth her ex. Seems like I should definitely meet her.'

'Whatever for?'

'I'm just looking into things to help Rainbow. We need to give the police some other suspects so they move off her.'

'In that case, Ellie would be my first pick. Send them her way.'

I was actually going to send myself her way.

Chapter Eighteen

Leo

In the quiet of a late Sunday in the police station, Leo reviewed the reports and evidence gathered so far on Kelly Ann. The day had been such a rush, he just needed time to lay it all out for himself. The scene-of-crime officers had turned up some interesting evidence on the prints on the blade used to slit her wrists. The marks were the victim's, but several has been partially wiped as if then handled by someone else, possibly wearing gloves or holding it in a cloth. He put that to one side: the physical evidence was mounting.

Rooting through the items removed from the cottage in Chipping Norton in the evidence room, Leo could find no trace of the champagne bottle the victim was said to have brought home with her. That was the second piece of evidence that someone else had been in the house on the evening she died.

Opening a box of papers and documents, he struck gold. They had found a notebook that Kelly Ann had used as a diary. It had been under the pillow on the side of the bed she didn't sleep on – not a place that someone might have thought to look if they had been quickly searching for anything before leaving the crime scene. Already skimmed once at the cottage by a detective constable looking at the last twenty-four hours of her life, it had yielded nothing that suggested suicidal thoughts or arrangements to meet anyone on Friday evening. Leo, however, was looking for something different and further back in time. Scanning it, he saw that these pages were where Kelly Ann had felt able to put down her private thoughts, giving a window on her life, one she hadn't expected anyone else ever to look through. Significant then that no suicidal impulses were registered. For confidential information she had adopted a basic code of referring to people by their initials – hardly difficult to crack. Having never met her in life, Leo was now confronted by an involved and somewhat angry woman. No one had mentioned her anger.

18th January 2018

Finally talked alone to LT today. Luckily, I caught her at work on a day when she was ready to talk. She'd just received bad news from home. Her father has passed away but she can't go back to his funeral as she doesn't have her passport. The fact that she wasn't reconciled before he died is the worst, she said. Poor girl.

LT? Checking his notes, Leo couldn't find a current

employee with those initials. He'd have to look back through the records. He read on.

She told me the story of what led her to seek a life abroad – a remote village – third daughter, not valued. She hadn't wanted to leave home but her family paid for her to be sent here. Her debt to the SMs is still huge.

Reading between the lines, Leo guessed that LT had owed money to the people who smuggled migrants into the country. The SMs? Could they be the Stanton-Milbecks? They were the ones in haulage for the designer outlets in Bicester Village, weren't they?

He checked the Stanton-Milbecks against the police database but they had traded so far without gaining a record. There had to be something though. They were moving goods – possibly people – across borders. Following that train of thought, he put in a call to a colleague from Immigration.

'Leo, long time no hear!' said Gerry Fulwell. They'd met on one of Leo's earliest cases when he was just a sergeant and Gerry a raw recruit to the Immigration services. 'How are you?'

'Good, thank you, Gerry.'

Gerry laughed sourly. 'Let me guess: even though it is Sunday, you're in the office? It wouldn't be like you to make a call just to chat.'

Gerry was right: Leo rarely called anyone just for a conversation; he only called when he wanted something.

He really needed to have a look at his work/life balance. 'It's murder I'm afraid.'

'It nearly always is with you. How can I help?'

Leo sketched out the details he'd gathered so far. 'Have you come across the haulage firm?'

He could hear Gerry consulting his computer, the little staccato taps as he navigated his way through the information.

'Not me – I'm on the Irish border, at the moment. Bloody Brexit. But, yeah, we've got flags against them. Ongoing investigation. I'll send you what I've got. But don't balls it up, Leo, and make me regret telling you.'

'I'd be looking at them in any case as their name has come up.'

Gerry sighed. 'Well, keep us in the loop then. I'll tell the team in charge that you are sniffing around. They'll probably know more than I have here.'

'Thanks, Gerry.'

'Next time, call because you want a beer, OK?'

'I will.'

Gerry sounded sceptical. 'See that you do.'

Leo put his phone down. He would call, wouldn't he? Gerry was a nice guy and they had work in common. But Leo rarely made the first outreach to any of his friends, his reclusive side winning out when he looked at his contact list and decided against messaging.

And his record as a boyfriend?

He shook off thoughts of his failed weekend away – no time for that now. He had to look after Kelly Ann, not agonise about his character defects. He turned back to the diary.

I told her to reject the so-called contract with the people who had brought her here but she's scared. I also said she should tell the Ks that she was no longer going to work for them. The spa work was fine, but the extra things they expected of her weren't.

What was Kelly Ann hinting at here, this 'extra'? He wished she'd been more explicit.

The Ks and the SMs have a reputation in the club.

There was his best evidence that the initials very likely led to his existing suspects. It tied up with her emails.

If I can find proof of what they are doing to these girls, I'll happily sink them. Some of the girls look barely 18, maybe younger. Those parties, the older men disappearing with them to God knows where… It's disgusting and it has to stop.

And what was the betting that the Ks referenced here were the Kanons and their links to the sex industry? The notebook was evidence that Kelly Ann had discovered what they were up to in the shadows of a seemingly respectable club and yet her attempt to start the process of exposing them had resulted in them getting a prized membership from the Birbecks, giving them a free pass at the owners's discretion, and Kelly Ann ended up dead a year later in the bath. What had gone down here? How had she mishandled her attempts to bring the Kanons and the Stanton-Milbecksto justice? Why had she gone on after this righteous entry to accepting what looked like hush money from the club owners, which she'd happily invested in her pension or whatever? Leo corrected himself. Maybe not happily – maybe she'd taken it with fear and resentment – but the money had gone into her investments, hadn't it? He had to know why.

'You want to interview Jeremy and Chester Birbeck?' asked Superintendent Thaxted. 'You don't ask for much, do you? You know they were both made OBEs in the last honours list?'

'I wouldn't ask, ma'am, if I didn't think they weren't central to the death I'm investigating,' Leo said, keeping his tone respectful but steady.

His boss had come to the station to see him on Sunday evening even though both of them were theoretically off-duty. He had told Claire Thaxted that his investigation was taking him into politically sensitive waters and they needed to discuss it in private. The police HQ was quiet this late on a weekend night. Leo's team was finishing up their work but with no suspects in custody they were not against the clock, not like the team in Banbury interviewing Rainbow. Leo hated the thought of his friend in interview. He would have to leave soon if he were to be at the station to collect her when promised. But first he had to win over his commanding officer for the next stage in his investigation.

Claire toyed with the strap of her Fitbit. She'd come straight from her run. 'Explain again what you think they have to do with this?'

'My victim, Kelly Ann Porter, collected the membership fees for the club. She clashed with the Birbecks when she recommended ending the membership of two sets of their contacts who are involved in murky business locally – she cited reputation risk to the club as a reason.'

'Was she right? What do we have on them?'

'They've not got a police record, but the Kanons used to own a number of adult shops in the area. They've diversified online now.'

'I didn't think many people paid for pornography any longer.'

'Premium chatrooms. Stripping and other voyeuristic sex acts. Porn films.'

'And the other ones?'

'The Stanton-Milbecks. They provide logistical support to Bicester Village – they move surplus stock from the designer warehouses to the outlets.'

'That sounds above board.' A frown line appeared above her nose – he was losing her on this. He knew he didn't have much yet.

'Which made me wonder what our vic could have found. Drawing a blank with HOLMES, I reached out to Immigration. They're already looking at the haulage firm. From the reports my contact sent me, they suspect it's part of a chain used by people traffickers, specifically young women from Central and Southeast Asia who end up in nail bars, massage parlours, and prostitution.'

'I see. Interesting. Which takes us back to the Kanons. There's a link?'

'That's what I'm exploring. The Immigration investigation is not public knowledge so our vic must have found her own evidence.'

Claire drummed her fingers. 'Someone at the club talked to her?'

Leo nodded. 'A victim identified by initials. We're looking into past employees and taking another look at the young women on the staff in the spa. I'll also be interviewing the couples, the Kanons and the Stanton-Milbecks.'

'All right.' Claire made a note for herself. 'If there's anything in this, then there's more damage for us if we don't look, than if we do.'

He was relieved she saw it that way. Proved right, a case like this would be a coup for the superintendent. Claire had her eyes on that prize. But they both knew there would be nothing but career-ending embarrassment if he wasn't meticulous with his evidence trail. The money in Kelly Ann's account and the diary were a start. Now he made to prove the links.

There was something else to consider. If the activity that upset Kelly Ann had been going on in the underbelly of the club with the tacit approval of the owners, Rebecca had to have known, hadn't she? Leo worried over that fact; had he gone too easy on her because she was a good friend of his friends? Just because he knew her a little didn't mean she wasn't capable of being party to criminal acts. One of the first things you learned as a policeman was that criminals were 'us' not 'them'.

Claire's thoughts had been travelling a parallel problematic path. 'But if you're right that there's a darker side, Leo, that would be explosive if the press got hold of it. This area is known for its highly placed politicians and celebrities and most of them belong to the club.'

'And our politicians are never caught in sex scandals?'

She sighed. 'You're handing me a grenade with the pin pulled out. How do the Birbecks fit in?'

'The Birbecks chose to offer both the Kanons and the Stanton-Milbecks one of the memberships they have in their gift rather than follow Porter's advice to cut ties. That indicates a relationship between them and the Birbecks, perhaps existing business ties, which Porter might not have known about.'

'So she kicked the ants' nest and later got stung: that's your theory?'

'Exactly! Porter found something serious enough to suggest cutting them off, evidence rather than conjecture, perhaps even uncovered incriminating information about them.'

'Have you found out what?'

'Working on it. Aside from the notes in her diary, there's still her electronics to analyse. These are with forensics. I've asked them to look for any files she created on the couples I've named, especially any kept on her home computer. But following the evidence in her diary and her objection to their membership, it seems clear they were aware she knew something in 2018, else why try to buy her silence? Did she threaten to go public? I don't know the "Why?" yet, but I do know she received a huge bonus last year. Evidence points to the Birbecks buying her off as there was no business reason to reward her.'

'If she was bribed to keep silent, why get rid of her now and in a hazardous way that might unravel, as it's currently doing?'

'Perhaps she renewed her threats, or turned up new evidence? That's what I need to find out. What could be contained last year with a bribe appears to have become a matter over which someone might kill.'

'And you're sure it was murder? There wasn't something else that tipped her over the edge? Some personal tragedy?'

'It wasn't suicide. Too many wrong details. The champagne bottle is missing and there were partially wiped prints on the knife used to slit her wrists.'

'The victim's?'

'Yes. How it reads is that her fingers were pressed on the handle – perhaps post mortem – but then partially wiped as the killer handled it with gloves or a cloth. If Kelly had done it, I would expect the blade to be found in the water with her, not carefully placed on a surface beside her, far side of a glass, no blood splatter.'

Claire got up and paced, arms folded. Leo could tell she was coming over to his view that it was murder. She'd been a detective before being promoted above the rank where she had her own caseload. 'We need to be extremely careful, Leo, that we're not rushing to judgement. I believe the trafficking exists, but that might be a separate matter to the death. I've not heard you mention a personal motive in the killer – a spurned lover, or angry relative? I assume you've considered that?'

He nodded. 'She lived a quiet life, and was looking for a partner but not currently in a relationship. She hadn't been for a while. No close living relatives beyond a sister, no family feuds. There's not a whisper against her in the local community. The only logical place for a motive to have arisen was where she spent the majority of her life: at the club.'

Claire sat back and pushed her chair away from the desk. 'You can't escape the press stories about the ruthless business practices of the gentlemen in Guernsey. I can see why you might lean that way. But murder?'

'I'm not saying they ordered it. I just need to know where they fit in the picture.'

'And how will you achieve that by asking them? You risk tipping them off that you're looking at them and you do realise they are amongst the most influential donors to our current government?'

'I'm aware of that, but I'm also trying not to allow that knowledge to get in the way.'

'No fear or favour?'

'Exactly. And I won't tip them off. I will present my questions as ones they will wish to answer, ones that will help protect their business from unfortunate rumours.'

Claire walked to the window and looked out at the dismal lights of a February evening. She touched her fingertips to her lips in a praying gesture and tapped thoughtfully. Then she turned around.

'All right, Leo. Request – *very politely* – a meeting with the brothers but make clear it's a fact-finding interview only on the sad death of an employee and that you are not accusing them of anything. Present it as you say: that you wish to protect the good name of their establishment. Do not, for heaven's sake, hint that you are digging underneath for the dirt. I imagine there will be some delay in granting that request for an interview, if not a flat-out refusal. Use that time to follow up your other leads. I would be much happier if you had more behind you when you talked to them.'

Leo concurred with that. 'And if they agree to speak, will you sign off on a trip to Guernsey?'

'One trip, so make good use of it. Don't upset them.'

'I hope I don't disappoint you.'

She gave him a grim smile. 'So do I, Leo.'

Leaving messages with the Kanons and the Stanton-Milbecks that he would appreciate a meeting early on Monday, Leo closed down his computer for the night. He'd not heard from Rainbow so decided the quickest route was via the solicitor. With his professional conflicts to consider, it would be best if it wasn't him doing the asking.

He messaged Jess to make the enquiry. She replied ten minutes later, sending him a copy of the reply she'd received. It was bad news. The solicitor, Brook Musgrave, had replied that the police had contacted the Crown Prosecution Service and it had been decided to charge

Rainbow on the physical evidence of tampering with the generator. They were keeping her in overnight until bail could be arranged.

Leo slammed his phone down on the desk, regretting it immediately as the last thing he needed was to break it at this critical point.

A call came in from Jess:

'You got my message?'

'Yeah. I don't know what's going on up at Banbury, Jess – seems such a stretch to blame her.'

'I know. Are you still at work?'

'Yeah. We've had developments on my other case. Sorry.'

'What do you want me to do, Leo? I phoned Brook and she says the decision to charge is mainly on the physical evidence but that's not strong as Rainbow lived with him. Your colleagues are arguing she also had the motive.'

'What motive?'

'Domestic abuse.'

'Christ.'

'And opportunity before leaving for the club. I dispute the last. She came back with us. She didn't have time to go around slapping duct tape on air vents inside.'

But could this have been done this earlier? Would they have noticed? Leo wondered.

Instead Leo went with what he could be sure of:

'Rainbow is not a killer.'

'I get that. But someone did set up the kill zone, either Lloyd or someone he allowed inside. Your friends have given me other names to investigate. There's an old lover who sounds mad enough.'

'Any connections you can see to my case?'

'Not with the ex as far as I'm aware. But you were following the money for your victim. Maybe that works here too as a motive? Lloyd worked for the Birbecks, once, didn't he?'

He would have to think how it might fit in. It was bloody inconvenient to be kept so far away from Lloyd's case.

'Maybe. Thanks, Jess.'

'See you tomorrow?' she asked hopefully.

'I have some club members to interview so not till much later.'

'OK. Let's keep in touch and work something out. Will you still collect Rainbow?

Tomorrow looked like it was shaping up as another impossible day. 'I'll try but can you be on standby? You've got my key.'

'Yes. I can collect her and keep her company, if you think she'd like that?'

'That would be great, and maybe Janice or one of the others can also be with her? Thanks – you're the best.'

'I'll remember you said that. Good night. Don't work too late.'

He ended the call and sent a new group message to his Durham friends telling them the bad news.

Chapter Nineteen

Leo

The Kanons had agreed to see him at their home in Chipping Norton. One of the largest properties in the old centre of town, Leo noted that it was only a five-minute walk from Kelly Ann's rose-covered cottage. He drew up at the gates of the Kanons's mansion and pressed the buzzer. Through the black iron railings he could see the many chimneys and gabled roofs of Oak Manor Farm. It was the kind of home a Jane Austen family like the Bennets might've inhabited. What Lizzy and her sisters wouldn't have had was a large modern conservatory and outdoor swimming pool round the back. There was not much in the way of landscaping, though the mature trees had been kept for privacy.

The intercom crackled. 'Who is it?'

'Inspector George, Thames Valley. I have an appointment.'

The gate swung open, closing quickly after he had driven through. He parked on the gravel by the front steps, next to a navy-blue Porsche. Glancing inside, he spotted tennis rackets on the back seat.

The front door opened without him having to knock. A grey-haired man in his early fifties stood in the entrance. He was tanned, medium height, and with the distinguishing feature of being slightly boss-eyed so one eye wandered while the other looked at you. Leo found himself thinking of a vicious cat his mother's had briefly owned when they lived on a canal boat, whose eye had never recovered from a kicking one of her boyfriends had given it. Kanon was dressed in smart casual – yellow cashmere jumper over tailored white shirt with pale trousers.

'Mr Kanon?' asked Leo.

'Correct.' His gaze swept Leo, assessing the visitor as Leo had done him. 'Come in. I have to admit that my wife and I are perplexed as to what brings you to our door.'

'I'll explain. Will your wife be joining us?'

'She's waiting in the conservatory. We thought you might like coffee in the daylight. Easy to get starved of Vitamin D at this time of year.'

'So they say.'

Kanon led him briskly down the corridors to the modern extension at the back. Leo had a chance for a quick look through open doors at the interiors. There was nothing to suggest this was the home of a couple who made their money from sex, unless the large number of photographic nude studies and sketches on the walls were connected to that.

Kanon noticed where his gaze was directed. 'My wife's work. Got several into the Royal Academy exhibition over the years.'

'Very impressive. I understand there's stiff competition for a place.'

The lady herself was waiting for them in a wicker chair with a large round back, like a peacock's tail spread behind her. Hothouse plants framed her – a banana tree, several palms, a lemon bush in a terracotta pot. Marta Kanon was a few years younger than her husband, with glossy brunette hair falling in waves, and a Botox-smooth face. Her lips were suspiciously plump in that way of those who opted for lip-filler. A teardrop diamond hung from the end of a gold chain around her neck, two matching ones in her ears. She got up to offer a hand, the closely fitted pink dress revealing curves that probably owed much to a plastic surgeon or superb corsetry as they were too pertly abundant to be natural. Every inch of her was lush and sensual. If she was used to men reacting stupidly to her flaunted sex appeal, she was going to be disappointed in his case. Leo's taste didn't run to this Hollywood Wives kind of femininity.

'Inspector.' Her voice was deep and sexy. If they had phone lines in addition to their online activities, that tone alone would be worth a fortune.

'Mrs Kanon, thank you for making time to see me.' He took an armchair opposite her.

'Coffee?' She gestured to the tray freighted with a silver coffee pot and sugar bowl – modern design – with fine china cups, also contemporary.

'Thank you.'

'Josef?'

It wasn't a question of what he wanted but an instruction. Mr Kanon poured.

'Your husband was asking why I wanted to speak to you. I'm investigating the death of an employee at the Piccadilly People Club, Kelly Ann Porter.'

'Ah, yes, we heard,' she said.

'You heard?'

'Local grapevine.' She waved that away as if no more need be said. 'So sad. But I understand there were no children or partner. I guess it was her right to decide when to go.'

'You assume it was suicide? Did you know the victim?'

Marta Kanon glanced at her husband. 'Wasn't it?'

'We are investigating the exact circumstances of her death,' said Leo. 'Did you know her?'

'Not really. We corresponded some time ago.' Marta leant forward to reach for the sugar, dress gaping. 'She didn't like us.'

Kanon sat back in his chair, cup in hand, and crossed his legs. 'You will know, Inspector, that we own a business that sells adult services.'

'I did know that.'

'It's completely legal, but some prudish people around here still have a problem with sex. Probably because they aren't getting any.'

'Darling, you mustn't speak ill of the dead,' said his wife, though she was smiling at his quip.

Kanon smirked. 'Miss Porter complained about our business to the owners of the club.'

'The Birbeck brothers?' said Leo.

'Exactly. They agreed with us that old-fashioned views shouldn't stand in the way of legitimate business and they arranged matters so we didn't have to deal with her again. That's why it's ironic that her death brought you to our door. We've had nothing to do with her for years.'

Leo pulled out his notebook. The inference that he had the facts written down usually made it harder for people to avoid answering. 'You had trouble paying for your membership fees in 2018. That was what started the confrontation with Kelly Ann Porter?'

Marta's smile turned icy. 'Temporary cash-flow problems. Rapidly resolved, but she used it as an excuse to attempt to get rid of us. I would've shaken the dust off my heels and found another club if Gemma hadn't loved the tennis courts. So convenient for a serious player.'

'Our daughter is in the junior GB squad, Inspector,' said Kanon.

'I had heard that. Congratulations.'

'She's at training camp now. We're hoping she'll make selection for the junior competition at Wimbledon this year.'

'I wish her luck with that. You use the courts at the club a lot?'

'Most days,' agreed Marta.

'And the other facilities?'

'Their restaurant is the best in the area.'

'When were you last there?'

Kanon looked to his wife. 'Friday, wasn't it? Jamie invited us.'

'That's Jamie Paxton?' clarified Leo.

'Correct. Legal bod at the club. Nice chap. Went to school with a friend of ours. Not a bad tennis player either.'

'How long did that dinner last?'

Kanon shrugged. 'Can't say I watched the clock but I think the reservation was for eight and we got home around eleven. Would you say that was about right, darling?'

Marta crossed her legs and sipped her coffee, taking her time. 'About that. We ate a little later than usual as I had to run Gemma into Oxford to meet up with the rest of her squad.'

That gave plenty of time for any of them to have paid a call on the victim and staged the suicide.

'Have you ever been to Kelly Ann Porter's house?' asked Leo.

'Good God, why would we? I didn't even know where it was until the police tape went up outside. You know, those pretty cottages opposite the almshouses?' She directed that to her husband.

'The woman lived down there, did she? Must be worth quite a lot, a property in that road.' Kanon looked over at Leo, one eye looking a little to the left as the other focused on him. 'I take it you are considering us as suspects in some way, Inspector? I find that insulting. Our tiff with Miss Porter was hardly the stuff to go killing someone over.'

'I'm establishing the movements of anyone connected to the case, not making accusations,' said Leo evenly. 'Do you know Tony and Gaia Stanton-Milbeck?'

'Of course we do. We often play them at mixed doubles. They're good friends,' said Kanon.

'Do you have any business relationship with them?'

'No, Inspector. They are in shipping and we are in sex.' Marta almost purred the answer.

'They also had trouble paying their club fees in 2018. Were their difficulties connected in any way with the reasons you struggled to pay?'

Leo caught a glint in Marta's eye: knowledge of something she wasn't going to share with him. 'I presume we were both in a rough patch. Things have been very up and down for a lot of businesses – Brexit, austerity – we weren't the only ones.'

'Would you be willing to share a list of your employees since 2018?' He wasn't expecting agreement.

'Not without a warrant.' Marta smiled complacently.

He kept moving, hoping to wrong-foot them with quick changes of subject. 'Have any of your employees ever turned out to be here illegally?'

Marta bristled. 'We fill out all the necessary paperwork, have all the permits for what we do. What are you suggesting?'

'But, on occasion, have you had anyone fall foul of immigration rules?'

'Not that I can recall,' she snapped.

That wasn't the same as 'no', was it? 'Thank you. One last question: do you know a man by the name of Lloyd Rumbold.' He shouldn't really be asking but he had to for Rainbow's sake.

'Never heard of him. Will that be all?' said Kanon.

But Leo was watching Marta. 'Mrs Kanon?'

'No, no, I don't know him,' she said, but the pause was too long.

'He was a financial adviser.'

'Was he? I don't think we've met.' But she was lying and, from the expression on her husband's face, he hadn't known and caught the lie, too. 'Not that I recall. I do meet such a lot of people.'

Her failed recollections were apparently saved for the things she wanted to cover up. How had she known Lloyd? A fling? Come across him in business? 'Are you sure, Mrs Kanon?'

'Yes, I'm sure. Now, I hope we've been helpful but I really have to get on.' She stood up. 'I'll see you at lunch, Josef.' She headed back into the house.

'Home studio,' said Kanon absently as his focus was on the back of his wife. 'I'll show you out.'

Leo excepted the dismissal. It was a shame he couldn't stay to hear the reckoning between the couple but maybe Kanon wouldn't challenge her? It would take guts to confront a woman like Marta and Kanon didn't seem the type.

Reluctantly, Leo got back in his car and headed for his next appointment: the Stanton-Milbecks.

During the thirty-minute drive to Bicester village – the designer outlet on the edge of the town – Leo checked for updates on Rainbow and cursed. She'd messaged him that she was to be released at noon and could he please please come for her?

He called Jess instead on hands-free.

'Leo? Any news?' she asked at once.

'They're releasing Rainbow on bail. Only problem is, I can't be there to fetch her until one at the earliest as I've another interview to do. Could you go in my place and take her back to mine? Get a taxi – I'll pay you back.'

'It's OK. I signed up for one of those electric-car-share services. There's one near me. I'll take that if it's not booked out.'

'Good. Will you let the others know and make sure she's not alone?'

'Yes. I can do the searches I need to do at yours.'

'Searches?'

'I'm hunting down Lloyd's exes, remember?'

'Oh, yes. Then you might like to add in Marta Kanon as a possible. I got the sense her path had crossed his. Maybe sound out Rainbow if the name rings any bells?'

'Will do. I'll see if Janice can come and share Rainbow duties as I have an address to check out for the bunny-boiler.'

'The what?'

'The crazy ex. The dog poisoner. Ellie. She did away with his boxer because it farted too much – that's according to Rebecca. Oh, and she'd got a pronounced kink that he apparently shared.'

'Don't take any unnecessary risks, Jess.'

'I won't. Only the necessary ones.'

Chapter Twenty

Jess

I used the code to open the little electric car and checked the last person had left it on charge. We were good to go. I could drive up to Banbury and back in time to meet Janice at Leo's house. Rainbow didn't really know me so I thought she'd be happier with her old friend to talk to. My time would be better spent trying to exonerate her.

The drive to Banbury was mercifully free of difficult driving moments (I'm not a confident driver). I pulled into Banbury police station – an unlovely red brick building – and found a spot in the visitors' parking area. Had this building been designed to tell offenders that crime was tedious and procedural, so as to make it as unsexy as possible?

'I'm here to collect Rainbow Williams,' I told the receptionist.

She nodded and passed on the message to the custody officer. After a five-minute wait, Rainbow appeared through the swing doors, her arm gently held by the police officer escorting her. He was guiding her with care, treating her more as victim than suspect – more proof of the frequent claim I heard that everyone liked Rainbow, even after charging her with murder.

'Rainbow?' I said.

She gazed around her. 'Where's Leo?'

'Held up by work. He asked me to take you home. Is that OK?'

'Yes, yes, fine.' She was quivering like an aspen leaf.

'Finished all the paperwork?' I asked, knowing that you didn't walk out of a police station on bail for murder without providing a filing clerk with several hours of work.

'Miss Williams is all done,' said the officer. 'The CPS has looked at her case and agreed that she can be released on bail, as we do not consider her a danger to the public. She must remain at the address in Iffley we were given until her court hearing.'

'Understood,' I said.

'There you go, Miss Williams. Let your friend take you home.' His tone was like that used to speak to a distressed child.

'Thank you, Sergeant Chaudri,' she said politely.

He gave her a nod and disappeared back to his less attractive felons.

The foyer was no place to discuss exactly what had happened in police custody, nor did I think she wanted to linger any longer than necessary.

'I'm parked just outside.' I took her arm where the officer had held it when she showed little sign of moving. He'd been keeping her on her feet, I realised, as she was in deep shock. She wasn't tracking properly. 'Janice is going to be at Leo's to look after you.'

'Janice? Oh, I don't want to be a bother to anyone.'

'You're not a bother.' I led her to the car. 'Now buckle up and we'll have you at Leo's house before you know it. You probably need to rest. Cells are the last place for a good night's sleep.'

Mutely, she nodded.

'Have you eaten?'

She nodded again.

'Is there anyone you'd like to call? Your family?'

She shook her head. 'I don't want them to know. I don't want anyone to know.'

'They will find out, though, won't they?' I said, gently.

'But not today. I couldn't bear it!'

Fair enough. I'd probably keep it from my mother in Rainbow's place. Mum would rush over and make everything ten times worse for me, as I'd have to cope with her pain as well as my own.

'Let's just get you to Leo's then.'

Drawing up at his little brick house in Iffley – a pretty village suburb of Oxford – I saw Janice had beaten me to it. And Phil. Of course, she'd gone home with him and didn't have her own car yet.

'Hi, guys,' I said, helping Rainbow out of the car. 'One very confused Rainbow for you.'

Janice hugged her. 'You poor thing. It's too much.'

'Fucking pigs,' growled Phil. 'Anyone with any sense can see they've made a mammoth mistake.'

I opened the front door, finding it odd to do so without the owner being the one to greet guests. I stooped to pick up his post and set it on the radiator shelf. This was a stage further in our relationship than we had yet gone: me acting as if his home was mine to share.

'I imagine Leo would want you to have the spare room, Rainbow. I'll dig out some sheets and make up the bed. Janice, Phil, make yourself at home in the kitchen. There's probably something for lunch if you have a look in the fridge.'

'I'm not hungry,' said Rainbow, faintly.

'Well, I am. You can keep us company,' I said firmly. Between us, I was sure we could get her to eat something as I didn't trust her nod that she had eaten while in the cells.

Bed made, I returned to the kitchen to find them sitting around a plate of toasted cheese, which had been cut into small squares. From the drift of the conversation, I deduced that Janice had said they would answer Rainbow's questions for every square Rainbow ate.

'Someone really killed him?' asked Rainbow, nibbling a square.

'That's what it looks like. The details are sketchy. They're looking at you because your fingerprints were on the duct tape,' explained Janice.

'Of course they were. It's my tape, from my toolbox.'

'When did you last use it?' I asked, sitting down next to her and filching a square of toast.

She shrugged. 'A few days ago. I had a vase to send and I used it when boxing it up.'

'So, you use it a lot?'

'Yes.'

I made a mental note to try to find out if the police had matched the torn-off strips on the ventilation to the last piece taken off the roll of tape left behind. It would be very illuminating if the last strip had been used on the parcel sent to a client, rather than on the wall vents. 'I wonder if your client still has the parcel?'

'Oh, I think I sent it tracked.' She wrinkled her brow in the struggle for coherent thought. 'It should be arriving today.'

'Could you ask them to save the box?'

'Why?'

'Because if the cut on the tape matches the last piece taken from the roll the police have, it means it couldn't have been used to seal up the vents.'

'Oh, I see!' Her eyes brightened. 'Yes, I'll send a message.'

'Great. We might get lucky.'

I found some grapes in the fridge and put them in a bowl for us all to pick at.

'Did Lloyd ever mention a woman called Marta to you – Marta Kanon?' I asked, trying not to make it sound too much like an interrogation. She would've had her fill of that the last twelve hours. 'In fact, have any of you heard of her?'

'Not me,' said Phil.

'Me, neither,' said Janice. 'Who is she?"

'Just someone who might have been a local contact of Lloyd's,' I said lightly.

Rainbow took a grape. 'Marta? I don't know. There were so many people – Lloyd knew so many people. I didn't even try to keep up. He had a lot of women.' She was visibly wilting and it felt cruel to carry on asking her questions.

'Why don't you take the rest of that upstairs with a cup of tea? We'll call you if anything happens. Don't forget to message the client.'

Janice got up and picked up the plate and mug. 'I'll make sure she does. Come on, Bow. I'll see you to your room.'

'I don't want to be alone,' she said, plaintively.

'You're not. We're all here for you.'

'Lloyd's gone – really gone?'

'Yes, he is. And it's tragic, but not your fault.'

Phil and I could hear them going over this same territory as they mounted the stairs. Rainbow was feeling guilty for not dying alongside him. An understandable survivor's guilt, unless…

Phil would give me a straight answer.

'You don't think she did it, do you?' I asked, my tone making it plain this was a genuine question.

'Rainbow? Kill Lloyd? No way.' He wasn't angered by

my enquiry. His rage of yesterday had simmered down. 'She meant what she said just then – Lloyd had a lot of women… sexually.' He flicked his gaze to my breasts. 'He didn't go in for monogamy and preferred open relationships. This Marta could've been one of them.'

'Up here, Phil.' I tapped my face. He grinned, unapologetically. 'And Rainbow was OK with this?'

'Doubt it. She would've thought she'd be the one to change him. She's starry-eyed enough for that. When she realised that she would never be his one and only, she might've left him, but it would have been a messy will-I-won't-I thing that would've gone on for weeks. That's how things ended between us way back when we were students.'

'How long did you date?'

'For four months in our final year. My fault that ended. I think being with someone so good made me bad, do you understand what I mean?'

I did as I had that weakness, too: behaving badly just because goodness made me antsy, like the urge to shout in a silent room. Leo hadn't seen that side of me yet but I worried it would surface. 'Yeah, I do.'

'I don't believe for one moment Rainbow would've gone through with leaving him this weekend, no matter what Janice says. Even if she felt desperate, she certainly doesn't have it in her to take such a ruthless way out as murder. We've all known her since we were eighteen. She can't have fooled us all for so long that she was gentle and kind when really she was a killer.'

But even sweet, kind people have their breaking point.

'I just wondered. But maybe the police were right about her having enough cause?'

Phil grabbed a fistful of grapes. 'Lloyd could be a bastard but I got the impression he rated Rainbow, knew she was a good soul. The bastard didn't deserve her and he knew it.' Phil got up and put a couple of pieces of bread in the toaster. 'Want some?'

'Toast and Marmite will do for lunch. I'm hoping to track down one of Lloyd's exes, the dog killer.'

He got the Marmite ready and found a knife for me, his version of encouragement for my investigations on their behalf. 'Did you find out where she lives, then?'

'Yes, and that's interesting because it's not far away. She's in East Oxford now. Cowley.'

'Close enough to go up to Chippie and finish off the old partner if she was still bearing a grudge? Good one.' The toaster delivered the slices with an energetic spring. He put the toast in front of me.

'Thanks. One thing I have to ask, while we're alone and just to get it out of the way: Phil, you didn't do it, did you?'

'Christ, you're blunt. No, I fucking well didn't,' he said, without rancour, as he slathered honey on his slice. 'As I said yesterday, I would've preferred to have him around to make him suffer. Dead, you're free of all this shite.'

'I wanted to ask you directly because, with your views, I thought you wouldn't hide the fact if you did.'

'You're right about that.' He pointed the table knife at me. 'If someone gave me sufficient cause, I'd take my pound of flesh and be proud to face the consequences.

Losing my money? Lloyd didn't pay enough in my estimation, going to sleep like that. So you can cross me off your list of suspects.'

I gave him a grin. 'Nope. You're still on there, but maybe not at the top.'

He shook his head at my stubbornness and munched on his toast. 'I wasn't the only one who had it in for Lloyd,' he said through a full mouth.

'I'm rather getting that impression. Janice wasn't a fan.'

'Not just her. Have you asked Lauren and Freddie what they really thought of him?' Phil's expression was impishly gleeful.

'Why? Is there something you want to tell me?'

'Problem with old friends is we know far too much about each other. Ask them. I'm not saying for one minute that they wished him serious harm, or would've done anything about it, but I just want to point out I'm not the only one with motive. When you come down to it, Lloyd was not a good man and a fucking terrible friend. I wouldn't be surprised if your list of suspects came down to everyone who ever met him.'

'Bar Rainbow?'

'Yeah, bar her.'

Pondering this view of the case, I got back into my little electric car. I had enough battery juice for a run to Cowley but then I'd have to return it to its parking place to recharge. I rejected the idea of asking Freddie and Lauren outright what Phil might mean, not on the phone at least. I would wait until we met again and try to winkle it out of them. They weren't good at keeping secrets so I thought the odds were high that I would succeed. There was talk of them coming over this evening to commiserate with Rainbow and see what I'd found out, so I wouldn't have long before I got my chance to question them.

I parked in a supermarket near the target's house and hoped I wouldn't get spotted by the Tesco parking wardens. Walking to her road, I took stock of her surroundings. My colleague Jennifer lived around here. It was the most multicultural area of Oxford, signalled by the more obvious outward signs of hijabs and saris, a variety of ethnic restaurants, and a more exotic range of fruit and veg available in the greengrocer's. Ellie lived in a pebble-dashed semi in Horspath Road, facing the recreation ground. Property round here wasn't cheap but neither was it high-end, suggesting her styling business was pulling in enough without leaving her flush. Her dreams of hitting payday with a loaded husband hadn't yet materialised. You could find houses like this in every town in the country – decent but not distinguished. I was hoping the occupant would be rather more exciting than the exterior.

I pulled a clipboard out of my messenger bag and put a survey I'd mocked up on the top. I'd used this ploy before and, though I often got the door shut in my face, I rarely met with outright hostility. Clipboards are usually quelling. I rang the bell. Footsteps inside sounded promising. The woman who opened the door fitted the photo Freddie had sent to me – a cluster of brown curls – though, today, she had it bundled up in a silk scarf like a Land Girl from World War Two. Big green eyes flawlessly made up. A smart blouse and well-cut navy trousers. Today's style theme: dig for victory. She had a pencil tucked behind one ear.

'Yes?' She glanced at my clipboard. 'I'm full up on charities, thanks very much.'

'No, not a charity,' I interjected quickly before the door closed. 'I'm conducting a survey for an academic who's working with the council. He's a planning expert and my job is to get people's views on the local area and any antisocial behaviour you've noticed – parking on the pavements, dog-fouling, misuse of cycle paths, and so on. Those are just some of the things your neighbours have mentioned. If you want to have your say, I'll only take five minutes of your time.'

She leant against the door. Most people didn't want to be left out if others had spoken. All enjoyed having a moan. 'ID?'

I held up my staff pass for St Nick's. Fortunately, she didn't ask for the name of the academic.

'OK, then. Come in for a minute. I was due to take a break.' She led me to the kitchen.

'I'm sorry. I didn't mean to interrupt your work.'

'Just a design for a client. I'm a stylist.'

'Like hair and makeup?'

'The whole works – lifestyle for home, personal appearance, website, social media.'

'That sounds fascinating.'

A cat came in through the flap in the back door and

wound round my ankles. 'You're a cat person?' she asked. 'Versace doesn't normally take to strangers.'

'I love cats. And dogs.' I scratched the feline on her white throat.

'*Ugh*. I can't abide dogs.' She put a glass of water in front of both of us.

'Oh? Have you ever had one? My spaniel is very friendly. I wouldn't be without her.'

'No place for them in my life – sorry. Cats suit me better.'

'Even if they claw the furniture?'

'I had her declawed.'

'Isn't that illegal?'

Temper sparked. 'Why? Are you going to report me?'

I was tempted. 'Of course not.'

'It's not illegal in America.'

Poor cat. I totally believed Ellie had killed the dog. Struggling to overcome my disgust, I calmed myself by stroking the purring animal.

'Your questions?' she asked, unaware of my emotional battle.

'Right. Questions. Can you give your top-three examples of antisocial behaviour that you've witnessed in the last three years, please?' Besides cat mutilation.

'I haven't lived here that long. I moved in 2017 – from London.'

'And where did you live in London?'

She paused.

'For comparison's sake,' I coaxed her.

'Kingston upon Thames.'

'And would you say that there were more incidents there, fewer, or about the same.'

'Fewer. It was a very nice area.'

So, she considered she had come down in the world. 'Going back to your top-three complaints in this area since you arrived, what would they be?'

I was unsurprised when she came up with dog-related gripes and untidy neighbours leaving broken kitchen appliances in their front gardens.

'What about parking?'

'A nightmare. I'm lucky I have a drive.'

'You have a car?'

'I do.'

I'd already taken of photo of it, and would ask Leo to check whether it appeared on any CCTV near the motorhome on the night of Lloyd's death. 'And how often would you say you used your car? More than once a day, once a day, once a week, or other?'

'Once a day. What relevance do these questions have to antisocial behaviour?'

I shrugged. 'I'm just the messenger. I think the council is considering tightening up on traffic using local roads, bringing in bus gates and further parking restrictions. They want to know how much the locals use their own cars and how inconvenienced they would be if through routes were restricted.'

'You mean we wouldn't be able to drive from our own homes?'

'Not quite but you might have to go the long way round to get to where you want to go, like the hospital, supermarket, or out for a weekend drive, things like that. Do you often drive out of Oxford for work or pleasure?'

'Yes, of course. I visit clients.'

She was hardly going to confess to driving out to murder someone, was she? But I'd had to ask. 'So would you or wouldn't you be in favour of new restrictions?'

'Not if it puts local people at a disadvantage. Bad enough sitting in the traffic as it is.'

I gave a big tick on my survey sheet. 'Thanks, that's it. Unless you have anything you might wish to add?'

'No, nothing.'

As I stood, I noticed she had a picture of Lloyd and her on the window ledge, a romantic shot taken on a beach somewhere. That answered the question as to whether she still had feelings for him. If she didn't kill him, did she know he was dead? I could hardly drop it into the conversation, so I had to leave without saying anything.

Back in the car, I waited in the car park to send my message, waving off a guy who wanted to wash my vehicle. I included her car registration. Leo replied virtually straight away.

> ***Me:*** *Any chance you can check if bunny-boiler was anywhere near Chipping Norton area at the time of Lloyd's death?*
>
> ***Leo:*** *I can if I can stretch that it's relevant to my investigation. I'll add it to the list of vehicles I'm looking for in relation to my victim. Impressions?*

Me: *Not enough to go on in this first interview, but I can confirm she has it in for dogs and still has feelings for Lloyd. A picture showing both of them has pride of place in her kitchen.*

Leo: *Good work.*

Me: *And see – I escaped unscathed.*

Leo: *This time.*

Chapter Twenty-One

Leo

The warehouse used by Stanton Logistics was tucked around the back of the Bicester designer outlets. Leo walked through the paved shopping centre with its faux village feel. Hard to believe but this was the biggest tourist attraction in the country, according to the latest statistics. Easy to reach from London, people flocked here more than to the Tower of London or Windsor Castle. In that awkward stage between Christmas and the next big shopping festival, the planters were full of early daffodils and trailing ivy, whimsical chicks announcing the beginning of the Easter season and the expectation of thousands of overseas visitors to come in 2020. Even today, there were a fair number of shoppers braving a drab February day, mainly from Arab and Asian countries. No one left without a couple of upmarket paper bags with rope handles. No one apart from him.

He made his way as instructed down a narrow alleyway between a perfume shop and a boutique. Empty trolleys partially blocked the path so he had to thread his way past them. At the end was the lorry park and the warehouse. The big doors were open as men in blue overalls unloaded the latest consignment. The company used unmarked white HGVs. The one in the docking bay had Turkish number plates.

Leo headed to the reception. This had no pretensions to fancy, just a desk and a bored young woman on duty. He held up his warrant card.

'Detective Inspector George to see Mr and Mrs Stanton-Milbeck.'

The girl – she looked like a recent school leaver – furrowed her thick eyebrows as she tapped on the computer keyboard.

'Oh, yeah, Inspector, they're expecting ya. I'll just buzz their PA. Take a seat, will ya?'

Leo sat on one of the metal chairs pushed up against the wall. The coffee table held a small selection of magazines of the *Motor Trader* kind – nothing to tempt him. Fortunately, he didn't have to wait long for the PA to fetch him. She had ten years on the receptionist but could've been her older sister, sharing the same thick eyebrows, round face, and long blonde highlighted hair. She had a smart cream-coloured suit – probably picked out of one of the shops in the village… unless it came as a perk of the job, because it looked pricey even with a discount.

'Inspector? This way, please,' she asked, using a politer tone than her receptionist sister.

He followed her along a brown carpeted corridor, up a flight of concrete stairs, to a slightly more comfortable area where the furnishings were soft and the flooring less industrial. She showed him into a conference room that had windows looking out over the top of a row of white lorries and to the Oxfordshire countryside. Two people were already seated at the far end – his hosts, he assumed.

Tony Stanton-Milbeck stood up as Leo came in. He wore a black shirt with rolled-up sleeves, no tie – businessman casual, someone who could go down on the warehouse floor and not look out of place. A powerfully built man, he had short black hair, a heavy beard shadow and eyes set deep and close to his narrow nose, like they'd retreated there for shelter. Leo was reminded of Novak Djokovic but that was probably only because the Kanons had talked so much of tennis. Gaia Stanton-Milbeck was the opposite of the earth mother name she'd been given. She was full of sharp points: bleached hair spiked up, dagger-like pendants hanging from her exposed earlobes, silver-painted nails filed to talon length. Her eyes snapped with blue fire as they took him in – appreciatively, Leo realised. His suit had made an impression.

'Inspector, how can we help you?' Tony asked, gesturing him to take the seat opposite Gaia. He returned to his seat at the head of the table. 'Can we get you anything?'

'No, thank you. And thank you for seeing me. It's about the death of a member of the Piccadilly People Club staff, Kelly Ann Porter.'

'The woman in Chipping Norton?' said Gaia, talon tapping on the polished tabletop.

'That's correct.'

'Wasn't she an accountant or something?'

'That's right. She was in charge of membership fees. Did you ever come across her?'

Gaia turned to her husband. 'It's that awful woman, Tony. The one who made a fuss because we were a little late with our fees one year. We'd been members since the beginning of the club in 2010. You would've thought our loyalty would've bought us more latitude.'

'Did you ever meet her in person?'

Gaia's earrings shivered as she shook her head. 'Don't think so.'

'We might've crossed paths at the club, I suppose, but we never spoke. Our exchanges were by email,' said Tony.

'Have you ever visited her at home?'

'Absolutely not. Inspector, why all these questions? We had barely anything to do with the woman.'

'As you may have gathered from the local news, the circumstances surrounding her death are suspicious. We are questioning anyone who might've had reason to dislike her.'

'In case we felt like bumping her off? Isn't that a bit farfetched, Inspector?' Tony's tone was acidic.

'A lot of police work is about elimination, Mr Stanton-Milbeck. Just because I'm asking questions, doesn't mean I'm accusing you of anything.'

Gaia poured her husband some water and pushed it towards him. 'He's just doing his job, Tony.'

'Yes, yes, I get that.' With a sigh, Tony sat back. 'Do you

have any more questions for us now you've established we barely knew the woman?'

It was interesting how often he said 'the woman' like he refused to grant her the dignity of a name. Most people were more respectful to a dead person even if they didn't care for them alive. Kelly Ann had clearly got under his skin.

'I understand that the result of your exchange of emails with Miss Porter was that you were offered a Birbeck membership, a direct gift from the founders of the club?'

'That's right. Jeremy and Chester were most apologetic and gave us membership as an apology for the hassle we were put through.'

'What kind of hassle?'

Tony rubbed the side of his glass.

'My husband is referring to that woman's accusations that our business was dealing with unsavoury people,' said Gaia.

'Unsavoury in what way?' They didn't answer. 'We're getting access to Miss Porter's work emails. We'll find out anyway but I'd like to hear it in your own words first.'

'All right then – not that we enjoy repeating this rubbish. The stupid woman had some elaborate scheme in her head, that we were trafficking Russians and Asian girls into some kind of white slavery! I think she'd been watching too many thrillers – got herself all worked up over nothing,' said Gaia.

'Trafficking girls for whom?'

'Oh, the whole thing was so foolish, I really don't want to say.'

Leo nodded as if sympathetic. 'I can help you there. She accused the Kanons, friends of yours, of being involved. Were they the people she thought you were working with?'

Tony got up abruptly and walked to the window. 'Yes, she did.' He swivelled to face Leo, his arm making angry, chopping gestures. 'Look out there, Inspector. We carry goods from factories working for the top fashion brands. We make good money doing so. Why would we need to risk it all to get involved in something like human trafficking? The very idea is preposterous!'

Why risk it? Because people always wanted more, thought Leo. But his task today wasn't to alarm them that he was looking seriously at the trafficking angle but to confirm what he already knew had gone on between the feisty accountant and the three couples who were so much more powerful than her. Kelly Ann had stood in the path of the Kanons, the Stanton-Milbecks, and the Birbecks: it was hardly surprising their juggernaut had mown her down.

'Thank you for your candour. It's helpful to get a fuller picture of the victim,' he said placatingly.

'Victim? Are you sure she didn't do this to herself? She was clearly half-cracked,' said Tony, not hiding his sneer.

'On another matter, are either of you familiar with the name Lloyd Rumbold?'

Tony shook his head but Gaia smiled.

'Lloyd?' she repeated. 'I think I've seen him around. Why? What's he done?'

'Can you remember where?'

'Some of our friends used him for financial advice – and

later, other services.' She left just enough pause to let the innuendo creep in. 'I hear he gave great satisfaction.'

Tony frowned and stalked back to his seat. 'What's this? Why have I never heard of this?'

She patted his arm. 'That's because it was a secret we girls shared, not with you. He got quite a name for himself as providing what we called "economic stimulation". I hasten to add that I never took him up on it so this is hearsay.'

'Can you speak a little plainer?' said Leo. 'Are you saying he slept with clients?'

Gaia smiled, catlike. 'He was a rare example of a failed Birbeck hire. He worked for their investment firm and many of us put our money with them, but Lloyd's fund was a dud.' She was enjoying spilling the local gossip, Leo could tell. 'He, however, was apparently not a dud between the sheets and got quite a lot of custom that way – those who were prepared to overlook the fact that he'd lost their money.'

Lloyd had been so strapped for cash that he'd turned to a form of prostitution with clients with whom he'd already had an affair? That might explain the glint in Marta's eye when his name had come up, realised Leo. She seemed the sort to enjoy a walk on the wild side.

'Did he lose your money?' Leo asked.

'You're not talking about that fucker who lost our profit in 2018, are you?' asked Tony.

No wonder the Birbecks had felt obligated to dish out memberships if it had been another of their firms to blame, thought Leo.

'I am.' His wife smiled serenely.

'Christ, I'd purposely wiped him from my memory banks. And your coven of women friends were all sleeping with him? Jesus, I've always said you're like bitches in heat!'

'Not me, darling. He wasn't to my taste.'

Tony rolled his eyes. 'Thank God for that or I'd be calling our solicitor.'

She didn't seem perturbed by the threat. 'I understand he liked to… how can I put this? Play with his food. I don't need to look elsewhere for my fun, but the adventurous ones felt it was a way of getting some of their money's worth. And they got a kick out of making him debase himself, throwing money at him for his favours.' She turned her blue eyes back on Leo. 'It's a powerful aphrodisiac making an authoritative man bend to your will, as you might know.'

Leo kept his face blank, though, clearly, she was taunting him.

'Jesus, Gaia, do you have to do that?' complained her husband.

Pleased with the reactions she'd elicited, she continued: 'Marta even persuaded him to appear in some of her little films recently. Quite the revenge.'

'Lloyd Rumbold made a porn film for the Kanons's adult services company?' asked Leo, genuinely surprised. He would've thought Lloyd would avoid having anything like that recorded. He had to have been desperate.

'He did. It's called something like *The Money Master* – Marta likes to tease with her titles.'

Leo realised with a sinking feeling that he was going to have to seek out and very possibly watch this title. That was the very last thing he wanted to do for someone who was an acquaintance.

'He didn't use his real name, of course. He didn't want to sully his reputation.' She laughed at the idea. 'As if losing half a billion hadn't done that already.'

'Are you sure about this? Mrs Kanon didn't appear to remember his name when I asked her this morning.'

Gaia smiled. 'Ask her about Rudy Tuesday. She remembers him. I don't suppose Lloyd will deny it either if you can track him down.'

'I'm afraid I can't do that. He died on Saturday night near the Rollright Stones. My colleagues from Banbury are investigating.'

Her amused expression sobered. 'I'm sorry to hear that. I didn't mean to make fun of him. He might've been a terrible investment manager, but he was an entertaining lay – reputedly.'

Leo revolved the new information in his mind as he drove back to Oxford. Lloyd had fallen back on his client list in a novel way. Leo could just imagine Lloyd blustering that sleeping with the women was just a way of making the most of his remaining assets; he wouldn't have even thought of it as prostitution, more of a verification of his masculinity which had taken a blow with the loss of his job. He might even have boasted to his male friends about it –

he'd never held a very high opinion of the opposite sex. But from Gaia's description, it sounded like the women believed they had played him for a fool, and even recorded him doing it. And what had Lloyd thought in his heart of hearts, sitting there in the dark motorhome, aware that his latest lover was thinking of leaving him? Had Rainbow had any idea what was going on?

The details of the relationships with former clients had to reach the Banbury team but they would not be pleased (an understatement) to find Leo had been sniffing around. Still, it couldn't be helped. And it had been primarily in connection with his own case that he'd been seeing the couples in question. He put the headlines in an email for Inspector Edmonds. It was a good angle that might take attention away from Rainbow. He could see it adding in two ways: either Lloyd was depressed by the depths he'd sunk to and ended his own life; or one of these sexual partners or their spouses – people who blamed him for losing their money – might've taken their revenge once they heard he was in the area. With Rainbow away for the night, he might've even invited someone over for sex and given them access to the generator and vents that way. Had Lloyd's blood showed that he was drugged before passing out? It was infuriating not being able to pull up the data that his colleagues undoubtedly had. If Lloyd had been drugged, it would be a method like the one used on Leo's victim, strengthening the case that the coincidence of two staged suicides was no coincidence at all.

He pulled into the drive of his house, noting that Phil's

car was parked outside, reminding him of who would be there to greet him when he went in.

Of course, his Banbury colleagues could consider it further motive for Rainbow. They could claim she had found out that her lover had been unfaithful with multiple women, culminating in humiliating her by appearing in a porn film, and so she planned her revenge. Evidence rarely pointed solely in one direction.

Chapter Twenty-Two

Jess

There isn't really any social etiquette to help with what to do when one of you is accused of murder. I took refuge in Leo's kitchen while Rainbow's old friends gathered around her in the sitting room. I don't think they knew what to do either as they simply went round and round the same few facts we had, like a frustrated person attempting to make a puzzle piece fit in the wrong hole by turning it all ways. I was relieved to see that Rainbow had rallied a little, losing the floaty shock and taking more charge of her situation. She'd already rung her mother and consulted with her lawyer – I took these as signs of the stronger person she was underneath it all.

Lauren came into the kitchen, bringing their used cups to the dishwasher.

'Everything OK?' I asked.

'Considering the circumstances, Rainbow's doing exceptionally well. Where should I put the teabags?'

'Here you go.' I passed her Leo's compost caddy.

'Oh, this is full. Maybe I should empty it?'

I had wanted an excuse to get her on her own with no chance of interruption. 'I'll show you where the heap is. Take this.' I passed her a coat that hung by the back door. As it was Leo's, it was huge on her. I zipped up my cardigan and shoved my feet into outdoor shoes. 'Follow me.'

We stepped out into Leo's miracle of a garden.

'Oh how lovely! He's done so much to this since I last saw it,' said Lauren, turning in a semi-circle to admire the paradise he had coaxed from Oxford earth. 'He hadn't made that hedge – and the path… just look at that path!'

I shared her appreciation of the blue-slate pebbled path with a gulley that trickled with clear water. There was a scent of wet grass and damp earth, and perhaps just a hint of winter having turned the last corner, heading out of sight. Most gardens looked dead and untidy at this time of year; Leo's looked expectant. 'It's amazing, isn't it? I can't wait to see it in the spring.'

'That's right,' she said, as if reminding herself, 'you've only been with Leo since December. Do you like gardening?'

'I'm hoping I can develop the taste.' I laughed self-deprecatingly.

She touched a white spray of the winter jasmine that spread over an arch leading further into the garden. 'But you've cleverly managed to share his work with him, perhaps you'll find you've got green fingers too?'

'Let's hope so. I don't think I've ever been entrusted with something more complicated than a cactus.'

I led her over the little red Japanese bridge to the grove at the end of the garden. The compost heap was tucked beside his greenhouse and shed.

'If I had lots of money, I'd by him a pagoda to replace that,' I said, pointing at the practical but unlovely outhouse which he'd inherited with the house.

'Be careful: never touch a man's shed without permission.' She tipped the peelings and old tea bags into the green bin.

'Speaking from experience?'

She tilted her head to smile up at me. 'Not really. Freddie is so easy going.'

I sat on a rustic bench positioned to look past the pond and Japanese garden and back up to the house. I patted the place beside me. 'Let's just enjoy this a moment.'

'It's getting dark – and cold.' But she sat, pulling the coat closer about her.

I wasn't going to get a better opportunity. 'Lauren, can I ask you about Lloyd, about some stuff you maybe didn't want to put on the group chat?'

'If it will help.' Her tone was more defensive than normal. Phil was right: there was something I didn't know.

'Was there any history between you and Lloyd, besides friendship?'

She dropped the empty caddy on the grass at our feet, shoulders slumping, and groaned. 'Who's been talking?'

'Does it matter?'

'I suppose not. It's just that not many people know. It's not nice remembering.'

'Can you tell me? I promise I'll keep your secrets.'

She curled her legs up to hug them to her chest. 'None of it is exactly a secret, more an embarrassment to remember.' Silence fell and I wondered if she would dare to go any further. 'Look, you didn't know Lloyd or even meet him for long enough to know what he was really like, but believe me when I tell you that he had charisma. Freddie and I were engaged, new to London. Lloyd was one of the first friends Freddie made, he got to know him through his gym. Soon Lloyd became part of our circle, pretty much with us at every social gathering.'

I constructed a mental timeline. This was mid noughties. 'Was this before he met Rebecca?'

'Oh, yes. That was a couple of years later, when I took up yoga and got to know her.'

'OK, back to the young couple in London with new exciting friend Lloyd.'

She laughed sourly. 'You got it right. See, I'd never been with anyone else, only Fred. But then Lloyd swooped in and he, well, he seemed just so switched on. Showed us the best bars, introduced us to cool people, took us out on his expense account – it went to my head. I was only just making it in television and he seemed to fit that world. Poor old Fred seemed to have no sparkle in comparison. He could even be a little embarrassing with his enthusiasms.'

I could see where this was going. 'You had an affair with Lloyd?'

'Yes. Brief, torrid, but, God, it was fun – until I realised how many people I was hurting, Freddie above all. The worst was that I had hormone problems at the time and was on a pill holiday, relying on condoms. Lloyd and I had a mishap – not surprising considering how we went at it – and I got pregnant A total fuck up. You see, I thought I'd be fine, play the Russian roulette and win. Didn't even think of taking the morning-after pill – probably couldn't with the other medical issues going on.' She shook her head at herself. 'Idiot. I had to tell Freddie, of course. I even ended our engagement and said I was sorry. He was…well, he was Freddie about it. No recriminations, said it was better to learn now that we weren't suited than find out five years into a marriage. I knew even as he said all this that I was letting a good man slip through my fingers but I didn't deserve to keep him.' She twisted the wedding ring on her left finger. 'I'd betrayed him.'

'Then what happened?'

'We didn't tell our friends – most of them didn't know about Lloyd – just said we were having difficulties. And when I told Lloyd, well he was spooked that he might have to step up and take responsibility. He'd always said it was just a little affair, fun on the side from the main business of our lives. He was far from ready to settle down. But he was kind, too. Don't get the wrong impression: he wasn't the villain of the piece. Once he learned that there was a baby on the way, he made the right noises about sorting out finances, looking to the future, if I didn't want to have an abortion.' She stopped talking, gazing up at the lit windows of the house. 'And I couldn't do that to a child, not by the time I'd taken a breath to think it through. I was already fourteen weeks. I didn't have it in me. He might even have carried through his promises. I think, once he got used to the idea, he wanted the child more than he wanted me; it suited his self-image as a virile man,' she said after a moment. 'You know, I'd forgotten that.'

'But you ended up married to Freddie?'

'Yes.' She turned to me. 'You see, Lloyd was right that our affair was an aberration. We were completely unsuited to each other, both strong willed, always butting heads. Having a family together would've been a disaster. But we didn't have to find that out.' She let another pause stretch in which I could hear the distant trickle of water and the call of an owl by the river. A siren from some far-off calamity recalled the fact that we were at the edge of a city. 'I got knocked down by a motorbike on my return from an antenatal appointment, of all things. I lost the baby.' She swallowed. 'I was in a coma for a few days.' She lifted her hair to show the scar on the side of her neck. 'Head injuries, abdominal too. I very nearly died. When I woke up in the hospital, it was Freddie sitting there, not Lloyd, and that felt right. Every other bloody thing felt wrong – losing the baby, losing my self-respect – but Fred? He felt right. We picked up the pieces and carried on from there. We married eighteen months later, Josephine came along after that, and the rest, as they say, is history.'

I would have to ask Leo what he remembered of the accident. He had to know about it, even if he didn't know about the baby. 'But you remained friends with Lloyd? Isn't that rather odd considering?'

'Is it?' She shrugged. 'There was some coolness for a while between Freddie and Lloyd; I kept my distance too, but by then our social group was so intertwined it would've been hard to cut him out entirely. The I met Rebecca and I kind of threw them together, thinking that would dilute things. It worked for a while. Lloyd married Rebecca so there was no longer any question of us...well, I think Freddie felt better after that. Our feelings mellowed, it all seemed so long ago and the emotions that had driven the affair had vanished. But it also meant we were spared investing with him. Freddie refused. And he was right. I've always loved Freddie far more than I ever loved Lloyd. He was the quintessential fling – exciting, dangerous and very, very stupid for both parties; Freddie was the forever one.'

I could see how that might be the case. I was still friends with my ex, Michael, from whom I had parted in spectacular fashion in the middle of a murder investigation. When the dust from that had settled, our friendship resumed when he was paralysed and he was now dating my best friend, Cory. I was equally guilty of complicated personal connections.

'And what does Freddie feel about all of that now?'

She rocked slightly. 'It was me who hurt him, not Lloyd. It was my weakness that mattered because I was the one who had made the commitment.'

Not in my book. Friendship was also a commitment. It should at the very least include a clause 'Thou shalt not sleep with a mate's fiancée'.

'But he got past it?'

'You're not looking at Freddie for this are you?' Her tone sharpened.

'Of course not.' I was considering it. 'I'm just curious.'

She nodded, mollified. 'The thing to understand about Freddie is that he doesn't really think he deserves to be treated well. There's low self-esteem underneath that manner of his – comes of being in the shadow of a very outspoken older brother, a Tory MP, can you believe it? I've spent my marriage trying to make Freddie see just how deserving he is. I think he's learning. I think so.' She turned to me again. 'You won't make him dig all this up, will you? He's upset enough as it is.'

Careful, I warned myself. 'If I'm to do the investigating you asked me to, I will have to talk to him about Lloyd but I won't raise it unless he does.'

She nodded. 'That's fair. And if he doesn't mention the affair and the baby, it will be because he's protecting me. He's sweet like that.'

'How much does Leo know about this?'

She uncurled and bent to pick up the caddy. 'Leo? He knows about the accident of course. He visited a couple of times – took Freddie out to give him a break – but I doubt very much he knew about the baby. He wouldn't ask, would he?'

'He does struggle with that. I think he fears that kind of intimacy. He thinks that if he asks you too many questions, then you'll ask them back.'

'He's probably right. We are a nosy lot. Freddie has made it his mission to reel him back in. He worries about Leo being lonely, after his awful mother and everything. He was the closest to Leo in Durham at some of the worst times, when we thought he might… you know?'

Kill himself? Leo had briefly mentioned that he'd come close a couple of times in his teens. My estimation of Freddie rose even higher.

'And would you mind if I told him – about you and Lloyd?'

She shrugged. 'I suppose not. I've come to terms with what I did a long while ago. It showed me that I was not as nice a person as I had assumed. That was a good lesson. It makes me try harder to deserve Freddie and the children. I want to be my best self with them, not the worst.'

That was exactly what I felt about my relationship with Leo. 'Lauren, thank you. That must've been hard to tell me.'

She smiled. 'Not so hard. You look like someone who understands the fuckups we make.'

I pointed at my chest. 'Me? Queen of Fuckup Land. You, Lauren, are but a visitor passing through my kingdom.'

That made her laugh and we strolled back to the warmth of the house.

Leo had arrived in our absence. I found him sitting at the kitchen table, pile of post in front of him, while Rainbow made him a cup of tea. From the sounds coming from the sitting room, Freddie and Phil had found something to watch on TV, sound up so Leo and Rainbow could talk with some privacy. Of Janice there was no sign until I heard a shower running upstairs. She had already announced that she was planning to stay over.

In Leo's house.

I was not pleased.

I pressed my cold cheek against his. 'I'm glad you're home.'

'Me too. Thanks for holding the fort.' He brushed his lips over mine.

Rainbow put a cup in front of him. She'd made it too strong but I noticed that Leo didn't complain.

'Do you want a cup, Jess?' she asked.

'Not in the mood for tea.' I got out a bottle of white wine from the fridge. 'I feel about ready for this. Lauren?'

'God, yes.' Lauren moved to the cupboard and grabbed some glasses. 'Rainbow, why don't we take these through to the guys and give Leo and Jess a chance to catch up?'

Rainbow fluttered at the sink. 'Oh right, yes, of course. I'm in the way. I've invaded your home. I'm sorry, Leo.'

'You are not an invasion and not in the way,' Leo said gallantly, even though I was thinking that she was a little. Having so many people in Leo's house was odd after months of it just being the two of us.

Rainbow was shepherded away by Lauren, and I got a glass for Leo and a fresh bottle of wine and put it down by him. 'Do you really want that?'

He smiled and shook his head. 'Irish tea – that's what Rainbow always called it at college. Then she'd go on to say something like "strong enough to make your chest hairs curl", some saying of her grandmother's.'

I unscrewed the lid of the wine. 'I'll have to check later. So,' I sat down opposite him, 'how was your day?'

'One of my best friends got charged with murder, I learned that another is managing a club that appears to have murky links to prostitution and trafficking, and last but not least, Lloyd made some money sleeping with women and appearing in a porn film, which I may now have to watch to see if it's true.'

'Things are looking up then.' I toasted him ironically. 'Tell me how you know all that.'

He gave me a run-down of his day and I reciprocated with what Lauren had told me by the compost heap.

'An affair? Christ, I didn't even guess – so used to them being the perfect couple.' Leo frowned into his wine. 'So that was why…' I could see him reconsidering what he knew of the accident and Lauren's time in hospital. 'I would never have suspected…poor Freddie. That must have been gutting.'

'He hid it well, according to Lauren.'

'Yeah, he'd do that.'

I topped up his glass. 'Look, don't jump down my throat when I say this, but you don't think that Freddie might've had motive to do away with Lloyd?'

His reply was instantaneous. 'Absolutely not. I can't see why you would even suggest it.'

'I'm not accusing him—'

'I'm relieved to hear it.'

'Just running it by you. It's only that he had the opportunity –with his car nearby, he could've slipped away during the time in the casino, with no one the wiser. He knows about generators and heaters – he said as much when we discussed it yesterday. He could've seen the generator during our visit and realised he had a golden opportunity to get his revenge.'

'But the affair was years ago!'

'It was twelve years ago – that's not that long. Lloyd stole the love of his life, got her pregnant, and didn't even visit after the accident and loss of the baby. I can see Freddie thinking of it as defending Lauren. If he was playing the long game, that would explain why he pretended to stay friends despite there being so many reasons to end the relationship.'

Loud laughter of the TV-audience kind came from the sitting room. Leo gave the door an anxious glance.

'I'm not saying he did it. I'm just trying to be methodical and go through everyone who had sufficient motive.'

'Jess, he's my best friend— or was - at college.' Leo looked like he was only just realising he really didn't know even his best friends very well.

'I understand that.'

'I know him better than I know anyone and I can tell you he wouldn't wait a decade to do something like this. He might've done something asinine like challenge Lloyd to a fight in the immediate aftermath because he was hurt and upset, but he would've made a hash of that because Lloyd would've laid him out with one punch. Forget this.'

I swirled my wine, some of it slopping over the edge onto my fingers. I was aware it was a mistake to press, but I was crap at holding back; I had to get this off my chest. 'And Lauren? Pretty tough thing to deal with at her age –

her second boyfriend leaving her in the lurch, meaning she's spent all her married life feeling less worthy than her husband. And I didn't see her at all in the casino. They said she was playing baccarat but I couldn't find her.'

Leo rested his head on his hands. 'Jess,' he said wearily. 'Investigations are supposed to be careful, meticulous processes. You can't just throw accusations around at anyone who was unaccounted for.'

I thought that was very unfair. I wasn't making my thoughts public, I was bringing them to him as a sounding board. And he wasn't making allowances for the fact that his affection for his friends could well blind them to their flaws.

'These aren't accusations – these are lines of enquiry.'

He just shook his head, which infuriated me. Just because he had the warrant card, and I a mere certificate for a private investigator qualification, didn't mean I couldn't sift through the facts as well as he did.

'You're not even going to ask Lauren and Freddie for their alibis, are you?' I said.

'I don't need to. I know they didn't do it.' Leo picked up a letter from the pile on the table. The address was handwritten but it was a business envelope, not a card. He ran his finger under the seal and took out the sheet of folded paper.

'You're not listening to me.'

'I am but you're following one of your impulses – a reckless, unsound one that could shatter the trust with my best friends.'

'I thought you said a lot of detective work was

elimination. Won't you even take the steps to rule them out?'

'I already have.' He shook out the letter and read it, turned it over, and stared at the signature.

'On emotional grounds, not logic.' Fed up with him not giving me due attention after all I'd done today for his friends, I stood up. 'I'm heading home.'

He didn't respond, just stared at the letter.

'Leo, I said I'm heading home. I'd appreciate a lift. Leo?' I twigged that the letter had carried a heavy punch of news. I softened my tone and tapped the page. 'What's wrong?'

He spread the letter flat on the table but covered the contents with his palm. 'It's from...he says he's my father.'

Chapter Twenty-Three

Leo

Leo knew he was handling Jess badly. She was right to have questions but asking them of the only people who had been consistently good in his life was like pressing on a bruise. If he doubted Rainbow, Lauren and Freddie, then he would doubt everyone.

And now, on top of everything, this letter.

What did it even mean? He was in his mid-thirties, far too late for a father to walk into his life. He had grown used to navigating around the absence, the dad-shaped hole that had made a regular appearance during childhood in the playground and on Father's Day. 'Who was your father?' his friends had asked. 'He died when I was a baby', had been his standard answer to cut off further enquiries. All he had ever known about that mysterious person was that his mother had had a brief affair with a man she called 'George'; she had refused to tell him any more detail than that, pretending forgetfulness whenever he had raised the issue. Eventually, he had bought her story that she genuinely had no more details to share. More fool him. Now a man called George Saito was writing as if to pick up on an ongoing conversation he assumed he'd been having with his son through the intermediary of his mother.

Decades of conversation of which Leo had been in complete ignorance, his mother pretending to be a conduit when really she had been a dead end.

Dear Leo,

I am returning to England for the first time in many years for work and was hoping that you would be prepared to meet me this time.

This time? That suggested there had been previous requests and previous denials, no doubt from his mother. Leo's temperature rose with every line.

As you'll know, I've long respected your wish to call your foster father your real dad and not have to deal with a man who only knew your mother for so brief a while.

What foster dad? Had Haven claimed one of her feckless – and in one case abusive – boyfriends had become his surrogate father? The idea made Leo sick. She'd probably just not wanted a responsible male invigilating her record as a mother.

And of course there was that difficult time in your teens when she warned me away from you.

He'd wanted to reach out when Leo was at his lowest and his mother had stopped him?

But then I saw your name come up in connection to the investigation into the Red House deaths in Oxford at Christmas and that prompted me to make this direct appeal. I'm not getting any younger. I decided that it would soon be too late if I didn't make an attempt to change matters between us.

Leo's vision tunnelled as anger clouded the edges.

I'm afraid I've lost track of your mother's current whereabouts. We lost regular contact after I finished paying for your college and gave the lump sum for you to get on the housing ladder. I hope these were useful? She sent me pictures of your first apartment and passed on your thanks.

He had never seen a penny of any of that – and the flat had been rented, if Saito meant the one Leo had lived in when he started working for the police.

After some investigation, a legal acquaintance of mine was able to give me your address – I hope you will forgive me for infringing on your privacy like this?

He could feel Jess watching him as he struggled with his

rage. She was bursting to find out what was going on. If he said anything, he'd probably regret it.

I'm pleased to see that you've made a success of your chosen career – I'm proud of you.

What right did he have to say something like that? This man who claimed to have sent him money for years, been a responsible if absent parent, channelling everything through Haven Keene, or was this all another variation on the kind of emotional scam his mother was best at? She played the caring mother for the cameras; was his father now doing the same act? Was this person even real or was it just another of his mother's roundabout ways of getting under his skin? They'd parted on difficult terms in December.

'Leo?' Jess asked, tentatively. She clearly couldn't restrain herself any longer. It was a small miracle she'd held off so long.

He pushed the letter over to her. She read it quickly, eyebrows disappearing under her fringe. Next she googled the name while he sat shaking with anger.

'George Saito, he has a *Wiki* page. Half-Japanese on his mother's side. Born in Hawaii, now lives in California. Award-winning filmmaker. Most famous film was an early one. an indie thriller called *Timed Lives*, made in the UK and released in '86.'

That was the year after Leo was born and might explain how George's path had crossed with Haven's. An actress, she might even have been involved in the project. He'd never seen the film. His father's award-winning film.

'There's a photo of him, if you want to look?' She angled her phone towards him and he glanced down at the salt-and-pepper-haired man with a dark moustache and eyebrows, big round glasses and an Asiatic profile. His features appeared to be carved from smooth sandstone, barely lined by age. If this was some fabrication of his mother's, she'd picked a convincing subject. 'I think you have his eyes,' said Jess.

'You believe this?' He gestured to the letter, a little impatiently because he didn't want it to mean so much.

'Believe that your mother could've milked your dad for every penny? Yes, I believe it.'

'He makes it sound as if I'm the one who's been keeping him away.'

'Don't get me wrong, he's not won any father-of-the-year awards from me. If he were any judge of a person's character, he'd've checked in with you, despite what Haven said was the deal at your end. He's either gullible or didn't really want to know if she was lying.'

Leo took the phone from her and scrolled down to the notes on Saito's family. 'It says he has three children from his marriage, a granddaughter and two step-children. One of them is my age. He was probably too busy playing happy families to wonder about the son left behind.'

Jess shrugged. 'It happens. You know that, Leo. You've seen that.'

He had. He came across too many fatherless children whose parent moved on to a new family and neglected the old. Usually there wasn't a lot of money around, mothers struggling to stay afloat. Chaotic families, like his own.

'What are you going to do?' Jess asked quietly. He put the letter back in its envelope. 'Will you see him?'

'For what purpose? I don't need a father. It's too late.'

'I wouldn't write him off so quickly. I know he wasn't there for you when you did need him to be your dad, but maybe now you could be something else with him? Your own kind of late-arrival family. There aren't rules on this stuff.'

He knew she had a point but he couldn't help feeling annoyed with her – an urge that he knew sprang from his hurt. 'Let's drop the subject, OK? I just can't think about it now. There's too much else going on.'

'You could at least tell him your mother nicked all the money he sent.'

'To what end? It's long gone.'

'So she doesn't get any more out of him. Don't reward her theft with silence.'

Jess was again correct but he couldn't sort it out now, not while he had such a full plate trying to clear his friend and solve the murder of Kelly Ann. 'I can't talk about this.'

She moved back, retreating in both words and with her body. 'All right. I won't push you.' But she would – he knew she would.

'I just need you to leave this alone, Jess. Don't do anything.' It was entirely within her character to contact George Saito herself on some whim that it would help heal the divide.

'OK.'

'I mean it.' Their arguments tonight had pushed their relationship severely off-kilter, he could feel it – the first time since they started dating.

'I heard you the first time, Leo.' She picked up her messenger bag. 'I'm off home if you don't need me.'

He should be giving her a lift but he couldn't move. There was too much to process.

'I'll ask Phil to drive me, shall I?' She hovered, expecting something more but he couldn't find it in himself to give it.

'Yes, good idea,' he said.

'OK, then.' She left without kissing him.

He heard voices and then the front door closed. No one came into the kitchen which suggested that Jess had told them to give him space. He was grateful for that at least. Leo sat and looked at the envelope.

A life he might've had – a father he might've known; half-brothers and -sisters out there in the world. Yet another betrayal by his mother. It was too painful to contemplate.

Tucking the letter in a pocket, he put on his gardening jacket over his suit and went out to dig the vegetable patch.

Chapter Twenty-Four

Jess

I suppose it was inevitable. Phil had been a decent human being for a few hours so he was due a relapse. He pulled up on a double yellow as close to my house as he could manage in the sclerotic street and cut the engine.

'Thanks, Phil, appreciate it.' I unbuckled my seatbelt, thoughts still back in Leo's kitchen, where he was still coming to terms with his letter. There weren't many people around on this unpromising February evening, just a dog walker dragging a reluctant collie for a last pee.

'Hang on a second – don't rush off.' Phil turned from the steering wheel to face me. 'There's something I want to say, Jess, while we're alone.'

'OK,' I said, warily.

'I like you.'

Thankful for the lift home I was in a generous mood.

'That's great. You're not so bad when you aren't being a dick.'

He put his hand on my forearm, stopping me from reaching for the door handle. 'I mean, I *like* you.'

I wasn't stupid. Of course I knew what he'd meant. I was just hoping he'd let it slide so I didn't have to say the next part. 'You do realise that I'm with Leo, don't you?'

He laughed knowingly. 'Yeah, and how long's that going to last? Be realistic. Leo's one of the good guys, almost puritanical. For him, there's black and white, where others see shades of grey. You, Jess, are grey to the core. Either you'll do something to piss him off or you'll get fed up with that soon enough.'

'Know me so well, do you?'

'Let's say that I recognise you. We're birds of a feather, you and I. Not good people, but not all bad. I'd know how to keep you interested.' His hand dropped from my arm to my thigh, curling around to the sensitive skin of the inner side. I hated the surge of excitement that told me I was enjoying this out-of-order flirtation more than I should.

You are not your bad impulses, I reminded myself.

'Phil…' His fingers brushed against my crotch and I yelped.

He looked pleased by the result. I hadn't slapped him, had I? Why hadn't I? His voice was husky. 'That feels good, doesn't it?'

It did, damn him. I revelled in naughty.

Be your better self. With an effort, fighting against my instincts, I grabbed his hand and pushed it away. It was harder for me than it should've been. 'Thanks for the lift, Phil, but you shouldn't take tips on your woman-handling from American presidents.'

He dropped his head back on the rest. 'OK, Jess, I can take "no" for an answer – for now. But I'm here when, you know, you need me?'

'That won't ever happen.' I got out.

'Won't it?' He moved off the moment I closed the door, leaving me with the feeling that he had won the encounter.

Stomping up the pavement to my own door, I fumed at myself. I was with Leo. LEO. Not some right-wing builder from Birmingham. Describing Phil like that made my ardour cool right down. I unpicked the reasons why I'd felt even a moment's temptation. I was frustrated. Leo and I had not had a chance to sleep together since before the weekend – well, we'd slept together in the attic room at the cottage, but only slept, nothing more interesting. To be frank, I liked sex and when I didn't get it I got antsy. Add to that, I was feeling bruised by the last few days and Leo's distance from me. He belonged more to his old friends than he did to me at the moment. And Phil had paid me the compliment of seeing me. Attention was seductive.

I stopped in the action of putting the key in the Yale lock. *Fool*. Think about it as a psychologist. Phil and Leo had an old rivalry. What better way to hurt an old enemy than to make a move on the new girl? *Phil doesn't see you, you slutty numpty, just a chance to get one over on Leo.*

I clattered upstairs to my room at the back of the house overlooking the tattered garden that snaked down to the canal. Our landlord had not redecorated since the noughties so the walls were scuffed by the passage of miscellaneous furniture, boxes, and suitcases as generations of tenants came and went. Fellow tenant Kristie had left a note on my door.

Your dog chewed the laces of my new trainers. I will bill you.

That gave me a split-second warning of what had been locked inside my room in punishment. Flossie threw herself at me like a North Korean missile on a successful launch day. I rubbed her in vigorous welcome.

'Did you eat Kristie's laces? Very bad dog.'

I think my discipline might lack something as my scolding was taken as effulgent praise.

'Let's get you something you are allowed to eat.'

Taking Flossie down to the kitchen, I continued to think about Phil's less-than-stellar motives for his front-seat groping. Another reason he did that might well be his philosophy of take-all-you-can-get sovereign-citizen crappery. He saw a curvy blonde and thought, 'hey, I like' so tried it on, almost a reflex action. He would be driving away now with no regrets or any sense of guilt. Extending that, maybe he saw in Lloyd an annoying guy who had lost a lot of his money and he'd thought 'there's someone who needs punishing'. That meant he'd be fully able to act today as if nothing was weighing on him. He took action, Lloyd died, no biggie.

The only flaw was Rainbow. I still was unconvinced Phil would do something that would rebound on her.

Unless he expected to get away with it and so acted accordingly? After his pass at me, I could well believe that.

Leo's emotional reaction to any mention of his friends being involved was clouding my own analysis of the situation. Maybe I was too ready to suspect Phil because I knew Leo disliked him, whereas I found it hard to think clearly about Rainbow, Lauren, and Freddie because he was so much on their side? I decided a second opinion would be of use to regain some objectivity so I invited myself round to Michael's for a breakfast consultation on my way to work on Tuesday.

It was raining as I chained my bike to his fence. He must've seen me arriving in my neon-yellow waterproofs as he had the door open and a towel waiting for me.

Once I was no longer dripping, I bent down and gave him a kiss on the cheek. Seriously injured in our involvement in my first murder case, Michael had been in a wheelchair ever since, though recently he had been able to get about on crutches for part of the time. He now lived in an adapted home in a new estate of mock-Georgian houses on the other side of the canal from me, and was an academic psychologist at Magdalen College, specialising in sociopathic and psychopathic disorders.

'Michael, thanks for making the time,' I said, noting that he looked well, his auburn hair glossy and recently trimmed. He was a favourite studio guest as a commentator on violent crimes thanks to his photogenic face: a handsome man pronouncing on ugly events was a mesmerising combination.

'It sounded intriguing from your message.' He led the

way down the wide corridor to his kitchen. 'Can you get the croissants out of the freezer?'

I rummaged in the freezer drawer, noting that Cory had been keeping it well stocked with home-cooked food – overspill from her family bounty. That suggested things were still chugging along nicely between them. I preferred to ask her rather than Michael for updates as…well, things had been complicated between Michael and me for a while.

The oven hummed and the kettle boiled. I slid the croissants into the heat on a baking tray and set the table while Michael made the coffee. He liked to keep up standards so I knew he expected plates, knives, butter in a dish, and upmarket-brand strawberry jam before he'd be able to settle to hear my story. Finally, everything was prepared to his satisfaction and we sat opposite each other, coffee pot between us, pastries baking.

'I'll start at the very beginning, shall I?' I suggested.

He gave me a wry smile. 'I'm told it's a very good place to start.'

'OK, here's what's been going on.' And I told him about the weekend of the two potentially staged suicides, the connections, the gaps, and how suspicion had fallen for the second death on a woman her close friends all thought the least likely person to murder her partner. I gave a thumbnail sketch of each of the friends in turn so he would know with whom I was dealing.

Michael made some notes on a pad, keeping track of the timeline, names, locations of the people involved. 'Have I got this right? The thing connecting the first victim and the second as far as you know is the Birbeck brothers' businesses and a couple of the people associated with them – most notably the ex-wife Rebecca Crawley, manager, and these shady people…what were they called again?'

'The Kanons.'

'The wife, Marta, was having an affair with Lloyd and using him in a porn film?'

'An affair gives the wrong impression. I think Leo considers it more of a male-escort deal, Lloyd getting money for sex from old clients. He probably went back to those who had responded to his flirting during the initial business meetings.'

Michael wrote that down. 'I've not come across that before in a man – interesting.'

'Maybe it happens more than we realise? It's been the fallback for women since time began. Why not men? Sugar Mummies. I should probably copyright the term.'

The oven pinged and I got up to remove the croissants.

'I think we have two options to consider,' said Michael. 'One, the deaths are not linked; at least one of them was actually a suicide, which means you should be looking at them separately, as the police are doing.'

'Or?' I used a tong to serve his croissant, then, not waiting, pulled mine apart with my fingers, wincing at the heat.

'They are linked, as Leo suspects. I suppose the way forward is to look at your death first, make a list of those who had the motive, means, and opportunity, then see if any of the names would fall on the list Leo must be generating.'

'OK, that's sort of what I've been doing, but it's helpful

to be methodical about it. We have lots of motives and precious little physical evidence so far.'

Michael gave a significant look at my messenger bag.

'What?'

'Haven't you got one of your notebooks in there?'

'The kind full of Post-it notes, underlinings, and flow diagrams that you teased me about for years?'

He smiled. 'Yes, that kind.'

'I haven't had a chance to start. It's all in here at the moment.' I tapped my forehead.

'God help us all then.' He reversed from the table and disappeared down the corridor.

'Michael?'

'Just getting something.'

I poured a second round of coffee and made inroads into the jam and butter before he got back. On his return, he dropped a black hardback notebook in my lap.

'A present. I've gone mostly over to digital notes so you can have that with my best wishes.'

It was lovely: thick, creamy pages, a ribbon bookmark, a little pouch at the back for clippings. 'Thank you.' I took out a ballpoint pen and clicked it with enthusiasm. 'Right. Let's line them up.'

The first thing we did was work out the window of opportunity.

'We left Lloyd at around two in the afternoon. That meant he was alone from then until the following morning when he was discovered by Leo and Rainbow. Running through our activities, I can account for most people most of the time but there are some obvious gaps: when I was out on the boating lake with Freddie, while we were dressing for dinner, during the casino games when I only saw people intermittently, and then after we went to bed. No one had a solid alibi. I can say I didn't kill him, neither did Leo as he was with colleagues working on his case, but that's about it.'

Michael ran a finger down his initial jottings. 'And what about Rebecca Crawley? Normally, you look first at a spouse – ex-spouse in this case – and she's got the strongest link to the other victim.'

'We didn't see her all that much. I think she was busy all day sorting out the aftermath of her colleague's death. She came over for tea but wasn't at the dinner that evening. I can't remember what people said but I assume it was her night off and she was planning to spend the following day with us.'

'So where was she?'

'I guess at home with her elderly mother? You're right, that's something I'll need to check. Perhaps I'll drop round and see if I can speak to the mother.'

'The police may have a better idea of time of death, though in this case it could've been set up earlier and the killer would be long gone before the victim was overcome by fumes.'

'Leo can't get any more details – not without risking his job.'

'You could ask Rainbow's solicitor if she knows what evidence they're sitting on. Or maybe I could try some of my contacts in the police who use me as a consultant? They won't be as suspicious if I ask. I can come up with some excuse as to why I'm interested.'

'Would you? That would be great.'

He looked down at his pad. 'That leaves the other suspects not in the friendship group – the Kanons, and other unknown cheated-on husbands and defrauded customers.'

'I was warned I might find more enemies than friends.'

'But only a small number of those will have been in the area and know that there was a chance to kill him. He was inside the motorhome all the time, correct?'

'As far as we know he had no plans for a walk. He was going to watch the football and have an early night.'

'Do we know the time of the game he was watching?'

'I'll check.' I should've already thought of that. I did a quick Google search. 'Eight-o'clock kick-off.'

'And the scene Leo found suggests that whatever happened wasn't violent: he was on the sofa, TV still on, toxic fumes still pumping?'

'Correct.'

'The duct tape was applied to vents inside the vehicle. One thing I wanted to ask: why were they using a portable generator?'

'Rainbow said they added a portable as the vehicle engine's battery couldn't cope with the extra demand of heating during the winter weather, particularly when they were stationary for long periods and not recharging the battery. There was no electric hook-up where they were camping. I didn't see the generator but I think it was at the back of the vehicle somewhere. They weren't stupid people. They must've been aware of the risks in confined spaces which is why it wasn't in the living area and was in a ventilated place.'

'And in what way had it been tampered with?'

'Again, not sure. That's another thing that would be helpful to know if your contacts feel like sharing. Maybe the timer was changed so it didn't turn off? Lloyd could've had the windows shut, expecting it to have closed down for the night. If it came on again while he was dozing…?'

'He wouldn't have woken to know there was anything wrong.' Michael nodded, underlining something on his pad. 'Looking at it from a psychological point of view, that's one thing that definitely connects both deaths: on the surface, both look peaceful. There are more violent ways to commit suicide if you wanted to stage one. In both cases it's almost like a mercy killing, a "sorry, you had to go, here's a gentle way out". I don't get any sense of hate or revenge, unless the killer is running very cold and calculating. If that's the case then this is a sign, not of compassion for the victim, but meticulous planning. I can make an argument for both kinds of mentality by framing my analysis slightly differently. We need more evidence to rule either way.'

'Cold, clever killer or an apologetic one?'

'That's it exactly. If it's murder. Have the last croissant.'

I pushed it back towards him. 'Couldn't possibly. You have it.' I was normally temptable but my mind was too busy. 'We have lots of people with motives, no one with a cast-iron alibi unless we have a narrower window, so how am I going to make progress on this?'

He buttered the croissant. 'Facts rather than theories. Let's start with your victim. From what I can tell from your description of the physical evidence, his death was a result of using the motorhome's stock of duct tape; he was sitting inside with no signs of struggle, and that frustratingly still doesn't rule out suicide. You mentioned a life crisis – no money, partner threatening to leave him, loss of self-esteem, reduced to selling sex, aware his contemporaries despised him – that's quite a list. Choosing to go out with his old friends as his witnesses has a dramatic flair that would fit with his persona.'

'But there was no note. Wouldn't he have written a "sod you" to them all if that was his reasoning?'

'I think so, from what you've said about him.'

'The police must have more to have dismissed suicide so early,' I mused.

'Perhaps the toxicology turned up something more damning? I'll see if I can find out. What about the prime suspect? Do *you* think Rainbow is the killer?'

'Could she be?' I closed my eyes and summoned up the jumbled events of the weekend. 'I think she was the last to leave the motorhome so I suppose it was possible she rushed around slapping duct tape on vents, risking someone surprising her in the middle of her master plan, risking Lloyd seeing what she had done.'

'That's a good point. I would imagine whoever covered the vents did so when he was already sleepy, or even drugged. If he were *compos mentis,* he would have checked if he heard the generator come on unexpectedly, or not shut off – I know I would.'

'Then it's too risky for Rainbow to have done it mid-afternoon. So filling in the blank where our possible murderer is, it seems more likely someone visited during the evening. A booty call? I could imagine Lloyd ringing up one of his girlfriends and saying the coast was clear and did they want to come round for a little athletic session with him. Marta Kanon or one of her ilk?'

'That fits with the absence of violence indicator. Whoever covered the vents did not have to fight to get in.'

'Or running the scenario another way, an old friend knocked on the door with a couple of beers. "Come to watch the footie, mate, heard you were in a rough patch with Rainbow and I'd had enough of those women."' I put on roughly a Phil kind of accent. 'Door closes. A few drinks later, Lloyd gets drugged or drunk. Sleepy. Whatever. Lloyd's out for the count. Fix the vents and generator and walk out. Neat.'

'I can see that fits the facts too.'

'Oh, and there's the bunny-boiler – Ellie – lives in Cowley. Old flame who still carries a torch for him. Two things that make me like her for this: she's into erotic asphyxiation – or claims Lloyd was – and she kills or mutilates small animals. Isn't that a classic serial-killer practice-ground?'

Michael's brows rose. 'And this was a suffocation of sorts. Yes, she does sound worth a closer look. Let's grant her the motive – jealousy – and character to do such a thing, but does she have opportunity?'

I wrinkled my nose in thought. 'That's a weakness. I can't say that she knew he was in the area. But maybe Lloyd's booty call was to her? He must've known that she would drop everything to run to him. That would've solved the opportunity issue. Plus she's a lifestyle adviser which involves interior decorating among other things. She would know about the basic regulations required to keep a home safe and ventilated surely?'

Michael looked interested by this theory. 'I'd like to meet Miss Bunny-Boiler.'

'Ask for her to consult on your lifestyle image and see what you make of her. She's got no reason to connect the questionnaire lady with dashing TV personality, Dr Michael Harrison.'

He shook his head at that description but he liked it really. 'Leave me her name. I might do that. If we lean that way, though, it weakens the connection to Leo's victim. It becomes purely personal.'

'Unless she's linked to the club too? Lifestyle stylist – wouldn't she want to get in with the Piccadilly People set, trawling for customers? I can see her sacrificing the dosh to get on the membership list.' The frail link I was building collapsed under the weight of my supposition. 'But that's not enough.'

'And we don't know much at all about the other victim. I'd like to talk to Leo. Do you think he'd be happy to discuss it with me?'

I thought of Leo reeling from his father's outreach. 'I don't know. I'll suggest it.'

'And I'll tell Eleanor Fanshawe that I'm in need of a style makeover.'

His cat, Colette, jumped on my lap and nestled for crumbs. 'But don't you dare take her advice and change your look, Michael. Cory would never forgive me.'

Chapter Twenty-Five

Leo

Sleep was fitful that night. It was hard to give Rainbow's distress its due while his thoughts kept sliding away to the letter currently burning a hole in his pocket. He didn't know what he was going to do about it and digging the vegetable patch hadn't resolved the dilemma. His 'father' had included an email address so Leo could end the lifetime lack of communication in seconds if he so wished. But did he? Was he ready to open up a whole new chapter in his life when he had just reached the point where he was happy with what he had created for himself?

The emotion he felt around his lack of a father when growing up had nothing to do with a person. He didn't bear his progenitor a grudge, didn't really hold any strong feelings about him at all. He could understand how a chance encounter between a young film director and an actress could result in him, but there had been no emotional engagement on either side of the couple, and not much on the mother's part to the resulting child. His own feelings for his mother had gone through cycles of love and hate, having settled now on dull despair that she would never be what he had wanted her to be. In fact, he now suspected that she was worse than that, taking away his chance to know his father for her own selfish reasons. They were a dysfunctional trio, this mother, father, and son. Jess had said he could write a whole new set of rules for a father-son relationship begun thirty-plus-years late, but why would he want to do that? He wasn't after a handout or even awkward gatherings on big holidays. He was used to functioning without relatives.

Jess would say to think positive, that he might find something he didn't know he wanted, but really? How likely was that?

Leo decided to leave it for the moment. George Saito had waited over thirty years to reach out; another few days would make no difference.

No one was up when he had a quick breakfast, a promising sign that Rainbow had managed to sleep. He found it almost a relief to leave his friends as he went to work. They'd all stayed over – Janice in the spare room; Freddie, Lauren, and Phil checking into the hotel across the road for the night and planning to reconvene to comfort Rainbow that morning. Freddie had taken extra leave and Phil appeared to be his own master. Lauren had called in sick. Leo was impressed by how they went out of their way to support Rainbow, but court cases were very long, drawn-out affairs. They could only keep this up for a day or two then they would have to find a solution for where Rainbow was going to live while the investigation continued. Not back in the motorhome obviously as this would be impounded. Janice was house-hunting. Lauren and Freddie had a houseful of kids. Phil was – well, he was Phil – hardly the right shoulder for her to cry on. She had registered her address with Leo for bail so it looked like he would have her as a house guest for the short term. This could only be a temporary solution: either she was exonerated quickly or, if this went to trial, she'd have to move out as he would have an obvious conflict of interest. It already existed but his superiors would probably give him a few days to sort out another arrangement, knowing this had swept up on him unannounced. He just hoped the press did not get wind of the fact that the prime suspect in a murder investigation was staying with a detective from the same police force that had charged her. The firewall between the two investigations would surely be questioned and his own position at work compromised.

The superintendent called him in on arrival. For a moment, he feared that she had heard the specifics about Rainbow's living arrangements and decided to take action to remove him from his case. Fortunately, her news was better than that.

'Leo, I finally got through to the Birbecks. They've agreed to see you, but it will be at their club in London rather than on Guernsey.'

The sense of making progress lifted some of his despondency. 'When, ma'am?'

'This afternoon. I'll get my PA to send you the details. They're attending a dinner in Park Lane – an awards evening for innovation. You took onboard what I said about diplomacy, I trust?'

'I did.'

She shuffled the papers on her desk. 'Take DS Wong with you.'

Leo had already decided that himself. Superintendent Thaxted sometimes forgot that her job wasn't to micromanage decisions that were his responsibility. 'Of course.'

'Do you have any more clarity on their involvement?' She looked up over the top of her reading glasses.

'Only more possible dirt. Do you know if there have been any investigations into the Birbecks's clubs worldwide, ma'am? Not just about trafficking but any other unsavoury transactions?'

'I've been putting out some feelers to trusted colleagues in other forces, but so far nothing like we are looking at here. Either we are the first—'

'—Or they are very good at burying the truth?'

'They are also good at burying the careers of those who cross them. Be careful.'

'Yes, ma'am.'

Leo spent the rest of the morning with Suyin going through interview prep. The superintendent had also laid down some more detailed ground rules. He'd had to leave Harry Boston – not his first choice – working on the Kanons and their porn sites, asking him to cross-check young female members of club staff, particularly those from overseas, from the last five years with the women who appeared in the material generated by the Kanons's adult services. Names would in all likelihood be changed so it would have to be facial recognition. If Kelly Ann was right that they had been asked to do things beyond their official duties in the spa, it was worth checking to see if these were on record. At least Harry could scope out exactly what might have been going on. So far, sex work in private chatrooms, pay-per-view stripping, and escort introductions at club events to interested clients had been identified. All of these were ephemeral encounters. The gossip on Lloyd, though, suggested there might be a more permanent record if Marta had used the same girls in her film enterprise.

Leo recalled the woman sitting in her peacock throne. Was Marta the spider in the middle of this web? She connected Lloyd and the club activities that had possibly doomed Kelly Ann. It was a thread definitely worth following but he needed more before he could apply for a warrant to look at what other material she might have kept in the home studio of hers.

'Inspector?' Harry came in, tie askew, sleeves rolled up. 'I found that man you asked me to keep an eye out for. Not that's he's hard to spot on account of his great presence.' He wiggled his eyebrows so no one could mistake his meaning.

'Thanks. I'll come and verify.'

In the office turned over to Harry's team, one monitor was frozen on a scene from *The Money Master*.

'Hardly the biggest budget blue movie I've ever

watched,' said Harry. 'All the action happens in one room. This time it's decked out like an office with the indebted client paying her way with sexual favours from the boss man. In others, it's a bedroom, or a restaurant, or – my favourite – a hairdressing salon. That was unexpected – must've required quite a bit of set-up to plumb in the water.'

'I imagine so. My information is that these are all made in a small home studio as a sideline, probably more an amusement for the creator. The Kanons's main income is from live sex chatrooms and stripping, all of which can happen remotely, as we know, in many locations around the globe. What definitely has to happen in our territory are the introductions. They also provide escorts, possibly via the clubs we're looking at.'

'That makes sense. The films are,' Harry rolled his shoulders, 'I dunno, dressed up tastefully, I suppose you'd say, promising a high-class brand? Even the thumbnails for the movies hide the content, make them look erotic rather than hardcore pornographic. But everything says "rich guy, come shop for a hot girl". It all fits together as part of the same image – all except the actual content which is definitely over the line from erotica to porn. But maybe that's intentional, too?'

'Because no matter how you dress it up, sex is a primal function?'

'It's not a bad business model,' continued Harry. 'Try her out first virtually in the privacy of your own home and then have your wet dream on your arm at the next function.'

Harry zoomed in on the man's face in the office scenario. 'Is this your guy?'

Lloyd was lightly disguised with his hair coloured black and a sculpted beard, but it was him. He was leading his client to his desk while he loosened his tie.

'Does this unfold normally?' asked Leo.

'How do you mean?' Harry fast-forward a few frames. Lloyd was now engaged in a vigorous coupling on the leather-topped surface. The woman he was having sex with was slim, dark-haired, but it would be hard to pigeonhole her nationality.

'Any erotic strangling, breath play?'

'Funny you should say that.' Harry zipped to the last third. 'He's quite creative with his tie.' The film paused on a scene where the client was now on the glass coffee table, hair splayed on the surface, as Lloyd used his tie to restrict her breathing. 'Never seen the attraction of this stuff but she seems to enjoy it.'

'She leaves the encounter alive and well?'

'Yeah.' He went to the end to show the woman buttoning up her white shirt and walking out with a foxy smile. 'Fairly mainstream porn as these things go.'

'OK. Tag this and send it over to the team investigating the death of Lloyd Rumbold. Invite them to consult with me on the way in which it crosses with lines of enquiry I'm pursuing, but add the caveat that this is sensitive territory so they shouldn't just go rushing in. Christ knows what would happen if they go stomping all over the Kanons and the club with the Birbecks waiting for our least mistake. If

Banbury want more details they should talk to Superintendent Thaxted.'

'They're not going to like that.' Harry closed the file and made a copy. 'They don't like you up there.'

'Oh?' But Leo wasn't surprised.

Harry, as an old hand, had contacts in most of the police stations in Thames Valley. 'They think you're only doing this to protect your friend.'

'Then maybe this evidence will persuade them to listen?'

'And DI Edmonds is so well known for her listening skills.' Harry rattled off an email with his stubby fingers and pressed Send. 'I wait with bated breath – unfortunate choice of words, sorry.' He grinned.

Suyin also had news for him when Leo returned to his desk. She came in, already in her coat, ready to leave for London.

'Sir, this came in from the forensic accountants while you were with Harry. I've printed it off so we can read it on the train.' She showed him an analysis of Kelly Ann's finances. 'I had a quick glance as it was coming off the printer. It seems that what we thought was a pension pot isn't that at all.'

Leo shrugged his way into his overcoat. 'Then what is it?'

'When I called up the full tax return, I found it was down as a charitable deduction rather than a pension contribution. Kelly Ann set it up for the benefit of an organisation she created working with women asylum seekers. In effect, it funds a house in Reading that offers shelter to trafficked women while their applications for leave to remain are considered. The house currently has four official tenants, names withheld on public documentation, but there are photos of them on the fundraising page. They all appear to be from the Far East.'

'So Kelly Ann didn't accept the so-called hush money for herself but used it to provide practical help to victims of trafficking? Maybe that was her price for her silence?' Leo packed his laptop in his bag and pocketed his phones.

'It fits better with what else we know about her. She was a woman of principles. She might've settled for a way to help the victims she knew about and a promise that these activities would cease.'

'Did she believe them?' wondered Leo. 'She must've realised she was seeing only a small part of the whole operation.'

Suyin shrugged. 'Perhaps she was realistic? One small accountant against the Birbecks and their allies. It was a win for her, wasn't it?'

'I suspect she was biding her time, digging in, carrying on getting more evidence against them. That was what made her a renewed threat. And that suggests there is yet more evidence to find. Tell the team to keep looking. Kelly Ann has done a lot of our work for us, if only we can find it.'

'What about the women in the Reading house?'

'Send the images to Harry in case they appear in any of the material he's looking at. We might get lucky. And what do you think about a stop in Reading after our meeting with the Birbecks?'

Suyin followed him to the car. 'I was going to suggest the same thing myself. Do you want me to ring ahead?'

'I think in this case it might be better to arrive unannounced. They might get scared and scatter if they know the police are coming. I'd prefer to reassure them in person that we mean them no harm.'

Chapter Twenty-Six

Leo

The Piccadilly People Club, the original location that gave its name to the worldwide chain, was in Golden Square, a short walk from Piccadilly Circus. It occupied several of the large terrace houses on the north side. Looking it up on the train to London, Leo was not surprised to find the square, designed by Christopher Wren, was built on the site of an old plague pit, somehow fitting if what he suspected about corruption in the club was true.

They were greeted by a top-hatted doorman, nut-brown face nestled between the white collars of his dark-green livery like a conker in its casing. He opened the glass door but used his bulk to deny them further entrance. A hushed interior of exclusive privacy lay behind him, architecturally bearing scant resemblance to the façade. The interior had been gutted and replaced with a modern foyer and atrium.

Perhaps a Blitz bomb had made that choice because there seemed precious little left of Wren's building.

'Can I help you, sir?' he asked.

'We've an appointment with the owners,' said Leo. 'Thames Valley Police.'

'Ah, yes. I was told to expect you.' He moved back and clicked his fingers. A female bellhop slunk out from behind a pillar, pillbox hat set at a rakish angle, livery a little too tight and with a low neckline – the first hint that anything else might be on offer here to those that knew to ask. 'Bobbie, please see the lady and gentleman to the owners' suite.'

A sleek and well-run concern, that was Leo's verdict as they were ushered through the lobby and upstairs with minimum fuss. Anyone visiting the club that hour would have been unaware that the police were at the door.

The bellhop led them through a library, which was also done up in a contemporary style, modern art works that splashed and swirled, Scandinavian furniture, and shelving that framed the books like pictures. The newspapers were stored in a pyramid of ceramic pipes marked with their names, a novel way to deal with the clutter they otherwise would've produced. The windows looked down on the square, framed by the bare twigs of the hornbeams. Even the trees seemed to be obeying the design ethic as the winter skeleton of a hornbeam was pleasingly symmetric.

Bobbie the bellhop (Was that her real name? Jess would love that, thought Leo) opened the door to a room at the far end, a conference room that continued the theme of the library. A bare oak table stretched the length. Two men waited at the far end, one seated in a white cup-shaped chair, the other standing at the window, looking out. Both men were in their sixties. The one seated, Chester, the elder by two years, had a lopsided smile that came off as smug. Grey-blue gaze, clean-shaven, greying fair hair, only faint lines around his eyes and mouth, he looked polished, like the table that faintly reflected him. His brother at the window, Jeremy, looked rougher, his resemblance closer to the trees in the square. More lines scored in his face, grey-streaked russet beard brushed to a point under his chin, he exuded less persuasion and more force. Neither, though, were to be underestimated. They were billionaires and moved in a circle well above the touch of a police officer, or so they would think. Personally, Leo thought no one was above the law, but he'd agreed to abide by certain conditions set by his boss before she let him loose for this interview. The most important had been not to piss them off.

Chester stood up. Not a tall man, he did not let that cow him as he held out a hand to Leo and Suyin.

'Inspector George, Sergeant Wong, please, take a seat.'

Jeremy came to the table and also shook hands, his grip distinctly tighter around Leo's palm than his brother's had been. He seemed to ease off for Suyin though, making the gesture more gallant.

'Thank you for seeing us,' said Leo. 'We appreciate that you are both busy men. And congratulations on your nomination in tonight's award ceremony.'

'Thank you, Inspector,' said Chester, continuing to take the lead. He remained at the head of the table while his brother sat at his right, slantwise to the table as if he was going to leap up at any moment. Leo and Suyin took the chairs opposite Jeremy. 'Club networks like our own have changed the way people travel. You are never far from home now, even if you're in Singapore or Sydney.' Introductory tap dance complete, he got down to business. 'Now, if you'd like to tell us what this is about?'

Leo led them through the events leading up to Kelly Ann's death and the conclusion that it wasn't suicide but murder staged to look that way.

'That's very shocking. It is always sad to lose an employee but to do so as an act of violence is doubly upsetting,' said Chester. He was making the right noises but he didn't look particularly upset. The very softness of his voice was chilling.

'During the course of our investigation, we came across some unusual aspects to Kelly Ann's employment with you,' Leo said, venturing into the more difficult territory. Unusually for him in an interview, he felt the flame-lick of nerves as he was well aware of the price he might pay if he took a wrong step.

'Indeed? Like what, specifically?' Cool eyes did not shift from his face. A predator lurked not too far from the surface.

'In 2018, Kelly Ann objected to the membership of Mr and Mrs Kanon and Mr and Mrs Stanton-Milbeck.'

'Inspector, we have a worldwide membership of over fifty thousand.' Chester spread his hands in a gesture that indicated the vastness of their empire.

'She emailed your headquarters about both couples. I've

spoken to the four people in question and they said that you had granted them the membership that lies in your gift as recompense for these complaints. Does this match your recollection of events?'

'I don't think I know them. Jeremy?' Chester batted this to his brother.

Jeremy was tapping away on his phone, slightly slumped in his chair, legs negligently spread. 'Member numbers 91 and 95. They were part of the New Moon investment fund. We gave them the Birbeck membership because we felt partially responsible for their temporary financial difficulties and thought the complaint against them unfounded.'

'Ah, yes. The fund. That was a sorry business.' The ghost of Lloyd hovered in the room briefly but Leo had been forbidden to mention him. His superintendent had pointed out that would leave the door open to the Birbecks's lawyers, welcome mat saying 'Sue Me for Conflict of Interest'.

'Did you investigate Kelly Ann's claims against the four?' asked Leo instead.

A flicker briefly lit Chester's otherwise flat gaze. 'If we excluded everyone who didn't obey our own moral code, then we'd halve our membership list, maybe cut it by ninety percent.' Chester met Leo's eyes with his strange unfeeling smile. 'We're vegetarian. For environmental and health reasons. That's why our clubs pride themselves on providing first class vegetarian options, but we continue to offer meat for those that aren't. As I'm sure you'll know.

You dined at our club on Saturday night, did you not, Inspector?'

Now that was interesting. Chester had done his homework, and had been waiting to slip in that he knew Leo had been a guest at the club, but he had not got the full story.

'Unfortunately, I was unable to enjoy that restaurant booking as I was already working this case.'

'But your credit card was used…' Chester let that hang out there, insinuating that Leo was lying.

'For my partner. She said the meal was excellent. So, returning to my question, you haven't met either the Stanton-Milbecks or the Kanons?'

'We aren't often at the Oxfordshire club. They don't sound familiar. Jeremy?'

The younger Birbeck shook his head, not looking up from his phone. 'If we do know them, it is only a little – in passing.'

Which wasn't quite a 'no'. It covered their backs if photographs of social events cropped up online.

'Did you or your brother ever meet Kelly Ann Porter in person?' asked Leo.

Chester wrinkled his smooth brow in pretend thought. 'Can't say that I have. Of course, she might have been at an event at which we were present, but I'm fairly certain we've never had a meeting with her.' Another lawyerly answer.

'She wasn't very senior, Inspector,' broke in Jeremy. 'We tend only to meet the most senior staff from our establishments.'

'Of course. I understand.' He and Suyin had thought

long and hard about the next question, but it was the essence of what they wanted to ask so he couldn't avoid it. 'Forgive me if I don't understand the ins and outs of business…'

Chester waved that away. 'Please, go on.'

'Can you explain to me why Kelly Ann was in receipt of such an exceptional bonus, this employee whom you'd not met and whose performance reviews, though good, were inline with those of her colleagues who did not get the same treatment?'

There was a pause.

'What kind of bonus?' asked Chester.

'Over a hundred and fifty thousand,' said Suyin, speaking for the first time. She pushed over a copy of the figures they'd gleaned from Kelly Ann's meticulous accounts.

'We do occasionally reward extremely good work with such sums,' said Chester.

'But you never met her in person. It comes across as a little unusual that she should be singled out like this,' said Leo. 'How did you decide?'

'We are known for being generous employers, with a maverick streak. If we felt like giving her this bonus, then that was what we'd do. It keeps our employees on their toes, hoping similar bounty might come their way if they do something that makes us sit up and notice them.'

'What did Kelly Ann do to make you notice her?' asked Suyin, head cocked in seemingly innocent interest. She'd picked up on exactly the right question to follow on.

'I don't remember the details.' Chester feigned a frown.

'I'd have to look them up but that would delay you. Jeremy, do you remember?'

The younger brother put his phone away and turned to the table. 'I'm thinking it might've been when we were in Mauritius?' Jeremy was spinning his tale, using a forceful tone to make up for the absence of truth. 'We'd been drinking. I threw a dart at the list of names of those we employ and she might've been the one that came out as the winner. Yes, I think she was.'

'My brother likes his games,' said Chester.

'But no one else knew – not even Kelly Ann's manager?' said Leo. 'Surely, such a windfall would be publicised, to encourage the rest of the workforce that they might also win one day?'

Jeremy shrugged, his free leg bouncing on his knee. 'No, I don't think we did say anything. As I said, it was a whim.' He wasn't even trying to make it sound convincing.

'That does seem unlikely for two such successful businessmen as yourselves,' said Leo, 'to run your HR like a casino.'

'When you're successful, Inspector, you can do whatever the hell you like with your money,' shot back Jeremy, unamused at being questioned.

'We wouldn't know,' said Suyin, placatingly. 'Not being in business.'

'Do you have any more questions?' asked Chester, glancing at his Rolex.

Leo chanced the last roll of the dice. 'We've discovered that Kelly Ann used the largesse you sent her way to fund a charity that works with victims of human trafficking. Do you have any idea why she might've done that – with your money?'

'It was her money by then, wasn't it, Inspector?' said Chester, a hint of venom in his soft voice. He was as angry as his brother but hid it better. 'That was admirable of her. It makes her loss even more of a tragedy. I hope you catch the party responsible.' He stood up. 'Now, you must excuse us, we have some press interviews before the event tonight and we really must get on.'

Leo and Suyin got to their feet. The Birbecks had agreed to this interview in order to be able to say they were being cooperative. They had no intention of giving any real answers and everyone in the room was aware of that. Adapting what Chester had said about his brother, the Birbecks liked their games.

'Thank you for your time,' said Leo formally. 'Good luck this evening.'

Chester smiled lopsidedly. 'Oh, I think it's in the bag. They wouldn't get us here for anything less.'

With that dismissal, the detectives walked out, finding the bellhop waiting for them in the library beyond. A group of journalists were poised on the low chairs around a kidney-shaped coffee table, talking in low voices. Leo would have liked to give them a real story, get them sniffing around the clubs for misdeeds, but knew Superintendent Thaxted would never forgive him.

Out on the street, Leo took a deep breath. That had felt like narrowly avoiding a stampede, though in this case, rather than horns and hooves, it would have been lawyers and legal action.

'Well?' he asked Suyin. 'What did you make of that?'

She walked quickly to keep up with his longer stride. He slowed a little. 'It went much as we expected, sir. They were busy in cover-up mode.' The two officers headed for the Underground entrance near Eros. 'But why the story about Mauritius? That just seemed like too much embroidery. They could've just stuck with "she was a valuable employee".'

'Left up to Chester, that's what we would've got, but Jeremy runs hotter. He could see they didn't have an explanation so took it upon himself to make one up. As a result, we got more than I expected.'

'We did?'

He nodded. 'For all the polish there were frayed edges. We got that they know the Stanton-Milbecks and Kanons; otherwise, they wouldn't have added that rider about maybe meeting at some social function. That was because they expect such pictures to exist. Chester also let slip that Kelly Ann's objections were moral – we hadn't said that.'

'He did, didn't he? I missed that.' Suyin seemed unhappy with herself for not catching this nuance.

'And we got that they knew exactly who Kelly Ann was well before her death but wouldn't tell us why she'd come to their attention. They would've done better saying she was an outstanding talent who they recognised above other staff members, rather than pretending not to know her and then giving that ridiculous dartboard explanation for special treatment.'

'That was the most obvious failing in the conversation on their part.'

'There's more. We also got confirmation that their lives were entangled with the Stanton-Milbecks and Kanons through the financial investment firm. That's our direct link to Lloyd Rumbold and shows the Birbecks conduct business as if they connect even though the two companies are supposed to be separate.'

They crossed the road onto the busy lower stretch of Regent Street. Buses sat in a line waiting for the lights to change, sides advertising the latest films to hit the cinemas. The electronic display boards on the Circus splashed messages from banks and brands at the crowded street, dragging all gazes up. This was what made it a prime spot for pickpockets and he spotted one young woman, white, five-five, dark hoodie, weaving her way through the crowds but he didn't witness her lift any purses. She must've felt his gaze on her because she gave him a hostile look before sliding away. Last time Leo had been here, he'd been with Jess a few weeks before Christmas and she'd told him about her time as a teenager on the streets. How he'd left things the night before rushed back to him from the place he had stuffed it during the interview. It had been mostly his fault that he'd given her the cold shoulder. He'd just felt so off-balance. It was hard to concentrate today when he was aware of this weakness undermining him. He wished he could steady their wobbling relationship, but how?

'*Sir,* do you want me to look into the Rumbold connection?' Suyin sounded like she was having to repeat her question.

'Sorry, I was just thinking.' He forced himself back to his

case. 'In normal circumstances, I would say yes but you know what's going on there… my personal involvement.'

'Thinking outside the box, sir, could Rumbold have staged the Kelly Ann suicide? He was in the vicinity and still had links to people in the orbit of the club. He might've owed them favours, or done it for money. We've only thought about him as a victim, but perhaps he was still working for the Birbecks at some level? He was desperate enough from what you were telling me.'

Leo considered it for a moment. Lloyd a killer? The man had already been in a terrible position, vulnerable to blackmail. Participating in that film had shown that he'd already gone very far to placate those he owed. Could they have bent his will further to encompass murder?

He would have to ask Rainbow if Lloyd had been absent at all the night of the first death. If Lloyd had been involved, then he could've invited the one who commissioned the crime over to the motorhome for his pay off – Leo was picturing Marta Kanon coming over to hear the report. There was a Cruella de Vil aspect to her that made her easy to imagine in such a role. He mustn't fall into the trap of letting the obvious blind him to other suspects. Maybe Marta, or some other person, had then killed the killer to make sure he never had a chance to say anything, the classic snipping of a loose end. Lloyd wouldn't have questioned taking a drink from her. How easy it would've been to get him out of commission, set the scene as an accidental death or suicide, and walk away. The miscalculation had been that Leo had been called in to investigate the first death and knew the second victim, thus instantly making the link.

Marta (or whoever) would not have known that would happen. Leo hadn't even been supposed to be on duty. Chance, and the new virus that had struck down his colleague, had played a part in arranging that.

'Valid questions, Suyin, though I can think of myriad objections, like how he got Kelly Ann to undress and take a bath.'

'Well, the obvious answer is sex. He did have a thing going with women associated with the club.' They descended into the Underground, threading their way through the people coming up the stairs.

When the crowd cleared, Leo fell in step with Suyin again. 'True. I'd been thinking of the clients, but he could've expanded to encompass others by word-of-mouth referrals.' He sighed. It all felt sordid and desperately sad. 'I'm not sure Kelly Ann was the type to call in a male escort.'

'Women have sexual drives too, sir, and she wasn't getting it any other way according to her friend you interviewed.'

That didn't feel right, not with the lavender cushions and frankly spinsterish feel of Kelly Ann's house. She wouldn't have left her diary under her pillow if she was expecting sex. 'Whatever the case, we don't have any evidence that our two victims ever met – at least, none that I know of. There's no payment to him on any of her accounts for his services.'

'Cash? She didn't have time to pay?'

'Both possible. We really need the other investigators to take us seriously on this and share what they've found. The evidence is mounting that the two deaths could be connected.' He tapped his card on the ticket pad. 'But how exactly Banbury are going to fit in with our team is the question.'

Suyin unzipped her winter coat in the warmth of the Tube station. 'I can't see DI Edmonds bringing her work under your banner. She'll argue to take over, not least because of your personal interest.'

'But if there's a link then it makes absolutely no sense to continue to believe Rainbow Williams is the culprit. She has no connection to the Birbecks.'

'I know, sir. I'm just saying what I would do in Inspector Edmonds's place.' Suyin grinned at him as they waited beneath the signboard for the train to arrive.

He returned her smile. 'I know, Suyin. You did well in there.' The train was approaching; he had to raise his voice or be drowned out. 'Let's visit that house in Reading, get back to Oxford, and debrief the team. I'll let the superintendent know when we're on the train that we didn't sink the force under a salvo of Birbeck writs.'

The doors rattled open and passengers descended.

Suyin stood back. 'Not yet, sir. Give us time.'

'You think they're part of this?' he asked.

'Yes, I do. For trafficking if not the murder. But I'm just wondering if they're too big for one small police force to take down?'

That was an excellent question.

Chapter Twenty-Seven

Jess

Grabbing some time for the enquiry while at work, I had my lunch at the Old Bank on the High. Opulent Victorian shrine to money, it had been turned into a hotel, and was just up the road from Michael's college and mine. Among the tourists, a few locals could be found enjoying the café in the old banking hall. I considered it expensive but I'd made friends with the maître d' and, if they weren't too busy, he let me have a table and a cut-price sandwich. It's amazing how finding a loved one for someone gets you discounts for life.

Michael rolled in a few minutes later.

'Breakfast, now lunch – Cory will get jealous,' I said, cheerfully, as he parked his chair opposite me.

'Dr Harrison, the usual?' asked the maître d'. I hadn't known Michael had also made this his local.

'Thank you, Connor. No fries today.' Michael pulled out

his phone, turned it to the Oxford Mail's website and passed it to me. 'Fifth article.'

I tapped on the piece in question and saw a factual write-up about the discovery of the body of Lloyd Percy Rumbold. There was a picture of the Rollright Stones and another of the motorhome.

'And you're showing me this because…?'

Michael poured a glass of water from the carafe on the table. 'You'll understand in a minute. I followed up with Ellie Fanshawe this morning. She's very keen on new business because she returned my call immediately.'

'Maybe the market for lifestyle gurus is a small one?'

'Or she doesn't get many referrals. Anyway, we went to video as we were using Skype.'

'OK. And what did you make of her in the screen-flesh?'

'Firstly, she makes her calls in a room that suggests a much more glamorous house than a semi. Nothing wrong with a semi, of course, but she has a green screen backdrop of a modernist building that looks like it should be in California not Cowley.'

'I didn't know you could do that. You can change what's behind you?' That might solve my problem about conducting my business calls from my bedroom.

'Apparently so.'

'You wouldn't need to bother because you have Magdalen as your backdrop – academic tomes and gargoyles. Some of us aren't so lucky.'

'Jess.'

'Yes, I know, I'm digressing. The green screen – go on.'

'Well, I picked up on it because it doesn't track quite true but if you weren't studying her so closely, you'd probably not question it. It helped that I knew where she was from your interview.'

'OK, she cares about self-presentation. How did she seem to you? Was she still channelling Land Army girl?'

'No, I'd say it was more West Coast realtor – business suit jacket buttoned over a neckline that didn't suggest a blouse underneath. She was probably matching her outfit to what she thought I would want.'

'A sexy lady to tell you what to do?'

He gave me a reproving look. 'I was looking for traits that indicate a lack of empathy, one of the key indicators of a psychopathic individual.'

'Yeah, I did your course, remember?'

He smiled wryly. 'Sorry. And I do. Vividly.'

I was not touching that comment. That academic encounter had got us both into a lot of trouble.

'Anyway, we chatted about my image and I dropped into the conversation that I had been let down by a former partner, bruised and battered by that experience, and was only now slowly getting my act together.'

I hoped he wasn't talking about me still because that was one way of describing what had happened between us. 'Go on. How did she react to your tale of woe?'

The waiter arrived with our lunch – chicken salad sandwich for me and a hamburger in a brioche roll for Michael. He faffed around with dressings and offers of drinks but finally he stepped away.

'She was very interested in my story. Started on her spiel about how a lifestyle adviser was really a lifestyle counsellor. There was a narcissistic element there because she wanted to make it about her, but I think she understood the emotions I was describing; in fact, she went so far as to tell me she'd felt something very similar when she broke up with her last partner.'

'Lloyd.'

'Lloyd,' he confirmed, 'but he wasn't mentioned by name. It's what happened next that I found most revealing. While we were talking, I saw her glance down, she paled, and then apologised hastily that she had to end the call. This seemed out of character as she had been putting everything into landing me as her next customer. Once she'd rung off, I checked. The police released the name of the victim at 10 o'clock this morning.'

'She had a Google alert set for his name?'

'That's my conclusion.'

I mopped up some salad dressing with a crust. 'I suppose in some Machiavellian universe I could make an argument that she already knew because she did it and it was useful to her to have a witness to her distress. If so, nicely played.' Michael was tucking into his hamburger, unimpressed by my spinning of the facts. 'Yeah, I know. It's easier just to think she was genuinely shocked, that this was nothing to do with her.'

'You'd just like it to be her because she killed a dog.'

'And ripped the claws out of her kitty. But, yeah, I think I'm prejudiced.'

'There's more.'

'Boy, you have been busy.' I pronged a green bean with my fork.

He gave me a sweet smile. 'Teaching undergraduates can be the epitome of dull.'

'Whereas helping in a murder hunt never is?' We were both, in our own ways, adrenaline junkies for weird psychological cases.

'I called my contact in the police force. You were right. The toxicology report on Lloyd tells us that he was drugged before he died – a common form of sleeping tablet: Zopiclone; it's prescribed to help people with bad insomnia. It boosts gamma-aminobutyric acid, the stuff that calms the brain to let us sleep.'

'I bet you practiced that so you wouldn't trip over the name.'

'You can call it GABA.'

'Thank you, kind sir. And did they say if he had a prescription for it?'

'No, he did not.'

'But would you need to knock yourself out if you were happily going to sit there and fume yourself to death?'

'I'd say not. This suggests he was helped into unconsciousness.'

'And the rationale is that he would only take this from someone else if he trusted them, probably in food or drink?'

'It comes in tablets usually, but you can get a liquid form if you have trouble swallowing. But it's fast acting. It's lights out in under an hour.'

I wiped my plate clean with a final piece of chicken. 'I wonder what Leo's victim took to make her cooperate with her bath death? This is really helpful, thank you.'

He dabbed his mouth with the serviette. 'It's a pleasure.

Perhaps you and Leo would like to come to dinner with Cory and me next week?'

'Oh.' I had a sudden vision of that awkward foursome.

'Something the matter?'

'It's just that Leo is really busy and—'

'Jess, I know when you're lying. If you don't think it's a good idea, just tell me.'

I caved. 'Look, we're in a difficult patch at the moment. Leo really does have a lot going on but he doesn't like me investigating his friends, even though he should've realised that's what I'd do when he asked me to help Rainbow.'

Michael nodded. 'That would feel very personal to him. He's a private man so I imagine he holds the few he lets close as especially precious.'

'It's not that he spends a lot of time with them or anything—'

'I get it. He has an idea about them that he doesn't want challenged. From what I gathered about his background, he doesn't have family behind him. Friends have taken that place, his safe haven.'

Unlike his hazardous Haven of a mother.

It was on the tip of my tongue to tell him about Leo's father but I couldn't do that to my guy, not with my old partner. Even I understood that was inappropriate.

'What do you think I should do?' I asked. 'To placate Leo?'

'Follow the facts. I've given you some new ones. He can't object to those.'

Chapter Twenty-Eight

Leo

The train finally shook off London as it went under the M25, passing through stretches of green fields, small woods, and business parks, before the next stop up the Thames at Reading. Suyin was filing a report of their meeting and Leo had already reported in to the superintendent. That left him a moment to return to his father's letter.

He didn't need to get it out. He just let his hand rest on his pocket. Why now? After so many years? Was it really just work bringing George Saito to the UK that prompted the outreach or did he want something from Leo?

Leo couldn't be naïve. He'd seen plenty of families with toxic relationships. He couldn't just take George Saito at his word. So what to do?

Wasn't the answer obvious? He should investigate Saito like he would any other case that crossed his desk.

First place to go for a statement was the other person in the equation. Leo rarely initiated contact with his mother but he would have to break that silence if he wanted answers. *Never let her know that the answer matters to you,* he told himself. She would withhold information like a hostage. It was better to get her worried. He composed his message.

I received a letter from my father. Where is the money he sent to you meant for me?

That would put her on the back foot. Her lies – if the money had existed – would tell him more than her so-called truths ever would. If she came back with the name of George Saito (he'd purposely left that out) then that would be useful confirmation of the relationship.

He pressed Send on the message and forced himself to put the subject away for the moment.

The women's refuge was in an end of terrace house in York Road, just five minutes' walk from Reading station. It was a pleasant area of primary schools, suburban roads, and playing fields leading to the banks of the Thames, some houses given over to families, others split into student accommodation. It would feel safe and anonymous, thought Leo, to group of women who had struggled out of the clutches of human traffickers. It was hard to imagine something bad happening with so many pushchairs and trampolines in the gardens.

Suyin rang the doorbell. Both of them wore plain clothes, so Leo hoped that their arrival wasn't a signal for the inhabitants to bolt out of the back and over the fence.

The door opened a crack. 'Yes?' A woman's face, mostly just the eyes, appeared in the gap. These were cinnamon brown and rounded with suspicion.

'Hello, there. My name is Suyin Wong,' began the sergeant in a friendly tone. 'We're from Thames Valley and we'd like to talk to you about Kelly Ann Porter. May we come in?'

There was quick-fire muttering behind the door. More than one person was in the hallway. The first woman came back to the gap.

'What is Thames Valley?'

'That's the name for the local police force – but don't be alarmed,' Suyin held up a warrant card, 'we're only here to talk about Kelly Ann. I'd prefer to explain it to you inside.'

Predictably the word 'police' had raised the alarm level from amber to red, but Suyin couldn't lawfully conceal their identities just to get inside.

'No, we not speak. Kelly Ann said so.' The woman made to close the door.

Leo stepped forward and put his hand against the frame, slowing the closure. 'I'm sorry but Kelly Ann is dead. We need to come in.' He hadn't wanted to announce it so crudely but he could see that they were not going to get in any other way.

Wails broke out from those who had heard, passing to

the others as the news spread. The woman no longer guarded the door and it swung open. Four young women were propping each other up in a group hug in the hallway as they expressed their grief. Their cries mounted, unrestrained, genuinely deep. A sisterhood of victims.

With a glance at him, Suyin gingerly entered first.

'We are so sorry for your loss.' There was a renewed burst of sobs. 'Please, if you'd like to help Kelly Ann, the best thing you can do now is speak to us. The inspector and I are here to get justice for your friend.'

The woman from the door turned from the huddle, wiping her eyes on her sleeve. The crying was subsiding so Suyin's voice could be heard. The woman looked to be about twenty, long, dark hair, mid-brown skin, and a high forehead. From her face shape, Leo would guess she was from one of the East Asian countries. He couldn't identify which language they were speaking but it didn't sound like any dialect of Chinese he knew.

'How did Miss Kelly Ann die?' the woman asked.

'We will tell you. Please, may we come in?'

Suyin's request this time was met with a nod. The woman led them through to a kitchen at the back, Glancing into the front room as he passed, Leo saw that it was used as a bedroom with bedding rolls on the floor. There were clearly more than four women finding shelter here.

The woman gestured to a small kitchen table. 'Sit, please.' Her friends crowded the doorway, evidently electing her to speak for them.

'Do you all understand English or do we need a translator?' asked Leo.

'No, we understand,' said the woman quickly.

Leo turned to the others who were behind him, positioned where he couldn't see them. Shuddering breaths told him that at least one was still crying. 'Is that true for everyone?'

'We speak English. All of us,' said a second woman.

'We had to learn for our job,' said another.

'My name is Detective Inspector Leo George.' He placed his warrant card on the table for them to see. 'This, as my colleague already said, is Detective Sergeant Suyin Wong.'

'You are from China?' asked one woman agitatedly. 'You look Chinese.' The others hushed her.

'No, no, I'm not,' said Leo. It was unfortunate to find his father's face swimming into view just when he needed to be most focused.

'But all of my grandparents live in Hong Kong,' said Suyin. 'Both the inspector and I were born in the UK and are British police officers.'

'We investigate serious crimes,' said Leo.

'We are *not* from Immigration, in case you were worried,' added Suyin. 'May we ask your names?'

The women exchanged glances.

'It really will help us investigate Kelly Ann's death if we have accurate information,' said Leo.

The woman across the table from them, nodded. 'I understand.' Her gaze flicked up. '*We* understand. My name is Ly Tien. She is Phuong Vu,' she pointed to the smallest and youngest of the group, 'Chi and Kim Nguyen. They are sisters.' The family resemblance was strong and they appeared about the same age – again, no more than twenty. Twins maybe? The three in the doorway gave the impression of delicacy, almost willowy frailty, in the way they clung to each other, but Ly had the bearing of a confident woman, a school teacherly control beyond her age.

'Miss Tien, as I mentioned on the doorstep, I regret to inform you that Kelly Ann Porter was found dead at her home on Saturday morning,' said Leo. 'She died Friday evening. We believe her death is suspicious.'

'What does this mean? Suspicious?' Ly scowled even while tears matted her lashes.

'It means that we don't believe that she took her own life.'

Ly shook her head vigorously. 'No, Kelly Ann would not take her own life. It was against her beliefs. And she had so much to live for. We—' She broke off.

'Please, go on. Tell me what you wanted to say.'

Tears glistened in Ly's eyes. 'I say *we* had so much to live for. She said she fight for us.' She clenched her fist and pressed it against her heart.

'In the course of our investigation, we have learned that Kelly Ann was an exceptional woman. She provided the money for this house, didn't she?' In the back of his mind, Leo worried how they were going to pay their way now she was gone.

'Yes, yes, she pay our rent. She pay our lawyers,' broke in one of the others behind Leo, he didn't see which. The others shushed her, seeming scared to give anything away.

'We believe that what you can tell us will lead us to her

killer,' said Suyin. 'It is vitally important you don't hide anything from us.'

'You will not tell others where we are?' said Ly, nervously plucking at the skin on the back of one hand.

'We won't tell anyone,' Leo promised, though he now worried that the charitable donations made by Kelly Ann could be traced to this house. He'd have to put the local station on alert. He had told the Birbecks that Kelly Ann donated to a charity for trafficked women. If she was listed as a trustee with the Charity Commission… 'Do you believe you have reason to be afraid?'

Ly hugged her arms to herself. 'Yes. Kelly Ann was killed.'

That was undoubtedly true.

'I'll leave you with our numbers. If you have any reason to feel concerned for your safety, then you must call one of us immediately – and the local police station. Stay with each other and don't allow strangers into the house. Are there any others here at the moment?' asked Leo. 'What I mean is, how many are using this as their address?'

'There are another two but they are meeting with their solicitor today,' said Ly. 'We had another but she decided to return home. Her family sent for her.' She didn't look as if she considered this was a good choice.

Leo thought the house could probably hide more than six but that was all she was going to admit to now. She probably felt she had good reason to conceal the others, for example if they were undocumented.

'Make sure everyone knows to take care,' he said, putting a business card next to his badge.

'Where are you from originally?' asked Suyin.

'We are from Vietnam.' Ly swept Leo with a dubious look, suspicions rising again. 'You are not here about that?'

'No, we're not, Miss Tien,' said Leo firmly. 'If you have applied for asylum then that procedure will take its own course. We have no intention of interfering with due process.'

'Good, good. Mr King said that we have a good case. We should not fear.'

Leo was less sanguine about the justice in the immigration system. 'Mr King is…?'

'Our lawyer.'

'You are welcome to tell him about our visit and he can call me if he has any questions. Miss Tien, we need to know if any of you worked for the Piccadilly People Club?'

Ly grimaced. 'Yes, we worked there. That is where I met Kelly Ann.' Her words confirmed for Leo that she was the LT mentioned in the victim's diary. 'What happened to Kelly Ann, sir?'

'You are saying that you worked at the club near Chipping Norton?'

'I did. The sisters did. Phuong worked in London club. The youngest ones always go there. Please, you talk of a killer? What happened to Kelly Ann?'

'Someone went to a great deal of trouble to make her death look like suicide. Do you understand what I am saying?' She nodded. 'We think they were trying to hide something, or stop her speaking about it. Do you have any idea what that might be? Did Kelly Ann tell you what she found out?'

'This is not safe, Inspector.' Ly looked to her friends again. They had the bearing of a flock of sparrows about to take off at the slightest snap of a twig.

'It is safe to tell DS Wong and me. We'll do everything in our power to ensure the information is used to bring a murderer to justice.'

Ly put a finger to her mouth and bit the nail. Catching herself, she dropped her hands to her lap and folded them tightly together. 'I do not know what she found. Two weeks ago, she said that she was close.'

'Close to what?'

'To proof that what we said was true.'

'What did you tell her?' asked Suyin, gently.

There was an explosion of chatter in Vietnamese but Ly held up her hand so she could say it in English.

'We come from Vietnam with promise of good job in beauty parlour or hairdresser. I was told I would be receptionist.' Ly rolled her eyes, presumably at her own naïveté. 'We get here and find it very different job.'

'How did you get here? I'm talking about the last part of your journey when you crossed a British border,' asked Leo.

'In lorry. We were all in same lorry. We did not know each other before. It was a bad journey. So long time. We were in a space behind boxes of clothes and shoes. No food, no water, for days. I thought we would die there.'

'Stop then start. Stop then start,' added one of the sisters. 'We had no idea when it would end.'

'Then we arrive in a warehouse and we are taken away by a lady and given food and water. She say, yes, we will be working in beauty parlour, but we also do extra work. We are to do what we are told.'

'And what was that?' asked Suyin.

'We were to meet men who wanted us and then…' Ly looked away.

'You were told to have sex with them?' said Suyin.

Ly nodded.

'They like young girls, these men. They have parties. They are told we want to be with them. We are supposed to say they are so good, so rich, so attractive.' The Nguyen sister's tone was acidic. 'But if they so good, why do they need girls brought to them?'

'Were you told what would happen to you if you didn't agree to participate in these parties?' asked Leo.

'They say they take away jobs. They pass us on to people in London and then we will see what real prostitution is like,' said Ly. She sounded like she was quoting someone when she said that.

'How old were you when you were brought here?' asked Suyin.

Ly tapped her chest. 'Seventeen. Chi and Kim were sixteen. Phuong was fifteen. We were told to say we were twenty. *Yes, sir, I am twenty. Vietnamese women look young for age.*' She adopted a hands-under-chin pose, the kind adopted by dancing girls on posters advertising their country's culture.

'If we showed you some photographs would you be able to identify the people who met you at the warehouse, and the people who told you what you were expected to do?' asked Leo.

'Yes, we know their faces.'

'I'd like to arrange for some of my officers to return tomorrow with pictures for you to look at. If you can see any of the people in them, you are to tell us. You can tell us the names then.'

'We can do that,' agreed Ly.

'And the men you slept with, do you know who they were?' asked Suyin.

Ly shrugged. 'They were just old men. We were told first names only. Bill. Richard. John.'

'But if we arranged more photographs could you pick them out?'

'Maybe, maybe not.' Ly made a wobbly hand gesture, expressing her doubt.

'I remember some of them,' offered Phuong, speaking for the first time. She was so quiet, it was hard to hear her. 'And there were cameras. Maybe you find pictures?'

'You were photographed?' asked Leo carefully.

'They film without saying, but we knew,' said Phuong. 'They tell us it was to keep everything secret.'

Meaning that the organisers of the sex ring would threaten to blackmail anyone who had a crisis of conscience about sleeping with an underage girl?

'Who said this?'

Phuong wrinkled her nose in disgust. 'Bad woman. Big hair like this.' She mimicked a hairstyle that could well be Marta Kanon. 'She the worst. Not nice like the man.'

'Who was the man? What did he look like?' asked Leo, thinking of Josef Kanon.

'I don't know. Old. Grey hair. Like all the others,' said Phuong.

'But you'd recognise him if you saw his photo?'

'Yes,' but then she added, 'he was in charge. It all was done for him.'

Chapter Twenty-Nine

Jess

Booking out the electric car again, I drove to the Rollright Stones after rush hour. I was intending to call on Rebecca and meet her mother, but first I wanted to return to the scene of the crime and see if it had any more to tell me.

The entrance was closed for the night but that didn't stop a keen person climbing over – it was only a five-bar gate. The motorhome had gone but even in the dusk I could see the stamped earth where it had been parked and the evidence of multiple tyre tracks. I'd already spotted the police signs appealing for witnesses that were posted in the lay-by on the road and at nearby junctions. It was highly unlikely anyone would have seen a person approaching the motorhome as it was screened from the main road by the hedge. Would the killer have parked in the lay-by? That would have been ballsy, but maybe the police would get lucky.

I walked into the middle of the stone circle. The constellations were pinprick bright, the moon waning. A line of bright stars (or were they planets?) filed along the horizon. I wished I knew more about the names of the constellations to understand what I could see overhead. Unlike the riotous dance I had done with Rainbow and Lauren just a couple of days ago, when the stones had been stripped of awe and mystery by daylight, I could now feel their ancient power. That was partly because I was alone, but it was also just the thought of their age. They had stood here so long, witnessed so much – the arrival of Romans and other invaders, the passing of kingdoms, legionaries and monarchs, the overflight of birds, planes, now satellites and space stations – yet still they waited. There was also something unnerving about the human-scale of the megaliths. It was like you were always catching sight of someone moving just out of the corner of your eye.

I was drawn to the centre. You had to stand there at least for a moment, didn't you? Had this been the spot occupied by druid priests in the ceremonies? Had the faithful processed around the ring, torches flaming? I could almost see them, or their ghosts, if I opened myself up to my imagination.

Then one of the stones moved.

A whispered curse slipped from me. There was no cover in the centre. Why on earth was I standing here in the open after dark? Even without a murder, that would be an idiotic thing to do. I was a sitting duck for a crazy person or sex pest.

'Hello?' I called, pretending this was entirely normal, willing the person who was half-hidden by the rock to step out and reveal themselves as someone ordinary – a walker, a tourist, a modern-day druid come to perform a rite. As long as it wasn't human sacrifice.

The shape resolved itself into a woman in a long winter coat and hood, reminding me of the model for the Scottish Widows Pension adverts. I couldn't quite make out her face, but it was pale. Definitely a white woman.

Not a ghost. Absolutely not a ghost. *Jess, be sensible.*

I wondered for a moment if Rainbow had slipped her bail leash and decided to come here to mourn.

'Rainbow?' My voice limped out with little conviction.

The figure turned away.

'Rebecca?'

She paused, then pivoted to face me. 'Not Rebecca,' she said and pushed the hood back. With an unpleasant swoop in my stomach, I saw that I was talking to Ellie Fanshawe. She held a bouquet of flowers which I guessed she had been intending to lay at the place where Lloyd had died – until she'd seen me and come to investigate.

'Oh.' Crap, this was awkward.

'You— You're the woman taking the survey?' Unfortunately she had a good memory for faces and decent night vision. I hadn't disguised myself, not expecting to meet her again, and certainly not under these circumstances. 'What are you doing here?'

It wouldn't take her long to reject coincidence as an

explanation, so I decided to come clean. I didn't want her to think I was here alone. She had to believe there were people who would miss me – not that I had told anyone my plans for the evening because I didn't think Leo would approve. An oversight, now I came to think about it. I hadn't entirely dismissed my instinct that Ellie was a person prepared to hurt another.

'I'm a private detective, Jess Bridges. I'm looking into the death of Lloyd Rumbold.' That sounded official enough, didn't it?

On the mention of his name, she let out a sob and clutched the flowers to her chest. I took a step closer.

'No, stay back!' she warned, raising the bouquet, making a stop gesture.

I went still. It was like a bizarre game of grandmother's footsteps. I dared not wobble in case it set her off.

'I'm sorry for your loss.'

'Who killed him?' she asked, her voice sharp. 'Tell me what you know!'

I had to admit she wasn't behaving like a murderer, more a distraught lover.

Unless she was repeating the pattern of returning to the scene? I wished my mind would make itself up about her.

No. I had to get over the damage to small animals and think clearly. She might've been capable of violence but she genuinely appeared not to have known about his death until the announcement was made today. That made sense of her coming with flowers now and not earlier.

'All I know is that Lloyd died of carbon monoxide poisoning. The police think it was deliberate – that the ventilation in the motorhome in which he was travelling was tampered with so he suffocated.' She shuddered. 'He wouldn't have known or suffered,' I added quickly. 'He would've just gone to sleep and not woken up.'

She struggled for a moment then found her voice. 'Who hired you?'

'His friends. One of them is being blamed but she didn't do it.' *Probably*, I had to add silently, keeping myself honest. 'They've asked me to see if I can find out what really happened.'

'That's Rainbow – the name you called out?' So, Ellie had been keeping tabs on Lloyd's love life and the local news about the decision to charge a woman.

'Yes.'

'She didn't do it?'

'No. She was with us all evening.'

'And Rebecca – you said Rebecca?'

'I did.'

'His ex-wife?'

'Yes.'

'Why would she be here? She hated him.'

I hadn't got that impression. 'I didn't recognise you. It was just a guess.' I risked taking a step and Ellie didn't object. Of course, she had been as scared as I had been, finding a stranger in so remote a place.

Ellie looked around her. 'Do you know where the camper van was parked?'

I guided her to the spot in the field beyond the stones and stood back while she placed her bouquet on the fencepost nearest to the flattened grass. No one else had come to lay flowers. I could hear heartbroken, raw sobs but didn't feel I could intrude. I did wait, though, for her to finish.

Finally, after about ten minutes of standing vigil, she stepped away and came towards me.

'Why did you visit me?' she asked, her brain having caught up with the oddity of my appearance at her home. I could smell alcohol on her breath. She probably was over the limit and functioning on Dutch courage. Had she been drowning her sorrows since news broke?

'I'm looking into all Lloyd's contacts,' I said, hoping she wouldn't push further. 'When did you last see him?'

'Christmas,' she said at once. 'That was the last time.'

I was under the impression their relationship had ended long ago. 'Do you mind telling me where you met – and why?'

We headed together to the lay-by where I saw her car parked next to mine.

'He came to me when his girlfriend was in Wales. We continued to see each other when we couldn't get what we needed from others.'

'And what did you need?'

She played with the key in her hand for a moment. 'He said his current lover didn't like to experiment – that he was bored.'

'Whereas, you did like experimentation?'

'I'm not ashamed of my sexual nature.'

'I'm the last person to suggest that, believe me. But you and Lloyd enjoyed what kind of sex? Sorry if this sounds intrusive – I'm just trying to understand.'

She shrugged. 'We shared a taste for some aspects of BDSM.'

'Such as?'

She said nothing.

'Look, we're the post-*Fifty Shades* generation. We're all a lot more educated than we used to be.'

That comment annoyed her. 'That book is ridiculous, no guide to anything. You don't have to be an abused child to like the lifestyle.'

'All right, I hear you.'

'Look, we liked breath play, OK? That's one of the reasons why we clicked. And Lloyd was very good at it – never went too far.'

If he'd gone too far, she would've been dead, so, yeah, that was fair.

'Did his current partner know he was seeing you?'

'I didn't ask, but Lloyd, even when I was with him, he was never faithful. He never promised that.'

What a player. 'OK, thanks, that's helpful. Do you think he was the same in his marriage?'

'I know for a fact he was because I was one of his girlfriends when he was married to Rebecca. She's lying if she claims she didn't know about us.' She clicked the key and opened the car door.

'Should you be driving?'

'Oh, fuck off.' The car started. 'If you're looking for someone who wanted him gone,' said Ellie though the open window, 'then you should look at Rebecca. She pretends to be a straight arrow, but according to Lloyd she had her kink too.'

'Which was?'

'Pain,' said Ellie, before shutting the window and driving away.

That gave me plenty to think about as I drove to the village of Great Rollright in search of Rebecca's house. I had found out the address from Lauren, but she had not yet visited Rebecca at home because she had only fairly recently moved in. It took me a while to find the address, partly because I couldn't believe the huge property, a double-fronted eighteenth-century farmhouse, could be hers. Then I remembered she had her mother with her. Perhaps this was in fact the old family home and she had moved in to look after her parent?

I rang the bell on the gate. Even though it was the electric sort that allowed the householder to check who was at the door, the gate swung open without challenge. Rebecca must've recognised me. I crunched down the shingle path to the front door. You could hardly see this as it was guarded by two big evergreen bushes. The secretiveness of the entrance was totally at odds with the ease at which the gate had been opened. I knocked. After a little scuffling on the inside, it swung open, and I found myself looking into the childlike gaze of a little old lady. Now, I'm no giant, but Rebecca's mother had never seen five feet in her life and was rapidly shrinking, like Mrs Pepper Pot.

'Hello, is Rebecca in?' I asked, keeping well back so as not to scare her.

'Rebecca? No, no, she's at work,' said the woman, opening the door fully. She had dandelion-fluff hair and apple cheeks, quite adorable really. 'Come in, come in.'

I was more than a little alarmed that she hadn't even asked my name. Would she treat any stranger the same, even without her daughter's name as a reassurance?

'I'm Jess Bridges, a friend of Rebecca,' I said in explanation. I followed the old lady inside and into a beautiful hallway decorated with antique furniture and paintings of country scenes. A walker was the only out-of-place element but the lady seized that and started her slow way further into the house.

'I'll make you a cup of tea,' said the woman.

'Mrs Crawley—'

'Call me Ma. Everyone in the village does.'

'Oh, er, Ma, please don't put yourself out on my account.'

'It's no trouble, dear. I like company.'

We arrived at our snail's pace in the farmhouse kitchen. I could see that Rebecca had left notes all over the place for her mother. They said things like *When the bell rings, take the blue pill* – that was on an electric timer. Containers were labelled with their contents: *Your tea. You take one spoonful*. The butcher block was empty of knives – perhaps a precaution to stop her mother cutting herself while Rebecca was out. A Tupperware box sat on the table with a label: *Supper – put in microwave for 3 mins.* An egg timer stood next to it. The box hadn't been emptied.

'Do you want me to cook this while you make tea?' I asked, pointing to the container.

'Is that my supper?' She put the kettle on the Aga without filling it. I went over to lift it surreptitiously, just to check there was some water inside. Fortunately, it was heavy, so she hadn't boiled it dry today.

'I believe it is.'

'Would you be a dear? I don't like the buttons on the microwave. All these newfangled appliances drive me mad. Why I can't put it in the oven, I don't know.'

Because it was in a plastic box and she would need to tip it into an ovenproof one. I imagined Rebecca had had that conversation a number of times. I quickly dealt with the supper and then found the teapot and emptied it. It contained an almost full pot of tepid tea. Had she made it and then forgotten it? Mrs Crawley sat down at the oval kitchen table, content to let me take over.

'It's a lovely house you've got here,' I said.

'Too big,' she said. 'Very hard to heat.'

'That's true.'

'It's my daughter's.'

'Have you been here long?'

'No, not long. At least, I don't think so.' She looked confused for a moment. 'Rebecca's looking for sheltered accommodation for me but there's always a waiting list.'

'That sounds like it would be nice, not so lonely.' As well as cut down the likelihood that she'd let in a gang of thieves and invite them to tea. 'Rebecca is often out in the evenings?'

'Is she?' Mrs Crawley looked about her, then saw that it

was dark outside. 'Yes, I suppose she is. Always at work. That girl works too hard. She needs a nice man to come home to, not an old woman like me.'

The kettle whistled and I made the tea.

'Who did you say you were again, dear? She likes to know who calls round but I forget names so easily.'

'I'll write it down for you, shall I?' I looked around and found a pad of club notepaper by the phone. Taking the ballpoint pen, I wrote down my name.

Mrs Crawley peered at it. 'Nice name, Jessica. My great-aunt was called Jessica, but we all called her Jessie.'

'And people tend to call me Jess. It's one of those names destined to get shortened.'

'Rebecca never wanted to have her name shortened. She refused to answer if I called her Becky.' The old lady smiled fondly. 'She's such a good girl. Looks after me so well. I must be so much in her way.'

'I'm sure she doesn't think that for one moment.'

The lady chuckled. 'Oh, she does but she's too kind to say anything. She gets cross when things don't go her way – always has – but she's an angel with me.' Her expression clouded. 'Did I ask to see your identification? She tells me again and again to ask to see a badge before I let people in.'

'No, you didn't – and she's right.' I got out my staff pass. 'Here's my name and my picture. See, it matches what I wrote down here.' Handing the pass to her so she could take a good look, I poured the tea. The microwave pinged. 'That's your supper. One moment.'

I fetched it from the microwave and upended it on a plate. Steam rose from what looked and smelt like beef stew. After a little experimentation, I found a knife and fork in a drawer and set it before Mrs Crawley.

'Careful. It'll be hot.'

'Oh, I can't eat alone.' The lady looked quite distressed at the idea.

Taking a side plate from the drainer, I scooped a little onto it and set myself a second place. 'There, we can have dinner together. Tell me about your family, Mrs Crawley. Do you have any other children?'

We ate slowly while she regaled me with tales of her marriage. As was common with a failing memory, the past was easier to recall than the present. I got the impression her husband had been a stern man. There was another child – a son – who was in Australia (probably fleeing the father). The thought of that brought tears to her eyes.

'I've grandchildren I never see,' she said. 'I'm too old now to go all that way and Chris says he can't afford to bring them back here. I think it's that wife of his stopping him. I never liked her.'

'Rebecca was married once, wasn't she?'

'Oh, yes, to Lloyd. He was quite the charmer!' Her eyes sparkled with mischief. 'I can quite see why she fell for him. Rebecca has always been so... well, shy with men, I suppose you'd say. Never seemed to feel much for any of the boys who came calling. But Lloyd? He was different. Swept her off her feet. I think they were happy – for a while. But she said he wasn't faithful. Men like that never are. Perhaps the divorce was for the best.' She yawned. 'Gosh. What's the time?'

'Nine o'clock.'

'Past my bedtime, then.'

I took the hint and cleared the plates and cups, stacking them in the dishwasher.

'You will remember to lock the door after me?' I said, stifling my own yawn. I always found yawning catching.

'Yes, dear.'

'I'll wait until I hear the key in the lock,' I warned her. 'And don't forget to buzz me out at the gate.'

I did as promised. It took her a long time to remember to release the gate lock, but she did eventually. Rubbing my eyes – it had been a long day and a busy weekend – I got back into my car and headed for home.

Blasting myself with cold air from the car air vent, I forced myself to stay awake for the journey. If the police were relying on Mrs Crawley for an alibi, then that would be worth precisely nothing. I didn't think the old lady knew which year we were in, let alone what had happened a few days ago.

Chapter Thirty

Jess

I barely remembered how I got home, and woke next morning feeling sluggish. I also had a text telling me off for failing to plug the car back into the electricity point, making it useless for the next customer. If I did it again, I was going to be chucked out of the car club. As it was, I'd incurred a penalty charge.

Well, good morning to you, too.

I struggled through work. My colleague Jennifer noticed how I was finding the day more difficult than normal.

'I hope you're not coming down with that virus,' she said, as we stuffed envelopes together. This mindless task was about all I could manage.

Rumours were spreading about this illness but I was banking on it all being just hype in the media. We'd all been scared stiff of swine flu and I didn't even remember which year that had been now. 'I don't know anyone just back from Italy – or China. Do you think it's serious, this virus thing?'

'Hard to say, isn't it?' Jennifer cleaned her glasses and re-seated them on her nose. 'If it comes here, I can't see us shutting down like Wuhan, can you?'

'Do you think it will come to that? No way would the British public be so obedient. You saw our Olympic opening ceremony compared to Beijing – that about sums us up as nations.'

'Sorry?' I often left Jennifer behind with my allusions.

'You know, lockstep dancing and perfectly choreographed crowds, versus the Queen skydiving with James Bond and kids bouncing on hospital beds. We just wouldn't shut down like they have – too many ragged edges to us. God, I hope we don't have to.' I couldn't think of much worse than having to stay indoors. I'm a restless soul.

'The events of the last few years have taught me that anything is possible,' Jennifer said, cheerfully. 'Especially the worst-case scenario. Brexit. Trump. Boris. I'll be stocking up, just in case.' She was a Labour Party supporter. The last few years had been a vast disappointment.

'Then I know who to come to for loo roll when I run out. I suck at forward planning.' I tapped the envelopes into a neat pile. They were invitations to the summer events. 'I mean, it'll be sorted out before the May ball surely?'

'You'd think.' With that cryptic remark, Jennifer carried the mail to the post room.

I felt better by the afternoon so decided the mystery

virus was not circulating around my system. I messaged Leo but didn't get a reply. In fact, now I looked, he'd not responded to the last four messages. I knew I messaged a lot, and I didn't expect him to answer every one, but I did hope to get some kind of response in a twenty-four hour period. And, my brain added helpfully, his old flame Janice was in his spare bedroom holding Rainbow's hand. At least, I hoped she was in the spare bedroom and not his bed.

I wished I hadn't thought that. Thoughts of disloyal Lloyd had soured me. And disloyal Lauren. The Durham friends seemed horribly prone to two-timing each other.

My last message was to say that I was going to call round after work and update everyone on my progress. I'd managed to eliminate Ellie Fanshawe to my satisfaction, deciding her grief was real and the timing of when she heard genuine. I also wanted to ask the others about Rebecca's house. It was a very large property in this area of millionaires. Did she come from money?

While I was putting on my cycling gear and considering all this, Rebecca herself rang me.

'Jess?'

'Oh, hi, Rebecca. You got my note?'

'Note? I saw your name written on a pad at home but Mum couldn't explain it. That's why I'm calling.'

'Oh, I should've realised. Sorry. I popped in as I was in the area, to see how you were doing, but obviously you weren't there.'

'I was working.'

'So your mum said. A lovely lady.'

'Did she ask who you were before she let you in?' Her voice rose a little.

'No, and that worried me, I have to admit. Maybe you should get one of those remote bells where you can see the visitor?' I suggested.

'I think I'll have to.'

'Anyway, we had a nice cup of tea together and had some supper. Good beef stew, by the way.'

'You ate the stew. Oh, God.' I could hear the distress in her tone.

'What's wrong? Only a little – your mum had most of it.'

'It's not that. It's the only way I can get her to take her medication. She's up all night, otherwise.'

'So that's why I've been propping up my eyelids with matchsticks all day. I'm *so* sorry.'

'I'm just relieved you didn't crash your car.'

'How is your mum today?'

'She's fine. Pottering around the house making me tea every five minutes. Well, half making.'

'It's not my place, but do you think you should get in a carer?'

'I'm looking for a home,' Rebecca said, defences up. 'We like the one in the village but there's no room at the moment. I want her close by.'

'I meant as a stop-gap. Sorry. It's none of my business.'

'No, it's not.'

'Well, best wishes to your mum. I enjoyed meeting her. You have a lovely house.' I left that hanging, hoping she would say something more about it but, instead, all I got was: 'I've a call on the other line. I've got to go. Goodbye.'

'Bye.' But she'd already ended the call.

I put the phone in my pocket and considered. Rebecca? The ex-wife, connected to both victims, flimsy alibi – definitely worth a closer look. But why do it? That was the part I couldn't work out.

Chapter Thirty-One

Leo

Leo knew he was heading for a storm when he saw DI Edmonds waiting outside Superintendent Thaxted's office.

'Kesha,' Leo said, nodding to her.

'Leo. I don't appreciate you shoehorning yourself into my investigations.' The accusation rattled out. Kesha was wearing a silver-grey trouser suit today that made Leo think of a machete. She clearly intended to slice and dice him.

'That's not what I'm doing. I'm just following the evidence.'

She folded her arms. 'Really? So that's why your girlfriend got Williams's last customer to send the packaging from a recent consignment to me, is it?'

'I'm sorry, what are you talking about?'

She spoke slowly, as if to a dim pupil: 'Rainbow Williams contacted the person to whom she had sent a decorated vase and asked them to return the box in which it had been posted.'

'Because…?'

'She claimed it would match the last strip of duct tape from the roll we have in evidence.'

What a brilliant idea. Leo mentally applauded Jess. 'And have you?'

'Have I what?'

'Matched the duct tape?'

'It's at the lab now – and, yes, the technicians have. But, so what? Even if the tears on the tape do match the last one taken from the roll in the motorhome, what does that prove? She could've had another roll somewhere and thrown it away to cover her tracks.'

Some of the tension that had felt like a squeeze on the back of his neck eased. 'It proves quite a lot though, doesn't it? At the very least, it means that her lawyer will argue that the physical evidence you have of fingerprints on the roll of duct tape are meaningless. We just have evidence she used it to package up something recently. Were there fingerprints on the tape on the vents?'

'No, they were wiped.'

'But the killer forgot to do the same to the leftover roll? Doesn't that make you wonder, Kesha?'

'Why are you so desperate to see Williams cleared? She was the last person to see him alive, for God's sake! She had the motive – and the means.' She squared up to him, leaning in as Jess would say.

'No, the last person to see him alive was the killer. I have to wonder why you're so desperate to see her convicted?

You charged off after the obvious suspect and didn't do your job properly. You must realise you've not got enough – you'll have to drop the charges sooner or later. Sooner, surely, is better?'

The door opened and the superintendent stood in the entrance.

'I thought I heard voices. I do not appreciate my senior officers arguing about sensitive matters pertaining to active and ongoing cases out in the hallway.'

She was right. Leo had let his temper get the better of him.

'I apologise,' he said. His phone buzzed in his trouser pocket but he ignored it. It was likely to be Jess. He owed her several responses.

'I'm sorry, ma'am,' said Kesha. 'It won't happen again.'

'Come in, both of you.' Claire gestured to them to take seats opposite her. 'Right, the Porter and Rumbold cases. DI Edmonds, have you reviewed the material Leo's team has shared – the link to the porn industry, the human-trafficking angle, the involvement of the Birbeck brothers?'

'I have, ma'am.'

'And what do you make of it?' Claire pushed back from her desk. She looked relaxed but Leo guessed she was far from it. She was juggling sticks of dynamite.

'I find the links interesting – there's clearly a good case evolving around Inspector George's victim concerning the finances of the club and the individuals involved in trafficking. However, the connections to my victim are old. Rumbold left the investment firm in 2018. He did not appear to find his role as a male escort problematic and seems to have participated in that film willingly. His bank accounts show that he was in the red but his position was improving thanks to low-cost living, courtesy of Williams's motorhome and her income as an artist. In short, he was living off her and cheating on her at the same time. There are no records of any renewed contacts with the Birbecks or their employees. So my question to Inspector George is why would anyone kill Rumbold now? If they are running an operation that thrives in the shadows, what did that achieve but to bring a public light to bear on their activities?'

Claire shifted so her attention was now on Leo. 'Do you have an answer, Leo?'

Thanks to the house in Reading, he did. 'I think the motives behind both murders can be summed up as money and secrets. From what the women at the refuge said, Kelly Ann was close to exposing this operation. That meant she had to die. I believe Lloyd was killed because he also knew too much, but being familiar with the way he thought, I doubt very much he was going to bring it to the authorities. I believe he would've sought financial gain and, pursuing this, he may have approached the wrong person and asked to be paid to keep silent.' He decided to hold back on Suyin's theory that Lloyd could've been the killer of Kelly Ann.

'That's all very well, but how would Rumbold know what was going on?' asked Kesha. 'He had been out in the cold for a couple of years, no longer part of the Birbeck empire.'

'Not exactly,' corrected Leo, 'he'd been roped back in via the sex work.'

'That's an unfortunate pun, seeing the content of some of those films,' said the superintendent, sardonically.

'What I mean is that he was seeing the underbelly of the operation. He had become close to Marta Kanon – was in all likelihood her lover – and certainly an actor for her.'

'I can't see Marta Kanon indulging in pillow talk,' said Claire.

'No, but what about the woman in the film? We think we've identified her as one of the trafficked Vietnamese asylum seekers – not one of the ones I met yesterday but I'm hoping they will give us her name. I've officers at the house this morning going through photographs with them. In the intimate conditions of filming, hours spent together, I think Lloyd heard enough to work out where his co-star came from, and pieced together what the Kanons and the Stanton-Milbecks were doing. If he suspected it reached the club, this presented him with a way of getting back at the men who had fired him. He would've relished the power.'

'If he tried blackmail,' said Claire, 'who would he approach?'

'My chief suspect would be Marta Kanon, as she was the person in the group that he knew best. The Kanons's car was caught on CCTV both Friday and Saturday night passing through Chipping Norton so we know they were out. They live close enough to Kelly Ann to have walked there. Their alibi on Friday night is that they were having dinner with the legal adviser at the club, Jamie Paxton, but it's not a complete one, and I imagine he has an interest in covering for them. Did you get any witnesses coming forward in response to your appeals on local roads?' he asked Kesha.

'I haven't yet been ordered to share my information with you,' said Kesha. 'You have a conflict of interest and I do not wish to jeopardise my investigation. Superintendent?'

'Answer Leo's question, please.' Claire leant on the desk, arms folded.

'There are no reports of vehicles parked in the lay-by. A late-night visitor – an amateur astronomer who went to observe the stars – said that he had been annoyed by the presence of the camper van. This had been parked close to the Rollright Stones. Lights were on inside which ruined his night vision so he went across the road to the King's Stone instead.'

'That means he would've walked past a car in the lay-by,' commented Claire.

'Only his own was parked at the time. When he finished his observations, he noticed that the lights in the motorhome were off.'

'Does he have a time for this?'

'Yes. He arrived at 11.13 and left at 11.56. He was able to be very precise because he was recording data.'

'The lights were off when we found the body,' said Leo.

'I had made that connection,' Kesha said stiffly.

Leo was trying very hard not to make this personal but she acted like he was out to sabotage her. 'This might indicate that there was someone with him who left during that period of forty or so minutes.'

'Forty-one minutes – and it doesn't need to mean that at

all. It might simply mean he'd turned them off because he was settling in for the night after watching the match.'

'The match would've long been over at that time.' Leo addressed his boss. 'Rainbow Williams doesn't have a car and she was with people all evening – certainly without a gap long enough to get from the club on foot and back again at that time of night. Not only do her friends remember her being there but she is also on the club CCTV.'

'Been doing my job for me, have you Leo?' said Kesha. 'Superintendent, this isn't something I should have to put up with. Inspector George is out of line. My case is not that Williams left the club, but that she set things up before she went there, making sure she was alibied by a number of friends all evening. This has no bearing on the charges we've brought.'

'But the duct tape does,' said Leo. 'You've updated the superintendent about that?'

Claire held up her hand. 'Leo, Kesha, enough. Kesha, Leo is correct in saying that there are enough threads that bring these two deaths together to justify them being under one investigatory team.'

Kesha stood up. 'In that case, ma'am, in light of Leo's personal involvement in this, I request that my team take over leading this investigation. Otherwise, we are in danger of prejudicing the case and opening ourselves to legal challenge.'

Claire ignored the formality of Kesha's stance, deflecting her attention to a file that was on the desk in front of her. 'I've read the report on the duct tape. You have to know your best piece of physical evidence is now null and void.

You only have supposition that there was a second roll that the accused removed. But the fingerprints were the linchpin in the decision to charge her. The CPS are going to drop the charge.'

'But, ma'am—'

'A probability that someone is guilty, circumstantial evidence, and plenty of provocation, aren't enough. Rumbold takes no prizes as a partner, I think we can all agree on that, but I haven't seen a shred of evidence that convinces me his girlfriend took the risky option of setting up a suicide that would be triggered hours later. And you haven't accounted for how the drugs got in his system.'

Kesha began to speak but Claire cut her off.

'You'll say it could've been put much earlier in the whisky bottle, but again that is very tendentious. He might've had a beer instead – or not drunk anything at all. No, it isn't enough. Rainbow Williams is no longer our prime suspect.'

There were times when Leo was grateful that Claire had been a detective. She saw through the holes in a case in a way that many officers resented, but he personally welcomed. Especially today.

'That removes the conflict. Leo's knowledge of the many characters in these two cases, the work he's done so far, makes the decision for me. I'm putting him in charge and I'm ordering you to send over everything you've gathered to date. Am I understood, Inspector Edmonds?'

'Yes, ma'am.'

'If you prefer to move to another investigation and let

your sergeant join Leo's team for continuity, then I'm sure we all would understand.'

'No, I'm happy to join the team.'

Leo wished she wouldn't. DS Connaught was a much easier person to get on with. 'I appreciate all the help you can give me, Kesha,' he said politely.

'This is a big case if it goes as far as we believe. Plenty of work for everyone,' said Claire, bracingly. 'I'll be keeping a very close eye on what steps you take. I don't want any action against the Birbecks without my explicit permission. I don't think you'll be surprised to hear that the chief constable himself will be giving final sign-off.'

Just what they needed: more layers of command.

'Yes, Superintendent,' said Leo.

'Right.' She rubbed her hands together. 'How are we going to nail these bastards?'

Chapter Thirty-Two

Leo

After a coordination meeting with his new team, Leo headed back into the field. The Banbury team were continuing to follow up the leads from passing motorists on Lloyd's case, as well as getting themselves up to speed on the connections to the club. Harry was walking them through what the Oxford team had found so far, a process that Leo did not anticipate either Harry or DI Edmonds would enjoy. Their only common ground was dislike of him.

Asking Suyin to drive, Leo took the chance to check his personal messages. Five from Jess. He couldn't deal with them now. She said something about going around to his place later so he sent a thumbs-up and moved on. He knew this was shoddy treatment but he had only so much mental and emotional energy. He then came across an email from his mother.

Well, he had invited it, hadn't he?

Leo,

That money was sent for your upkeep and was spent on you. Where do you think your clothes and food came from, as I couldn't work while I was looking after you?

That was a laughable rewriting of history. She'd worked until she stopped getting parts, leaving him with a succession of unreliable carers and very often on his own long before an age when he could be expected to cope. Did she expect him to have forgotten?

George didn't lift a finger to help us out.

Her casual use of the name 'George' also bore out that she knew full well who had been in contact. Her years of snowing him that she didn't remember who his father was melted away so easily. She didn't even acknowledge their passing.

As so often in the last few days, it was hard to concentrate because of the rage he was feeling.

In fact, I spent far more on you than he ever sent me, so he owes me. I will be in touch – you tell him that!

Now that was interesting. An experienced brawler, his mother had started swinging before George Saito could come after her. Should he just step back and let his parents go at each other like a sober patron moving out of the way of a drunken bar fight? There was some pleasure in that prospect.

I don't know what lies that man is telling you but I think it's best that we discuss this in person. I'll be over this weekend.

Mum x

Oh, no, she wouldn't. And he really didn't want that kiss.

He tapped out a reply.

I'm working all weekend. I have a houseful of people you really don't want to meet filling up all available space and I will instruct them not to let you in. Anything you want to say to me can be put in a message.

Leo

He could imagine her wails of 'but I'm your mother!' – her go-to complaint when he did anything that she felt slighted her. It was therefore quite a surprise when her immediate response was rather more measured.

Please send me your new phone number.

It was satisfying to reply:

I haven't changed my number.

He hadn't blocked her – though he'd been tempted. He'd just ignored her calls and now only communicated through email. Let her infer what she liked from that. He put his phone away.

'Everything all right, sir?' asked Suyin, doubtless aware of his angry messaging as he was sitting beside her.

'Just a minor family crisis,' he said. 'Where are we starting?'

'I got a call from the local officers moments before we left. A resident of the almshouses has just got back home. She's been in hospital for a hip replacement since early Saturday which is why she was missed on the first round. They followed up as soon as she got back and she has something to tell us that we'll want to hear.'

'Excellent. About time, too.' The lack of witnesses in a busy market town, albeit it on a side road, had been frustrating.

Parking close to the little row of cottages, Leo and Suyin joined Sergeant Wilmot outside the one at the far end. It seemed too small – almost doll's house-sized – to accommodate all three of them, but they were invited in by a carer to join Enid Pemberton in her front room. Painted sage green, the light through the mullioned window was dappled, a little like being under the sea. An elderly lady was sitting up in a hospital-style bed that had been installed for her recovery. Knitting rested on her lap and she was wearing a handmade bed jacket, pink with scalloped edges – something Leo didn't think he'd ever seen before outside of a period drama. Little gold specs rested on her nose. Leo had a fleeting image of Little Red Riding Hood's granny from a childhood book; he hoped that didn't make them the wolves.

'Mrs Pemberton, thank you for agreeing to speak to us,' Leo said after introductions had been made.

'Sit down, officers, sit down. I apologise there's not much space. We had to clear out all my good chairs to make room for this.' She tapped the bed guard. 'Can't manage the stairs for a while.'

'I hope the operation went well?' asked Suyin, moving a pile of craft magazines from an upright chair.

'Yes, thank you, young lady. Praise God for the NHS. I'll be running laps with Mo Farah soon – or maybe that centenarian Sikh. Did you see him? Mr Singh in his splendid turmeric-coloured turban?'

'I did. Well over a hundred now, isn't he?' said Leo. Whatever else was wrong with this lady's body, her memory was as sharp as a tack.

'Nice to have someone in the news who makes me feel young. How can I help you?' She cocked her head, alert like a garden bird watching the gardener dig.

'Mrs Pemberton, I think Sergeant Wilmot here explained why we wanted to talk to you,' said Leo.

'Yes. It's about poor Kelly Ann, isn't it? She was such a lovely girl. She brought me eggs every Sunday if her hens had been laying. I do like a fresh egg for breakfast now and then.'

'You were here Friday night?'

'I was. I had to be nil by mouth before my operation so I didn't go out to my book club like I was supposed to, but the space on the surgeon's list came up unexpectedly.

Probably some other old dear popped their clogs.' She reached for her water. Leo leaped up to bring it nearer. 'Thank you, Inspector. I knew I wouldn't have the willpower to refuse a glass of wine. Raoul and Matilda can be so gung-ho about such things. You can't talk about books without wine, don't you find?'

'So my partner says. I don't belong to a book club,' said Leo, once again reminded that he really had to grovel to Jess – and soon. It was no good feeling apologetic if she had no idea that he regretted brushing off her views so coolly.

'Well, you should. It's very good for the brain cells. We were discussing *Maxwell's Demon*. I had to join in on Skype.'

'I'm always on the lookout for a good read. Is that a ghost story?' asked Suyin. 'It sounds like Stephen King.'

'Good gracious, dear, no! James Clerk Maxwell? Only Physics' most brilliant mind – and I mean that with no disrespect to Einstein. He would agree with me.'

'Mrs Pemberton – or Professor Pemberton, I should say – is a retired Professor of Physics from Oxford University,' murmured Sergeant Wilmot, enjoying Suyin's consternation that she might've been caught patronising the lady because she looked like a nana from the back of a cereal packet. 'She's well known in Chippie, famous for her scientific knitting.'

The lady held up her needles. 'Oxygen today – I'm knitting atoms for my display at the school science fair.'

Leo recalibrated his approach. He too had been guilty of making assumptions as to the lady's IQ, which was clearly much higher than his.

'Professor Pemberton, can you tell us what you saw on Friday night – and where you saw it from?'

She nodded, as if he were a passably intelligent pupil asking the right question in the seminar. 'Yes.' From the pause that followed, she was clearly waiting for something so he got out his notebook. That was the right move. 'I was in this room by the window. It was just after six-thirty because the Radio 4 news had finished and I turned off the comedy programme. Kelly Ann arrived home. She had someone with her. I waved but she didn't see me.'

All the officers went on the alert at the new information. This was the first mention of a second person coming home with her.

'Can you give a description of the other person?' asked Leo.

'I apologise that my eyesight is not what it was and it was getting dark. I can tell you that I am certain it was a woman of around the same height as Kelly Ann. She was wearing a dark winter coat with her hood up so it was hard to make out more details. Work shoes with a heel, not flat – another reason to think it was a woman.'

'How did she seem to get on with Kelly Ann?'

'I'd say they were friendly.' She thought a moment. 'Yes, friendly, solicitous. She was the one driving.'

'She drove Kelly Ann's car?'

'Correct. She parked, helped Kelly Ann out and gave her a basket to hold while she dealt with the keys.'

Another detail that confirmed this was a Friday-night sighting. 'Can you describe the basket?'

'Yes. It was eye-catching. A gift hamper wrapped in

cellophane, though the wrapping was undone and fluttered about in the breeze.'

'And did you see the contents?'

'No, Inspector George. Just some colourful boxes.'

'Any idea why the other woman might have been driving?'

'I assumed Kelly Ann felt she was over the limit. She did look a little tipsy – and she was holding a bottle that she kept upright. There was torn foil at the top –it caught the light. It looked like she'd been celebrating something with a bottle of bubbly and I thought "good for her".' The lady's voice quavered a little. 'I regret not going out to see if she was all right. However, I did wonder if it was a Valentine's gift and speculated that Kelly Ann had a new lady-friend – not that Kelly Ann ever mentioned that she was gay.' She waved that away, impatient that she was getting off topic. 'Anyway, I felt bad about what might've been seen as spying if it were a date so I did nothing.'

That wasn't a line of enquiry they'd yet considered, having taken Elizabeth Benfield at her word that the two friends were looking for male partners. And Valentine's Day had just passed. Leo tried to imagine the scene. 'So Kelly Ann was juggling two things – the basket and bottle?'

'Yes. She was giggling because it was quite a handful.'

'And the other woman?'

'She was angled with her back to me but she steered Kelly Ann to the front door.'

'Then what happened?'

'The stranger opened the door and stood back, gesturing to Kelly Ann to go first. It was all so fleeting I didn't have much time to form an opinion. It's very frustrating I didn't see the stranger's face.'

'Please, go on.'

'There's not much left to say. The front door closed. More lights went on, upstairs and downstairs.'

'Including the bathroom at the front?'

'I didn't see that go on, but there was a little glow up there later when I next looked. I took it to be candlelight. It's distinctive.'

'Did you see the woman leave?'

'Yes, at about the time of *The Archers*. I turned the radio back on for that and noticed her go.' The radio sat on the window ledge within reach of the bed which explained why she had been at the window at those times.

'Just after seven,' Leo clarified for Suyin. 'Which way did she go?'

'Well, that's hard to say. She didn't appear to be in a hurry. I saw her head towards the church but I'd describe it as unhurried, flapping along in that black coat of hers. She would've scared a few feebleminded people in the churchyard if they caught sight of her. I suppose she might have got back to the main roads on one of the footpaths down there.'

'Did she come back, to your knowledge?'

'I'm sorry, Inspector, but I don't know. It was fully dark by then and I drew the curtains. That's when I noticed the candlelight upstairs. I then went onto the computer, talking to my friends in book club. I didn't look outside again.'

'Understood. Thank you. You've been very helpful.'

She fretted with the blue yarn with which she was

making oxygen. 'My neighbours here all say that you think Kelly Ann was murdered. Is that right or are they getting the wrong end of the stick? That's not hard for most of them.'

'They are correct. It's possible the person you saw was responsible.'

'People are such terrible beings under a thin veneer of civility.'

She wouldn't find many police officers who would argue. 'I'd be grateful if you would sign a statement about what you've just told us.'

She pulled the blanket up to her chest. 'Anything to help Kelly Ann.'

'It would also be helpful if you don't share what you've told us with anyone else.' Leo didn't want the killer to get wind of the fact that there was an eye-witness. They might take it into their head to arrange another accidental death.

She looked over the top of her glasses at him. 'I'm not one to gossip, young man.'

'No, I don't suppose you are.' Leo stood up to leave. 'Thank you for your time, Professor Pemberton.'

Back in the front garden of the almshouses, Leo took Wilmot aside and had words about arranging a close eye to be kept on the frighteningly bright Professor Pemberton. They were already keeping the victim's house under surveillance so that would be no trouble for the local beat officers.

In the car once more, Suyin pulled away from the curb. 'Well, I certainly felt like the dunce of the class.'

'It's a hazard of working in Oxfordshire, meeting

witnesses whose brains far outstrip yours. Which makes me think she wouldn't be wrong about a scintilla of her evidence. We are looking for a woman.'

Suyin grimaced. 'Bang goes my theory about Lloyd coming round for sex.' They drove towards the Rollright Stones. 'Marta Kanon? She's got that gap when she supposedly was taking her daughter into Oxford and before dinner – that leaves plenty of time unaccounted for. The daughter was dropped off at five-thirty.'

'But Kelly Ann didn't like her. Marta made no bones about the fact that she didn't like Kelly Ann. It's hard to imagine them hanging out together on a Friday night.'

His sergeant wrinkled her brow in thought. 'Unless… unless Kelly Ann wanted to get closer to Marta to gather evidence to bring down the trafficking ring? She could've taken the money, pretended she was compromised like them, and claimed she'd got over her qualms, all to position herself to get more information?'

He appreciated the way his sergeant thought; she was good at generating new angles. 'Go on. What about Marta's attitude?'

'When you talked to her, Marta would obviously claim not to like her, or even know her, if she killed her. She could have suspected Kelly Ann's motives and held up her part of the fake friendship - until she was ready to strike.'

That did fit the facts but Kelly Ann's diary had not contained any suggestion that this was the strategy she was following. Leo had been working on the supposition that the evidence she'd been amassing was documentary, gathered at work. That seemed something an accountant might do, rather than trying to embed herself in a hostile organisation – that seemed too high stakes. 'I suppose one thing in favour of that theory is that Marta could easily have walked home from here. But we've no evidence they were both playing this dangerous game with each other.'

'But we do have evidence now that Kelly Ann came home impaired and with someone who was able to walk in when she was invited.'

'The drugs found in her blood were probably already lowering her inhibitions. If someone suggested she take her usual bath while they let themselves out, she might well not have questioned it. All they had to do was wait for the tranquilliser to work and they could do the rest.'

'The drinking must've started elsewhere. At work?'

'We'll have to re-interview the staff and ask if anyone saw her with a woman fitting Professor Pemberton's description that afternoon. A large dark coat. Same height.'

'How tall is Marta Kanon?'

He remembered her best in her peacock chair but she had stood up briefly as she left for her studio.

'About your height.'

'And I'm about the same as Kelly Ann.'

'Let's find out what winter coat Marta's wearing this season,' said Leo. 'Not that she will volunteer this if she felt it would incriminate her.'

'Or she'll show you one of her ten other coats. She should be on club CCTV if she's a regular.'

'Including for the dinner on that Friday night. OK, let's go back there and see if we can catch her on film.'

Chapter Thirty-Three

Jess

I was a little later than I intended reaching Leo's because my bike had developed a puncture halfway down the Iffley Road and I had to wheel it the rest of the way. Despite this, I still beat Leo home. Lauren and Freddie had returned to their children at lunchtime, but Janice and Phil had stayed to keep Rainbow company. I was less happy, though, to see Rebecca had also driven over and was in the process of loading the boot of her car. Before I could ask what was going on, Rainbow hurried over to me.

'Jess! Oh, bad luck,' Rainbow said, noticing the very flat back tyre. 'The rear ones are always a pig to change.'

'Tell me about it.' I stacked the bike against the fence. 'How are you doing, Rainbow?'

'I'm good.' And she looked it, standing straighter and without the crushed-petal air of the last few days. 'Very good, in fact. My lawyer rang me to say they were dropping the charges.' She was smiling, though her eyes were brimming. She dashed a wrist across her face. 'Sorry. I'm up one minute and down another. I just feel so relieved.'

'That's great.'

'I messaged you as soon as I heard.'

That would probably be in the bunch of recent notifications I hadn't looked at because my hands were covered in oil from the bike chain. 'What happened?'

'It's all down to you. The duct tape saved the day.'

I mentally patted myself on the back. 'I'm so pleased it hadn't gone out to recycling.'

She put her hands to her cheeks. 'I know. So odd to think my freedom hung on so little a thing. Thank you, Jess.' Uncaring of the oil, she hugged me. 'Thank you.'

Phil and Janice emerged from the house, Janice with a bouquet of flowers and Phil another suitcase. He winked at me but I pretended not to see.

'What's going on?' I asked.

'I can't impose on poor Leo any longer,' said Rainbow. 'We decided this before I got the news but I still think it's for the best. He's a policeman and, even with the charges dropped, I'm still part of the case as a witness.'

'Decided what?' I realised the belongings being packed were Rainbow's eclectic selection of canvas holdalls and battered suitcase.

'Rainbow's coming to live with me for the foreseeable future,' said Rebecca.

'She is?' No, this was a terrible idea. I'd just begun to suspect Rebecca wasn't all she seemed and now we were sending Rainbow into her clutches?

'It's so kind of her, isn't it?' said Rainbow. 'And she said it was your idea.'

'My idea?'

'Not directly,' said Rebecca with a little laugh. 'I was just thinking about what you said about my mother needing a carer until I can get something more permanent sorted out for her. Then I thought of Rainbow being homeless for the moment and it just clicked. There's plenty of space at mine – loads of room for a studio so Rainbow can work. Mum doesn't need constant supervision, but someone to check on her every so often. Rainbow will be perfect. Everyone's a winner.'

Rainbow sniffed. 'It's really helped me out of a bind. I didn't know how I was going to afford to rent somewhere. All my money is tied up in the van, and I never want to see it again.' The last was tearful.

Rebecca put an arm around her. 'You won't have to. Once this nightmare is over, it can be sold and you can start again. I'll be in no hurry to get rid of you.'

Why were tingles running down my spine on that statement? Because I felt the exact opposite might be the case. Not immediately, but give her a few days…

'But I'm sure Leo would be delighted for Rainbow to stay here,' I said, in a last-ditch attempt to stop this plan going ahead.

'No, he isn't,' said Rainbow. 'I know him well enough to understand that, even if it weren't for this case, he'd be uncomfortable sharing his space with anyone. He's an introvert through and through.'

That certainly put a different light on my hopes I could one day share a home with him.

'I really don't think this is the best solution,' I tried.

'Jess, sorry, but you're a newcomer among us. I think we really do know each other best,' said Rebecca. 'Rainbow and I get on well. We understand what we've both lost better than anyone else can. It will be healing to do our grieving together.'

'Healing,' echoed Rainbow. 'I've left a message for Leo but tell him thanks when he gets home.'

'We'd better run. Mum is waiting for her supper.' Rebecca got in, but not before her eyes met mine with a look that was lethal. Her guard had slipped fractionally and she knew it. She turned her smile up a notch, acting as if nothing had happened. 'Bye, everyone.'

'Careful what you eat – Rebecca drugged me,' I said as a joke that wasn't a joke. How was I going to get her out of this?

'Only because you ate Mum's food,' said Rebecca with a spiky little laugh.

'Come and see me when you can,' called Rainbow, making the comment general.

'I'll be over soon,' promised Janice.

Phil raised a hand, not promising anything. I had the impression he was relieved that it looked like the immediate aftermath of the death was passing and normal life could resume.

Janice waited for the car to drive out of sight before turning back to the house.

'Are you still planning to come in?' she asked me, making it plain I wasn't welcome.

'Yes. I'll wait for Leo.' I had to get him to see what I saw in Rebecca, otherwise I'd just sound crazy. I couldn't say an exchanged look was proof. 'What about you? Are you and Phil heading off now?' *Please, please be heading off.*

She walked straight through to the kitchen where she rummaged in the fridge to find some bread, cold meat and cheese and set them out on the table. 'I thought I'd hang around in the area for a few more days, keep Leo company.'

I really wanted to say that he didn't want or need her company, Rainbow had just told us all as much, but that would sound petty.

But I felt petty.

'What about you, Phil?' I asked instead, thinking I could possibly bear it if he was present, dampening the chances for romantic feelings to reignite.

'Nah. Not throwing more money away at that hotel when I've got a perfectly good bed back home.' He gave me a look that made clear the bed was available to share if I should so wish.

'That's a shame,' I managed.

'I knew you'd come round to liking me.' He risked a little rub of my neck when Janice's back was turned.

I was just about to tell him to step away, when we heard Leo's keys in the front door. I'd positioned myself badly – Janice was closer to the hallway so was first to greet him.

'Leo darling, you're back. You've just missed Rainbow. Rebecca whisked her away to her house. Here, let me take your bag.' Janice came back into the kitchen bearing the messenger bag in triumph. Phil squeezed my shoulders. That could've been sympathy or a 'don't forget what I'm offering' consolation prize.

Leo followed her, looking shattered. This case was demanding a lot from him and I felt a twinge of concern until I remembered I was pissed at him. 'Oh, hi,' he said. 'Phil, you're still here, too?' Hardly the most ecstatic of welcomes from my lover.

'Yeah, but I'll be going shortly,' said Phil. He still hadn't moved from behind me. I wriggled my shoulders away. 'Jess came up with the idea of Rainbow being a carer for Rebecca's mum, solving both their problems.'

'I think it's a terrible idea,' I said. Should I just blurt out my suspicions? Considering how Leo had reacted last time I mentioned theories involving people he knew, I had to wait until I could get Leo on his own and really listen to me.

Janice poured him a beer from his own stock in the fridge. 'Here: you look like you've earned it.'

'Thanks.' Leo sat down without coming round to kiss me. 'What a day.'

'Can we talk?' I murmured.

He was about to reply when Janice piped up:

'They dropped the charges on Rainbow, did you hear?' Janice pushed the bread and cold cuts nearer to him.

'Yes, I knew that was in the works.' He made himself a sandwich. He looked up and caught my gaze. 'Sorry. Didn't get time for lunch. I'm starving. Do you want some?'

'No, you go right ahead.' He'd totally failed to understand my look had everything to do with him not protesting Janice's takeover of his kitchen and nothing to do with not sharing.

'This is great. Just what I needed. Thanks, Janice.' He was eating his own food, for heaven's sake!

'You didn't think to tell me about the charges?' I asked instead. 'I was still working on it for Rainbow.'

'I couldn't. Professional conflict. I knew you'd hear from the solicitor.'

'No, she told Rainbow. I only just got the news.'

'Right, OK, then sorry.' He didn't sound it, not around the mouthfuls of bread.

'At least Rainbow's somewhere safe,' said Janice, brightly. 'How about I call for a takeaway for us? Then we can get an early night. I'm exhausted, too. I think it's all the emotions we've been going through. What a roller coaster!'

'You're staying?' asked Leo.

'Well, I don't have anywhere else to go at the moment. I'm due to start house-hunting in London, remember, but put it off.' Leo's gaze flicked to Phil but neither took the hint. 'And I'd like to stay close by,' she continued, digging in, 'just in case Rainbow needs me again. So what do you feel like? Chinese? Indian?'

'Jess?' *Now* he remembered me. Me the girlfriend and partner he'd begged to look into the case.

'I don't want a takeaway,' I said sullenly. 'I'll—'

'Then I'll run you home,' said Phil, stepping in too soon before I could volunteer to cook something. 'I can chuck your bike in the back of the car. I could even fix it for you, if you have a puncture kit.'

That was seriously helpful. Annoyed by Janice's

manoeuvrings as I was, I wasn't going to pass up the chance to get the tyre sorted. I didn't have the energy for the kind of territorial battle I imagined she was thinking of staging. 'I think my flatmate does.'

'I've got a kit somewhere,' said Leo, half getting up.

'Stay where you are, Leo. Phil's great at these things. Let him have his moment to shine,' said Janice. 'Ah, I've found a restaurant that has good reviews and they're running an offer on meals for two. Let me just order it. What do you feel about spice?'

'I like things spicy,' he said – dumb-ass.

'That's good as so do I.' She gave a little shimmy and went to her bedroom to fetch her credit card.

'What was that?' I asked. 'I like things spicy?' I mimicked his tenor voice. 'Jeez, why don't you just leave the bedroom door open and throw back the duvet while you're at it?'

Phil moved back, hands up. 'I can see you two need a moment. I'll be putting your bike in the car, Jess.'

As soon as Phil left, Leo shook his head. 'Please, Jess, not now.'

'Leo, your ex-girlfriend has just taken over your house and as well as what you bloody well eat right in front of me, your current girlfriend: doesn't that strike you as a tad wrong?' Sarcasm wasn't clever but it was satisfying.

'I get why you're upset—'

'Do you really? I've been working two jobs the last few days, my usual and trying to clear up your friend's mess. You've been singularly unhelpful even though you asked me to do so. Then when she no longer needs my services, no one even bothers to tell me!' I ran my fingers through my hair, annoyed that this wasn't even what was really upsetting me. 'Look, I'm not happy Rainbow has gone with Rebecca. Things just don't add up around her – Rebecca, I mean. Why is she living in that great big house that must cost a million at least? It's hers, not her parents'. I checked. Her mother is worse than useless as an alibi. She doesn't know what day it is – completely away with the dementia fairies.'

Leo pressed his temples with his fingers. 'First it was Rainbow, then Freddie, then Lauren. Now you've decided Rebecca is the one. Are there any of my friends you don't want to accuse? That might make for a shorter list.'

'Excuse me? It might've escaped your attention but one of those so-called friends ended up dead. I have every right to question the motives of everyone who was involved with him – that means your friends. Rebecca was his ex-wife. She links to your case, too.'

'But we've developments to the Chipping Norton death that I can't share with you. I can tell you we're not leaning Rebecca's way. We've another suspect who links both cases.'

'Can't share with me? Oh, you've changed your tune quickly!'

'I have to tread very carefully. DI Edmonds has been put under my command and I have to watch everything I do. She's breathing down my neck, waiting for a mistake.'

'Which means you just dump me as an investigative aide? But I was the one who got the charges dropped on Rainbow!'

'I know – and I thank you for that. We all do. You have more than earned whatever we can pay you.'

'Pay me? You really think I'd take money for this?'

'But you said…?' He looked flummoxed.

'I only asked to be engaged through my business to give me official standing when I approached people. I didn't want money to help someone close to you. I don't want to profit from other people's misery.'

'I apologise. I misunderstood.'

'What a pile of crap, Leo! I thought you knew me better than that?'

'I did – I do. But could you please just step back now, let me finish this?'

'Step back? Oh, yeah, I see how that will go. I step back and, *wow*, look who steps in. Miss Durham 2002!'

'Jess—'

'You know what?' I shoved back my chair. 'I deserve more than this. At the very least, I should come first on your list of things to take care of, not last. I'll step away all right – step right back to my own life on the other side of Oxford, with my dog, my hostile flatmates, and my stupid little detective agency that's so beneath your consideration. See you around, Inspector George.'

I swung out, only to spoil my exit by bumping into Janice as she headed in.

'All done. I've ordered some extra naan as you're so hungry,' she said brightly, though I knew – oh I knew – she'd been listening at the door, waiting to make her entrance.

Leo had got up. I hoped that was a sign that he had intended to stop me, but Janice got in his way too.

'I'd really like your guidance on where's best to look for a house in London, Leo. I've been away so long that I've lost touch with what are the safest areas.' She pulled out a chair beside him. 'Oh, you've finished the bread. You really must be hungry. I'll make you another snack while we wait.'

'I just need to talk to Jess—' he began.

Phil hooted the horn outside.

'Sounds like Phil's raring to go. So kind of him to offer to mend your bike, Jess.' She gave me a look that said she had won this round and knew it.

'Fine. Text me later,' I told Leo, 'if you remember.'

I walked out, not exactly clear as to whether I had just broken up with him or not. I thought maybe I had, and I hadn't wanted to at all.

Chapter Thirty-Four

Leo

It was gone eleven-thirty by the time Leo had managed to shake off Janice and retire to his own room. And, no, he did not leave the door open and the duvet thrown back as Jess had taunted him. He was tempted to send her a photo of the closed bedroom door but decided he was feeling too annoyed to humour her ridiculous accusations.

She had, however, been right about Janice's intentions. Janice had first attempted to seduce him over the curry. If he hadn't been so tired, he might've been aroused by her sensuous eating and provocative remarks; she was certainly fascinating to watch. It wasn't her fault she was working with the equivalent of damp matches and wet wood. She would've done better to order in oysters and champagne. Excellent actress though she was, even she struggled to make a kitchen table covered in little plastic takeout boxes romantic.

After the meal, her onslaught had switched to reviving old memories but that was counterproductive as it merely served to remind him how distant they were from those younger selves. Their first time together had been in her college room while listening to Avril Lavigne's 'Complicated', a song he had felt at the time summed him up. Eighteen-year-old Leo had thought Janice ineffably sophisticated – her posters of *Breakfast at Tiffany's* and *On the Waterfront* part of a world of classic films he knew nothing about, despite having an actress for a mother. He'd fallen for that world of finer things and imagined then that the lyrics were Janice's subliminal message to him that she wanted him, but with hindsight that had been reading too much into the moment. It had probably just been what was on her iPod. It was strange to find now that Janice remembered the moment but without any details that had been imprinted on his mind. She thought they'd listened to Justin Timberlake, been at a friend's party and that he made the first move. He let her spin her version as it was too exhausting to set about correcting her. Besides, he knew from his police work that it was entirely possible for two witnesses of the same event to describe it in completely different terms, each convinced they were right. *He wore red. He wore blue. She held a knife. She was unarmed.* It was frightening how easy it was for the mind to supply details that weren't there if they fitted the narrative the witness had created.

'Maybe you'll feel more like it tomorrow?' Janice had asked as he resisted her kiss good night.

He held her wrists to remove her hands from his face. 'I'm with Jess.'

'But you broke up.' Had they? He was so tired he wasn't sure what was going on. 'You're free, Leo. And I'm free. It needn't be complicated.'

He pushed her away gently. 'It's always complicated.'

'You'll regret not taking your opportunity.' Backing up to the entrance to her room across the corridor from his, she unbelted her silky robe, revealing a short slip nightdress beneath. Her legs were world class. Leo's mouth went dry. 'I'll leave the door unlocked.'

She was beautiful and for a moment the wicked part of him wanted to take what was being dangled before him. She would tempt a saint. But he wasn't his mother – or his father. He didn't just take an offer of sex because a body was available.

'Good night, Janice.'

Sitting on his bed, he felt the weight of the day crash down on him, like a surfer misjudging the wave. That wasn't a bad description of what had just happened. He'd thought he'd been on board with Jess and now his board was bobbing up beside him, tied only by the weak strap around his ankle, pulling in another direction. She wanted to go after Rebecca? But on what evidence? Knowing both victims, yes; having a big house, OK, the money needed to be looked into. But where was the motive?

He might have been readier to start a whole new line of enquiry if his own case hadn't been coming together so quickly. The team in Reading had succeeded in getting the women at the refuge to pick out Marta Kanon and Tony Stanton-Milbeck in the line-up of photos they'd presented them. Marta had been the one who told the women what was expected of them, trained those that knew nothing about sex in how to entice a customer. Tony they had only seen once, and that had been on arrival. The lorries containing the illegal refugees had been unloaded at night with only two other men present – the driver and someone to work the forklift truck. From the warehouse they'd been taken to another much smaller premises on an industrial estate somewhere, this one rigged up as a dormitory. There they'd been briefed by Marta and sent a week later to the club that had been designated for them.

Most interesting of all, and what had made him late home, was the fact that the man for whom it had all been arranged was not Tony Stanton-Milbeck, or even Josef Kanon. Every woman had picked out Chester Birbeck. The implications of this were keeping the top brass up this evening, discussing what to do next. The Home Secretary was being sounded out, without betraying any details. Leo was expecting to be called back at any moment. A domestic drama was the last thing he needed.

The Birbecks were the very definition of a big game trophy for a police force. When looking for the man in control of the operation, Leo has been anticipating Jeremy might be behind it, being the one that in public showed an appetite for women. He was never without a model on his arm in the society pages. His brother was supposedly happily married to a woman from Guernsey who rarely appeared in the papers, apparently busy raising their family of three daughters. Officers specially trained in dealing with victims of sexual crimes were now interviewing the witnesses to find out just how far Chester's involvement has gone. Had he been organising these sexual services purely as a business sideline, or had he done it to feed his own predilection for young girls? If so, they could get him on that, with other charges to follow.

The issue, and the reason for Leo's feeling of exhaustion, was the battle that would come over the credibility of the witnesses. It was all right to claim in theory that the victim got listened to in this new enlightened post-Savile age but the police force had had their fingers burned after the high-profile cases of wrongfully charged men. A good lawyer – and Chester would have the best – would paint the girls as willing participants in an illegal scheme to get themselves jobs in the West. Their accusations would be presented as their attempts to get leave to remain because they could demand to be treated as victims not offenders. There were enough cynical people out there who would believe that, particularly in certain sections of the press whose readership hated migrants. Chester, as an impeccable family man, would doubtless jettison his co-conspirators, the Kanons and the Stanton-Milbecks, like a rocket parting from the fuel tanks, then sail off into an atmosphere of untouchability. *How terrible that such things had been going on in the clubs, Inspector. Didn't know a thing about it. The girls just latched onto me because they knew my name. Such a big business empire, bound to be some illegal workers but thank you for bringing it to our attention.* Leo didn't need a screenwriter for that script.

What the police required for their case was to catch all

the players in the act and record them doing the deals so that no one could deny their part in the trafficking network. The evidence was sufficient against the Stanton-Milbecks and the Kanons now that the women in Reading were testifying against them in great detail in their statements; he was less worried about them. There would be financial evidence too, particularly if he could find the material Kelly Ann had to have stashed somewhere safe. What he really needed a way of proving Chester Birbeck was not only aware but deeply involved. He had to have more than their words against his. But how to achieve that?

Setting his phone on the bedside table, he saw the screen light up.

Oh, God, Jess! He should've messaged her.

He picked the handset up and saw, not a message from her, but one from his father.

Leo,

I'm in London and would love to see you. Please don't hesitate to contact me so we can set up a time that suits you. I'll make sure I reorganise my schedule to accommodate you.

How had he got Leo's email? Scrolling up, Leo saw a long message from his mother he hadn't opened. In it, she justified her spending of the money George had sent her while accusing him in the same breath of neglect. What Leo hadn't realised until now was that she'd side-copied it to him, thus giving George Saito a direct line to his son.

I can be reached on this email address or at the Piccadilly People Club, Golden Square.

Leo gave a hollow laugh. Oh, the irony! Yes, his dad with his screen credentials was exactly the kind of international celebrity who made up the clientele of the worldwide club membership, but still…

There is so much I'd like to learn about you. I don't want to interfere in anyway in your life, I would just value the chance to get to know a little about it.

Leave a message with Reception any time day or night and they'll make sure it gets to me.

Dad/George

Leo put the phone face down while he thought. He'd been wondering how he could find out how the sex ring worked and here he was presented with a person no one but he and his mother knew had any connection to him. Could he? It was a very strange way of taking the olive branch his father had extended to him, but it would tell him a great deal about the man who claimed he wanted to know his son.

Leo picked up the phone again, but this time to speak to his superintendent.

Chapter Thirty-Five

Jess

I checked my phone at midnight. Leo hadn't messaged me and it was now officially no longer 'later' this evening. He was out of time. OK, then. That meant we had split up. I had gone with the impulse to say something radical and it had backfired. I now had to suck it up as I, after all, had initiated it.

Phil took the cap off another beer as he studied me from his armchair. He'd stayed to watch TV with me and my flatmates, quite content with our diet of reality-TV shows. In fact, he'd fitted in well – much better than Leo ever had. He watched Ru Paul without a sneer but cheered the contestants on with a whatever-floats-your-boat attitude to drag. He seemed well versed in who was snogging whom in the Australian *Love Island*. With a few arch looks in our direction and a promise that they wouldn't be back downstairs tonight, Kristie and Sally had gone to bed twenty minutes ago, leaving us the front room.

'Face it, babe: he's just not that into you,' said Phil, mockingly echoing something one of the contestants had told another when their dreamboat had sailed off with another.

I put my phone down.

'How many of those have you had?' I asked, just catching up to the fact that he had a row of bottles in front of him.

'Five. Maybe six. Can I crash here?' He yawned and stretched, displaying his toned stomach.

I could hardly turn him out into the night to face a drink-driving penalty, not after he made an impressive job of mending my puncture. Sad to admit it, but I found a man who knew his way around a toolbox very attractive.

'OK, I'll fetch you a sleeping bag.'

'I could share your bed.' He gave me the puppy-dog eyes. 'I'll keep to my side and I'm told I don't snore.'

'Good try, sport, but I'm not that girl.' I stood before him to start collecting in the empties.

He snagged me to sit on his knee. I lost balance and ended up in his lap. 'You mean you don't want a rebound guy? Oh, Jess, why not? I won't tell anyone and it'll make you feel better.'

Temporarily, it would scratch an itch, true, but would I be able to face myself in the morning?

He began stroking my thigh in the circles that had worked the day before. You had to give this guy points for persistence.

'Look, Phil, you don't really like me.' I tried to get up but a hand sneaked around my waist, anchoring me.

'Just wait a moment. Put those down.' He relieved me of the bottles and dropped them on the carpet. 'I do like you. You're smart, for one thing – look at what you did about that packaging! Left to Leo and his stormtroopers that would've been missed – or thought of too late. Rainbow would still be accused of a crime she didn't commit. We all owe you for that.'

I sagged back against his chest. 'Yeah, I did do that. I feel pretty great that it worked.'

He nipped my chin. 'And you're funny. I like how you stand up to me.'

'Your ideas are ridiculous, you know that?'

'See? That's what I mean. You call me on my bullshit – which isn't bullshit, by the way, but I know why you think it is.'

'Oh?'

'You're conditioned by society. You're angst-ridden like everyone else. Twist yourself up like pretzels. See what's happening here? You could have sex with me tonight and neither of us should feel guilty about it. I could have you naked and orgasming on that sofa in twenty seconds if you'd just let that stuff go.'

'Twenty seconds, huh?' He made a move as if to prove it. Oops. 'No, what I meant was that stuff, as you call it, is what I call my morals. I have commitments – people I don't want to betray.'

He toyed with the buttons on my blouse, undoing a few them and slipping his hand into my cleavage. I took a shaky breath, which only made more room for him. I hadn't meant to do that… had I? 'I can't see how you'd be betraying anyone. Leo was stupid enough to let you walk out tonight. He's probably having consolation sex with Janice even as we speak. She's my friend but I have to say that woman is a tiger – she pounces on the best-looking guy and drags him back to her bed. I've seen it again and again. She's already bagged Leo once; she won't have any trouble getting him again.'

'What do you mean?' Even though I asked, I could already see it all too clearly.

'At college, the girls were all after the tall, dark, handsome fresher, the one with the tortured past and look of a brooding hero. That's catnip to Janice. He didn't stand a chance then and I can guarantee he's no man if he doesn't fall for it again. Have you seen what's she's packing under her clothes?' He ran his hands over me. 'But you've got your own charms, haven't you, babe? And as I always say, what's sauce for the goose can be saucy for the gander.' He tweaked a nipple.

I squeaked.

'Feels good, doesn't it?'

It did. I was in big trouble here. I liked risk, loved doing things that crossed lines. And I'd made no move to shift his exploring fingers, my high ground eroding with every passing second as I was finding the low ground so very seductive. Especially *that* low ground. He now had my breast cupped while the other hand fumbled for the bra hooks. He slipped those free and my bosoms dropped a little into his palm. 'Perfect,' he breathed into my ear. 'Soft, beautiful – the things I can do with these.'

'Phil, I—'

He kissed me to stop my words. 'Just one night, Jess. No recriminations. Just pleasure. And if you like it, then maybe there will be more.'

'Oh, God.'

He slipped my bra off completely, taking my blouse with it. 'Look at it this way, if Leo doesn't care enough to keep you, then let someone else show you how you should be treated.'

Chapter Thirty-Six

Leo

Debate with his superiors about the wisdom of the course he was suggesting didn't end until the early hours. Leo grabbed a few hours' sleep, his alarm set for six. There was a lot to get done today.

When the beeping started, his limbs still felt heavy, the covers like concrete setting on them. He rolled out of bed and staggered to the shower where he stood under the most powerful blast it managed. The water ran cool for a while until the hot kicked in but that was good as that did more to wake him up than anything else. Butterflies fluttered in his stomach as he considered what he had planned. It could be a disaster or a master stroke. If it went wrong, he'd probably find himself on traffic patrol for the rest of his life, or eased out of the force altogether.

As he turned off the taps and grappled for a towel,

soapy water stinging his eyes, a hand stroked his chest. He slapped his palm over the groping fingers.

'Mmm, you look good, Leo. Quite the man now,' purred Janice. She pressed against him, only the thin slip between their bodies. 'Look at that six pack.'

Anger flared. He pushed her hand away and wrapped the towel around his middle.

'For God's sake, Janice!'

She pouted, trying to pass it all off as a joke. 'I'm just admiring you. Nothing wrong with that.'

'There is and you know it.'

'I was only paying you a compliment.'

'How would you react if a man broke into your shower and made comments about you when you were naked?'

'Depends if I invited him or not.'

'Exactly. I did *not* invite you.'

She put her hands on her hips. 'You didn't lock the door.'

'Because this is my house. I don't usually have to lock it – I live alone.'

'You don't have to be alone.' She reached for him.

'Maybe I like it that way. Did you think of that?' Turning his back on her, he walked past and slammed the door to his bedroom. Breath heaving, he struggled to regain his temper. He was tempted to yell at her to leave but he wanted to have that conversation when he was dressed.

Fuck! Jess! He'd forgotten to text her. Could this day get any worse?

He dashed to his phone on the bedside table. No

message from her. Hopefully, she was still asleep and hadn't been waiting for him to contact her.

Sorry I forgot to message you last night. Let's talk. Busy today with a work thing but I'll let you know as soon as I'm free. You're right – I have been neglecting you. Sorry again. x

Not his most eloquent apology but something was better than nothing, right? In the stew of feelings he'd been going through the last few days, he was aware that, under it all, he was missing her with a constant ache. He'd fallen into the trap of taking her for granted as she always made it so easy for him – fitting in with his work schedule, cheering him up when he needed it, coming to meet his friends even though she hadn't really wanted to. And how had he reacted? Not gratefully, that was for sure. She was the one important person in his life and he'd treated her like she didn't need the same consideration as those who weren't so essential to his heart. He'd proved once again the old adage that we treat those we love the worst.

His phone whirred. A message in reply from Jess. That was early for her.

I'm sorry too.

Nothing more. No kiss. No 'you're a rat, Leo'. Just these three sad, little words.

He tried calling her but she didn't pick up. That was a first. Seeing the time, he knew he had to get to work, so he sent another message.

I'm prepared to grovel for your forgiveness. I love you. xx

He waited. No reply. Slipping the phone in his jacket pocket, he went to work deeply troubled.

George Saito had been waiting for Leo's message. Of course he would meet him. And, yes, he would come to Oxford. No problem cancelling his meetings. Don't even mention it.

Leo had thought hard about where would be good to hold this first encounter. He didn't want to meet his father anywhere near one of the Birbecks's clubs, not even in London if the Birbecks were keeping an eye on what he was doing. It had to be somewhere they would expect Leo to go. That was why Leo had suggested the garden centre near the police headquarters. He doubted very much any spies would pay much attention to his movements once he arrived at work. The garden centre was close enough for him to slip away to without being seen, especially as he borrowed a colleague's car. The narrow country roads that led to it made a tail impossible.

'Elaborate security protocol, Leo,' said Milly, PA to the superintendent, who had volunteered her car keys. She was aware of what was afoot.

'I found out on my last big case that people with money don't play by the same rules as the rest of us. An abundance of caution is called for.'

She dropped the keys into his hand. 'Don't put a scratch on her.'

As Milly's Fiesta was a collection of scratches and dents – her teenagers were learning to drive in it – he didn't think she'd notice even if he did.

Arriving fifteen minutes early, Leo wandered for a while among the tables of evergreens and climbing plants to check no one was following him. The good thing about February was that there were few visitors to the plant section, only the keen gardeners after some early spring colour. It was calming to be amongst growing things. He lingered in front of a clipped yew, wondering if he should put something on his doorstep. A bay tree perhaps? Two either side?

A big garden wall clock showed him that it was time to make his meeting. He joined the short queue of pensioners and wheelchair users with their carers who made up the clientele at this time of day, ordered a black coffee, and looked around for a table.

He was caught by surprise when he spotted George Saito had preceded him. He was sitting in a booth with papers spread on the table in front of him, but he wasn't reading. He was looking right at Leo.

Their eyes met. For a moment, Leo just registered the similarities between himself and the father he'd never known. Jess was right: they did have the same eyes. George also had his hair, the way it curved into a slight widow's peak in the centre of the forehead. When he stood up, Leo saw that he was also tall, answering the question from where he got his height.

Encumbered by his tray, Leo crossed what seemed like acres of café floor to put it down on the table.

'Leo?' George asked in an emotion-filled word.

'Yes, I'm Leo. Thank you, Mr Saito, for coming out all this way to meet me.' Leo shook the proffered hand, their first touch. It felt like sparks were running down his arm to his spine, then down the backs of his legs. He had to shove away all the might-have-beens that crowded into his mind – the missed school events, the good-night hugs, the graduations...

'Call me George, please, and no thanks necessary. I wanted to be here. I would've gone to Timbuktu if you had set that as your condition.' George retook his seat. He also was drinking black coffee.

'It wasn't a condition.' Leo slid onto the bench seat opposite him.

'Your mother said you bore a grudge. An understandable grudge. I've been afraid of this meeting for years.'

'I never knew who my father was until you wrote to me.' Leo let him absorb the implications of that for a minute. His eyes fell on the papers his father had been working on – a script. 'Is it...er...going well, the film?'

George gathered up the pages. 'It is kind of you to ask but I don't want to talk about the movie. It'll get made – or not. It's not important. What's important is you.'

Leo shrugged, then regretted it as that felt too much of a teenage thing to do. He measured his words out carefully.

'I don't bear you a grudge, sir.' He couldn't quite manage 'George' and 'Mr Saito' would sound like a rejection. 'I know that I was the result of an accident. You didn't walk out on me as a baby, didn't abandon me. You barely knew I existed. I was a theoretical child you'd had with someone you didn't really know. You had your own family to consider.'

George studied Leo's face. 'You worked out then that I had a partner at the time I was with your mother?'

'Your eldest daughter is the same age as me. It doesn't take much to deduce that.'

'I don't want you to get the wrong impression. I was a stupid boy when I did these things but I wasn't irresponsible. I'd split from Mia before coming to the UK. When I returned from filming, we got back together and Felicity was our new start. I only heard that I'd left behind more than just a… dalliance when your mother announced she'd had a baby boy. The news came on the day I was in the hospital with Mia having Felicity. It was… difficult to take in.'

'I can imagine. Did you tell your wife?'

'She wasn't my wife then, only a year later. No, not then, when she was holding our newborn in her arms. I couldn't do it. I'm afraid I pushed it away. I only told her when you turned five and I was sending money for your schooling. I thought she would notice the large amounts leaving our account. It almost ended our marriage – she didn't begrudge the money but she hated the lies of omission. Never hide anything from a person you truly love.'

'You should know that I never saw any of that money.'

'But your mother said—'

'We lived on other people's canal boats, I wore second-hand clothes and went to state schools. Government benefits would've covered my costs. I don't know what she did with it, but that money wasn't spent on me.'

George's jaw firmed as if he was gritting his teeth. 'I should've known.'

'My guess is she spent it on maintaining her image. She always looked good and had several operations to make herself look better. That would've been expensive as she used the best plastic surgeons.'

George shook his head. 'Unbelievable.'

'Not really. I assumed she'd earned the money for them from her acting, but this makes more sense. You have to understand, she's like a child with her hand in the cookie jar.'

'Me being the cookie jar?'

Leo nodded. 'She doesn't see beyond satisfying her needs. I'm not sure I'm even a person to her.'

'God, Leo, I'm sorry. I should've done more.'

'Why? Because you had a fleeting encounter with a pretty woman? It was her decision to go ahead with the pregnancy. I'd imagined that keeping me was the one brave act in her life but now I see that it was all part of her narcissism. She had me to keep the cookie jar full.' He sipped his coffee. 'If you don't realise it already, she really is an appalling person.'

'I'll take her to court – I'll punish her for what she did!' And he did look ready to spring from his seat and take on the world right there and then, head held in a defiant tilt.

Leo laughed mirthlessly. 'And achieve what? The money's gone. All you would do is make her famous – she'd love that. I truly believe she thinks bad press is better than no press. And there's always the possibility she'll persuade some parts of the media that she was badly treated by you. She'll drag you and your family through the mud.'

'And you.'

'Believe me, I don't think she can do any more to me at this point. I don't advise taking legal action unless you are prepared for it to blow back up it your face.'

George looked grimly into the dark depths of his coffee. 'Tell me she was kind to you, at least.'

Leo kept silent.

'I'll need to think about this but I know already that I am profoundly, deeply sorry for my negligence. I can't excuse myself. I could've looked closer but I didn't. I was too busy, too caught up in my career, my family, my business ups and down. I see I have thirty-five lost years to make up for,' said George, pulling himself back to a more cheerful place. 'If I hadn't been by chance scanning the British news and seen your name… I don't know that I would ever have changed the situation. That says something awful about me, which I don't think I've come to terms with.' He shook himself. 'But this isn't about me. What can I do for you now, Leo?'

Leo wished he could say 'nothing', get up, and walk out, but he had engineered this meeting precisely because he did want something from him.

'There is something you can do for me,' George's face brightened. 'In fact, not just for me but for the British police.'

'That sounds ominous.' Dark eyes sparkled with humour. 'And I can't imagine what your next sentence is going to be. That's quite exciting.'

'How long have you been a member of the Piccadilly People Club?'

A frown line appeared at the top of George's nose. His glasses slid forward and he pushed them back. 'Since 2011. I was one of the early adopters as they had a branch in Singapore where I was filming that year.'

'Do you know the owners?'

'Chester and Jeremy? Yes, a little, but only from the occasional club event.'

'Do you have any financial dealings with them?'

'Not that I'm aware of, beyond my annual membership, of course. They may have a stake in some of the media companies I work with, but again, that's not something they've brought to my attention.'

Leo nodded. That was good enough. His superiors had stressed that they couldn't risk revealing elements of what they had found out to someone who might have exposure to a Birbeck business failure. The temptation would be to tip them off to avoid personal loss.

'I'm working a case.'

'I imagine you always are. An inspector – I was so proud when I saw what you did in December. I've been looking up your other cases, too, since then. I'd love to talk to you about them – absolutely fascinating.'

'This case might well be the biggest one yet – if we can get the proof we need to show what's going on.'

George took a moment to think. 'It involves the Birbecks?'

'It does.'

'What are they into? Some financial fraud?'

'No. Sex trafficking.'

George had unwisely sipped his coffee at this point and spluttered some of it back into the cup. 'You're not joking.'

'No, I'm not.'

'That's... that's one hell of a story you've got there. I call dibs on the film rights.'

Leo smiled, warming to his father a little. Maybe there was a man with a sense of humour here that he would like to know? True, he'd been careless with his family but he might not be irredeemable as a person. 'You'll probably get them as you could have a role in it if you agree to do what I'm going to suggest.'

'Sex trafficking? I know nothing about that. I really can't see how I can help.'

'Let me explain.' Leo told him about the chain of events that had led to the conclusion that there was a secret sex ring introducing select customers to underage Vietnamese girls in the guise of escorts or companions. The real agenda was prostitution.

'You think this is going on at the clubs?' George frowned.

'Do *you* think it is? You've been in and out of them for years.' They had debated whether George was possibly already part of it before approaching him but Leo had argued that the risk was worth the potential benefits. He was therefore relieved that his father's shock appeared genuine.

'I would never have thought of it, but I suppose... I have noticed that there are a large number of well-groomed young women at some of them, ones you see at events but don't see on Reception or in the restaurants and bars. I just assumed the girls, and boys, were there as part of a training scheme for the hospitality industry. Don't tell me I've been as blind to what's going on as I was to your mother's activities?'

'It's subtle. The victims say the introductions are carefully managed and happen at private events that are not open to all members. If you saw them only in passing in corridors and in the public areas, you would have no reason to suspect that anything else was going on. That is rather the point. The gloss of the clubs encourages you to assume they are totally respectable. What businessman wants his wife to know her husband has been staying at an establishment notorious for its escort services?'

George paled. 'My wife is going to be livid.'

'Exactly.'

'And she did so like using the club facilities when we travelled together.'

'It's the times when you were apart she might be most cross about.'

'Indeed. I don't have a stellar record, do I?' He gave Leo a significant look.

'I was the only mistake?'

'You were. I learned my lesson early on in our relationship.' He rubbed his hands together, his wedding ring shining. 'So, what is my part in all this?'

'We'd like you to persuade Chester Birbeck to introduce you to a young lady friend to keep you company while you're in London. We'll have you wired – with your permission. We want evidence that he's part of the arrangement and fully cognisant of the illegality of what he's doing. He's making money from prostitution for one thing, as well as pimping out children.'

'May he burn in hell for that,' said George fiercely.

'Indeed.'

'I'm not sure you can understand. I have daughters. Men like that should not be allowed to live.'

'We're looking for an arrest. Will you be able to keep your disgust hidden?'

George sighed. 'I can try. There's a bit of an actor in every director.'

'OK, then. Would you be willing to play your part in bringing him down?'

George reached out and covered Leo's hand with his. A lump formed in Leo's throat at the tenderness in the gesture. 'You're right. I'll do this – not for you but for those girls. This is not me paying you back in any way, this is me standing by you and doing the right thing.'

'Thank you,' Leo cleared his throat, 'George.'

Chapter Thirty-Seven

Jess

'Why the long face?' asked Jennifer as I unwrapped my scarf and shrugged out of my red padded winter coat.

'I feel like shit.' I couldn't face another day at my computer pretending to care about rich people leaving St Nick's money in their will. 'And, no, I'm not sickening for anything. We've already had that conversation so don't start.'

'Ah, an affair of the heart,' my colleague said knowledgeably. 'I'll put the kettle on.'

I went through the motions, switching on the screen and booting up the machine. I scanned through the most urgent emails and considered moving them to Spam. At least then when someone asked me why I hadn't replied, I could 'find' their super-important message in the Spam folder. Brilliant, hey? Paul might get suspicious, though, as most of them were nagging ones from him about deadlines.

A mug of tea appeared at my elbow.

'Right. Paul is at a meeting on this epidemic so he won't interrupt. Tell me what's up.' Jennifer had a grandmotherly air to her, a correct impression as she had lots of grandkids, but she'd also had a life before motherhood, living it to the full in the 80s, as she had cheerfully admitted in the past. I'd not yet managed to shock her.

'I did a bad thing,' I stated baldly.

She offered me a chocolate digestive. 'Just one?'

I wasn't sure if she meant the biscuit or the thing, so I took two in answer.

'Ah… Are you going to tell me what you did?'

'Probably. I'm terrible at keeping a secret, especially about myself.'

She smiled at that. 'Well, you do keep me entertained. You are much more interesting than Sheila.' I was the maternity cover for the new mother. 'Happily married to a childhood sweetheart, never had any love complications that I can tell. She's a sweetie but boring, if you understand me?'

I did. 'OK, then. Let me then say I am not boring. I've got that going for me.' I dried up at that point. Saying it out loud to someone else would make it more real.

Jennifer tutted. 'The way I see it, you either tell me or you go to Sanyu. I've heard him say that he believes in the mental-health benefits of confessions so he'll keep it sacred.'

'*No!*' I was blushing. I could not possibly talk about this in front of the genial Sanyu Masane, the college chaplain. 'No way am I telling him.'

'Then, it's me. Let me just say, first, even before I've heard a thing, "I'm sorry" is probably your way out of this.'

'I'm not sure there is a way.' I explained how I had quarrelled with Leo and thought I'd ended it. When he'd failed to message, I had taken it as confirmation.

'I then did something incredibly stupid.' I nibbled the chocolate off the top of the biscuit, showering myself with crumbs.

'Oh, yes?'

'I made out with his old college rival. You see, Phil fixed my tyre for me—'

'I'm liking him already.'

'Yeah, I know. The whole competent-with-his-hands thing is a real button for me. Well, he was there and into me and I was feeling upset so…'

'So?'

I sighed. 'We did a Bill Clinton.'

'You gave him a…?' She twirled her hand towards an imagined crotch.

'Yeah. Just as a thank-you for what he did first to me. I drew a shaky line at more and managed to keep to it but… Oh, God, I had sex with him, didn't I?'

'Well, it's certainly a "sex act".'

'I was telling myself it was heavy petting, but that's crap. I two-timed Leo, like all his other pathetic friends keep doing to each other. I'm just like them. He's the only one with any standards.'

'Can you be two-timing if you thought you'd broken up?' Jennifer asked reasonably.

'I hadn't broken up with him emotionally. I'd said the words but I didn't mean them. That was the second stupid thing I did. I didn't answer his calls and apologise immediately, you know, confess to the whole shit-show and let him end it properly? I've just left him hanging.'

Jennifer offered me the biscuit packet again. Yes, I did need comforting.

'The worst thing is I know that Phil only got it on with me to hurt Leo. I realised this but I still let him charm me out of my panties.'

'Some men are like that,' Jennifer said, nodding. 'They make girls lose their heads.'

I did a double-take. 'But you haven't…?'

'Thirty-five years is a long time to be married to someone. There have been ups and downs along the way, times when communication has broken down and we wanted to hurt each other. A plausible man coming along at the right time can do a lot of damage.'

I never would've suspected. She seemed so… so married. 'How did you get back from that?'

Jennifer didn't rush to answer. She sipped her tea for a moment and considered. 'You both have to want to salvage the relationship, that's the first thing. Sometimes one partner is looking outside the marriage because what they really want is an exit. Do you want an exit?'

'*No!*'

'OK, then. Once you've established you've got something worth saving, then you have to lay all your cards on the table and hope the other can find it in their heart to forgive you. They usually can if they are aware of having done something bad themselves.'

I shivered. 'Is it wrong to hope Leo did sleep with his ex-girlfriend, then?'

'Do you think he would?'

'Not really, no. He's the good guy – I'm the bad one.'

'Jess, you can't have a relationship with someone who makes you feel that.'

'He doesn't make me feel that; I make myself feel that.'

The phone rang on her desk, so she got up to answer it. 'You still need to talk – and by the sounds of it, you should do it before this Phil person gives his version of events to Leo.'

'Crap! I hadn't thought of that.' I grabbed my phone and returned Leo's call.

It rung out.

I could hardly leave a message, could I? *Sorry I had sex with your enemy.* Classy, Jess, really classy. Instead, I hung up and texted him the next best thing.

> *Mutual grovelling will be in order. I'll try to make it up to you. Xx*

I then rattled through the emails without dumping them in Spam and pondered how I could catch a killer for him.

Chapter Thirty-Eight

Leo

The Met police would've loved to take over the investigation as soon as they heard Thames Valley wanted to take down Chester Birbeck on their territory. It had required some quick procedural tap dancing by Superintendent Thaxted, and George Saito's point-blank refusal to work with anyone else, to keep Leo in charge of the sting operation. He still had to put up with an Inspector Randall from the Met's CID breathing down his neck – *literally*, as he was sitting beside him in the listening post that they'd established in an empty office building opposite the club. If they got enough to make the arrest, the Met would do this but Leo would get the first crack at interview.

They had had to move fast to get the joint Thames Valley–Metropolitan police operation off the ground. The Birbecks were still in London but were said to have plans to return to Guernsey that Friday. Wednesday night at the club was traditionally a members' meet-and-greet, which meant any member present for the evening was encouraged to come to the exclusive bar on the rooftop and talk business and socialise with other equally well-heeled types. Networking was part of what sold the clubs to their members. If the owners were in town, they too made a point of attending.

'George, are you ready?' asked Leo.

Leo focused his binoculars on the terrace. Bright flares of outdoor heaters and fairy lights marked out the bar. His father came to the railing and touched his ear in a prearranged sign that he was in position and could hear what they were saying in the mic that had been fitted on him earlier.

'That's your old man, is it?' said Randall, snacking on a pack of almonds.

'Yes.'

'You kept that quiet.'

Leo was hardly going to explain the background to a stranger from another force. It had already been an ordeal to go through it with his own bosses. 'Why would anyone want to know?'

Randall rolled his eyes. Short, with dark blond hair, he had a common-man appeal about him, the Martin Freeman of policing. 'In case you haven't noticed, you've earned yourself a bit of press recently. A connection like that, to one of the Hollywood names, would've pleased the hacks no end.'

'I didn't realise my fame had travelled so far,' said Leo, dryly. He made a point of not following what was written about him.

'Others might not have noticed but I did. I took an interest as I have the misfortune of being the officer who arrested Michael Harrison for murder.' He pulled a face. 'What a fuckup that was. Could've killed my career if we hadn't caught the guilty party in the end.'

'Ah, that explains it. Yes, Dr Harrison has been very helpful with a couple of my enquiries now he's in Oxford.'

'Have you spoken to him about this one?'

'No time. It's developed so quickly from a suspected suicide to something so much bigger. There's not been a psychopathic angle to explore, which is why I usually go to him.'

'And how is Miss Bridges?'

'You know her, too, do you?' Jess's first involvement with a murder case had been as a suspect, though it was Michael who was the one to spend time under arrest until he was exonerated. 'Small world.'

'Not if she keeps getting mixed up in murder.' Randall smiled in reminiscence. 'I developed quite a soft spot for her, even though she was a total nightmare to deal with. Rough time for her, if I remember. Someone trying to send her over the edge with fucking scream masks.'

Jess had had a breakdown during the course of that enquiry. Leo sometimes forgot how fragile she was. He really had been too cavalier in his treatment of her, he thought guiltily. 'She's better now, thanks.'

'Tell her I said "hello".' Which meant that Leo's connection to Jess, too, had been reported in the press. None of this was welcome news.

Randall slapped him on the chest. 'Look lively: I think that's our guy.'

A limousine drew up at the steps of the club. Both Birbecks got out and went up the stairs, doors opened by the porter before they reached him.

'Chester and Jeremy are here,' Leo told his father. George left the rail and went to re-join the people at the bar. He chose a seat with a spare stool next to him and struck up a conversation with the bartender, their dialogue uplit from the illuminated surface of the counter.

'You don't half look like him,' mused Randall. 'I bet you get told that a lot.'

Randall's comment reminded Leo that he and George had not had time to discuss what they were going to say in public about their relationship. He was fairly certain his father would like to acknowledge him but the question was, did Leo want to claim him back? He couldn't shake the old idea that it was too late to acquire a father.

The Birbeck brothers didn't linger long in their private office. They emerged from the lift together and began their practiced circulation among their guests. It was intriguing to watch the shift in body language as people angled themselves towards the pair, or made a gap in their conversation groups to encourage them to join them. Jeremy went over to a knot of women he appeared to know well and rapidly got absorbed into their circle. One latched on to his arm.

'That's his flavour of the month,' said Randall, passing a photo from the social pages over to Leo. 'Charmaine D'Arcy.'

'No flavours for Chester?'

'No. He's always been said to be faithful and true to the missus back in Guernsey.'

Chester reached the bar. Leo had to commend his father – he hadn't been joking about his acting skills – as he timed his turning away perfectly so it looked like an accident that he ended up in Chester's path.

'George! Long time, no see!' said Chester in genial-host mode. His voice came through clearly on the microphone. He couldn't possibly keep track of everyone's names, decided Leo. He would bet Chester was given a run-down of who was in the club that night so he could flatter them by seeming to remember.

'Chester! This is an unexpected pleasure!' said George.

'What brings you to London, if I might ask?'

'The usual. I'm trying to put the financing together on a great new script I've optioned. It's all meetings, meetings, followed by maybe, maybe. It can be incredibly frustrating.'

'But that's the movie business for you.'

'Indeed. I just wish I didn't have to hang around so long on my own waiting for people to green-light things. It gets lonely, I can tell you.'

'That's what the clubs are for – to make the world a little less lonely. Here, let me buy you a drink.' They turned back to the bar and chatted about things that had come up in the news and about mutual acquaintances. George had been warned not to entrap Chester by making too bold a play for an introduction. The ideal scenario was for him to lay enough breadcrumbs for Chester to gobble up so he stuck his own head in the snare.

'How's your lovely wife?' asked Chester after George had enquired after his.

'Oh, I'm afraid we're not together at the moment,' said George, which was strictly true as she was in LA but, clearly, he was hoping Chester would infer more from that.

'Oh? I'm sorry.'

'My fault. Old sins coming back to haunt me, I'm afraid. I wasn't a very good boy in my youth.' Leo was impressed that his father was using elements of his biography to spin his tale. But perhaps that was what creatives did? Use what they knew to make it more convincing?

'Few of us were.'

George sighed. 'And after thirty-five years, I miss that man, you know? I got a lot of my creativity from being with younger people, living a little dangerously. I fear I've lost that spark.' He fluttered his fingers in the air like a sprinkle of fairy dust.

'You really think that? I thought you were still being put up for awards?'

'But I've not won any recently. I need to shake things up. Get back to my roots. Find my muse again.'

'What kind of muse?' asked Chester, his laser focus on George's face. Leo felt a pang of pleasure as he ate the first breadcrumb.

George looked over his shoulder, assuming a shifty air. 'In my early twenties, I found this sweetest peach of a girl.

She looked like an angel, so fresh, you know? Long dark hair, slim, adventurous.' George sipped his drink, appearing lost in his memories. 'I'm not shocking you, am I?'

'No, no, quite the contrary. I know exactly what you mean,' said Chester, encouragingly.

'Actually, it was here in London, over at the Ritzy Club, that I met her. It was quite a happening scene back then.'

Was this a version of 'how I met your mother'? wondered Leo, appalled. He hoped he would be spared any details.

'No one bothered with things like age ID then, not like now,' continued George. 'Anyone could come in.' He let that suggestion hang. 'God, we did things then that really excited me – they inspired me in fact to make my first movie.'

'*Timed Lives*?' said Chester. 'That's a great piece of work.'

'I just wish I could find someone like her again. But who would look at an old fossil like me, hey?' He took a sip of his drink.

Chester leant in. 'Women won't see a fossil when they look at you. They'll see a successful, powerful man and they'll want you, believe me.'

George snorted, sceptically. 'Oh, yeah? Where are these mythical girls who think like that?'

'Let me show you. Come to the after-party in my suite at about ten. It's not an event for everyone, only the discerning.' He slid his card over the counter. 'Just show that to the girl on the door.' With that, Chester slithered away and headed for another businessman who was drinking on his own. Leo wondered how many of those cards he would be dishing out tonight.

Pocketing the card, George came to the railing and pretended to look out over the nightlights of London.

'That was great, George,' said Leo. 'Great start. We'll need you to go to that party, though, to confirm that it is the kind of event we think it is. If you can get Chester to make the introduction himself to one of the girls, then that will close the deal.'

George gave a nod and headed out from the meet-and-greet to prepare for the next stage in the operation.

While they waited for ten o'clock, Leo briefed his superiors and checked everyone was in place for the next stage. Once that was done, he had a few minutes to grab a sandwich and take five for himself. Perhaps Randall's good wishes would be a smooth way of re-establishing contact with Jess, a kind of neutral topic?

He checked his personal phone and found she'd tried to call him earlier. That was a good sign. He also had messages from Rainbow, Janice, Freddie, and Phil. He sent Jess a quick greeting from Randall and a promise to call as soon as he could, then went through the other texts. Rainbow was just thanking him again for looking after her and saying that she was enjoying staying with Rebecca and her mother. Jess's accusations edged back in. Why did Rebecca have such a big house? What was the source of her personal wealth? He sent an email to Suyin to look into it for him just so he could put that to bed.

Janice's message was an apology that she'd come on too strong that morning. She explained that she had always carried a torch for him as he had been her first love and had let those feelings get the better of her. She'd found an apartment through an agent in London and was going to look at it if he didn't mind her staying on for a few more days while she sorted things out.

He texted that he didn't mind and that he didn't expect to be home much, if at all.

Freddie's message was interesting. He said that he and Lauren didn't think Rainbow staying with Rebecca was a good idea, not because of the reasons Jess had intimated, but because Lauren didn't think Rebecca would be good for Rainbow.

In what way 'not good'? Leo wondered. He almost texted the question but decided against it. He'd call tomorrow and ask to talk to Lauren. She knew Rebecca best and carrying this conversation on via Freddie as an intermediary was liable to end up like a game of Chinese whispers.

The last message he opened reluctantly. He couldn't remember the last time Phil had messaged him – probably on some pre-smartphone and just to arrange a squash match.

Finders keepers, losers weepers.

What the hell did that mean? Leo didn't have time to play word games with Phil.

What have I lost?

He didn't have long to wait for the reply.

Jess.

Chapter Thirty-Nine

Jess

A whole day had passed since the debacle with Phil, and Leo was still too caught up with work to see me. This wasn't something I could explain over the phone; I wanted something tangible to offer him when I broke the news I'd dallied with his frenemy. I wanted my apology to be in the form of proof that the cause of our rift – my accusations against Leo's friends – was actually warranted. It was a little like a cat dropping a dead mouse at your feet – a not entirely wanted gift – but it was the thought that counted, right?

But how could I prove that Rebecca was the one? I didn't know much about the first case in Chipping Norton, but I had a much better idea how Lloyd might have met his end at the Rollright Stones. He died while sitting watching the TV. A visitor either came before or after kick-off or was familiar enough to sit with him to share the viewing experience. I ran the likely evening in my head. What did I know about Lloyd's habits? Ellie had said they had continued seeing each other after they parted; might Lloyd not have had a similar arrangement with Rebecca? If her kink was pain, it might be tricky to satisfy that with sexual partners in Chipping Norton. If you asked the wrong person and then word got out that that was your thing, how could you go to the local supermarket again without everyone giving you a funny look? Going back to the person who you could trust to scratch that itch and keep it secret… that made sense.

So, Rainbow leaves in the afternoon and Lloyd knows she's planning to separate from him. He's feeling hurt and horny because she's also not sleeping with him. Hey, just down the road is the ex who is willing to come and let him feel like the big man if he provides her with what she needs. Coast is clear but Lloyd, being a guy, decides to arrange it so he can still watch his team lose one-nil to Liverpool. How would he make the assignation?

I had to get a look at her phone. My guess would be something like a WhatsApp message, encrypted end to end, seeming safe. The police had his phone so they would've checked his messages. She would've known that and couldn't remove it as that would give away the presence of someone else in the motorhome. She probably deleted the chat on both phones. Could I get them back?

I quickly googled for an answer. According to the advice, I had to delete the app then reinstall it, selecting the 'restore old messages' option.

That sounded simple. I'd have to remember that if ever I

wanted to hide something in future to delete the cache that was saved for a few weeks.

I couldn't get hold of Lloyd's but I could potentially snag Rebecca's phone. All I'd need was to add my own fingerprint in the settings so it could be used as ID for a new download. Thinking that practice makes perfect, I tried it on my own phone. As long as I knew her passcode, I could do this.

That was quite a few steps though. I needed to have some alone time with her phone, having got her code.

An idea came to me. It was high-risk, and unlikely to succeed, so it was my kind of plan.

I knocked on the door of Rebecca's house, having sent a last-minute I'm-in-the-area message to Rainbow.

'Hey!' I said brightly as Rebecca opened the door. 'I'm here to see how Rainbow's getting on.'

'*Jess!*' Rainbow came down the stairs, brushing past Rebecca to hug me. 'I'm so pleased you dropped round. We're about to have supper. Can you join us?'

'Thank you,' I said quickly, stepping inside before Rebecca could come up with an excuse. 'That's so kind of you. I haven't eaten all day.'

Rainbow conducted me through to the kitchen. 'This is Ma. I think you've met already?'

Ma inched forward on her walker. 'Hello, dear. What's your name again?'

'Jess Bridges. I'm Rainbow's friend.'

'How lovely.'

Rainbow pulled out a chair for the elderly lady. 'I'll just set another place.'

I produced a bottle of red out of my tote. 'I guess I should come clean. I was hoping you'd ask me to stay for supper.'

Rainbow whisked it away to open it. 'Wine is always welcome.'

'We're having fish. We should have white,' Rebecca said, the first words she had spoken since I invaded her kitchen.

'White doesn't agree with me,' I lied, 'not this late. It's red for me.'

I took my place beside her at the table. 'How is everything?'

'Good,' said Rainbow. 'Ma and I are getting along well, aren't we, Ma?'

'Yes, dear. Is it salmon?' she asked, blinking confusedly.

Rebecca took a baking tray out of the Aga. 'Yes, Ma, we always have salmon on Wednesday. I'm not sure this will stretch to all of us.'

'Jess can have my portion,' said Rainbow.

'I thought you were vegan?' I asked.

'No, that was Lloyd. I'm pescatarian when I get a choice.' She swallowed, remembering. 'I didn't mind being vegan, though. It's healthy.'

'Indeed, it is,' I agreed, hoping to stave off tears. 'Have you been out for any walks?'

'Not today. Too rainy.' Rainbow put the plates in front of each of us and we all sat down. I poured myself a red while the others opted for the white. I was pleased to see they'd used a tablecloth. That would help.

'I wonder what it's going to be like this weekend?' I said brightly. 'Anyone know?'

'I've been too busy,' said Rebecca.

'If only there was a way…' I said archly as I got out my phone. 'Oh, flat battery. Rebecca, may I have a quick look on yours?' It was lying by her plate, face down. I reached for it with an oily forefinger and, while fumbling, smeared the home button.

She snatched it back. 'I'll check.' She tried to open it with her fingerprint but the oil spoiled that. After several failed attempts, she was prompted to put in her passcode. She ran her finger round the outside edges in an L shape. 'More rain but Sunday looks fine.'

I let the conversation move on. I didn't want her to know just how interested I was in her phone.

'How's Leo?' Rainbow asked.

'Ah… we've had a bit of a falling out,' I said.

'About what?' asked Rebecca.

If in doubt, blame Phil.

'I got a bit too friendly with Phil – totally my fault. I'm hoping Leo will forgive me.' This also had the advantage of Phil backing me up if they cared to check this version of events.

'I'm so sorry. I bet it's my fault – all my business messing everything up!' said Rainbow.

I made a sudden move, as if to reach across the table to comfort her, sending my full glass of red flying over the tablecloth.

'Oh, God, I'm sorry! Quick, we need salt!'

Rebecca leaped up to fetch some.

'Damn – my clothes!' I grabbed her phone with a napkin and legged it to the bathroom.

'Just cleaning myself up!' I called over my shoulder. 'I got it on my jumper.'

Sitting on the closed toilet lid, taps running in the sink, I wiped the home button clean of oil with the napkin and dropped it. After entering wrong fingerprints a few times, it took me to the passcode. I then opened the phone with the L shape I'd seen Rebecca use – 1,5,7,8,9,9. Bingo! Quickly, I opened WhatsApp to check in case she hadn't deleted the messages. No, she had been careful. But not careful enough. I deleted the app, opened Settings, added my fingerprint, opened the App Store…

Banging came on the door. 'Jess, have you seen my phone?' My long absence had been noticed.

'Gosh, sorry, I think I might've scooped it up with the napkin I grabbed to dab myself down. I've stripped to the skin but will be out in a moment.'

'Could you just pass it out?'

'Wet hands – sorry! Won't be a moment. Don't wait for me – your food will get cold.'

I downloaded the app and selected the restore option. *Come on, come on!* And there it was: the exchange at 16:32.

> ***Lloyd:*** *Want to come round later? Rainbow's out. I've got something to tell you about the Bs that you'll want to hear.*

> ***Rebecca:*** *What thing?*

Lloyd: *Something big. There's money in it for us. Bring the flogger and we'll have fun while we plot their downfall.*

I took a photo of the screen and sent it to myself and Leo but I didn't have time for an explanation. I quickly deleted the messages again so Rebecca didn't see what I'd done, flushed the loo and returned to the kitchen, carrying the phone on the napkin.

'So sorry – I was in a panic. I don't think I got any wine on it but I've given it a good clean.' I handed it back.

Rebecca looked at it suspiciously, like an audience member after a magician has made their watch disappear and reappear. She opened it and checked for changes. Her home screen was a sunset shot of the Rollright Stones.

'Is it working OK?' I asked.

'Seems fine,' she said, grudgingly.

It was difficult to finish the meal, knowing that Rebecca habitually used drugged food and drink to get her way. I just had to hope I hadn't left her any time to plan something similar for me. I stood up as soon as I thought I could decently leave.

'Thanks so much for supper.'

'See you again soon?' asked Rainbow, hopefully.

Probably sooner than she thought. 'Hope so.'

'Drive carefully,' said Rebecca. That seemed more than a little ominous. She hadn't had time to tamper with my brakes, had she?

'I will.' I scampered out with my mouse of evidence, got back in the car, and drove away as quickly as I could, metaphorical tail-twitching. Just in case she decided to follow and run me off the road – my mind was throwing up all sorts of wild scenarios – I turned in the opposite direction to Oxford, drove for five minutes and parked up in a lay-by.

My heart was pounding and I was pretty sure the salmon was going to swim right back up.

When the moment of panic faded, I pulled out my phone. *Message failed to send*. The images had been too big to upload and Leo's hadn't gone through. Cursing, I drove on to find a place where I had a 4G signal and tried again. This time the message went. Now I would have to wait and see what he made of my mouse.

Chapter Forty

Leo

He had to put it away. He couldn't think about Phil's message. He just had to crack on and get this operation done and then he could work out if Phil was just messing with him or if he really had moved in on his girl.

It wouldn't be the first time. In Durham, Phil had made it one of his aims in life to cosy up to any girl Leo showed an interest in. That was why he'd gone out with Rainbow in their third year – to stop Leo asking her to a Valentine's Day party. If she hadn't said yes to Phil, Leo had often wondered if they might not have ended up together. She had been a much better fit than Janice had ever been.

'OK, Leo, I'm at the bastard's door,' said his father, breaking his thoughts.

'Copy that,' said Leo, biting back a smile. 'You know what to do. Get an introduction, leave with the girl, and you'll be met by officers, including an officer trained to deal with victims of trafficking.'

'Understood.'

Leo could hear that his father had moved into a crowded room. Big-band music played softly as an undertow to the current of conversation. He caught bursts of conversation but nothing substantial until Chester came into George's orbit.

'George, so glad you made it.'

'I must say, I've never seen this side of the club before.' George made his tone as slimy as Chester's.

'Gentlemen's clubs have been chased out of existence by the PC brigade. Nothing wrong with men meeting women, but they seem to want to make everything so difficult these days. Let me introduce you to some girls.'

There was another burst of conversation and music as the two men moved through the gathering.

'Who are these people?' George asked, as if marvelling.

'Likeminded friends of mine – and some ladies who appreciate their qualities.'

'Many of these girls look like they're from Asia.'

'Like yourself. Who knows, I might be able to find you one who speaks Japanese.'

'I was born in Baltimore.'

Chester laughed as if George had cracked a joke. 'Of course, of course. Most of them are from Cambodia, Vietnam, and Laos, in any case. And we've a few Russians. They appreciate the worth of a man, not like so many women you meet these days.'

'You can't give a compliment to a girl now without

being scared of a legal action,' said George, acting as though the Me Too movement was the worst thing that had happened to the industry. 'What they don't get is that sex sells. No point hiding the fact. If they're not sexy, then there's no point casting them.'

'And here is someone who I'm sure you'll agree does not disappoint in that area. Lin, this is George. He's looking for someone to keep him company tonight.'

'Mr Chester, it would be my pleasure,' said a very young-sounding female voice.

'Mr George is a very important man in Hollywood, Lin. Perhaps you two would like to talk movies together while you get to know each other?'

'I love movies,' said Lin.

Leo heard his father clear his throat. It sounded like he was struggling to keep up his act. *Hang in there.*

'Lin, it's a pleasure to meet you. My, you do look young. How old are you?'

'I'm twenty,' Lin said. 'Vietnamese girls always look young for their age.'

'Then I'm delighted to meet you. Let me buy you a drink. See you later, Chester.'

'Enjoy your evening, George. You do realise that this is a very special part of the club, don't you?' Chester's tone now held a warning.

'You mean…?'

'Yes, there's a charge, but I won't bore you with the details now. I'll be in touch.'

'Got him!' crowed Randall, slapping the table. 'And proof the fucker is in it for the money.'

Leo nodded grimly. 'That's better for us. All we need do is wait for the message and then we can arrest him.'

'Leaving now,' said George, sounding rather hurried.

'Mr George, is there problem?' asked Lin.

'No, my dear. I just want to get out of here. Don't like crowds.' Leo waited as the two wove their way through the throngs of people. Then the background noise dropped away. 'Package delivered,' said George.

Leo breathed a sigh of relief, not realising until then how anxious for his father he had been. George was brought up to the listening post by the plainclothes officers, who had intercepted him and Lin on the street. The girl had been taken away for questioning and, at Leo's suggestion, this would take place at the women's refuge in Reading.

'Do you want a coffee?' Leo asked his father, gesturing to the Thermos the team had on the sideboard. 'I have to warn you, it's pretty bad.'

'I'd love something to get that sour taste out of my mouth, so terrible coffee sounds perfect.'

They sat on office chairs across a table from each other. Events had happened so fast since their meeting in a garden-centre café the day before that it was dizzying. Leo was aware of his colleagues gathering up the equipment, uploading audio and video evidence, breaking down the temporary listening post. They left father and son alone for a private debrief.

'Did I get what you wanted?' asked George.

'You did. I was impressed. You could've had a career in front of the camera, rather than behind.'

George tipped his head to one side, considering. 'I

decided early on that that world wouldn't lead to success for me. Back then, there weren't many opportunities for Asian-Americans. We got cast as drug lords and inscrutable warriors.'

'Has much changed?'

'I hope so. It's taken decades too long.' He paused. 'Leo, I'd much prefer to talk about you. My career – the shape of it – is settled. It's an old story. You are what I find exciting – the unfolding tale of the crime-fighter!'

'You make me sound like a superhero.'

'God forbid, they are rarely interesting. I'd like to get to know you better if you'd let me. And my children… my other children,' he corrected, 'they'd like to meet you.'

Leo wasn't so sure about that. 'Let's just take this a step at a time.'

'What about the basics? Do you have a wife, or partner? Someone I should know about?'

'I'm not sure. There have been complications since this case started.'

'I imagine police work swallows up everything – a little like when we're shooting a film?'

Leo nodded but he knew it was more than that. There were cracks in the base of his relationship with Jess that needed more than papering over. They would have to rebuild or walk away.

'If you've got what you need here, what else are you waiting for?' asked George.

'One of the victims – a woman whom we believe was murdered for what she knew – dug up evidence about the trafficking ring that would help us make our case. She didn't keep it at the office or at her home – not that we've found.'

'Did the murderer take it?'

'Unlikely, as they missed other written evidence that a search would've turned up. Kelly Ann was careful—'

'She's the victim?'

'Yes. An accountant by training. I think she would've followed the money. We expect there to be records, perhaps data stored on a memory card, hidden somewhere.'

'That would fit that kind of personality – careful, looking at things via the numbers.'

Leo sat back and considered. His father had years of experience thinking through the motivations and habits of a range of characters in the films he made. 'Where would you think she would hide it?'

George pursed his lips. 'This coffee *is* terrible.'

'I did warn you.'

He rubbed his chin. 'If it were me, I'd hide it somewhere I could see it, somewhere I could check without anyone suspecting what I had. Possibly not in the house, though, if I thought that might be searched. Did she have a garden shed or a garage?'

Leo suddenly knew where he had to search. He stood up. 'Thank you.'

'What have I done?'

'Given me an idea.'

'That's all a parent can ever hope to do,' said George, smiling.

Leo started walking. 'I'll be in touch tomorrow.'

'Good hunting, Leo,' said George.

Chapter Forty-One

Leo

On arrival at Kelly Ann's cottage, Leo checked his most recent messages to see if George had got any communication from Chester. Nothing so far. Chester was probably waiting until George had 'enjoyed' his evening with his companion before presenting him with the bill. There was a danger that the missing Lin would scare Chester into not sending any further communication. Leo tapped out a quick message to Suyin, who was handling Lin's interview, to check what the usual practice was after a night with a client. He didn't want to ask Lin to return. They'd think of an excuse for her absence, if necessary.

Putting his work phone away, his fingers brushed his personal mobile. He'd had it switched off during the operation as per protocol. He now turned it on. While it was loading, he fetched his flashlight from the boot and went to visit some very sleepy chickens.

Where would Kelly Ann most likely have put a memory card? Not somewhere that the hens could peck at it, and not out in the elements. Slipping on plastic gloves, he lifted the lid and looked down on the roosting birds. There was no other way of doing this than by touch. He started rooting around in the straw under the warm bodies, a couple of times coming across eggs that were yet to be collected, and provoking a few ruffled feathers. Then, in the furthest corner, his fingers seized on a small plastic box. He pulled it out and prised off the lid. A data card.

'Thank you, Kelly Ann,' he said softly. He took a picture of where he'd discovered the evidence, dropped it in a plastic bag and replaced the lid. Once in his car, he sent an update to his team, saying he was going in to the office to see what Kelly Ann had left for them.

Just before he pulled out of his parking spot, his personal phone buzzed again. A message from Jess, only just received, though it had been sent a few hours earlier.

Don't keep putting her last, he told himself. He switched off the car and opened the image she'd sent.

Chapter Forty-Two

The knock on the door came at seven. Rebecca was already dressed for work and preparing her mother's schedule for the day to leave with Rainbow. As she went to answer, her heart missed a beat when she saw it was the police. Not to panic, she told herself. Probably just more follow-up questions.

'Yes?' she asked as calmly as she could manage. 'Can I help you?'

'Rebecca Crawley?' said the officer. He seemed familiar from Chipping Norton town hall meetings.

'Sergeant Wilmot, isn't it?'

He didn't respond with the social smile she'd hoped to elicit. 'Yes, ma'am. Can you confirm that you are the householder, Rebecca Crawley?'

'I am.' She knew a fraction before he said the words.

'I'm arresting you on suspicion of the murder of Lloyd Rumbold last Saturday night. Other charges may follow.'

'W-what?' She made to close the door but he put a boot in the way.

'I wouldn't do that, ma'am.'

A pyjama-clad Rainbow clattered down the stairs. 'Rebecca? What's going on?'

'I also have a warrant to search the property.' Wilmot passed her a piece of paper but the words swam before her eyes. She let it fall to the floor. Rainbow scooped it up and scanned it. Sergeant Wilmot pulled Rebecca forward so she was outside the house and turned her so that his colleague could handcuff her while he recited her rights.

'I don't understand,' said Rainbow.

Rebecca couldn't think of anything to say to explain. This hadn't been the plan. 'Look after Ma for me until I get back?'

'I'll call Leo – get this straightened out,' said Rainbow.

'What's going on?' Now her mother was slowly making her way into the hallway. That was the worst moment by far. Her mother had to be protected.

'Ma, go back into the warm,' said Rebecca. '*Rainbow!*'

That got her house guest moving. 'I'll make sure she's looked after. You can trust me,' Rainbow promised.

Rebecca let herself be led away. Whatever happened, Ma was not to be disturbed. Otherwise, none of it would have been worth it.

Chapter Forty-Three

Jess

I was invited to help police with their enquiries. That never had a promising sound.

I took the train to Banbury to spare myself the drive. Sitting in the carriage watching the fields with their huddles of sheep go by, I nervously checked my phone. Still no message from Leo. No acknowledgement – unless this was the acknowledgement? – of my breakthrough, on his behalf. He'd opened my message but that was all.

I wasn't kept waiting in Reception but shown straight to an interview room. I couldn't see Leo anywhere. Surely, he'd at least poke his head around the door to say 'thanks', for old times' sake?

Instead, DI Kesha Edmonds entered with her sidekick. What was his name again? DS Connaught, wasn't it? The one who didn't make the cut for a Holmesian designation. I was regretting that now as he didn't look very friendly this morning.

'Miss Bridges, thank you for coming in,' said Edmonds.

'No problem. Well, actually, it is a bit of a problem as my boss is making me take it as holiday, but there you are. The perils of being a public-spirited citizen.' I tried a smile but it fell like a shot pheasant to be snapped up in the jaws of the gun dog.

'I'll get right to it. You sent a photo of an exchange of messages from the phone of Rebecca Crawley. Can you explain how you had access to her phone?'

Then the purpose of this interview crashed down upon me. Leo had repeatedly warned me that my tendency to ignore pesky laws on such things as the legal collection of evidence could get him in trouble. My mouse had revived and bitten him on the nose.

'I can.' What could I say? I tried edited truth. 'I went to Rebecca's house last night for supper. During the meal, I spilt some wine so dashed to the loo. I only realised when I unfolded the napkin I'd grabbed that I'd also taken her phone with me. My eyes fell on the messages and I realised that this was key information that you didn't have – so I snapped a photo, sent it to Leo, and returned the phone to Rebecca.'

'She said the phone was locked. How did you break in?'

I wasn't going to answer that. 'She'd just been using it to check the weather. It must've still been unlocked.'

'She also said she'd deleted the messages. They weren't on the phone when we examined it earlier.'

I shrugged. 'Then she might have suspected her mistake and deleted them after I left, I guess.'

'No, I meant she had deleted them days earlier.'

'I don't know then. I'm not great with computers.'

Edmonds willed me to confess with her fixed stare but her gaze didn't work on me.

'You do realise that compromised evidence is not admissible in court?' she asked.

That was what Leo had tried to tell me again and again. 'Yes, I do know that.'

She shifted in her seat, opened the file in front of her, then closed it again. I'm fairly good at reading body language and this was a flashing sign to me that she was preparing herself for what she really wanted to ask.

'Did DI George ask you to obtain the evidence against Rebecca Crawley?'

Oh, no. She would not get me to sink the career of the man I loved – albeit very imperfectly, seeing how I'd behaved.

'No, he did not.'

'Come on, Miss Bridges. We know you're his girlfriend and he involved you in investigating the death of Lloyd Rumbold. It's logical, therefore, that you took this daring step to break into a suspect's phone as part of that case. You can't expect us to buy the "it just fell into my hands" excuse.'

I held up my index finger. 'OK, stop right there. I really need a paper and pen to keep up with all the wrong things you've just said, so I don't forget to rebut all of them. I was asked by Rainbow's friends – in fact, engaged by Freddie

Forrester and Lauren Westbourne – to try to exonerate her. I have the paperwork.' Thank God I'd put that in writing. 'If you remember, I did clear her because it was my idea to retrieve the parcel she sent and prove that the duct tape was last used legitimately and not to commit murder. You wouldn't have done that and would still be thinking Rainbow was the guilty party.'

Edmonds didn't like that, but, hey, I wasn't here to make friends.

'Secondly, as I've already said, I didn't break into Rebecca's phone.' I totally had. 'But you have my statement on that so I won't repeat myself.'

'Rebecca Crawley said you barged in without an invitation.'

'Wrong again. I was invited to supper by Rainbow, who was feeling very grateful to me for, you know, getting her off a murder charge?' That felt like getting in another jab and I was in danger of enjoying myself too much.

'And what about DI George's part in all this?'

That punctured my little helium balloon of happiness. 'Unfortunately, DI George and I had an argument a few days ago and we broke up – well, sort of. We've not had a chance to speak for days.'

'You expect me to believe that you conveniently broke up with Inspector George just before you undertook an illegal operation to collect evidence?'

'There you go again – I haven't done anything illegal. I happened upon something that I knew would be of interest to the police. Or would you prefer me to have ignored what I saw? Wouldn't that be accessory after the fact?' I looked to the silent DS Connaught. 'You guys know these things. That's an offence, isn't it?'

He gave me a nod.

'DI George told Superintendent Thaxted today that you are still his girlfriend,' Edmonds growled.

Aw, had he? My hopes rose a little.

'Yeah, as I said, we had sort of broken up but were due the final talk about it.' Would he prefer me to pretend all was fine or save his career? I went with the truth this time. 'Look, I was with someone else Monday night. He can confirm that I thought Leo and I were no longer together.'

'How can he confirm this?'

'Because he heard me tell Leo that we were finished and, well,' I swallowed, 'he was my rebound guy. Leo doesn't know and if you make him feel the least uncomfortable about my failings, embarrass him in any way, I will make it my next mission to use all legal means at my disposal to make your life equally, if not more, miserable.'

She bristled. 'Is that a threat?'

'No, a consequence.' I folded my arms.

'I'm a police officer and I will not stand for being threatened during the course of my work.'

'And I'm a well-known personality in this area who will get plenty of airtime in the media outlets your bosses most care about. Imagine what it would be like if I go to the press to tell them how you missed two vital bits of evidence – the deleted messages and the duct-tape packaging – and then tried to shoot the messenger. You will come out looking far worse than DI George, whose only sin is to pick an imperfect girlfriend. Are we done here?'

Edmonds glared at me as if she wished she could shred the flesh from my bones. DS Connaught stood up.

'Ma'am, shall I escort Miss Bridges out?'

'Do that.' Edmonds grabbed her files and flounced off.

I cocked my head to one side. 'Did you arrest Rebecca?'

DS Connaught glanced up at the camera which was still recording. 'A thirty-six-year-old woman is helping us with our enquiries.'

'Excellent.' I followed him out. 'You should put in for a transfer. That lady knows how to bear a grudge.'

'Lestrade always has to make a fuss when he's bested by Holmes and Watson, doesn't he?'

We exchanged a handshake in Reception and I walked free from the police station.

Chapter Forty-Four

Leo

Even after his third cup of coffee, Leo was flagging. He tried not to think what was happening up in Banbury. His superiors had told him that he wasn't to communicate with Jess or any of the team interviewing the prime suspect due to the serious irregularities in how the evidence implicating Rebecca had been gathered.

Jess had done it for him, he knew that, but she never thought things through. He was expecting any moment to get the call that he was to go on gardening leave and be investigated himself, which was why he was ploughing ahead with the case against the trafficking ring to get as much of this done as possible before being escorted from the building.

The one silver lining was that Kelly Ann had gathered the financial data he required to tie all parts of the trafficking ring together. He now had payments from clients for 'special services' which would lead to the men involved being identified. He also had 'refunds' to the Kanons and Stanton-Milbecks coming from the administration in Guernsey. As they weren't paying a membership fee, and the 'refunds' were in the hundreds of thousands, it would be fair to surmise that this was how Chester Birbeck paid his middle men for their activities on his behalf. Leo wished he had met Kelly Ann in life. From her little office in the club in Oxfordshire, she had managed to get into the main server on Guernsey that ran the whole network. There were weeks of work ahead for forensic accountants but it was all here, certainly enough for the arrests to go ahead.

The saddest moment for Leo, though, was when he saw who she had gone to with her evidence. He came across a record of a personal email on the Friday she died, since deleted from the club system, to her manager, Rebecca, asking what the system was for whistleblowing. She had thought Rebecca her friend, not understanding that Rebecca was no innocent bystander, but paid very well to keep her silence. The payment in her case had been in the form of a house, bought as club property for the manager, then quietly transferred into her ownership in 2019. She hadn't directly dirtied her hands by being involved with the trafficking, but she had organised the events in the Oxfordshire club for the introductions and seen the women go through the club doors. She was an intelligent woman; she knew that Kelly Ann had stumbled onto the ongoing activities. Her golden goose was threatened so she had used her friendship to stage the suicide.

Superintendent Thaxted came into his office. 'Leo?'

This was it – marching orders. The image of him leaving with his things in a cardboard box whisked through his mind. He stood to attention. 'Yes, ma'am.'

'I think it only fair you see this after all the work you've put in. It's your case they're presenting.' She led him to her office where she was watching a live feed of the interview with Rebecca.

The sensation of the bullet missing him by a hair was rapidly replaced by intrigue at seeing if Rebecca would finally explain herself. She sat with her solicitor across the table from Edmonds and Connaught. She still looked well-presented, professional, though perhaps her auburn hair was slightly mussed at the back. Did she understand what she had done, he wondered?

DI Edmonds took a much gentler tone with her suspect than she did with her colleagues.

'As we explained,' said Edmonds, 'your cooperation now will help when this comes to trial. So please run through again what happened that Friday.'

Rebecca toyed with a cup of water. Her solicitor sat silently beside her. Rebecca cleared her throat. 'I think I went a little mad.'

'What was the trigger?' Edmonds managed to sound sympathetic.

'It was Kelly Ann. She came up to me that morning and said she had something she needed to ask me.' Rebecca fell silent again.

'What did you think she was going to ask?'

'I wasn't sure. In fact, I told her I didn't want to know but she insisted I listen.'

'You said you didn't want to know?'

Rebecca covered her face briefly with her hands then dropped them. 'Look, the Birbecks aren't nice people. You work for them and you keep quiet, then they reward you. It's understood. None of us can be that naïve.'

'But Kelly Ann was?'

'Yes! Can you believe it?' She appealed to Edmonds as if she should at least understand this much. 'She, an accountant from Chipping Norton, thought she could bring them down. She asked me what the process was for whistleblowing. Whistleblowing?' Rebecca gave a mirthless laugh. 'That only works when there is someone outside the company you can go to. We are all trapped in the system – that's the way they run their business.'

'So what did you tell her?'

'I needed time to think – I just needed time to think. So I told her to come and have a drink with me after work so we could work out what to do.'

In the superintendent's office, Leo shook his head. 'She means she needed time to plan. She must've drugged the wine, parked her car somewhere she could fetch it later after taking Kelly Ann home, made all the arrangements.'

Claire Thaxted nodded. 'I imagine Kesha is well aware.'

Leo wished he could be in there, asking the questions.

Fortunately, Edmonds had read the timeline he'd generated with his team. 'Come on, Rebecca, you can't expect us to believe that. You were a busy bee after that conversation – you took your car into Chipping Norton, telling your PA that you were buying more gifts for the gift baskets, and you left it in a side street. We've now got confirmation from the bus company CCTV that you were on the one-thirty service back to the club. And you spiked Kelly Ann's drink in the office – that took some preparation.'

'No, no, it didn't. I had Mum's prescription with me. I just wanted Kelly Ann to cooperate and tell me what evidence she had – to give it to me.' Rebecca was flailing, not realising that this version made it no better. 'She wouldn't say – got giggly, in fact, not like Mum. She'll do what you tell her when she's had her pills.'

'You drove Kelly Ann home?'

'Of course. I couldn't let her drive like that.'

'She's lying,' said Leo. 'I believe she intended to make Kelly Ann talk, but she was going to kill her whatever.'

'Agreed,' said Claire.

'Then what happened?' asked Edmonds.

Rebecca folded her arms, hugging herself.

'Whose idea was the bath?'

'She always had a bath – it was her Friday night ritual.'

'Did she think you were gone?'

Rebecca shrugged, a cagey look on her face.

'We know what happened next. You waited for her to fall asleep and then you slit her wrists.'

'I don't know.' She wouldn't look at anyone in the room.

'You do know. We've got enough to charge you with murder, Rebecca. What we don't understand is why. Is there anything you can say that will make us understand – make it less cold, calculating?'

Silence.

'Are you afraid what your family will think if you admit

to what you did – what your mother will think?' asked DS Connaught.

'Leave my mother out of this!' Suddenly, everyone could see where the killer came from – Rebecca's face was vivid with fury. 'Look, I did it to protect her – all of this. Kelly Ann was going to take it all away from us – the house, I wouldn't be able to afford the right care for Mum, it was all going to pieces! She's my mother – I couldn't – can't let anything happen to her! I had to just…just stop her ruining everything.'

'But you made a hash of it, didn't you?' said Edmonds. 'You messed up the scene so we knew it wasn't suicide.'

Back in her office, Claire shot Leo a rueful look. She had so very nearly ordered him to ignore it.

'Oh, you started well enough with the message you dictated to Kelly Ann that afternoon. Was it to apologise for some delay or other at the club?' Edmonds got no reaction from Rebecca. 'You then pretended to change your mind and came up with a new message and later retrieved the discarded one from Kelly Ann's pad. You thought you had the perfect suicide note. But then you made mistake after mistake. You didn't search her place properly, thinking that no one would look into her life once she'd been dismissed as a suicide. You had no idea just how much evidence she had collected, or even how long she had been investigating.'

And, despite Edmonds's tone, Rebecca was right to think she would have got away with it in most cases, thought Leo grimly.

Back in the interview room, Rebecca had clammed up.

Leo wondered if they'd get any more from her, offer of cooperation notwithstanding.

Sensing a change of pace was needed, Edmond refilled Rebecca's water from the jug on the side and set it down in front of her. 'OK, so tell us what happened when Lloyd got in touch saying he had something dramatic to tell you. You'd just got away with murder, did you wonder if you could do it again?'

The solicitor looked sideways at her client. 'My client has no comment.'

'Come on, Rebecca, why hide it? We've got most of it in your messages.' Edmonds leant into the table. 'I bet your first thought was that the terrible thing you'd done to cover up the scandal would be wasted if the news got out another way. What did you think when Lloyd told you what he'd discovered while filming with the Vietnamese girl?'

'Lloyd was upset – suicidal. I tried to talk him out of it. He was OK when I left but he must've changed his mind.' Rebecca said the words tonelessly.

'That isn't true. You were furious when he told you what he knew. But this time you had to work quickly with little time to plan.' Kesha put a framed certificate on the table between them. 'Your health and safety course certificate that you have in your office. Running a club with holiday lets: I bet you are well aware of safety issues around heaters.'

'Everyone knows they can be dangerous – not just me,' Rebecca said.

'I can see it was a simple plan. Walk over to see Lloyd as arranged. Pop a few tranqs belonging to your mother in the whisky, send him to sleep and set it up with duct tape you'd brought from home, walk back. It had probably seemed the perfect crime. You mistake was to think two staged suicides would not be connected by us.' That was rich coming from Edmonds. 'But why did you set up Rainbow Williams?'

'I didn't!' hissed Rebecca. 'None of this should have been questioned. They committed suicide – they both did!' She was panicking now. Her solicitor leant over and whispered something. 'No comment,' Rebecca ended bullishly.

It looked like they weren't going to get anything else from her but they had more than enough evidence to build a case against her. Edmonds tried a few more questions but got the same 'No comment' in reply. The interview ended with her being taken back to the cells.

Claire clicked off the screen. 'Impressions?'

'I think we were lucky that fate intervened so we linked the cases. Otherwise, where would she have stopped? Maybe Rainbow would have found out too much, or Rebecca would decide to kill her with a fake confession to throw suspicion on the dead? Let her mother go to sleep and never wake up because she got too much to handle?'

'You think she would have gone for her mother? That seems the only person about whom she has any real feelings?'

'Eventually. I think the psychologists might say that someone who had a short-circuit in the empathy area of her brain is capable of anything.'

'If I were her lawyer, I would definitely want an assessment, but from what we saw,' Claire nodded at the screen, 'she seems competent to stand trial.'

A call came through on Leo's phone. He glanced down. 'Superintendent, it's my father.'

She gestured for him to take it.

'Leo, you'd never guess what that fucker has done!' It was George, his tone ringing with vindictive pleasure.

'Tell us – you're on speaker with my superintendent.'

', well, now. Good afternoon, ma'am. I apologise for swearing.'

'Not at all, Mr George,' said Claire. 'Thank you for helping us. You've news, I take it?'

'Yes. Chester just sent me a message, saying how he hoped I enjoyed myself last night, including a photo of me leaving with the young lady on my arm. He heavily hints that this will be released to the Hollywood press if I have second thoughts about the arrangement. But as he is sure I will be delighted to carry on with the search for a muse, here's my bill for his special services.'

'How much?' asked Leo.

'Fifty thousand dollars. You've got him.'

'*We've* got him.' Leo would've punched the air if his boss hadn't been watching. 'Thanks, George. We couldn't have done this without you.' Leo took the phone off speaker as Claire started telling her superiors the news. He walked out into the corridor.

'I have to stay put, apparently,' George was saying, 'so as not to spook Chester before he gets the knock on the door later today, but we'll see each other again soon, I hope? We didn't have much time to get to know each other with all this going on.'

'I don't know, I think I got to know you very well.'

George paused, then laughed. 'You're right. No better way. Let's do more things together.'

'I'll look forward to it.' And despite the threat of disciplinary action still hanging over him, Leo felt joy about that at least.

When he went back into Claire's office, she was just putting the phone down. 'We're good to go. Let your contact in Immigration know as they'll want part of this. Let's bring them all in – the Kanons, the Stanton-Milbecks. The Met will tackle the Birbecks. I think we'll be looking for free cells before close of play.'

'They'll still let me have first crack at Chester Birbeck?'

'Absolutely. Let DI Edmonds and the rest of the team deal with the ones this end. You get yourself off to London. Good work all round.' He turned to go. 'Oh, and Leo? After the way the messages were discovered on Rebecca Crawley's phone, best not to contact Miss Bridges until we've got this wrapped up, understood?'

There was his reprimand. 'Is that an order, Superintendent?'

She smiled sourly. 'A strongly worded caution.'

And with that, Leo knew his boss did not doubt that Jess had crossed lines. Claire was merely relieved to have a reason not to notice.

Chapter Forty-Five

Jess

I watched the case unfold on television like the rest of the UK population. Chester Birbeck was led out of his London club looking grey-faced but defiant. Later reports said he denied everything in police interview, but when he appeared in Bow Street Magistrates' Court for his plea, he hobbled in on a walker, his lawyer claiming he had been unfairly hounded by the police and was a broken man. His brother was rapidly putting distance between himself and Chester and trying to salvage their business empire.

Public sympathy was not forthcoming, not once the stories of the victims came out. The journalists pieced together the events, fizzing up the trail of gunpowder like a spark on its way to a stack of dynamite and exploded with the heroic tale of murdered whistleblower, Kelly Ann Porter, and relatively innocent bystander, Lloyd Rumbold, both killed to keep the trafficking ring in business. The others involved – the transport agents, the sex-industry experts, the legal and finance people – they all got swept up in the same operation that took out Chester, like the Rollright Stones, caught by the curse that took out the king. Taking most of the TV-camera time on behalf of Thames Valley Police, was telegenic Leo George, the intrepid detective who had pieced it together, though he was always careful to credit the anonymous citizens who had assisted. I took that as all the thanks I was going to get.

OK, I got it. He was over me. Two weeks had passed and the country was moving on to the coronavirus news. Even a big sex-ring bust got pushed out of the headlines. I knew it was serious when I found myself buying an extra pack of toilet paper, just in case.

One drizzly late-February evening, I stood with Flossie watching the trains pass under the bridge leading to Port Meadow. Well, I was standing; she was doing her sniff and piss two-step that was the highlight of her day. I looked up from the tracks when someone came to stand next to me. It was Leo.

'How did you find me?' I asked. That really wasn't the most important thing I had to say but it just came out.

'You've not turned off Find My Friends on your phone,' he pointed out.

'Oh. Then I made it easy for you, didn't I?' I started walking because Flossie was pulling me towards the meadow.

Leo fell in step. 'I wouldn't call it easy.'

We reached the gate at the bottom of the little hill. I let Flossie off so she could rocket across the grass and roll in cow pats if she so wished, I just did not care. I'd dropped my mouse and he had made use of it, but ignored the giver. I got the message, but I still owed him an apology.

'I'm so sorry, Leo. I did something with Phil that I really, really regret.'

'I know.'

I looked up at him. 'You know?'

'Not the details, but Phil told me something happened in so many words.'

'You don't want to know the details, trust me. Enough to say, I thought you and me were done, I went to him for comfort, and I've felt like a worm ever since because I wasn't really done, whatever I told myself.'

He swallowed, ever the stoic. 'Did you sleep with him?'

'Full disclosure: we did… *something* on the sofa and then I went to my own bed and he slept downstairs.'

'Are you together now?'

'God, no! It was an idiotic moment. A stupid impulse.'

'Because I pushed you away?'

'Don't let me blame you. This is on me. I fuck up. This is probably one of the worst but, still, it's part of who I am.'

'You didn't fuck up about Rebecca. I did.'

'I almost did. Did you know that awful Edmonds person tried to get me to say you put me up to it? I had to tell her we weren't a thing any more when really I wanted to punch her.'

'Yes, I knew. She was just doing her job.'

'No, she was trying to get yours. Don't kid yourself.'

'But you protected me.'

'I told her the truth – about that part at any rate.'

We looked at each other for a long, agonising moment.

'Are we done?' I asked.

'I don't know. Do you want to be?' He looked away to where Flossie was arrowing down the path, heading back to us all muddied up. That felt like my heart racing towards him. He might well toss it, but I had to do the equivalent of throwing myself at him, muddy paws and all.

'No, I don't want that, Leo. Can we start again?'

He didn't reply but just opened his arms.

I stepped into his hug as we braced ourselves for the next hit.

Acknowledgments

Thanks to Kate and the wonderful team at One More Chapter, HarperCollins, for bringing the first four Jessica Bridges Mysteries from a chance conversation over coffee in the News Building to a four part murder mystery series in the Thames Valley.

One More Chapter is an
award-winning global
division of HarperCollins.

Sign up to our newsletter to get our
latest eBook deals and stay up to date
with our weekly Book Club!
Subscribe here.

Meet the team at
www.onemorechapter.com

Follow us!

 @OneMoreChapter_

 @OneMoreChapter

 @onemorechapterhc

Do you write unputdownable fiction?
We love to hear from new voices.
Find out how to submit your novel at
www.onemorechapter.com/submissions